Connie

TOO WILD TO TAME

Cotannah Chisk-Ko is banished from the Texas ranch she has always known as home, to return to the Choctaw Nation where she must learn to behave like a proper maiden of her tribe. Cotannah continues her outrageous flirtations, yet she can't seem to entice the one man she wants—the handsome, intriguingly remote shaman, Walks-With-Spirits.

TOO DANGEROUS TO LOVE

Walks-With-Spirits is consumed by desire for the beautiful woman who haunts his dreams. Her restless nature shatters his serenity, yet he cannot deny the powerful attraction binding them together. When Cotannah's wanton ways place her in danger, Walks-With-Spirits risks all to rescue her and his heroism results in an unjust punishment. Now Walks-With-Spirits must fight for his life if he is to save the love he has found with the woman who brings peace to his heart and fire to his b̶l̶o̶o̶d̶. With time running out, will t̶h̶e̶ ̶ ̶ ̶ ̶ ̶ ̶ vers discover a heaven on E̶ ̶ ̶ ̶ ̶ ̶ ̶ that will unite them

D0973838

GENELL DELLIN

After the Thunder

An Avon Romantic Treasure

AVON BOOKS ◆ NEW YORK

To my sister, Bonnie Smith Lytal
With much love and many thanks

AVON BOOKS
A division of
The Hearst Corporation
1350 Avenue of the Americas
New York, New York 10019

Copyright © 1998 by Genell Smith Dellin
Inside cover author photo by Loy's Photography
Published by arrangement with the author
Visit our website at http://www.AvonBooks.com
Library of Congress Catalog Card Number: 97-93793
ISBN: 0-380-78603-6

First Avon Books Printing: January 1998

AVON TRADEMARK REG. U.S. PAT. OFF. AND IN OTHER COUNTRIES, MARCA REGISTRADA, HECHO EN U.S.A.

Printed in the U.S.A.

WCD   10   9   8   7   6   5   4   3   2   1

Prologue

Cotannah turned and walked away from her older brother, Cade, all the way to the other end of the porch, but it didn't do a bit of good. Stubborn, bossy soul that he was, he stayed right on her heels and kept on berating her.

"I'm not putting up with your wild ways anymore, Cotannah. I've just fired one of the best vaqueros who ever rode for me because of you."

He was so furious he was shouting. She could not recall him ever being this furious before, at least not with her. Well, he had no right to be. She whirled to face him and shouted right back.

"It's not my fault! Can I help it if Tonio can't stay away from me?"

He answered with a glare so ferocious that she had to resist taking a step backward. What in the world was he so angry about? It wasn't as if he'd never fired a vaquero before and wouldn't fire one again.

But it wouldn't do to say that to him; Cade was in a

1

fit this afternoon like she'd never seen him. Well, if she knew anything, she knew a person could catch more flies with honey than with vinegar, so she drew a deep breath, smiled, and forced a conciliatory tone into her voice.

"Really, Cade, this isn't my fault—I clearly told Tonio that I'm not seeing him anymore!"

"Maybe in words. But then, no doubt, you batted your eyelashes and flashed him a smile to show that you didn't really mean it. You should never have been seeing him at all, Cotannah. You never cared one breath for him, yet you couldn't rest until he was pie-eyed crazy over you."

"That is not true! I did not!"

However, his harsh voice rode right over hers.

"What you did was go too far. You broke the man's heart and lost him his job into the bargain. Now, aren't you proud of yourself?"

Her conscience stabbed at her, but she ignored it.

"Tonio's a big boy. Twenty years old, the same as I am, so he can take care of himself! I'm sick and tired of hearing this lecture—first from Maggie and then Oleana and now you, Big Brother. Why can't you all see that I'm only growing up and learning how to be a woman?"

The look of scorn that swept over his face took her breath. He pushed his hat back on his head, placed his hands on the porch banister, one on each side of her, and leaned down so his face would be close to hers.

"Your education about womanhood is just commencing."

His eyes were like a stranger's, hard and black and completely empty of the love she usually saw in them; they made her want to shiver. She wouldn't, though, and she would not look away, no matter how much she wanted.

"What do you mean?" she asked, a little uncertain.

"I mean that I'm sending you back to the Nation so you can learn how to be a real woman in the old Choctaw way. Emily and Aunt Ancie and Auntie Iola will teach you."

The shock of it, the incredible cruelty of the idea, stopped the blood cold in her veins.

"Emily isn't Choctaw."

"But she's a real woman in the old tradition: she takes care of her husband and child, she helps the teachers at the school, she shares with the less fortunate, she contributes to Tay's position as Principal Chief. In other words, 'Tannah, she thinks of other people, not entirely of herself and what she wants from daylight 'til dark."

She struggled to make her brain work, to defend herself.

"So?" she cried. "Are you comparing her to me? Are you saying that I think only of myself?"

"Right."

"Well! Now I understand why Tay broke my heart and chose Emily instead of me—she's a saint, and I'm nothing but a selfish sinner!"

His face softened slightly but not his voice.

"Tay broke your pride more than your heart. He and Emily were destined for each other, you've said so yourself a dozen times, and what I'm saying is that if you want to find the man destined to stay with you for life, you'd better change some things."

"I'm not looking for a man destined to stay with me for life! For ten long years I thought Tay was that man, but I was wrong, so I'm never going to think that way again."

He snorted.

"You'd better start thinking that way instead of thinking one man after another is put in your path for you to use and then throw away. Someday you're going to cause a killing or some other disaster.''

The remark stabbed her, cut her deep.

''Better I should discard them than for them to discard me! I'd rather break their hearts than for them to break mine! I'll never let my heart be broken again, and I won't be humiliated again, either, so you'd better stop preaching and listen to me, Cade Chisk-Ko. I'm not going back to the Nation.''

''Yes. You're going.''

She set her fists on her hips and glared up at him, pure fury rushing over her skin hot and fast, washing away shame and guilt like a blistering rain.

''How embarrassing would that be, for me, of all people, to go and stay with Tay and Emily? My former betrothed and the woman he chose instead of me, won't that be a fine holiday for me? And for them! Are they to govern my behavior?''

''Yes. And Ancie and Jumper will be there to help them.''

''What! You're sending them, too?''

His expression hardened again.

''Naturally. You have to have a chaperone—we can't have you on the trail alone with a bunch of handsome vaquero outriders, now, can we?''

The implication infuriated her. And brought back the guilt she hated.

''I haven't done one iota of what you did in your young days! In your Wandering Year—which lasted for ten years—I begged you to come home and live with us and really be my brother! You have no call to be so self-righteous, Cade! ''

''I'm a man. There's a world of difference.''

''Oh, yes,'' she cried. ''There is a world of difference, isn't there? No man who was twenty years old ever got sent away from home like a naughty child in disgrace!''

"You disgraced yourself. This is the consequence of your own actions.''

"That's what you think. I'm not going!''

"Pack your bags.''

He wheeled and strode away down the length of the porch, his spurs ringing fast and loud.

Chapter 1

Choctaw Nation
Three weeks later

Crossing the Kiamichi River meant they were almost there. Cotannah longed to jump off her mare and into the water, into the deep, swift-running current and let it carry her far into the wilds of the mountains, where she'd never have to see another human soul. Especially not Tay and Emily.

Her hands shook with the effort it took to hold the reins and keep riding toward Tall Pine, where Cade meant to leave her for no telling how long. Never, not even in her most humiliating nightmare, could she have dreamed that Cade would make her a prisoner living in shame under Tay and Emily's charitable supervision.

Well, she didn't care if he had sent messages ahead to Tay and Emily and had surrounded her with eight outriders and Uncle Jumper and Aunt Ancie, all ten of them determined to fulfill his orders to the letter. Somehow she'd show him, she'd show them all. Cotannah Chisk-Ko did as she pleased; she was a woman grown, now, and they'd all have to learn to live with that fact.

The sudden crack of a rifle shot tore through the air. It sent her horse, Pretty Feather, bolting through the shallow ford toward the north bank of the Kiamichi so fast that for one, horrible moment Cotannah was afraid that the mare had been hit. She threw herself along her mount's neck as she scrambled up the rocky incline and ran her hands over every inch of sleek horseflesh she could reach. By the time they'd topped the bank and hit the road running, she'd decided that Pretty Feather was only scared. Her own heart was pounding as hard as the mare's hooves against the ground.

Juan Caldero, one of the two outriders who were farthest ahead turned back, shouted for her to take care. Then she heard the coach wheels behind her and Pretty Feather's frightened whinny entirely filled her ears. She glimpsed an animal, a dog or a coyote, darting into their path from out of nowhere and then the mare was skidding to a stop, rearing up onto her hind feet, rising and rising into the air, reaching for the sky as if she meant to tear down the sun. Cotannah, nearly unseated, clung to the horn and slid her feet from the stirrups so she could fling herself free of the mare if she flipped over backwards. Lord! Pretty Feather never, ever acted this way!

The mare's forefeet finally touched earth again but only for an instant because the wild animal or whatever it was ran right between her trembling legs the moment they hit the ground. She reared again, came down briefly and then raised herself wildly once more, this time staying up forever.

Suddenly, a man appeared, darted out of the woods and into the road. Cotannah locked her legs against Pretty Feather's sides and looked down from her vantage point in the air, caught helpless in a moment that wouldn't end. The animal—it was a coyote, she could see that now—ran in a frenzied circle beneath her and she caught a glimpse of gushing blood before it dropped to the ground directly beneath her horse. Pretty Feather snorted and started trembling worse than ever, scrabbling her hooves against the ground, swiveling and swaying, walking, actually walking on her hind feet!

How could a horse do that and not fall over backward? She'd be crushed at any moment! Her brain froze in panic. Should she jump now or cling to her mount with all the strength in her legs? She couldn't decide. She couldn't move, couldn't do anything.

The man ran toward the fallen coyote, she saw a flash of his hot, light-colored eyes and glimpsed a stunningly handsome, broad face beneath a knotted cloth headband. Somehow, he seemed familiar. And fearless. He ran directly underneath Pretty Feather's flailing forefeet! The mare took in a long, whistling breath as her instincts against trampling a human being made her shy from him, but she made no move to come down.

The man—wearing skin breeches with an old-fashioned cloth hunting shirt and shoulder-length hair with the headband, carried the look of the wild about him. He lifted his hand toward her teetering mount. Cotannah's breath stopped completely. The slightest unbalancing push could send them on over backwards and mash her to death beneath the horse. She stared, terrified, at his long, brown fingers as they touched, then stroked Pretty Feather's shoulder.

He was *talking* to the mare, she could hear a crooning of low-pitched Choctaw words beneath the roaring thunder of her own pulse beating in her head and the galloping of the vaqueros' horses as they rode back to see about her. Pretty Feather immediately, softly, dropped all four feet to the ground and stood quiet.

The woodsman kept stroking her, kept talking to her.

He had the most beguiling voice—deep and slow as an old wise man. The sound of it brought a sudden calm to the terror rolling deep inside Cotannah and she knew how Pretty Feather felt. Relief flowed through her like a warm river and carried the trembling from her body, out through her toes and the tips of her fingers.

The man glanced up at her, and she saw that he wasn't old at all, he was near her own age, heartbreakingly handsome with topaz-colored eyes, a straight nose, and a broad, sensual mouth. She'd never seen his face before or she'd remember. She managed a smile, made it flirtatious.

"I thank you for calming my horse."

He didn't answer. Immediately he bent over the coyote again, picked it up in his arms, turned and ran back toward the woods that lined the road. Just as he reached a thicket of redbud trees he turned and looked over his shoulder at Cotannah.

It was a quick flash of acknowledgment, a fast look to see that she was still all right and Pretty Feather still calm, but it was a look of such power that it stripped away everything superficial as though he could see straight into her heart. His strangely pale eyes seemed filled with light. Somehow, they captured hers in a gaze so strong and sharp that she could not have looked away if someone had thrown a rope around her neck and tried to turn her head.

He knew her. Deep down to her soul. For the first time in her life she was looking into the eyes of someone who *knew* her. It gave her the most peculiar feeling. It made her shiver.

Then she was staring at the yellowing leaves and gray limbs of the old, gnarled redbud trees and the woodsman was gone, vanished so fast it seemed, suddenly, as if he'd never been there at all. But he had been. And she knew him from somewhere, she did! But how could that be? She would have remembered that face! Maybe Tay and Emily would know him.

They had to know—he was too different from most men, too powerful in his looks and his manner to escape notice. Disappointment stabbed at her. He was different from most men, also, in that he hadn't smiled at her. Nor had he spoken to her. Not even to accept her thanks. He'd been too fascinated by that coyote, of all things! Any other man would be more interested in her than in a scruffy old coyote!

"*¿Señorita, como está?*"

Juan Caldero was talking to her, but his gaze was fixed on the trees where the woodsman had disappeared. Only then did she realize that she, too, was still watching that spot as if she believed the man would reappear. The coach clattered to a stop behind her and the rest of the vaqueros gathered around.

"*¿Quien es?*" one of them asked, staring, as she and Juan were still doing, at the last place the woodsman had been.

A spate of Spanish filled the air, and she caught enough words to know that all the men were as amazed as she that the coyote was being cared for instead of being hunted. Juan declared that the man was magic, pointing to Pretty Feather's sudden and continuing calm as proof. Aunt Ancie and Uncle Jumper agreed—they, too, had been near enough to see what he had done.

"There went an *alikchi*," Ancie declared, "like in the old days."

He was a man of magic or there was something else special about him. As they all started moving on toward Tall Pine again, Cotannah thought about the way he'd looked at her. She relived every moment of their encounter and made a solemn promise to herself as she rode that last mile and a half. The woodsman was specially sensual and magically handsome, and she was going to find out who he was and make him take notice of her or her name wasn't Cotannah Chisk-Ko.

Her chance to fulfill that vow came sooner than she ever expected. She had to blink her eyes and look again when they rode up into the front yard at Tall Pine, because there he was, kneeling, bent over the hurt coyote at the foot of the majestic pine tree that gave the house its name! He had arrived first even though he'd been on foot, so it must be that he could run like a deer.

Or maybe he had used medicine to fly through the air, maybe he was a shape-changer who'd turned himself into an eagle carrying the coyote in his beak. A new shiver passed over her. This was a man like none she'd ever seen before, and here he was, right in her path again!

Her heart skipped. Had he guessed that Tall Pine was her destination? Had he come here because he wanted to see her again? Perhaps he wasn't so different from other men after all!

Emily came around the corner of the house as Aunt Ancie and Uncle Jumper's coach pulled up at the steps and Cotannah brought Pretty Feather to a stop halfway between the porch and the tall pine tree. The sight of the woman who used to be her best friend carrying her and Tay's baby girl, Sophia—took Cotannah's attention from the woodsman and made her stomach give a strange, twisting lurch.

Tay had chosen unselfish Emily in spite of the fact that he'd ridden all the way to Texas to make Cotannah his bride. Unselfish best-friend Emily, who had betrayed her. Thanks to Emily, she had lost the man she had always planned to marry and the woman who was her one and only best friend at the same awful, bitter time.

Two years ago. Two years that seemed a whole lifetime ago, two years that had seen her grow wilder and bolder and completely distrustful of long-lasting friendships with women and romantic attachments with men.

Emily was smiling straight at her, though, that sweet smile that came straight from her truly caring and generous heart. How could she blame her, a small voice demanded from the depths of her heart. Emily and Tay *had* been meant for each other and Cotannah had said so many times, just as Cade had reminded her when he'd sent her here.

Emily was smiling at her as if they'd never exchanged a single hateful, hurtful word, as if Cotannah had never accused her of betraying their deep friendship, of deliberately stealing Cotannah's intended husband away. Emily was smiling as naturally as if Cotannah had never participated in that cruel, taunting testing of Emily that Auntie Iola and the other Choctaw women had used to torture her when they couldn't believe that Tay would choose a white girl as his bride.

Now here she was, the white woman, Emily Harrington Nashoba, wife of the Principal Chief of the Choctaws, Tay Nashoba, and mother of his child, not only accepted but beloved by his people. Cotannah's people, the People of the Choctaw Nation.

To her own surprise, though, she didn't feel as bitter as she had expected. Maybe Cade had been right about that, too—maybe it had been her pride that was broken more than her heart.

Her stomach settled right back into place and her hands relaxed on the reins. Emily was running to greet her, smiling a smile that she could never forget.

"Oh, 'Tannah," she cried, "get down from there and give me a hug. I thought you never would get here!"

Then Cotannah was on the ground and Emily was

hugging her hard with her one free arm while the baby flailed at her with two chubby hands.

"I'm so glad you've come to us," Emily whispered. "Cade's message said you've had some troubles of the heart and Tay and I want so very much to be able to help."

"I'm sure that's exactly the way Cade put it—troubles of the heart," Cotannah drawled sarcastically.

Emily pulled away a little to give her a solemn, measuring look. Then she grinned.

"We-e-ll, maybe those weren't his exact words, but I want you to know right now, 'Tannah, that whatever has happened, I'm not judging you one bit, not after what you've been through. I'm just glad that you feel comfortable coming to us."

Cotannah felt a twinge of the old, deep hurt, then, but when she looked into Emily's kind brown eyes it simply didn't grow. It stayed there, but it didn't get any bigger. How could she ever feel comfortable coming to Tay and Emily talking of other beaux, other courtships? Of course, in a way, if she were absolutely honest, she had to admit that Tay had never truly courted her at all, or been her beau, except in her imagination and his own thoughts and unacted-upon intentions.

"You and Tay were destined for each other," she said simply. "I've said that lots of times. And I've meant it. It's just been hard for me to accept."

"We never set out to hurt you," Emily said, as the baby leaned forward to reach for the stampede strings dangling from Cotannah's hat. "We're hoping you've forgiven us and all the hard feelings have faded away forever."

Yes. They have. No. They haven't.

Cotannah opened her mouth but she couldn't say either set of words. She didn't know how she really felt, and she didn't want to think about it. Emily—being Emily the peacemaker who loved to make everyone happy—was trying to get the big problem out in the open and disposed of as soon as she could so that things could be easy and warm between them the way they used to be before Tay ever came to Texas.

And why shouldn't they be? Tay was far in her past and she had captivated plenty of men since then.

"All of that was ages ago," she said, with a careless shrug.

She looked away from her old friend to tickle the baby's fat neck with the tips of the hat strings.

"This baby is so beautiful," she said. "Her looks are a combination of you and Tay both, although I'd have said that wouldn't be possible."

"Well, her behavior is a combination of you and Maggie," Emily said, laughing. "She's barely a year old and she's running everywhere and into everything."

Cotannah laughed, too.

"Is she as wild as Miranda?"

"Almost. Yes, I'd say it's a close contest between the little cousins."

"I can't wait to see them together."

"Neither can I."

Emily squeezed her arm.

"Come with me, 'Tannah, I need to welcome Aunt Ancie and Uncle Jumper. At supper I'll introduce you all to a friend of ours whom I think you'll find interesting."

Emily glanced over Sophia's head toward the woodsman beneath the tall pine tree.

Cotannah looked at him, too, glad to be reminded of her latest distraction.

"Do you mean him? Who is he, Emily?"

He was still bent over the coyote, but as they watched

him, he stood up. Just that one, simple, fluid motion
made the breath catch in Cotannah's throat. She waited
for him to look her way. He had to be aware she was
there, he couldn't be so wrapped up in that coyote he
hadn't seen or heard their whole noisy cavalcade ride in.
Obviously, she thought wryly, seeing her again was not
the reason he had come to Tall Pine.

He never even turned his head; he stared toward the
back of the house, instead, and never moved at all until
a girl appeared, running toward him with a basket in her
hands. He watched her intensely.

A hard, quick tug of jealousy, like the plucking of a
guitar string, pulled at Cotannah.

"And who is she?"

"My servant girl, Rosie. I had just sent her for the
medicines he asked for when I heard you ride up," Emily said. "He's trying to staunch the bleeding."

Cotannah didn't answer. The *alikchi* was watching
that servant girl as if he'd never seen a woman before,
yet he hadn't given her the barest glance since she'd
arrived here at Tall Pine. What an unheard-of turn of
events: a fascinating, handsome, young man paying
more attention to a coyote and a fourteen-year-old girl
than to her, Cotannah Chisk-Ko, the most sought-after
belle of the Nueces Strip!

She squared her shoulders. Well, she would just see
about that! She would not only make him notice her—
she would make him court her. A hum of excitement
began in her blood at the thought of such a challenge.
That gorgeous woodsman, medicine man or no, might
as well get ready to come calling!

"I'm glad he's a friend of yours," she said to Emily
as she watched him take the basket from Rosie and sort
through its contents, "I was hoping you'd know who he
is."

"You've seen him before?"

"On the road. Just a few minutes ago."

"Oh! Was his coyote wounded then?"

"Yes, and so scared it ran right underneath Pretty Feather. She spooked at the smell of blood and reared up so high I just knew I'd have to jump off or be crushed when she fell over backward. But then this man came out of nowhere, and he petted and talked to her a little, and she calmed down like magic."

Emily smiled and nodded knowingly.

"He seemed really . . . different . . . strangely powerful," Cotannah blurted, "Aunt Ancie called him an *alikchi*. What's his name?"

At the mention of Ancie, Emily again started toward the coach to welcome the older couple climbing out of it.

"Walks-With-Spirits," she said, over her shoulder, "because that coyote and a mountain lion go with him everywhere, like pets. Some people say they must be spirits because real animals wouldn't act like that."

"What do you say?" Cotannah called after her.

"Oh, they're real, all right."

Emily ran to Aunt Ancie and Uncle Jumper, and they all embraced. Cotannah turned to look at the woodsman again. Walks-With-Spirits. The name fit him.

And it was one she knew she'd never heard before. So why did he seem familiar to her? There was something about the way he moved . . .

He was on his knees now, mixing some medicine. His hands worked with a sure grace that looked swift but not hasty. He knew what he was doing, that showed plainly in every line of his sinewy body, and the coyote knew it, too, for it lay without struggling.

She hoped it lived.

The thought hit her suddenly, with a surprising force.

Why? Why would she care? It was only a coyote, after all, a predator that in hard times would eat people's livestock.

But she did want it to live.

Because of the intense way Walks-With-Spirits was trying to heal it, she supposed, because his broad shoulders—and they were broader than she had noticed during that moment in the road, wide and intriguingly muscular beneath his thin shirt—bent over the animal with an air of such pure purpose.

That was it. She wanted him to win. She wanted him to be rewarded for caring about his pet so much. When she cared about something or someone, she, too, cared with every fiber of her being.

The thought froze her heart. It made her turn away abruptly from the sight of Walks-With-Spirits and go to Emily and her aunt and uncle. No, that was wrong. She used to care with every fiber of her being. She didn't do that anymore; Tonio was proof of that. Caring was way too dangerous. Caring would break her heart.

Chapter 2

⟨⟨⟩⟩

"Ah, and here is this new Choctaw—look at her, Jumper," Aunt Ancie was saying, stroking Sophia's cheek and meeting her unswerving gaze. "*Holitopa*. This child is a darling, that's all there is to it."

Sophia took the endearment solemnly, as her due.

Then, without warning, she let go of her mother's neck and held out both her tiny hands to Ancie, who threw the end of her shawl over her shoulder and eagerly took her into her arms.

"You are a darling, all right, your old Aunt Ancie can tell you that."

Ancie snuggled Sophia against her wrinkled face. For an instant, Cotannah wanted to be the one who was holding the plump baby in her arms—she wanted to feel that warmth, that trust, that innocent sweetness so close to her—but then she turned away from that sight, too. She wasn't going to start caring a whole lot for Sophia, either, no matter how precious a baby she was.

As suddenly as she'd gone to Ancie, Sophia wanted to be put down. She began wiggling and struggling, fussing and demanding to be free. Ancie set her on her feet

18

and took her hand, walking with her toward the porch steps.

"Come with me, all of you dear people," Emily said, and linked her arm through Cotannah's as she used to do. "Come into our home and rest yourselves. You've ridden a long, long way to see us."

Restlessness—the stinging yearning for something, anything—for going, doing, for something to change, something she even didn't know how to name, rushed through Cotannah with a searing force. That sudden, venomous longing to be somewhere else, doing something else, she didn't know where or what, took her more often now, especially since she no longer had Tonio to distract her.

"No. I don't want to go in the house."

Emily stopped still and looked at her, her huge brown eyes filling with such dismay that Cotannah reached out to her. Emily, no doubt, was thinking that Cotannah didn't want to enter Tay and Emily's home—the home of the Principal Chief that once had been considered Cotannah's rightful place. But that wasn't it. It was the demons that drove her.

"I'll come in in a minute. I want to take care of Pretty Feather first."

Emily glanced at the Texas vaqueros dismounting all around them and at her own two stableboys, who had come running to see the new arrivals.

"You don't need to do that! There are Willie and Cornelius, and if she needs some special care, your vaqueros will know what to do . . ."

Her distress was touching. Cotannah never could bear for Emily to be upset—maybe because Emily always tried so hard to see to it that no one around her was disquieted in any way.

"Just give me a minute to get used to being here,"

she said. "I know I'll enjoy being your guest . . . and Tay's. All I need is a minute to realize I'm back in the Nation again."

She gave Emily a persuasive smile, and Emily smiled back with the old trust in her eyes. She squeezed Cotannah's hand, then let go to shepherd Ancie and Jumper and the baby Sophia toward the house.

"We have a surprise waiting for you," she called back to Cotannah. "I can't wait to see your face when you find it, so let me be the one to take you to your room."

"All right, I will."

Emily truly was one of the best, most generous people she had ever known. There wasn't a mean or selfish bone in her body, and she had never meant to hurt Cotannah by loving Tay. The knot in Cotannah's stomach eased a little. At least Emily and Tay were at peace and contented—it was nice to know that was true for some people. Come to think of it, so were Cade and Maggie.

So why could it not be true for her as well? Why was she destined to be in a turmoil all her life?

She picked up Pretty Feather's reins and started walking toward the handsome woodsman, who was still kneeling beneath the tall pine. No surprise waiting in her room could ever divert her half as much as a challenging man, she thought, as she bit her lips to make the color come to them—especially after she'd practically been a prisoner of decorum for the whole three-week journey under Ancie and Jumper's sharp eyes.

Yes. A lively flirtation with Walks-With-Spirits was exactly what she needed to quell the restlessness and keep thoughts of the past and the future at bay. Fortunately, the servant girl had returned to the house so they would be alone.

He didn't look up as she approached, not even when

she stood near him looking down at the coyote. Its wound was covered by a poultice now and the bleeding had stopped.

"Maybe you are an *alikchi*," she said. "When it ran underneath my horse out in the road it was bleeding enough to have died right there."

He murmured something unintelligible to the coyote and dipped his fingers into a gourd full of water, holding the drops so they'd fall onto the animal's panting tongue.

"Who says so?" His golden-brown eyes flashed up to her face.

"I say so," she said, bristling a little. "Even at a glimpse, I could see its blood gushing like a fountain."

"Anyone could," he said brusquely. "I'm asking— who calls me *alikchi*?"

Ah. So he was vain, and therefore subject to flattery and provocation. He wouldn't be such a challenge, after all—he wasn't so different from many other men.

"My Aunt Ancie, who is old-fashioned and my vaquero, Juan Caldero, who is superstitious."

There. That should provoke him into really noticing her.

It didn't. He kept right on with his ministrations to the coyote, then sat back on his haunches and reached into the leather bag he wore attached to his belt.

"And what do *you* say?"

"I call you a fearless and brave man," she said, intending to flatter him into noticing her if provocation wouldn't do it.

As soon as she spoke, though, she knew that she truly meant it. He couldn't have known that Pretty Feather wouldn't fall on him or strike at him, no more than he could've known that the coyote wouldn't be crazy enough from pain to bite him, yet he had rushed in and saved it from bleeding to death, taking time out to calm the horse and keep her from falling.

He looked at her then, gave her a quick, slanting glance, and the light deep in his eyes flared brighter for an instant. Ah! She was making progress!

She smiled at him, but he was already looking away, turning back to his pet coyote. He resumed dripping the water onto its tongue, adding tiny bits of the dried herb he had taken from the bag.

"I know you braved my horse's hooves for your pet's sake and not for mine," she said. "But you saved my life anyway—or at the very least you saved me from being hurt. I was fast sliding out of the saddle."

"Taloa is my friend," he said, in that same abrupt, faintly arrogant tone.

A great irritation took hold of her, made her want to reach out and take hold of him and shake him until his teeth rattled. He wouldn't even look at her, much less amuse her with a flirtation! He wouldn't even accept her compliments and her thanks!

"And just who is Taloa?"

He said nothing; he simply sat on his heels, smoothing the fur on the coyote's head.

It took a long moment for her to put it all together and realize that he was objecting to her calling the animal his pet. The coyote he'd named Taloa, which made sense, for it meant "songster" or "singer" in Choctaw.

"Well, excuse me!" Thoroughly piqued, she went on, "I could have called him your predator or your varmint instead of your pet."

That brought a vexed look from him—she was at least getting under his skin as he was hers. Good.

"Anyone can be called a varmint when they're annoying," he said dryly.

That fueled her anger like tinder thrown on a fire.

"If you're referring to me, I wish I hadn't bothered trying to give you compliments and thanks for calming my mount. After all, you owed me some help since it was your friend, Taloa, who scared Pretty Feather into rearing up and walking around on her hind feet like a person."

"Be glad Pretty Feather doesn't talk like a person," he said, glancing up at her again with a wry lift of one eyebrow.

Her anger blossomed.

"Not talking at all when you're spoken to—that's worse! It's downright rude."

"Worse than what?"

His topaz eyes found hers and held them.

"Than . . . than annoying a person by offering a sincere thank-you to a . . . an oaf who doesn't have the grace to accept it!"

"No talk is worth disturbing the healing spirits."

Fury boiled up in her. He was looking her straight in the eye and telling her in so many words what his actions had already said: that she wasn't as important as a coyote to him.

Good Lord, what was the matter with him? She set her jaw against the pure frustration that came boiling up inside her, turned on her heel without another word, and ran toward the stables, leading Pretty Feather at a pace that made the stirrups bounce and slap at her sides.

"He wants silence, then he gets silence!" she told the mare. "He'll be begging me to talk to him before I ever speak to him again."

She ran into the stable yard with Pretty Feather and waved away all offers of help from the stableboys and from Juan and the other vaqueros. A long, thorough grooming of the little mare would settle both their nerves and give her something to do with her hands while she blanked out her mind. Enough was enough for one day, and she wasn't going to give Walks-With-Spirits so much as another thought.

When she finally finished and put the brushes away, she tucked her arm around Pretty Feather's throatlatch and led her into the turnout pen. There she saw Emily waiting for her on the veranda. She let the mare go with a last pat on the rump and ran toward the house, her hat bouncing on its strings against her back.

"I was beginning to think you'd never come in," Emily said, smiling her warm smile as she opened the back door of the rambling two-story house for Cotannah. "Aunt Ancie and Uncle Jumper have deserted me completely to play with Sophia in the nursery, and I'm dying to give you your surprise!"

She put her hand lightly on Cotannah's arm and pulled her toward the stairs. They hurried upward, their heels striking rapidly on the wide oak risers.

"I have a surprise for you, too, packed in my trunk," Cotannah said, "Cole and Miranda sent you a drawing of Joanna's new foal. They spent all morning the day before we left the ranch sitting out in the pasture with their paper and pencils, one drawing the off side of the colt and one the near, 'so Aunt Mimi can see the whole new baby horse.' "

Emily's eyes filled with big tears.

"I still miss them so much," she said, "I can't wait until they meet Sophia."

She pulled a handkerchief from her pocket and wiped her eyes.

"I'm not going to think about who isn't here now, though," she said resolutely. "I'm going to revel in the fact that you are here and in the look on your face when you see what has miraculously come to light at last."

"Emily! You're too mysterious," Cotannah cried as Emily took the steps even faster. "You have to tell me what you're talking about."

"You'll see."

They reached the second floor, and Emily drew her across the brightly patterned carpet runner to a door standing open on the west side of the wide hall. She led her inside and into the middle of the large, square room, where she took her by the shoulders and turned her to face the mirrored dresser.

"Look!"

Emily pointed impatiently. There, on the stiffly starched white dresser scarf sat two tall combs of fancy cutout silver.

Cotannah stared. They seemed to brighten, almost to dance, before her disbelieving eyes. A strange sensation ran up the back of her neck.

Could it be? Could they really be the ones she'd heard about all her life?

She took a step closer. Yes. The open design was that of the sunburst enclosing a star.

Goose bumps broke out on her arms. For the last twenty years, ever since her mother died giving birth to her, Aunt Ancie had searched for this treasure.

Deep, turbulent feelings stirred, where she'd locked them away in her soul. The old longings, the wordless yearnings to see her mother, to know the feel of her mother's touch and the shape of her face, to hear the sound of her voice and smell the scent of her hair, the old need to look into her mother's eyes and see a boundless love for her only daughter shining there, all the ancient, hopeless cravings that went all the way back to a time before she could really remember filled her heart like a river rising. She opened her mouth, but at first she couldn't speak.

Finally, in a whisper, she asked, "Are they Mama's?"

"Yes! Can you believe it? Polly Two-Roads has had them all these years, your mother had traded her the combs for a wagonload of corn and a team when your father was sick and couldn't make a crop."

"But why . . . why now? Why didn't she say she had them a long time ago? I would have bought them from her . . ."

"Polly says you're just now old enough to appreciate them. When she heard you were coming to visit us she brought them here for you herself although she's so arthritic that she has to be lifted, sitting in a straight chair, in and out of the wagon."

"Aunt Ancie has searched endlessly for these. She asked all the neighbors and kin about them when Mama died, and she's looked for them ever since."

"That's what Polly said, too. She explained that Ancie's always been too flighty for her own good, ever since they were girls together, so she never would have entrusted something as valuable as the combs to her. She was waiting to give them to you when you grew up."

"Ancie? Flighty?"

They looked at each other through the tears that were welling up, beginning to flow down both their faces, and they laughed out loud.

"Ancie?"

"Yes," Emily said. "That was the word Polly used for our strict, extremely particular Aunt Ancie. Flighty."

Cotannah took a step toward the dresser, then another.

"This is like a dream."

"I knew it would be."

She touched one of the combs with the tips of her fingers. The silver was warm from the sunlight streaming in through the window, so warm she could pretend for one, flying instant that her mother had just laid them there.

"I'm going to wear them."

"Wear them to dinner tonight," Emily said, with a little catch in her voice. "They'll be gorgeous against your black hair."

Cotannah touched the second comb.

"I was here in the Nation two years ago. I was eighteen then. Didn't Polly Two-Roads notice that I was grown up?"

"She says no. She told me that she saw you at the election dance and she knew you were still a child. She says the Great Spirit tells her that now is the time in your life for the combs to come to you."

"Polly must be as opinionated and bossy as flighty Aunt Ancie," Cotannah said, her voice breaking completely on the name of the aunt who had raised her.

She scooped up the combs and held them clasped to her breast with both hands, her head bent over them.

"I'm going to leave you alone now, 'Tannah," Emily whispered. "Supper's at six."

Cotannah nodded and stood without moving until she heard the door softly close. The minute Emily was gone, she turned and ran to the bed, threw herself across it and let the tears pour out of her while she cradled the combs in her hands.

She wasn't crying about being an orphan who never had known her mother or her father, though. She wasn't even going to think about that.

No, she had been needing to cry ever since Pretty Feather had reared up and scared her so badly; ever since Walks-With-Spirits had looked into her eyes and seen all the way to her soul. He knew her, he really did, and he didn't care to be around her.

He had told her to hush, not even to talk to him, and

he had sent her away from him just as Cade had done.

If the truth were told, she had been needing to cry ever since Cade told her he was ashamed of her behavior and sent her off the ranch.

She sobbed harder and held the combs tighter, so tight that their slender teeth cut into her skin.

If Mama could see her today, if she knew everything Cotannah had said and done in the past two years, would she be ashamed of her like Cade?

Cotannah's spirits lifted considerably when she studied her reflection in the mirror just before dinner. Her deep yellow–colored dress with its low, curving neckline was infinitely becoming, and the silver combs in her hair set off its black shine. They were gorgeous, and they gave her an intriguing air.

Yes. She looked fine, plenty fine enough to make Walks-With-Spirits want to talk with her instead of telling her to hush—fine enough, certainly, to compete with a wounded coyote for his attention. Well, now he'd be lucky if he could coax one kind word from her lips!

It'd serve him right if she made him fall in love with her and then deliberately broke his heart the way Cade always accused her of doing, she thought, as she arranged her long, loose hair in artful disarray around her face, then reset the combs in the traditional fashion— one in the front to "frame her face" as Aunt Ancie and her friends called it and the other at the back of her neck. He deserved a hard time for treating her like a child.

She left the room, walked down the hall, and slowly descended the curving front staircase, hoping she was late enough to make an entrance in the dining room. There were boarders here at Tall Pine and always visitors for supper, mostly travelers. There was lots of business going on in Tuskahoma these days, Emily had

written in her letters to the ranch, yet the town still had
no hotel. Surely there would be other men to notice her.
It would hardly matter if Walks-With-Spirits was present. She could care less if she ever saw him again. Truly.

The big clock in the hallway struck six as she reached
the first floor, but even its loud chiming couldn't drown
out the laughter and talk that spilled from the wide double doors of the dining room. There were lots of different voices, mostly masculine ones, and they sounded
wonderfully festive to Cotannah after three long weeks
on the road with only Ancie and Jumper and her escort
of vaqueros.

She strolled down the hall to the wide doorway and
stopped beneath its arch.

" 'Tannah, you're just in time!" Emily cried. "Come
sit here beside me and after the blessing I'll introduce
you to everyone."

Walks-With-Spirits was the first person she saw, there
at Emily's right, dressed in a fresh, sky-blue shirt. In
spite of all she could do, her eyes went to him before
she even focused on Emily's face. He met her gaze as
she stepped into the room, and his eyes sent a sharp,
quick thrill right through her, as if his hand had touched
her skin. Yet he didn't smile, didn't even give any in-
dication he knew her.

She lifted her chin and made herself look past him.
At the man across the table from him. At Tay, who
looked exactly the same but who, to her relief, had absolutely no effect on her anymore. At the portly, blond
man who flashed her a welcoming smile.

Another young man smiled at her and inclined his
head as she walked past, his dark eyes devouring her
face. Another cleared his throat and stepped away from
his chair to pull hers away from the table for her. Emily

reached out and patted her hand in welcome as they bowed their heads.

When Uncle Jumper had finished with his usual, rather lengthy blessing, they all sat down. Cotannah fought to keep from looking at Walks-With-Spirits again as the bowls and platters of food were passed around the table, as Tay welcomed her and Ancie and Jumper to Tall Pine and he and Emily introduced all three of them to the other visitors. A quick glance told her that only one was a woman—she, Emily, Aunt Ancie, and a middle-aged white woman named Jane Trahorn, who boarded at Tall Pine while she taught at Pleasant Valley School, were the only women present.

Tay was still marvelously handsome, with his black hair and his sparkling silver eyes, and he still had his silver tongue; he always knew exactly what to say.

"I'm so disappointed that I wasn't home when you arrived, 'Tannah," he said, flashing a grin at her in his old teasing way. "I knew you were here, though, and more beautiful than ever because while I was riding home the sun dimmed, despairing of competing with you."

"And you're more handsome than ever," she told him, laughing with the others, "and just as full of nonsense."

They smiled at each other then, and she knew without a doubt that no shred of feeling save friendship was left in her heart for him. Not even anger or hurt at being betrayed. Not anymore.

Walks-With-Spirits's introductions came last because Emily had started at the other end of the table. He acknowledged each of them with a quiet nod, but said nothing at all to Aunt Ancie or Uncle Jumper. His intense, dark amber eyes met Cotannah's for the space of one heartbeat when Emily told them each other's names,

and for a moment she thought he would say something
to her. But he didn't.

"We've met, but not formally," she said, as a challenge. Then, with the finest shading of sarcasm in her
tone, she asked, "And how is your friend, Taloa, this
evening?"

"Resting, thank you."

Well, now. He could be gracious and polite when the
subject was his mangy animal instead of her and Pretty
Feather. She felt her cheeks grow hot.

Yet the sound of his voice was like cool water flowing
over her wrists, like a soothing hand passing over her
brow. Its music mesmerized her, it was as different from
the blatant noises of the other men at the table as the
ridges of the Nation's blue mountains were from the
rolling prairies of the Texas rancho. She had to say
something else, anything that would make him talk to
her again, never mind her vow to make him beg for a
word from her.

But he was concentrating on his plate, his gaze di-
verted from her and his mind clearly somewhere else.
As a balm to her pride, she glanced around to confirm
that several other of the men, however, were looking at
her, as she had expected.

So she spoke to the young man whose eyes had been
avidly following her ever since she came into the room.
Jacob Charley, Emily said was his name. Jacob Charley,
who also was about the same age as she and who possessed sparkling dark eyes and who was finely dressed,
more finely, even, than Tay. And he, unlike Walks-With-
Spirits, had noticed that he was a man and she was a
woman.

"Mr. Charley," she said, "are you one of the boarders here at Tall Pine?"

He smiled at her broadly, obviously pleased to be chosen for her attention.

"Only occasionally," he said. "When business brings me to Tuskahoma, I impose on the generous hospitality dispensed by our Principal Chief and his lovely Miss Emily here at Tall Pine. My home is a day's ride away."

"I live here, Miss Cotannah," the plump, older blond man said smoothly. "If ever you're seeking a partner at cards or a companion to sit on the veranda and watch the sunset, I'd be honored to oblige you."

Most of the company chuckled at that sally, but Jacob Charley turned to the man with a quick retort.

"You'll be too busy for porch sitting, Phillips," he said. "If you're keeping an eye on business for us, there's plenty of work to keep you in town until long after the sun goes down."

The man called Phillips beamed at him.

"Don't forget you have a few responsibilities for the mercantile yourself, lad," he said heartily. "I'll wager you'll be spending more time in Tuskahoma after our store opens than you ever have before."

"As long as Miss Cotannah is here, I'll agree that I will," Jacob Charley said, a teasing tone creeping into his voice. "I'll have to come to town to liven things up for her, since you'll be wearying her with your old man's card games and rocking chairs on the veranda."

"Why, thank you, Mr. Charley," she said, flashing a coquettish smile at him and then at Phillips, "but I'm sure Mr. Phillips's company wouldn't prove tiresome at all."

Then she glanced at Walks-With-Spirits, unable to resist trying to see whether he'd taken notice of her popularity with the gentlemen.

He had not. He was eating his dinner and making some quiet remark to Emily.

She felt Jacob Charley's gaze on her again and turned to meet it.

"Mr. Phillips and I are partners in a new mercantile venture in Tuskahoma," he said, "and I'd be most honored if you'd permit me to drive you in and show it to you, Miss Cotannah. It's to be the first brick building in town, and our brick just arrived today."

"How fascinating," she said. "Of course, I've only arrived today, also, Mr. Charley, so I must rest a bit from my journey and consult with my hostess before I begin making my social plans."

There. That would whet his appetite if he had to wait and work a little bit at persuading her to go out driving with him. Plus she could use the time to advantage and ask Emily and Tay whether Jacob Charley would be suitable to squire her around—that would be the diplomatic thing to do since they would soon be writing to Cade, and the more docile she appeared, the sooner he would lift her punishment.

"Now, Jacob, I need to be the one to show Miss Cotannah around the store since you haven't been there but one day all this week," Phillips said.

Phillips wasn't serious, though—he was mostly only teasing Jacob Charley and admiring Cotannah in an avuncular way. She smiled at him.

"I'm more interested in seeing the ribbon and lace counter than the bricks," she told him.

"And you shall, my dear. You certainly shall. I'll make you a gift of ribbons myself, just as soon as the freighter brings in our merchandise."

She smiled at Jacob again and met his frankly admiring look, but she kept wanting to glance at Walks-With-Spirits, wanting to see his reaction to these mild flirtations. Risking another quick glimpse, she caught his eye as he stopped talking with Emily and looked up.

Jacob Charley must have followed her glance.

"Hey, there, Animal Man," he said, in that same teasing tone he had used with his friend, Phillips, "I heard Miss Cotannah ask you something a little while ago. Was that one of your furry little buddies you said is resting? Somebody told me one of 'em got shot today."

Slowly, deliberately, Walks-With-Spirits turned his piercing amber gaze onto Jacob Charley.

"They don't belong to me," he said.

Jacob Charley stared at him through narrowed eyes as if trying mightily to read the meaning behind the words.

"Well, now. You all sure do stick close together, though, now, don't you? Maybe I got it backwards— maybe it's you that belongs to them, maybe you're the pet of the four-legged ones."

Someone chuckled, several people stopped talking to listen to Walks-With-Spirits's response. But he didn't speak, only looked at Jacob.

"It's got to be one way or the other," Jacob insisted, "because every time I see you, in town or in the woods or running the tops of the ridges, you're right in the middle of that coyote and that mountain lion and God knows what all else."

"You're never in the woods or on the ridges," Walks-With-Spirits said offhandedly. "If you rode a stone's throw off the road, your horse would have to find your way home."

More chuckles broke out, and all the other conversations died down.

Jacob Charley's grin broadened.

"At least I ride a horse, like a regular man, instead of tromping around on foot in between a coyote and a mountain lion with a bird nesting in my hair and a raccoon running up and down my arm!"

Cotannah giggled at the image.

"I didn't know you had a mountain lion, too," she said to Walks-With-Spirits. "Where was he today?"

"I don't have one."

Because the animals were his companions, not his pets. But he didn't explain that, and Jacob didn't understand.

"Everybody here knows that's not true," he said. "Why, nobody in the Nation would recognize you if you happened to be out by yourself."

Walks-With-Spirits gave a small shrug. "As you would not recognize the truth?"

A shadow crossed Jacob's face, and he bristled as if that remark had hit a nerve.

"The truth I see is that you're causing a lot of backward thinking around here with your talk of spirits and herbs and the old ways and the People arguing whether you're a witch or a shaman. This Nation has to forget all that nonsense and go to the white man's ways if it's going to survive." Jacob's color had risen and his voice had gone sharp but Walks-With-Spirits remained admirably calm.

"Survival is the spirit."

That reply agitated Jacob even more.

"Survival is getting people with money to come in here and start businesses. It's teaching our full-blood children to speak English. It's getting rid of superstition. It's cooperating with the U. S. government so they won't take us over . . ."

"Jacob, Jacob," Phillips said, smiling broadly and shaking his head in mock despair as he interrupted the tirade. "Now you're getting off onto topics that will be boring to the ladies." He picked up a basket of bread and passed it to Jacob. "Why don't you eat your supper now and let me entertain the company with stories of my many travels?"

It served Jacob right, Cotannah thought, and Walks-With-Spirits, too, with one of them making mysterious remarks that didn't make sense and the other preaching politics like he was running for Principal Chief. Good heavens! She deliberately gave Mr. Phillips her most flirtatious smile.

"Thank you, sir," she said, "for being such a gallant gentleman. I'm thinking that your company would never prove tiresome, no matter what Mr. Charley . . ." She paused to tilt her head and flash her eyes in coquettish reproval at Jacob Charley, then smiled at Phillips again. ". . . would try to lead us to believe."

She smiled at Jacob, too, then, and he smiled back at her as everyone laughed and began talking again.

There. Maybe that would strike a spark of jealousy in Walks-With-Spirits. Jealousy, she had found, was a wondrous force for driving a man.

Chapter 3

W alks-With-Spirits felt her glance touch his face,
lightly, like the brush of a bird's wing, time and
again, as it had done since she walked into the room. It
brought that new tightening once more to his gut. Beneath the banter and the renewed conversations, her attention was still fixed on him, and she was still
determined to make him take notice of her. How could
he not notice her when she prattled on all the time, raising a fuss like a mother bird trying to distract a weasel
from finding her nest?

And how could he not notice her, even when she was
not looking at him, when her dark lashes brushed her
creamy skin and the blackness of her hair shone through
the openwork in the silver combs like a midnight sky in
winter?

What a travesty, though, that she was wearing those
combs cut out in the sunburst enclosing a star pattern!
Chito Humma always said it was a mark of honor for a
woman to wear that design, and here was this silly, shallow girl sporting it as if she had earned the right.

She was unbelievably beautiful on the outside but she
had no center, no balance, no harmony, no purpose in

37

her spirit. So how could she have done a deed that would bring her that privilege? She wouldn't know how to begin, for all she did, as far as he could see, was try to attract the attention and admiration of men.

His breath came faster, and his heart thumped once, hard, against his ribs. He closed his ears to the talk at the table and listened for the Great Spirit's voice to speak to the center of him, waited for his inner harmony to deepen again. Taloa's pain was enough to deal with now. Later, when his balance steadied, he would consider Cotannah Chisk-Ko.

He tried to force it, but his mind refused to leave her, just as his eyes couldn't stay away from her face. She was still full of the pulsing energy and eagerness for life that had drawn him to her that night two years ago during Tay's election dance, but that fervor in her was different now. It had turned inward and it had gone brittle—she was so plagued by awareness of herself that she didn't recognize him, didn't even remember that they had ever met.

Yet she was drawn to him as he had been to her then. What could be the meaning of this strange affinity between them?

Jacob Charley's arrogant voice broke into his thoughts.

"Hey, Ridge Runner, you might want to visit the mercantile, too," he said, "as soon as we're open, come in and look over the gentlemen's clothing. Nobody's worn braids and buckskins since the Civil War. We wear citizens' dress now—did you know that, or has the news not traveled that deep into the woods?"

He used that friendly, teasing tone that he had used when he spoke to him earlier. He spoke in a charming way that said he didn't mean to give offense—just a bit of laughter. But he did offend. For some reason, Charley had a core of hate in him.

Jacob chuckled at his own wit and a ripple of low laughter came from some of the others. Walks-With-Spirits wanted so much to ignore the remark, but silence would only challenge such a person. No use pushing Jacob to make unpleasantness at Tay and Emily's table.

He glanced up and fixed his gaze on Jacob's small, black eyes.

"Fashion is nothing but vanity."

"Listen to that—you sound like a preacher," Jacob said. "You been preaching to the squirrels and the bears out there in the woods?"

"They already know that truth."

Jacob Charley laughed at that.

"Oh, they do, do they? So then what do you do wandering around out there by yourself? You making a little Choctaw beer or maybe some white mule?"

"That kind of spirits I have no need of."

The man was such a stupid one. He was smart in some ways and he had a clever streak, but when it came to truth, he was stupid and deliberately blind.

"Better watch your mouth, Charley," said the man called Phillips, "Walks-With-Spirits is a shaman."

Jacob Charley dropped his fork onto his plate with a little clatter.

"That's what he and all the old folks want us to believe," he said, "but I, for one, say not. That coyote of his is no spirit—it was bleeding this afternoon just like it was made out of flesh."

He flashed Walks-With-Spirits a challenging look.

"Am I right?"

His tone held an edge of satisfaction. Walks-With-Spirits stared intently at his face. Had he had something to do with the rifle shot that had struck Taloa? Had the wound been deliberate and not an accident caused by a hunter's bad aim?

"Am I right, Coyote-Man? Your pet coyote and your pet panther aren't spirits, at all, now are they?"

"We are all spirits."

"Oh, yeah, here we go again. How could I forget that already?"

Jacob Charley looked at Cotannah Chisk-ko, then, with an abrupt nod of satisfaction. So. Perhaps he wasn't so very stupid, after all. He, too, had sensed that her real attention was fixed on Walks-With-Spirits, and he was jealous.

"Now what kind of a notion is that?" he asked her. " 'We are all spirits.' How do you like being lumped right in with a bunch of wild animals, Miss Cotannah?"

Emily, ever the perfect hostess, spared her guest from having to answer.

"Perhaps you're simplifying things a bit, Jacob," she said gently. "We all need to look deeper in both what we hear and what we say."

"That's true," Tay said firmly.

"We all need to see the difference between a primitive throwback and a progressive member of the Nation," Jacob said pleasantly, looking straight at his host.

"We all have to make our own judgments," Tay retorted.

"Yes," Walks-With-Spirits said, "that is one of the ancient traditions of the Choctaw Nation—making our own judgments."

Jacob Charley sent him a fast, hard glance full of undisguised hatred.

"I tell it to you because you have probably forgotten most of our people's ancient traditions," Walks-With-Spirits told him, staring him straight in the eye. "You have lost your Choctaw spirit. You have become a white man.''

The words made Charley's sallow complexion grow ruddy and bright.

''You're the white man, Shaman,'' he said, snarling the words from between his clenched teeth. ''You're the one who's come into the Nation for the one and only purpose of dividing the people and turning them against each other.''

His small eyes glinted dangerously as he warmed to his subject.

''As a matter of fact,'' he said, ''some faction of whites are most likely paying you to weaken the will of the Nation, to set our people at each other's throats, one side yelling that you're a witch and the other crying that you're a shaman and a medicine man.''

A shocked silence fell over the room.

''I'd wager a good deal of money that I'm right about this,'' Jacob Charley said. ''Why didn't I think of this before? You're being paid to raise up all the old superstitions and beliefs among the People so that the United States will declare us hopeless savages and take our land without any compensation at all!''

Tay leapt to his feet. ''Charley, I can't have you insulting a guest at my table,'' he said. ''No matter how much I respect your father, I won't stand for that.''

''I'm going,'' Jacob Charley said, jumping up and throwing his napkin down. ''Don't worry, this won't happen again. I don't aim to sit down with the traitor anymore.''

It was hard to believe that the hatred hadn't eaten the man's heart completely by now and caused his blood to stop flowing, Walks-With-Spirits thought, as Jacob Charley rushed from the room. It was more than just hatred for him. It was much bigger than one man or one thing.

The dream came to him that night as he slept beside his fire at the cave where he lived with Taloa and Basak, the mountain lion.

He was trapped, caught in a tangle of vines that swung from the limbs of a tall oak tree and trailed in a wide, dark river. He never knew how he got there, but his limbs were wrapped tight by tendrils that wouldn't break, and cold water lapped at the nape of his neck. The vine held him helpless, with his head the only part of his body free to move.

When he looked down, the river gleamed in the night, glistening with the silver of the moon and stars, reflecting in wavy patterns the sky he would see if lifted his eyes and looked up. A woman's voice, one he didn't recognize, was singing somewhere far in the distance, too far away for him to understand any of the words to her song. Closer to him, a night bird called.

The river moved silently although it ran so strong he could barely keep his bare feet planted in the mud on its bottom. He tried to call out for help, but every time he opened his mouth the woman's song changed into the wild turkey gobble, the traditional Choctaw call of defiance, the sound of warriors challenging the enemy to fight.

After his fourth try, when the old war cry had finished echoing from the mountains and had finally died away through the woods, he no longer wanted to call for help. Instead, he was at peace, completely at peace, looking up into the night sky. Slowly, in the very center of his vision, a star began to form, a bright star surrounded by a sunburst of stars that reached out brilliantly in all of the four directions.

He looked down, then, and saw them in perfect reflection on the slow, rippling river. He stared at them until they burst into flame on the water.

He woke, bathed in sweat, to the fall night's breeze and the sound of Taloa's even breathing beside him. Basak's yellow eyes glowed from the darkness of the woods across the little clearing from the cave.

Walks-With-Spirits lay without moving, willing his racing heart to slow down, reaching deep inside himself for quietness of spirit. But he didn't find it right away, for that had been Cotannah Chisk-Ko's voice singing the ancient melody with its Choctaw words. He knew it, even during the dream somehow.

He met Basak's gleaming stare and let it comfort him as he thought about the dream. First, two years ago, he had seen Cotannah and had walked straight to her through a crowd of many people. They had danced, moving together as if they shared one spirit, and he had told her then that she would seek him out someday. He hadn't known those words were in him until they had fallen off his tongue. And now they had come true.

She had returned, and he did not know what it meant, this pull of a silent force between them. Oh, if only Chito Humma were still alive, and he could ask him!

Or Sister Hambleton, the missionary woman come from the East to live among the Choctaw, the woman who had been Chito Humma's unlikely best friend. Unlikely, his people said, and hers. Inappropriate. Ridiculous. Wrong.

But to Walks-With-Spirits, who knew them both better than anyone else, who was raised by them, mostly, because he was an orphan, theirs was the most right, the most natural alliance on earth. Both were teachers and healers, both were loyal to their own spiritual directions, and both sensed the need of the people for the Choctaw ways and the white ways.

When he was fifteen, a boy beginning to grow into a man in the Old Nation, in a community hidden deep in the wilds of the land the white men had taken from the People and named Mississippi, both had died from a terrible, quick-acting sickness that had moved through the land faster than the birds could fly. If only they could talk to him now about what he was meant to do with Cotannah Chisk-Ko.

Why, why, had he been drawn to her like a bee flying straight to honey when he first saw her at the dance?

He had come to that dance, to that great gathering of the People for the election of the Principal Chief, out of loneliness, for he had been younger then and not as accustomed to the company of the four-footed and winged ones, not as attuned then to the companionship of the wilds and the woods and the Great Spirit. Then he had still missed Chito Humma and Sister with a sharp, sad ache.

So he had come to the gathering of the People at a farm near Tuskahoma and he had eaten pashofa and tanfula and fry bread and he had talked to some people and he had listened to the music. Then he had stepped into the line of men who were going to do the Wedding Dance.

In the women's line he had seen that slender body of Cotannah's swaying to the music, fairly vibrating with life, and when she had turned his way he had glimpsed the line of her long, graceful neck that looked too fragile to hold up her proud head, with its mass of black hair; he had seen the flash of her white teeth when she smiled and the huge dark eyes in her pale face that made her a beauty bright enough to blind a man.

He had asked her name of the man next to him, and

he had hardly been able to wait until the music signaled for a man to step out of line and go claim a woman. Why had he been unable to look away from her? Why had they danced together like two feathers in the wind?

Why, when she walked away from him, had he told her that someday she would seek him out and known in his heart that he was telling the truth?

How could this be? How could the spirits pull him toward her and now why had he had this dream of her singing and of the sunburst and the star?

She was silly and earthbound and in turmoil inside; she was foolishly squandering the strength of her spirit now as she had been doing back then two years ago. Maybe she had some connection to the reason he had come to the New Nation here in the West in his wanderings.

There was much healing he needed to do here, he was beginning to feel that strongly. Somehow—how hadn't yet been revealed to him—he was to help the People in the struggle to keep their land in severalty. He had known that since the coming of *hashi loshuma*, the old of the moon.

He sat up and scooted a short way to lean back against a rock, took in several long breaths of the sweet night air while he thought about that moment again. He had gone into Tuskahoma for supplies with his friend, Tay, who had picked up a copy of the Boomer newspaper, *Oklahoma Star*, from the counter in Pushulata's General Store.

Tay and Billy Pushulata had agreed that it was best to read it regularly in order to know what the Indians' enemies were saying in their drive to dissolve the Indian Nations. Tay had read over the headlines, then handed the paper to him. The instant it chilled Walks-With-Spirits's fingertips, he had known that it held some portent for him in that fight to keep the land for the Nation. But how? He had no alliance with anyone, no real communication with any human beings except for Tay and his wife, Emily.

And now this feeling of connection with Cotannah Chisk-Ko. When he first saw her again—out in the road, sitting the horse he'd just calmed—he had seen the turmoil in her eyes and had thought he was meant to help her find peace. But now he didn't know. How could he do that if she was bringing disquiet to him, instead?

On her first morning at Tall Pine, Cotannah woke with the restlessness raging in her veins like a fever. She had slept deeply, but fantastic dreams had plagued her, dreams that ran through her head over and over again, with every detail as vivid as in life. She was running a footrace with Jacob Charley through the woods while, a few feet away out in the middle of the road, Juan and the other vaqueros drove Aunt Ancie and Uncle Jumper's carriage at top speed to try to beat them both to Tall Pine. She was riding a slow-moving wooden rocking horse on the veranda at Las Manzanitas while Peter Phillips and her five-year-old twin nephew and niece, Cole and Miranda, all rode matching ones beside her. She was walking across the night sky with Walks-With-Spirits, surrounded by dozens and dozens of animals and, incredibly, every step each of the animals took left a star behind for a footprint.

All that was enough to exhaust the most intrepid traveler, but she had no desire to stay in bed all morning as Emily had suggested last night at bedtime. Indeed, she couldn't imagine sitting still for a minute.

She got up as Rosie came in just after dawn with fresh water for washing, dressed, and went for a walk across the dew-covered grounds before breakfast. Then she reentered the house through the back door, found the kitchen and the cook, who introduced herself as Rosie's mother, Daisy, and begged a hot biscuit straight from the pan.

She was buttering it and filling it with honey when a sleepy-eyed Emily came in with Sophia on her hip.

"Cotannah!" Emily exclaimed. "Are my eyes deceiving me? Is this the real Cotannah Chisk-Ko, in the kitchen so early in the morning that the roosters haven't crowed yet?"

"Yes, they have," Cotannah said smugly, reaching for the glass of cold milk Daisy was offering her. "You're the lazy lie-abed, Emily Harrington Nashoba, and that's why you didn't hear them."

"Oh, it's like old times! Let's have our breakfast here, just the two of us," Emily cried, and then with a glance down at Sophia's honey-colored head, "I mean the three of us. I don't want to cope with everybody else this morning."

Cotannah took a bite from her biscuit and a drink of the milk as Emily sat down across from her at the table by the backyard windows and settled the baby on her lap.

"And then let's have Juan hitch up the carriage, and we'll all go into town," she said. "If Tuskahoma's getting a brick building, it'll soon grow as big as Corpus Christi, so I'd better go in and start learning my way around."

Emily gave her a speculative glance and started crumbling a biscuit on the plate Daisy had placed in front of her.

"You'd rather go to town with me and Sophia than with your new admirer, Mr. Charley? He'll be going in right after breakfast, himself."

"Let him wait a few days," Cotannah said, getting

up abruptly to go to the stove and pour coffee for each of them. "It'll be good for him. I can tell he's got a high opinion of himself."

"He made me angry at supper last night," Emily said, "deliberately taunting Walks-With-Spirits that way. Jacob is a boor sometimes, no matter how nice his father is."

"I noticed Tay mentioned his father when he was trying nicely to shut him down," Cotannah said, coming back to the table with the coffee. "Who is his father?"

"Olmun Charley. He's a fine man and a great Choctaw patriot and Tay just loves him. He's on the Council and he's a staunch supporter of most of Tay's policies."

"I know that name. Isn't Olmun an old friend of Ancie and Jumper?"

"Yes."

"So are you advising me against letting Jacob call on me?"

Emily rolled her eyes and shrugged.

"Oh, not really, I guess. I don't know. There've been rumors that Jacob's not always really honest in his business dealings, or he's too shrewd or something—I know he has a reputation of making enemies that way but I've never heard anything bad about him and the ladies he has escorted."

Emily sipped her coffee while Sophia picked up pieces of the biscuit from the plate and ate them, one by one.

"You have to admit that Walks-With-Spirits provoked Jacob, too, though," Cotannah said, smiling at Daisy as she set a bowl of scrambled eggs and a platter of fried ham in the middle of the table, then put plates and utensils beside them. "He might as well have been speaking a foreign language for all the sense he made every time he opened his mouth."

"I'll let you all wait on yourselves now, ma'am," Daisy said briskly, "while I see to it that that Rosie's taking care of the dining room."

"Forget us, Daisy," Emily said. "Just don't even tell anyone in the dining room that we're awake and up."

"Yes ma'am."

"Walks-With-Spirits makes a lot of sense if a person listens and thinks about what he says," Emily said defensively. "Jacob wasn't trying."

"Well, neither was Walks-With-Spirits," Cotannah said lightly. "I wonder how his coyote's doing this morning. When I went out for a walk a while ago, I glanced in that hay shed where he left him during supper, but there was no sign of them."

"He told me when he left the house that he was going back to the cave for the night," Emily said. "He only brought Taloa here when he was shot because it was the nearest place to find the herbs he needed. Normally, he eats with us about once a week or so but he has never spent the night here."

Again the need to move, to do something, hit Cotannah, and she got up to refill their small china cups.

"Where's his cave?"

The minute she asked the question she held her breath, wanting desperately to know. But why? What did she plan to do with the information—go out there and demand an explanation for all the mysterious remarks he made last night? Go out there and demand that he look at her and see that she was a woman, that he respond to her as a man and not some vague-talking philosopher?

"It's over there in the east side of Buckthorn Ridge," Emily said. "Tay says the People have always had summer gatherings and ball plays there because of the cold water springs."

"All right," Cotannah said, "I know where it is."

She returned to the table with the coffee.

"If Walks-With-Spirits is living out there alone and coming in to see you all but once a week, then why was Jacob carrying on so about him causing division and strife in the Nation? I don't see how that could be so."

"He does things, and people hear about them," Emily said. "Like stopping a disease that was making the deer sick by finding some kind of grass for them to eat and planting some seeds he brought from the Old Nation to revitalize some abandoned, worn-out fields."

"I don't see why that'd make anybody call him a witch."

"Mostly that rumor comes from his association with so many wild animals," Emily said. "When he does go into town—or any other time anyone sees him in the woods—he's walking around with a coyote and a mountain lion. People have seen eagles and ravens fly down and sit on his shoulder and raccoons bring bright pebbles out of the creeks and drop them at his feet."

"So then the other half of the People again say he's a shaman."

"Right. Especially when he knows ahead of time when a tornado will come and he can predict its path."

"And again, the other faction cries witch."

"Yes. And they say he should be run out of the Nation before he does something evil to someone. It's a growing controversy," Emily said, wiping Sophia's plump hands and setting the wiggling child on the floor, "through no fault of his own."

"Then he isn't going around preaching a return to the old ways as Jacob claimed?"

"No. Other people are doing that because they see his powers and observe that he lives in the woods as the People did in the Old Nation long before the white men came."

She sighed and got up to follow Sophia, who ran directly to the pie safe and jerked open its lower doors.

"Olmun is one of Walks-With-Spirits's greatest admirers. He thinks he's wise far beyond his age. He's eager to talk with him every chance he gets, and personally, I think Jacob is jealous because he's an only child and he has always been the light of his father's life."

"Ah," Cotannah said. "That explains a lot about the tempest at the supper table last night."

"Yes," Emily said, laughing a little. "Doting father Olmun has always thought Jacob was wonderful, but even he would never call Jacob 'wise.' "

"Miss Cotannah, Miss Cotannah," Rosie cried, bursting in through the door to the hallway. "Here's a message for you, and I'm to bring an answer right away."

"I told her," Daisy said, returning to the kitchen right behind her daughter and scowling mightily at her back. "I told her we was not to say that you ladies was yet up and about, but Miss Talking Tongue blurted that news right out."

"It's all right," Emily soothed, as she picked Sophia up. "Don't worry, Daisy. Our quiet breakfast is finished, anyway."

Cotannah took the note Rosie brought her and unfolded it. At the top, a deeply embossed monogram in twining, fancy script shone in black against the cream color of the heavy paper. J. N. C.

She read the bold scrawl of the message beneath.

I'm sending my carriage for you at noon. I promised to show you the new mercantile building. I will do that for you and much more.

Yrs. Most Attentively, Jacob Charley

The signature covered half the page. Its large loops and flourishes, gleaming black against the expensive, slick paper, proclaimed that the writer was not a modest man in any sense of the word.

"Look at this," she said, smiling, and handed it to Emily.

"Shall I write back that I already have plans for the day?" she asked. "Then we'll drive into Tuskahoma together, and I'll surprise him by appearing at his precious store on my own. But with you and Sophia and maybe even Ancie and Jumper."

"Yes, why not?" Emily said. "We don't want to let him think he's got the upper hand if he's beginning to court you."

"I like to be unpredictable," Cotannah said, smiling even more broadly now as she realized the full effect she had had on Jacob Charley. "But if there's any quality I do like in a man, it's confidence."

Somehow that remark made her think of Walks-With-Spirits, on whom she had had no effect whatsoever. He was a challenge to end all challenges.

Cold fingers of despair closed around her heart. Jacob Charley might amuse her for a short time, he might keep her mind busy for a little while. But he was going to be too easy. He couldn't keep her devils at bay for long.

Chapter 4

Jacob Charley stepped out into the street and walked backward, with his eye fixed on his new building until he could see the split-shingled roof clear against the sky instead of all mixed up with the overhanging tree limbs. A powerful wave of pride swept through him. Not only would his new mercantile be the first brick building in Tuskahoma; at three stories high, it would be the tallest building, too!

He smiled and gave a nod and an approving wave to William Sowers, the head carpenter, who had stopped listening to Phillips for a minute so he could look and see Jacob's reaction to how the roofing was going, to see if he wanted anything. It didn't matter what Phillips was saying, really—it was only natural that William would look to him rather than to Phillips for orders—Jacob was a natural leader, everyone always said so.

"It looks good!" he shouted over the noise of the saws and hammers.

And it did. It looked great. He stood still and ran his eye over the whole structure while the breeze rose and rattled the leaves on the trees. It carried the slight scent of rain from somewhere, rain and the cool air of fall.

53

Yes, fall was fast approaching, and sometimes it brought fierce storms.

No matter. The roof would be finished before this day was over, and the mason's crew would come tomorrow. Soon the bricks would protect the walls, and he wouldn't care how much it rained—except to hope that it didn't raise the creeks and muddy the roads until the customers couldn't get to town.

He smiled broadly. Yes, this was a building good enough to impress a St. Louis drummer or a Philadelphia lawyer. It was almost finished, and, when the brick was on, it would look like the home of a prosperous business, the property of a smart, successful, progressive, forward-looking man.

Which it would be as soon as he accumulated enough in his secret Texas bank account to buy out Phillips. He didn't worry about buying his father, Olmun, out of his third—all he had to do was wait and drop a few hints and the old man would give it to him. That was the good thing about being an only son, especially the only son of a soft old man like Olmun.

Slowly, reveling in the sight of his new dream taking shape in reality, he strolled back to Phillips, who was standing in the spot where the double front door was open wide. He would order brass plates and hinges for it and have it painted white, Jacob decided. That would show up the red bricks very well.

"We'll have to cut those tree limbs way back," he said to Phillips and William Sowers as he reached them. "They'll rot out the eaves eventually, and, what's more important, they'll cover up part of our sign if we don't."

"I don't reckon you'll much need a sign, Mr. Charley," William said. "This here will be such a fine place that there won't be nobody in the Nation nor out of it who don't know Charley and Phillips Mercantile, soon as you all are in business for six months or so.''

Yes. But in that six months or so the name would have changed to Jacob Charley Mercantile and Phillips would be gone.

He couldn't say that, of course, so he acknowledged the remark with a nod and a friendly clap on the shoulder. The young man had good judgment—he had to admit that.

''William, I've got some barns to build out on my place in Buffalo Valley,'' Jacob said, pretending for a moment that the huge farm was his instead of his father's, ''two large hay barns and a horse barn, as a matter of fact, and I'd like you and your crew to put them up for me, since you've done such a good job here on the mercantile.''

''It'd be a pleasure, sir,'' William said, his face lighting with interest. ''Would you want us to start right away, since we're all but done here?''

''Yes. I can keep you busy all fall and winter, depending on the weather being good, of course, and all of next spring into the bargain.''

''That'd be welcome work for sure,'' William said, in a grateful tone. ''Thank you, Mr. Charley.''

Mr. Charley. He loved the sound of that address. Usually it was his father who was called Mr. Charley. Well, the old man would just have to face the fact that he was sliding on toward the end of his days, and Jacob would be taking over everything pretty soon.

He felt a slight twinge of apprehension. This was the first time he'd gone so far as to arrange to have major work done, so far as to contract for a truly major expenditure, without talking it over with Olmun first, but he felt certain his father wouldn't contradict his orders. He had, most of the time, let Jacob do whatever he wanted, from the moment he was born.

William Sowers went back to work, and Jacob glanced past Phillips into the street again. His heart gave a great leap of anger.

"Damn his hide! Phillips, do you see what I see or have my eyes gone bad?"

Phillips turned to look.

"Yep. There's your old friend and supper companion, Walks-With-Spirits," he said, with a low, irritating chuckle. "If that's who your eyes tell you it is, that's right."

"The very sight of that mangy woods rat turns my stomach," Jacob said. "I don't know how I ever managed to eat with him sitting at the same table."

His pulse thundered, roared in his ears.

The so-called shaman was stalking down the middle of the street like he thought he owned the town, with that slinking panther right beside him. A little rush of satisfaction ran through Jacob. The coyote wasn't here, though, was it?

People on foot, riders on horseback, coaches and carriages rolling behind teams, none of them slowed the shyster one whit nor made him move one inch out of his set path. The sneaky pretender did, in fact, think the Nation was his to rule.

And why wouldn't he, when superstitious men like Olmun and Tay Nashoba and two dozen others plus a wagonload of silly women, too, believed that he was a shaman and a damned *alikchi*, into the bargain?

Jacob's blood fairly boiled.

"I'd like to send him and that cat straight to hell," he muttered.

"Where's the coyote?" Phillips said.

"I hope it died. Then maybe everybody'll come to their senses and stop saying that his stupid animals are spirits and that he's got powers."

"According to him, they're not his animals, remember?" Phillips murmured sarcastically.

"I'll make him wish he had admitted the truth," Jacob muttered, "that he's got no more powers than a bessie-bug. I aim to encourage the crowd saying he's got evil powers, though, because I want him gone. If they kill him as a witch, so much the better."

They watched in silence as the ignorant throwback to a red savage—his hair was tied in two braids this morning, for God's sake!—and his mountain cat began to angle toward the board sidewalk and Brown's General Store on the opposite side of the street.

"Looks like he's headed to Brown's for his monthly supplies," Phillips said.

Jacob clenched his jaw.

"Let's hope he keeps on trading with Brown after our mercantile opens. If he comes in our store, I can't say what I might do. I'm liable to leap over the counter and strangle him."

Phillips laughed, long and loud. The white bastard actually laughed at him, Jacob Charley!

"Don't be attacking our customers, now. We need all of 'em we can get if we're gonna pay for this building, remember?"

"We'll have this building paid for in no time," Jacob said sharply, "remember?"

At least I will.

How could Phillips make such a simpleminded remark when they both had the extra money coming from the Boomers? Phillips was stupid, that was the truth, and Jacob Charley and his business would be better off when the white turnip-head was gone.

But irritating as Phillips was, he couldn't hold Jacob's attention for long. His vision swam, he was staring so hard at the scene across the street. The woods rat and his big cat stepped up onto the boardwalk and vanished into Brown's Store. Imagine! Taking a dangerous animal into a business establishment! Brown ought to throw him out and not hesitate about it.

He ought to be wiped off the face of the earth. At the very least, he ought to be scared out of showing his ugly face in town, arrogant fake that he is.

When that thought hit him, the plan began to form in Jacob's mind almost faster than he could sort it out, and he spoke even before it was finished.

"William!" he shouted. "William Sowers!"

It took a moment, but then the man came bursting in through the open back door of the building and running toward Jacob with a deep look of concern on his face.

Jacob's chest swelled. The builder certainly wanted to please him, and he liked that.

"Go into Brown's and find that medicine man woods walker. Give him my invitation to come see our building—the first brick building in Tuskahoma—and to talk to me. I need to speak with him."

Phillips stared at him, alarmed.

"Now, Jacob, what do you have in mind? What're you planning?"

Jacob felt a great surge of anger. The arrogant white-eyes actually had the nerve to question him in front of an employee!

He clamped his lips together tightly and sent William on his way with a commanding gesture.

"I thought you were going to grab the medicine man and hit him at supper last night, abuse of the Chief's and Miss Emily's hospitality or not," Phillips said worriedly. "I don't hanker to be a party to trouble, and we don't need trouble here at our store."

Jacob forced his pulse to slow and his words to come out light and cool.

"That's why I want to talk to him. I'd better smooth over that disagreement from last evening—it didn't set too well with Miss Emily and with the Chief and they're liable to mention something to my father."

Phillips stared at him skeptically.

Fury, pure, pulsating fury that the man would dare to criticize him and then dare to doubt his word rushed through Jacob in a hot wave. He fought to keep it out of his voice.

"It's true," he said, trying to sound humble and concerned. "You know as well as I do that old Olmun is one of the true believers in that lumphead. He talks to the faker all the time, and you know how he drives me crazy preaching at me when he gets on a tear."

He used his man-to-man, friendly grin.

"We don't want any friction in this three-way partnership, now, do we, Phillips? Let's head it off before anything gets started, or Olmun will nag us both to death. Besides, we might lose the business of all the folks who believe like Olmun if word gets around that I've had words with the charlatan."

Phillips frowned.

"You may be right. We don't want that. But I'm warning you now, Charley, this had better not be a trick—you'd better not be getting him over here so you can start up that argument again."

"I'm not. Count on it."

"Well, one of us has to tend to business," Phillips said. "I'm going to check that shipment of harness. This store is basically done, and we'd do just as well to start stocking the shelves."

"Go ahead."

Jacob stepped out from under the doorframe as he spoke, heading for the back corner of the building where two huge sycamores grew. The scaffolding used in working on the second and third floors still stood in an L-shape, higher than the arm's reach of a tall man, its loose planks littered with pieces of boards and some of the bricks that had been brought in the day before. A stack of them balanced carefully in just the right way could come crashing down onto the head of somebody below.

He stepped into the dappled shade where he'd be less likely to be noticed and, with a quick look around to make sure that none of the workmen and none of the people in the street were watching, loosened one of the support braces. Then he upended a barrel and leapt up onto it. Faster than he had even hoped, the trap was set.

He jumped back down to the ground and thought quickly how to spring it. The so-called shaman was an animal lover wasn't he? How about a hurt fox right back in there in the thickest part of the underbrush? The natural place to hunker down and try to see into the dimness of the foliage was at the end of the scaffolding, and, while all the pretender's attention was taken up, Jacob could shake some bricks off on him or tip the other end of the board so they'd slide off down onto his prey.

He smiled grimly. Great. The idiot liked animals so much he could see what it was like to be hunted like one and caught in a trap.

Calmly, he walked back out into the sunshine. Phillips would stay in the store and leave them alone to talk, for Jacob to apologize—Ha!—and for them to make peace between them. Then, just like the snap of a finger, Olmun's wise man would be gone.

A broad grin stretched his lips. What inspiration! This would most likely take care of the mountain lion, too, since it stayed so close beside the man at all times, but if not, if it didn't run away from the clatter and the noise, if it tried to attack him, he had the pistol.

He patted the bulge in the pocket of his new dress coat. Yes. This was so perfect! An unfortunate accident was such a wonderful idea he couldn't believe he hadn't thought of it earlier—say the very first time Olmun had come home singing the praises of the crazy "healer" who was nothing but a throwback to two hundred years ago in the Old Nation.

Why couldn't Olmun and his old-fashioned friends have enough sense to see that progress was the only hope of salvation for all of them? The traditional ways were dead, and he, for one, intended to see to it that they were buried and forgotten.

He rounded the front corner of the store and saw a sight that stopped him short. An open carriage sat at the doorway of his building with two of those Mexican outriders dismounted beside it, a young woman accepting the hand of one of them as she stepped gracefully to the ground. Cotannah Chisk-Ko!

His pulse tripped and began beating faster. So. She hadn't been able to wait, after all! She got to thinking about his invitation and changed her plans for the day! She had come to him on the very next morning after they had met!

Her skirts blew against her legs and showed the shape of her thighs as she stood beside the carriage, but it was her breasts, high and firm and generously large compared to her tiny waist, that held his gaze. What a handful for any man! He'd never seen a woman who carried herself so proudly and had so much reason to do so.

At that moment, she turned and saw him, lifted her chin, and gave him that same cold look she had used on him when she walked into the dining room at Tall Pine. His loins stirred and began to ache.

She was challenging him. The most beautiful woman he'd ever seen was challenging him—of course, she had picked him out of all the men at the table last night in a heartbeat—and it was a challenge that no man, certainly not Jacob Charley, could refuse.

His breath came faster. He could not wait to get that little jade alone in the dark. Yes, oh yes! One time with him, and she'd forget every other man she'd ever known.

He settled his coat more evenly across his shoulders, touched the tie at his throat to make sure it was straight, and strolled toward her.

"Miss Chisk-Ko," he said. "What an unexpected pleasure."

She tilted her head and gave him an intriguing smile. A smile that held a lot of promise.

But damn it, the other members of the family were climbing out of the carriage and gathering around her. Jacob greeted them and visited with as much good humor as he could muster even though his blood was heating fast. He could go a long way toward getting her ready to bed if he could talk to her alone for a while.

And he wasn't going to worry about the fact she was under Chief Tay Nashoba's protection, either. This was a girl who was accustomed to taking care of herself; everything about her manner proclaimed that as a fact. Tay would never tell it, but Jacob would bet good money that a certain wild streak in her was the reason she was here. After all, she was twenty or more years old, and, from what he'd heard, Texas had a whole lot more men than women, so why wasn't she married by now?

He turned to Emily, determined to hurry the rest of them along and keep Cotannah behind with him.

"Are you here to get your supplies at Brown's, Miss Emily? If you'd like, I'll be glad to send my freight driver with a light wagon to haul your purchases home for you."

"Thank you, Jacob," she said, "but that won't be necessary."

She shifted the wiggly baby to her other arm and glanced up at his new building.

"I'm glad to see that the workmen are about to finish your new building," she said, examining it intently. "Didn't you say last night that the bricks have arrived?"

"Yes. And I got word that the bricklayers will be here today or tomorrow."

"Tay is so pleased that Wiley Stewart has started that brickyard at Durant's Station," she said, "and that you're using brick made right here in the Nation for the first brick building in Tuskahoma."

"I'm glad that pleases Tay."

Actually, he could not care less what would please Tay Nashoba, but he did want to keep on friendly terms with him so he could have whatever influence possible on the Principal Chief. It'd be foolish to think that the Chief would ever side with him against Olmun, though— Tay thought the old man hung the moon.

"Tay mentioned it before we retired last night," Emily said. "He would have said so to you at supper but there just seemed to be so much going on. We had quite a lot of lively talk, didn't we?"

She was smiling and speaking lightly, but in her own sweet way she was reproving him for causing the contretemps at her table. There was no doubt about it. He'd been right to think that word of it would eventually reach Olmun and that he would then hear a much stronger rebuke.

"Please do forgive me, Miss Emily," he said, in his most gallant manner. "I'm afraid feelings at supper may have run a little high last evening because of the stimulation of having the attention of so many beautiful ladies as yourself and Miss Cotannah and you, dear Aunt Ancie.''

He sketched an apologetic little bow toward the prune-faced old lady, but she never cracked so much as a ghost of a smile in return. From the corner of his eye, he glimpsed a teasing grin on Cotannah's full lips. She would love nothing more than for Ancie to take him to task, it said, and she loved knowing that she had had the power, simply by her presence, to stir the men into controversy—for she knew full well he had meant only her when he'd named them all.

Conceited little minx. Surely, in a few moments, he could get rid of the rest of them and get her off to himself. But even Uncle Jumper was sticking like glue, looking Jacob up and down as if he were a horse for sale.

''Lonely bachelors like me and Mr. Phillips aren't accustomed to having such beauty in every direction we look.''

''Well, don't you worry now,'' Emily said, leaning forward to let the baby go into Ancie's uplifted arms. ''You'll be getting used to it because Cotannah is with us for an extended visit.''

''I'm truly happy to hear that.'' For once, he did, indeed, mean what he said. He gave Emily a warm smile, then turned to look into Cotannah's laughing eyes. Generously, he smiled at her, too—she wouldn't be laughing at him long once he got that luscious body of hers beneath his.

''I believe I promised you a tour of our new premises, Miss Cotannah.''

He offered her his arm.

''You did, indeed, Mr. Charley, and we are *all* of us looking forward to seeing the first brick building in Tuskahoma before it actually dons its bricks.''

Smiling mischievously, she slid her hand into the crook of his elbow. So. This was the game she was playing this morning—tantalizing him but not letting him get her alone. Whetting his appetite was what she was doing, and well she knew it. Her laughing dark eyes said that she knew he knew it, too, and she loved having him in her power.

The expression in those big eyes would be different when he had her in his power.

"Isn't that right, Emily?" she said sweetly.

"Oh, yes, we would all love to see your new place," Emily said, beaming at Cotannah for behaving so circumspectly.

Poor Emily, little did she know!

And poor Jacob, come to think of it—with his trap all set and no chance to spring it! Oh no! Plus the fact that William would bring that gibbering fool of a false shaman over here at any moment, and then Jacob would be competing for Cotannah's attention again just like last evening! What a cruel turn of events!

But there was no hope for it; they were moving slowly along the front of the building, surrounding him, making him a prisoner in their midst. Losing this perfect chance to attack the woods rat and having to behave politely to the idiot would make him really angry if he let himself think about it, but that would never do. Somehow, he had to turn this situation to his advantage.

"Miss Emily, we were speaking a moment ago about our unfortunate abuse of your hospitality yesterday evening," he said, "and I want to apologize to you again. You might be happy to know that just before you arrived I asked my carpenter, William Sowers, to go across the street to Brown's and bring Walks-With-Spirits over here so that I could make sure that there are no hard feelings between us."

Cotannah's fingers tightened on his arm. She probably wanted him to look at her, to talk to her instead of to Emily. Good. It was gratifying to know that she was jealous.

"Oh, I'm glad you're going to talk to Walks-With-Spirits, Jacob," Emily said, her voice trembling with pure sincerity. "Our People are so divided right now about so many things that it's great you're making peace with him."

She smiled up at him. Emily was a pretty woman, but she couldn't hold a candle to Cotannah.

"I'm eager to see these bricks that are made here in the Nation," Cotannah said, restlessly beginning to walk faster in spite of Jacob's slow pace.

"There, you little wiggle-worm," Ancie said tartly, as she bent over to set the fretting little girl on the ground. "You go. Carry your own self, then."

The baby ran toddling ahead as Jacob escorted them around the corner of the store. The wind was growing stronger, and it blew around the building in swirling gusts, pulling at Cotannah's hair and lifting her skirts. How he wished he was out there in front of her so he could look up them!

"Well, Miss Cotannah," he said heartily, "right there you can see our Choctaw-made bricks from Durant's Station."

He led the way toward a stack of bricks resting on the ground, staying away from the scaffolding where he had set the trap for his enemy. The board wouldn't dump the bricks without being tipped or moved somehow, but there was no sense taking any chances.

"These look just as professionally made as any other bricks I've ever seen," Cotannah said playfully.

She let go of his arm, turned, and walked a few steps so she could see the full height of the new building.

"This is going to be a fine mercantile, indeed," she said.

He hardly heard her. All he could do was look at her and clench his fists to keep himself from walking up behind her and setting his hands on each side of that tiny waist of hers. His palms itched, his fingers ached to close around her—they could easily span her waist, easily, that and do so much more . . .

The next instant she glanced over her shoulder, but not at him, at the baby. The air was filled with the little girl's screams and he turned to see that the wind had taken her bonnet, was carrying it away from her, keeping it just beyond her reach. She screeched at the top of her lungs and ran after it, bobbling and stumbling, but never slowing, totally heedless of scattered boards and piles of sand, kegs of nails, and all the other construction clutter.

"Sophie, watch where you're going!" Cotannah cried.

She grabbed up her skirts in both hands and ran toward the child, covering the ground that separated them faster than he would have believed possible. Ancie and Jumper were hobbling behind her, and Emily ran a little ahead of them.

"Be careful, darling," she cried, "slow down so you won't fall on something that will hurt you!"

He looked for the baby again and his heart leapt up into his throat. Then, he, too, began to run toward her. The bonnet had caught on the scaffolding, high up, too far for her to reach, and she was grasping the leg of it with both hands, now, trying to climb up to get it.

The stack of bricks he had fixed to be too high and unstable was starting to teeter and sway. Cotannah glanced up and Emily screamed, a hair-raising, desperate sound.

He went cold all over, then hot. No! No! He had set

that trap for the woods rat, not for the baby of the Principal Chief! If she was hurt or killed, he and his mercantile both would bear a stigma forever, and Tay Nashoba, who had never given Jacob the respect that he gave to Olmun, would never forgive him even though it would be just a terrible accident.

The thought made him pick his feet up higher, ready to call out.

Too late. Cotannah ran into the space where the bricks would fall. He ran faster.

The wind was moving the large branches of the sycamores now, setting them swaying, knocking one of them against the opposite end of the board that held the stack of bricks. Damn it all to an eternal hell—it would be Cotannah who'd be killed!

Bricks began to fall, fast, hard. One of them, two of them, looked to be striking the child, others rained down on Cotannah, who was grabbing for her.

Then out of nowhere, a blurred figure streaked into sight from the opposite side of the building, coming at a noiseless run. A man. Braids streaming behind him.

And it was over while Jacob was still a half dozen yards away: the man reached Cotannah, who had just picked up the baby. He bent his head beneath the onslaught of flying bricks and pulled them both into his arms without ever slowing his pace. Then he hurtled sideways out from underneath the scaffold, whirling in a circle to keep his balance as he straightened up. Through some miracle he stayed on his feet and kept running to the shelter of the trunk of the big sycamore.

Underneath its swaying limbs, Walks-With-Spirits, Cotannah, and the baby stood safe, wrapped in each other's arms.

A rage exploded inside Jacob, a rage more murderous than any he had ever felt in his life. The man was a witch, he did have evil powers, for he had taken the trap Jacob had set and had turned it against him, had used it to make a huge fool of him!

He forced his legs to move faster. If he didn't hurry up he would look even more foolish because even the two crippled-up old ones would also get there before him. How would Cotannah look at him now? She had saved the baby, that wicked witch had saved her, and he, Jacob Charley, had done nothing but stand with his mouth hanging open, watching. He would be a laughingstock throughout the Nation and beyond it, even among the whites!

The panic that Cotannah always felt when any man's arms first surrounded her still didn't come, not even after they'd stopped against the trunk of the tree and she knew no one was hurt. Walks-With-Spirits was holding her trapped against him with muscles that flexed hard as iron ropes across her back, but she felt safe, completely safe, instead of scared.

Yet why wouldn't she? He had just snatched her from death. Her and Sophia.

"I thought this baby was going to die right in front of my eyes," she said, barely able to catch enough breath to talk to him past Sophia's curly head. "Then I thought we'd been snatched up by a . . . tornado. You're . . . as strong as one."

Walks-With-Spirits smiled, the light burning in his eyes warming her like a fire. Then her gaze drifted down to his mouth and stayed there, on his lips. His mouth was so sensual, so lush when he smiled!

Suddenly that feeling came over her again that she'd had out in the road, that tantalizing sensation that she knew him somehow. From somewhere. But she would have remembered, she couldn't have forgotten, if he had ever looked at her this way before.

"If I'm strong as a tornado, then you're brave as an eagle," he said. "You dived into a *hard* rain to save this little one."

"Those were the biggest hailstones I've ever seen."

They both laughed.

Sophia began to struggle between them, but Walks-With-Spirits paid her no mind—he didn't loosen his grip one bit.

"If . . . you weren't holding . . . us, I'd drop . . . her," Cotannah gasped. "My arms feel . . . weak as water. They're shaking."

He nodded and tightened his hold on her.

"I won't let you fall," he said. "Nor the little one."

"Where did you come from?" she asked breathlessly. "All of a sudden you were right there."

"I was crossing the street when Basak the mountain lion told me you were in danger."

Her mind reeled. Mountain lion? It had brought him to save her? Basak meant "snap" in Choctaw, she thought wildly. Had it snapped out the words to him?

"Me? Or Sophia?"

"Basak said 'babies.' 'Silly babies.' Why were you under that framework, anyway?"

Now he sounded irritated. Disapproving of her, as usual. She felt a stirring of disappointment.

He glanced toward the scaffold and so did she: the fallen board lay crazily at an angle, one end resting head high against the leg of the structure and the other end on the ground. Bricks, some whole and some broken, lay everywhere, with their hard edges gleaming red in the sunlight. An instant more, and they could have been red with blood. Sophia's bonnet had vanished, probably carried away by the wind.

"I was chasing the baby, who was chasing her bonnet."

"But why were you here at all?" he demanded, as sternly as Cade would have done. "Don't you know that a building under construction can be a dangerous place? That a scaffolding full of bricks is for workmen? What were you doing?"

I came here to flirt with Jacob. I brought Emily and Sophia and Ancie and Jumper here so I could start a real flirtation with Jacob Charley.

Now that seemed the stupidest reason in the world. Quick frustration surged through her.

"How could I know that the workmen were so sloppy they couldn't even build a scaffolding right? The store will probably fall down next."

Walks-With-Spirits gave her a reproving look as if she were a child making excuses. Then Emily threw herself at them.

"Oh, dear God, thank you! Thank you!"

She was pulling at Walks-With-Spirits's shoulder, and then at Cotannah's, clawing at them, trying to get her hands on Sophia, who suddenly let out a spine-chilling wail and began to scream. Walks-With-Spirits turned Cotannah loose, and, freeing the baby from her still-clutching arms, he gave Sophia to Emily. Only then did Cotannah hear the commotion that was growing louder and more frenzied and closer and closer.

Disembodied voices sounded from every direction.

"Are they all right? Was anybody hurt?"

"No. Walks-With-Spirits saved them."

Cotannah turned to see that two men, both wearing carpenter's aprons with hand tools hanging from them, stood near her and Walks-With-Spirits. They were staring at the wrecked scaffolding and the scattered bricks.

"That baby and the young lady could've been

killed," the short, older one said. "I was on the roof, and I nearly fell off it when I looked down to see what the screaming was all about."

Somebody else, farther away, called to a friend.

"It was a near thing! I was scared to watch, but I couldn't look away."

"What happened?" another man shouted as he hurried toward the workmen.

"The bricks fell off the scaffolding, Mr. Sowers—they were all stacked on one end," the younger one called back.

"No! That's impossible!"

The one called Mr. Sowers shouted the denial so loudly that the other voices quieted. Everyone turned to look at him. Even Sophia's screaming dropped to a moaning wail.

"I was returning to work on that scaffolding when Mr. Charley called me to the front of the building," Sowers said clearly, his quick, dark eyes searching out Jacob. "Those bricks were properly stacked on both ends of the board then. I've been up there on the platform with them all morning, finishing the window trims."

When that soaked in, all the people turned to look at Jacob Charley. They were quiet, as if waiting for him to give another explanation for the near disaster, since it was his store.

He glanced quickly around, in all directions. A trace of color began to return to his abnormally pale face.

"Well, no one would've moved the bricks while you were gone, William," he said nastily. "They fell. I saw them with my own eyes."

Uncle Jumper's aged, light voice called out.

"Jacob Charley, you were behind this store when we drove up here."

"So?" Jacob said defensively. "Are you suggesting that I climbed up onto William's scaffolding and started moving my own workmen's bricks all around?"

Dozens of eyes continued to stare at Jacob.

Sophia's wails began to grow louder again.

Uncle Jumper, also, continued to look at Jacob Charley.

"Did you see anyone else back here?" he asked, in his dry way.

"I was only walking around . . . looking to see what trees we'd have to trim," Jacob said. "I had my back to that scaffolding. Besides, I would never have looked up at it, anyhow—I hire men to take care of such as that for me."

Everyone continued to stare a him for a long moment more.

"This whole discussion is ridiculous!" he cried. "It was the wind."

Sophia gave a sudden, completely heart-rending scream, and Emily collapsed to the ground, doubled over as if she were the one in agony, carefully bending over the baby to set her down.

"Look," Walks-With-Spirits said, his fingers brushing Cotannah's arm in a touch that went right through her, "again we must help our little one."

Our little one. Again we must help.

Those intimately murmured words also went right through her as she dropped to her knees beside Emily. Lord! It was like he thought now they were connected or something. A strange, warm feeling spread across the back of her neck and down her spine.

People fell back from around them because Sophia's wails were growing more earsplitting with every breath. Someone let out a soft cry of horror, and then Cotannah saw why.

The small plump arm, her left one, that the child had held clutched against her, hung free now, dangling from her shoulder, bent at a sickeningly unnatural angle.

"Oh, dear goodness, it's broken," Emily cried, tears pouring down her face. "Oh, Precious! Mama didn't know your little arm was broken!"

Emily's hands hovered helplessly over the hurt while Sophie, screaming, leaned away from her.

Walks-With-Spirits reached past her.

"Now, now, Sophia," he soothed, in that voice of his that was like sweet, running water. "Listen, now. Hear your bones go back into their places again. They will be grown back together. Shhh, shhh! Listen to them, now."

His tone was so full of love you might think this was his own child.

It calmed her screams and he gazed steadily into her eyes, he sang a low, rhythmic chant in the Choctaw tongue, cupped both his huge hands around her little arm, stroking above and below the break for just a moment and then, in an instant that Cotannah didn't quite capture, he slipped her bones back into alignment. The baby gave a single, shaky sob, then, miraculously, she was quiet.

Who wouldn't be? The gentleness, the pure goodness emanating from him was enough to warm the world, and Cotannah felt it all over again, that deep, elemental knowing she was safe that had come to her when she'd found herself in his arms.

"Cotannah, untie my belt and give me one end of it," he murmured.

She did as he asked, but when she encircled his slender waist and her whole body came so close to his that her breasts brushed against his side, she was almost paralyzed by the urge simply to draw him to her and rest against him. No. Sophie. She must think of little Sophie and not of herself and Walks-With-Spirits.

But little Sophie was feeling it, too. She was watching Walks-With-Spirits's face with her heart in her eyes, tears drying on her round baby cheeks.

Cotannah's fingers trembled, but she managed to undo the knot in the cloth belt, woven in one of the old symbolic patterns, and unwind it from around him. She found one end of it and slipped it beneath his fingers which he lifted from Sophie carefully so as not to let the broken bones slip again.

Her skin burned where her hands brushed his.

He wrapped the tiny arm carefully, firmly, then glanced up at Aunt Ancie, who had stood watching him, reaching time and again to touch Sophie's hair over Emily's shoulder.

"You will add the bark supports to this arm at Tall Pine?" he asked. "You have done such many times, have you not, Auntie?"

She nodded.

"I have. I will do it."

"And I will come tomorrow to see her."

With a last, feathery touch on Sophie's cheek, he stood up to applause from the people gathered around. He nodded his thanks.

Then he turned to Cotannah and took both her shoulders in his big, warm hands.

"And you?" he said softly. "Are you sure that you were not hurt also?"

"I'm fine," she murmured, although she had never felt more unlike herself than she did at that moment.

Jacob Charley's voice struck at them like a weapon.

"Turn her loose, you false medicine man! Get your hands off her. You're not fit to touch Cotannah, and you'd better not do it again."

Immediately, Walks-With-Spirits was facing him, his

back straight and his feet set apart, his big, hard body planted firmly between Jacob and her. She couldn't see past him without leaning around, which she did.

"You are not fit to touch her."

"Ha!" Jacob shouted. "Who are you to say such a thing to me? Keep your mouth shut and get out of the Nation now. Don't come back. After this, all the People will know you for the witch you are."

Walks-With-Spirits stayed perfectly calm. He wasn't even breathing hard, he was just standing between her and Jacob, balanced lightly on the balls of his feet.

People fell completely silent, as they always did when two men in a crowd got ready to fight.

"Get out of my way!" Jacob shouted. "Let me see if you've hurt Miss Cotannah with your bad medicine!"

Walks-With-Spirits gave a dry, sarcastic chuckle.

"Unlike you," he said, "I pretend to nothing."

"What'n' hell do you mean by that? I'm not the one pretending to talk to animals and heal the sick and raise the dead!"

"Yet you only pretend to rescue babies and young ladies."

Jacob's face turned purple. "Listen to me," he snarled, "and remember what I say. Get out of the Nation and go back where you came from. It's not healthy for you here, and you are no good for the People."

"That's twice you have invoked the name of the People. Why is that? You have no respect for the People, nor for the Nation. You have no esteem for tradition." Walks-With-Spirits spoke flatly, calmly.

Jacob made an incoherent, guttural noise filled with rage.

"You have no use for the old ways," Walks-With-Spirits said, in that same implacable tone. "How can this be? Your father is one of the best-loved of the Choctaw elders.''

"You leave my father out of this!" Jacob smiled, then, a terrible grimace of a grin. "Of course, I can't say anything about your father, since no one knows who he is," he said, in a savage voice, "and no one can tell us your clan because no one knows who is your mother.''

Walks-With-Spirits clamped his jaw tight, and Cotannah saw the muscle jump along the bone.

"But I know who I am," he said, in a quiet tone that held so much cold it could freeze a man in his tracks. "And you cannot say the same. Is Jacob Charley a Choctaw or a white man? Who knows? Who can say?''

A shocked gasp ran through the crowd, which still was steadily growing larger. Every single soul who was within the bounds of Tuskahoma must have come running when they heard the screaming.

"Are you calling me some kind of a traitor?" Jacob roared.

Complete silence fell. Cotannah moved a step to the right so that she could see both men, and what she saw was a pistol gleaming in Jacob's hand.

"I'm not calling you," Walks-With-Spirits said. "I'm telling you. No one loyal to his people would show so much contempt for their old ways, for their traditions.''

"I'm telling you that you have eyes too pale to be a Choctaw," Jacob said derisively, "so you must be the white man here.''

"Many Choctaws have white blood, but that doesn't keep them from also having respect for the old traditions.''

Jacob advanced on Walks-With-Spirits, who didn't so much as make a fist to defend himself but who didn't yield an inch, either.

"Get out of the Nation," he shouted, waving the pistol in the air, "or I'll put you out. If you stay—you know what happens to witches."

Walks-With-Spirits watched him without a flicker of fear.

Cotannah's blood leapt. Who wouldn't admire a person who could stay as cool as that in the face of such venom? Such danger? Walks-With-Spirits carried no weapon, she was sure of it.

"Just as I thought," Walks-With-Spirits said. "You'd be too lacking in courage to try to kill me yourself; you would try to incite someone else to do it."

"You calling me a coward?" Jacob asked with a roar. His eyes were burning, fixed on Walks-With-Spirits. His hand shook as he leveled the gun and pointed it at Walks-With-Spirits's heart.

"The hate you love will kill you," Walks-With-Spirits responded.

Then, without a word to her or even a glance to see whether she was still there, he stepped out, turned his back on Jacob and the gun, and walked away. Basak sat at the edge of the woods watching, and when Walks-With-Spirits reached him, the two of them disappeared into the trees.

A strange, bereft feeling swept through Cotannah.

"You're a witch!" Jacob yelled after him. "But I'm not afraid of you. I'll run you out of this Nation if it's the last thing I ever do!"

How could she have felt so close to Walks-With-Spirits, there for that brief time? His real opinion of her—his and Basak's—was that she was a silly baby. Why did she feel so empty without him when he had lectured her as if she were a child and refused to see that she was a woman?

The even more terrifying question that was pulling at

her consciousness tried to break through then, but she pushed it back. Too much had happened in the past few minutes for her to be strong enough to think about that now.

Chapter 5

That night, Cotannah couldn't sleep. She tossed and turned in the lavender-scented sheets, then got up and paced the floor. She hung her head upside down and brushed her hair until her arm was so tired she couldn't hold the brush anymore. Finally she lit the lamp and looked severely at her face in the mirror. Nothing had changed that she could see, except that she looked tired. And who wouldn't, after finishing an eight-hundred-mile ride into exile one day and then having a bunch of bricks rain right down at her head the next?

You're brave as an eagle; you dived into a hard rain.

Walks-With-Spirits. He was why she couldn't sleep. And he was why she was worried about her face and her hair and whether she was still attractive to men. She had no power over him, none at all!

The restlessness came over her like a fire racing across a prairie. She turned away from the mirror and threw the hairbrush at the bed, then ripped off her nightgown and sent it flying, too, as she ran to the armoire where she and Rosie had hung her clothes. Her rose-colored silk had a neckline cut so low that she could never wear it when Cade was around—in fact, Cade had never seen the dress—and even the unshockable Maggie had commented dryly that she'd better have a bodyguard if she was going to wear it in public.

She smiled as she flung open the armoire's double doors. Tonio had loved this dress.

Quickly, she removed it from the hook and pulled it on over her head without bothering with underclothes, shivering softly as the silk came sliding down the length of her body to caress her skin. Looking at herself now would make her feel better—it'd help to remember it the next time her path crossed that of Walks-With-Spirits. He was different, yes, but he was still a man, and she could have power over him as she did over all men.

She closed the last fastener and settled her breasts barely halfway into the lace-trimmed bodice. As she picked up the lamp to throw more light on the mirror, somebody knocked at her door. What in the world! It had to be at least one in the morning.

"Who is it?"

"It's Emily. I saw your light."

Cotannah set the lamp on the dressing table and ran to open the door. Emily stood smiling, her nightgown and wrapper blowing in the breeze coming in through the window at the end of the hallway, both hands holding a tray filled with tea things. Her eyes widened when she saw Cotannah.

"Dear goodness! Cotannah! Are you expecting someone else?"

A quick, guilty resentment raced through Cotannah. Then a hurt shock. What had Cade written to Tay and Emily?

"Do I have that scarlet of a reputation now?"

"What in this world are you talking about?" Emily said, and entered the room as confidently as if she'd been invited, forcing Cotannah to step back and let her pass. "I'm only teasing you, you silly goose, and you know it."

It was true. Her tone had held no censure. Suddenly Cotannah was glad beyond belief to have her company.

She sighed and closed the door before she followed Emily toward the bed.

"Leave it open for the cool breeze, if you want—I don't care if we wake the whole household," Emily said. "I'm just so happy that you and Sophie weren't hurt today that I intend to celebrate all night."

"But if we wake the others, we'll have to share the tea cakes," Cotannah said, and ran to lift a napkin off a plate on the tray as Emily set it down on the rumpled sheet and threw the covers all the way back over the footboard. "We do have plain sugar tea cakes, don't we?"

"Most certainly. And with extra sugar sprinkled on top just the way you like them."

Emily had come home from their horrific afternoon and made tea cakes, just for her! And she was here, in the middle of this endless night, ready to resume their old friendship, ready to drive the loneliness away. Tears sprang to Cotannah's eyes.

"Let me get out of this dress," she said. "We're going to sit in the middle of the bed and get crumbs all over us and talk all night just like old times!"

"No, let me see you in it first," Emily demanded, stepping back to take her arm to turn her around, looking her up and down, front and back. "Where in the world did you get it, Cotannah?"

"In Corpus Christi. Isn't it the most disgraceful dress you've ever seen?"

"I think so. And I can't imagine where you'd wear it," she said, laughing, "except here in your room—but

Cotannah, I have to say just what I've always told you. You are a stunningly beautiful, striking woman, and that dress makes no bones about it.''

"Maggie says I need a bodyguard to wear it in public.''

"Have you ever?''

"No. I only wore it . . . well, for Tonio. He was . . . a vaquero on the ranch. I used to wear it under my cloak when I met him at the line cabin on Saltillo Creek.''

Emily didn't bat an eye.

"Was? What happened to him?''

Cotannah twirled around again, then picked up her nightgown puddled in a white pool on the oak floor, and began unfastening the dress at the waist.

"Cade fired him,'' she said. "He said it was my fault that Tonio wouldn't leave me alone after I broke up with him.''

Sudden modesty overcame her, and she turned her back to pull the dress off over her head and don her nightgown.

"Quick,'' she said, "prop up the pillows for us. I'll be right there.''

"Did *you* think it was your fault? That Cade fired Tonio?''

Cotannah threw the dress over a chair.

"No! It was Tonio's fault,'' she said defensively. "I told him it was over between us, and he knew I meant it.''

"Why was it over?''

Cotannah shrugged and began buttoning her gown as she walked to the bed. "I was tired of him.'' She sent Emily a defensive glance. "He didn't amuse me anymore, he was getting so serious, so demanding. He forbade me to even look at any other man, he was talking about marrying me. Incessantly.''

Emily gave her a straight look. She was sitting cross-legged in the bed, now, holding the tea tray in front of her with both hands so Cotannah could climb up into the bed without spilling anything.

"And you didn't want to marry him?"

"No. He didn't mean that much to me."

The words popped out before she knew she had thought them.

She hesitated, then laughed and reached out to help steady the teapot as she climbed in and sat opposite Emily.

"If Cade heard me say that, he'd say he told me so," she said. "I don't mean that Tonio meant nothing to me . . . I, well, I loved him, in a way, I truly did. But I'm not ever going to marry—I don't think I'll ever trust any one man to that extent."

She caught Emily's eye and smiled.

"I like lots of different men."

"Like them or hate them?"

Stunned, Cotannah stared at her.

"What do you mean?"

Emily uncovered the cups, picked up the pot, and began to pour.

"Cotannah," she said slowly, "in spite of what you said when I came in a minute ago, you do know that I would never judge you?"

Cotannah thought about that while she took a sugary tea cake from the plate and began to eat it, heedlessly brushing the crumbs from her lap into her bed.

"Yes," she said, and knew it was true.

"For one thing, after what I did to you—marrying the man you had planned for ten years to marry—I have no right to judge anyone. For another, I know from watching my mother be miserable for all the years of my

childhood that rules and social conventions can do as
much harm as good.''

Cotannah nodded impatiently.

''But why do you think I hate men?''

''It would be perfectly understandable if you did.''

Once more she was grateful for what was not in Emily's voice. This time it held no pity.

''After enduring the hell of Headmaster Haynes and
his whip when you were just becoming a woman and
then, such a few years later, the terror of being kidnapped by those *bandidos* and almost carried off to
Mexico—and, I must admit, after Tay came to Texas for
you and ended up with me instead—it'd be pretty surprising if you could trust men easily.''

She spoke as matter-of-factly, as if she were discuss-
ing the weather.

''Trust you to get all the old boogermen out in the
open,'' Cotannah said, with an ironic chuckle.

''You need to talk about them,'' Emily said. ''It's the
only way to be rid of them forever.''

''I can't. I push them all down so deep they never
come out except in dreams.''

''If you only could get it all out, maybe to me . . . I'll
listen anytime, 'Tannah.''

''Then you would have terrible dreams, too,'' Cotannah said gently. ''Besides, Mimi, you've done your part.
You helped bring me back from wanting to die after the
bandidos, not to mention the fact that you and Tay rescued me from them.''

''Well, if you see that as a debt, you repaid it a thousand times over this morning when you rescued Sophia,'' Emily said, her big brown eyes overflowing with
tears. ''If she'd been hurt, it would've killed us all. Oh,
'Tannah, thank you.''

Cotannah's hand shook as she remembered the terror

of thinking Sophia would die in front of her very eyes. She forced herself to pick up her teacup.

"I didn't do a thing," she said. "It was Walks-With-Spirits who saved us both. He's the one you should thank that you still have your baby."

As she said his name the feeling of being in his arms flowed through her again, so strong she could smell the woods on his skin and hear the deep, sure sound of his voice. The question she had been trying to avoid ever since came crashing through the defenses she had built around her heart.

She dropped the cup back into its saucer with a clatter, splashing hot tea onto her thigh through the thin fabric of her gown. It didn't even make her flinch.

"Why did I feel the way I did when he held me?" she blurted. "Oh, Mimi, I wasn't even scared!"

Emily stared at her.

"What do you mean, you weren't scared?"

"Oh, I was *scared*, about Sophia getting hurt by the bricks—or me getting hurt, but what I'm talking about is when Walks-With-Spirits snatched us up. I didn't even know anyone was near, I didn't see him coming, the first thing I knew he had grabbed me and locked his arms around me and I didn't even feel the panic."

"What panic?"

Cotannah propped her elbows on her knees and leaned across the tea tray toward Emily, searching her eyes for the answer to the question she was so afraid to ask even herself.

"Ever since . . . Headmaster Haynes, well, since the *bandidos* . . . whenever a man puts his arms around me, even when I'm expecting it—even when I've tantalized and encouraged him to do it—I get this horrible feeling of a smothering panic until I can hardly bear it, until I can barely breathe."

"Oh, 'Tannah!"

Now there was pity in Emily's tone and in her eyes, but it was too late. Cotannah had already said too much, and now she aimed to find out all she could.

"It goes away after a little while, after my mind gets used to what's happening to my body," she said. "And after my instincts realize that the man I'm with isn't going to hurt me." She drew in a deep, ragged breath. "But, Mimi, with Walks-With-Spirits, even though he shocked me so, I never felt it at all. Not one tiny twinge of it. From the instant he slammed into me and Sophia like a runaway train and scooped us up completely helpless, I only felt safe. Completely, thankfully safe, and I don't understand why."

Emily just looked at her, holding her cup frozen at her lips.

Finally she answered.

"Because you were in danger and he saved you from it."

"No!" Cotannah cried, her voice breaking with frustration. "That was an entirely separate thing, escaping the danger."

She reached out and took the cup from Emily's fingers and set it on the tray. Then she took her by the arms.

"Normal women don't feel that panic, do they, Mimi? But I have felt it with every man every time one put his arms around me."

She shook her a little, as if to shake the truth from her.

"So why not with Walks-With-Spirits? Tell me that!"

"Because he sees you as a person, not only as a woman, perhaps," Emily said, frowning in concentration on the problem. "He looks at everyone as simply people. People who have souls precious to the Great

Spirit, people who have brothers in each other and in all the animals.''

Cotannah shook her head.

"Maybe. But my instincts knew he was a man."

"Ye-es," Emily said thoughtfully.

"Plus he judges me every time he sees me," Cotannah said petulantly. "He told me I'm a silly baby, and he makes me feel like a brazen, clumsy hussy when I try to flirt with him."

Emily laughed.

"I don't think even your rose-colored dress is the way to make him notice you," she said. "He's just so . . . ethereal. I think he'd be more attracted to something wise you might say."

She shook her head.

"I don't know, 'Tannah, why you felt safe in his arms. He's just different from any other man, he truly is."

Then she pulled her arms free and took both of Cotannah's hands in hers.

"But you aren't so different from other women that you should call them 'normal' and not feel 'normal' yourself," she said. "You are a wonderful, incredibly beautiful woman, Cotannah, and some man is going to love you to distraction someday."

"We'll see," Cotannah said. "And if that's true, we'll see if I can love him back. In the meantime, I'm just glad I still have a best friend who loves me."

"It's true, isn't it?" Emily said, squeezing her fingers. "I was just thinking the same thing. How can I be so blessed as to have my baby and my best friend given back to me on the very same day?"

"I hope nothing ever comes between us again."

"It won't. It can't. We won't let it."

They looked at each other for a long time, then sealed

that pledge with a long hug that rattled the tray and spilled more tea on the bed.

"Well, it certainly won't be that I'm trying to chaperone you," Emily said, when they pulled apart and pushed everything back onto the tray. "Tay and I just want you to be happy, and so does Cade. You know that. That's why he insisted you leave the ranch."

"I should've known you'd be great. I never should've dreaded coming here, but Cade made me so furious, bossing me and judging me the way he did."

"Don't be mad at him, 'Tannah. I think only another woman could even guess at how you feel about men after all the hard knocks you've had."

Her understanding tone made a huge lump form in Cotannah's throat.

"I think Cade wanted you and Tay to keep me away from all men, but I do need to have a beau while I'm here," Cotannah said, "just for the principle of the matter."

"I know. You need to show everyone in the Nation that you have other suitors while you're living under my and Tay's roof."

Cotannah shook her head in wonder and smiled ruefully. "This is why we were true best friends for so long," she said. "You understand me better than anyone else in the world."

"And you me."

Emily righted things and poured them both some more tea.

"We'll be going to the horse races two days from now," she said, suddenly, "and Walks-With-Spirits will be there."

The suddenness of the remark made Cotannah laugh.

"You sound like a matchmaker, Miss Emily. And how do you know he'll be there?"

"He's been doctoring our bay mare, which is going to run. He'll come to look her over at the last minute to see if she's sound."

"After Jacob pulled a gun on him today he may be scared of getting shot if he comes back to town."

"Walks-With-Spirits isn't afraid of anybody or anything. I've seen him face down a dozen people without turning a hair, people calling him witch, yelling that witches have to be killed."

"Aunt Ancie says he's an *alikchi*."

"So do I and the half of the Nation who disagree with the other half, who say he's a witch."

Goose bumps sprang up on Cotannah's skin.

"That scares me," she said. "Somebody besides Jacob might try to kill him."

Suddenly, she couldn't think about that. She couldn't think about Walks-With-Spirits at all, anymore.

"What do the two halves of the Nation say about Jacob Charley?"

"Some . . . mostly men . . . say he'll never be the man his father is," Emily said, "and others . . . mostly young girls and their mothers . . . think he's a charming young man and a great catch."

"Jacob's earthbound, for sure. He's not ethereal."

"And he would notice you in your rose-silk dress."

They both laughed.

"Indeed he would. I have a feeling he would not let me out of his sight in my rose dress."

Emily broke a tea cake in half, then let both pieces lie.

"Be careful," she said. "He sounded really mean when he was arguing with Walks-With-Spirits."

"I will. I'm only amusing myself with him."

"Today in town it looked as if you can amuse yourself watching the two fight over you," she said pensively. "Maybe we're wrong. Maybe Walks-With-Spirits does see you as a woman, after all."

"Only briefly," Cotannah said, "for about one heartbeat when I was wrapped in his arms smashed up against that tree with Sophia between us."

"And maybe Jacob isn't mean," Emily said. "It was probably his hurt pride talking this morning—he must've been terribly embarrassed that he wasn't the hero of the day."

"You haven't changed one bit, Emily Harrington," Cotannah said, laughing. "Always trying to see the best in everyone and every situation. Always trying to make everyone happy."

"Neither have you changed, Cotannah Chisk-Ko, always trying to stir up some excitement."

They both laughed frequently as they emptied the teapot and ate every tea cake on the tray and talked of one person and then another, of Las Manzanitas and Tall Pine and every member of the family, sharing every detail they could recall of these past two years of separation. Then they cried together when they spoke again of Sophia and the danger of the afternoon just passed.

Finally, when the big clock downstairs began striking four, Emily clambered out of bed and hugged Cotannah good night.

"I'm so glad that we're friends again," she said. "I've missed you fiercely, 'Tannah."

Cotannah confessed the same and then, when her old friend had gone back to Tay, she wandered to the open window and lifted her face to the breeze. She could sleep now, for having Mimi's friendship again was a wonderful comfort against loneliness.

The thought of it made her shake her head in wonder that their old wounds were healed. Emily truly was the kindest, dearest person, and a wonderful friend who never stopped trying to make other people happy!

But it would take a miracle for her inveterate match-making to work out. Cotannah knew in her heart that she might as well forget about Walks-With-Spirits and concentrate on Jacob Charley or somebody else, maybe someone she would meet at the horse races. If Emily was right, she would never have any more power over Walks-With-Spirits than she did right now.

For she would be helpless trying to deal with a man who responded to her as a person instead of a woman. And she couldn't say something wise if she tried from now until she was ninety.

The horse races were still held in the same place Cotannah remembered from her childhood: the grassy flats south of Tuskahoma that stretched east from the Texas Road along the Kiamichi River. And the homey smells of fry bread sizzling and grape dumplings cooking, the sounds of children playing horse while they rode down the saplings that grew near the river and of the adults calling back and forth and making wagers on the running horses were all still the same.

Auntie Iola called out from her seat in the shade, demanding a hug before Cotannah had even dismounted, and that was still the same, too. She lifted her face to the breeze and let it ruffle her hair as she unsaddled Pretty Feather and turned her to graze with the other horses. All of it, everything, was still just as it had been in the best times of her childhood.

Except for her.

She pushed that thought away. The day was beautiful, and excitement crackled in the air the way it did only on Race Day and she was not going to let any guilt or regret sneak into her mind to spoil it.

"'Tannah, you come here this minute and give your old auntie a hug!" Iola called again.

That was something else that never changed. Iola wasn't really anybody's aunt except Tay's, but that was her title of respect and she loved it. She also loved ordering everybody around. Cotannah smiled and started toward her.

"Have you picked some winners yet, Auntie?"

Iola nodded vigorously.

"I've made my wagers, and I bet the most on Tay's bay mare, of course," she said, holding out her arms without bothering to heave herself up out of her chair.

Cotannah bent and embraced her, then sat down in one of several empty chairs placed in a half circle in the shade of a big oak tree.

"Where are all your friends? Where's Hattie?"

"Not here yet. Hattie's getting lazy in her old age. Where's the rest of your bunch?"

"Packing the food and getting the baby ready. I came on ahead to have a quiet ride by myself."

To have a chance to see what young men are here. To look them over and decide who my new conquest might be. To see if Jacob is here. To see if Walks-With-Spirits is coming to look over Tay's mare as Emily promised.

Iola gave a raspy chuckle.

"A quiet ride? Don't sound much like the Cotannah I know," she said, narrowing her beady eyes. "You can tell me the truth, girl. You're a'wantin' first pick of the young warriors, I'm a-thinking."

How could one old woman know everything?

She didn't say it to Auntie Iola, however. It would only puff her up and make her even more difficult to deal with.

"Just like you when you were my age," Cotannah said lightly.

"No, from what I hear, you're a bit bolder than the girl I was."

So. Iola did have the second sight. Or she'd had a letter from Cade.

But she said it in a tone so full of curiosity that Cotannah took no offense.

"What makes you say that?"

"Watchin' you makin' eyes at Jacob Charley. I was standing in the window of Brown's store the other day while you and him acted like Emily and Ancie and Jumper wasn't even there."

"I was not!" Cotannah exclaimed. "Jacob was the one making eyes at me!"

Then she remembered and who was flirting with whom seemed completely unimportant.

"The baby was there, too," Cotannah said, her heart sinking again as she remembered the sight of Sophia running beneath the tottering pile of bricks. "I tell you, Auntie, I nearly let Sophia get killed right in front of my eyes."

"I couldn't see you and her after y'all went behind the new mercantile," Iola said. "But I hurried over there when the screamin' started and got there in time to see Jacob pull his pistol on the *alikchi*."

She made a derogatory clucking sound and shook her head in disapproval.

"Jacob's just asking to be struck dead," she said. "For somebody who's suppose to be so clever he sure acts stupid sometimes."

"Walks-With-Spirits told me I was stupid for even going back there by the scaffolding," Cotannah said, and began to grow angry just remembering it. "He talked to me as if I were a backward child."

But mixed with her anger was the stinging admiration she'd felt when he'd stood up to Jacob so coolly. Jacob and his gun. She fought it off. She was not going to let herself feel drawn to him anymore.

"He made me so mad I don't care if I never speak to him again," she declared stoutly.

Iola turned quickly and looked at her.

"Underneath those words, your voice is telling me something different."

"No! It's true. I don't need anybody else picking me to pieces and telling me I'm wrong all the time. Cade did enough of that this spring to last me for years."

"Did you ever think that maybe you should listen?"

"No! He's unreasonable and bossy and so is Walks-With-Spirits!"

Iola looked at her sharply, but then Hattie's wagon came rattling down the incline in front of them and drew Iola's attention away. Once they'd both greeted Hattie and helped her settle into her accustomed place, Cotannah sat with the two of them only long enough to be polite. If she knew Iola—and she did—in a very short while she would go back to her original topic of conversation and there'd be two old women lecturing instead of one.

"I'll find you both again later," she said. "I want to go look at the horses before the first race and Emily sent a message to Tay."

Cade, darn his hide, did write to Iola, too, Cotannah decided, as she wandered off into the sunny field. Of course he had. He had mentioned Iola when he'd announced that she was going to learn to be a "real woman in the old Choctaw way," and he had written to Iola about every single one of Cotannah's sins and indiscretions.

Her face grew warm and her blood rose. No, she told

herself, just for today, for one nice day, she was not going to think about anything unpleasant. She wasn't going to care if Cade had told the whole world that she was a wild, heartless, shameless user of men.

She would just find some new man and use him, she thought with a mischievous grin.

Or she'd ignore all the men and pretend that she was a young girl again, saved from the white man's boarding school and its evil, perverted headmaster by her hero, her big brother, Cade. The old Cade, who would do anything for her and take her side on any issue; the old Cade who loved his little sister and thought she could do no wrong.

The ancient, constantly hovering question attacked without warning. As a young girl she had done no wrong. She had been shy and quiet with everyone except people she knew very well. So what had caused bad men, strangers, to manhandle her and abuse her? If none of the horror and humiliation with the headmaster, Haynes, and none of the terror and shame at the hands of the *bandidos* was her fault, if she was completely innocent, then why had such awful things happened to her in two different states at two different times in her life? They didn't happen to most women even once.

Cotannah stared out at the festive scene as she walked blindly across the browning grass. That chain of thoughts fell into the rut they'd worn in her brain over the years and started going around and around, dragging their load of guilt and regret and infuriating, unsolvable mystery. What was it that was wrong with her?

She pushed the question away. She could forget it if she tried, so she made herself truly look at, really see her surroundings and think about that.

The whole scene was still the same as it had always been. The running horses dotted the landscape, each one

the center of a swirl of activity by a whole gaggle of
people: owner, rider, handler, stableboy, friends, family,
and lookers-on, each group ensconced in a different spot
of shade. Over there, halfway across the field beneath
two huge sweet gum trees, stood Tay's tall bay mare
surrounded by her people.

Cotannah started in that direction. Iola would be
watching for her to find Tay as she'd said she intended
to do.

On her way, she waved to Hattie's daughter, Tulla,
and to Molly Leflore but luckily she was too far from
them to get caught in conversation. The restlessness was
coming upon her, now, bad, and she couldn't stand still,
couldn't force herself to listen to their chatter. No, she
needed stronger distractions than that to drown out the
nagging question in her head.

Distractions like the two young men standing straddle-legged up ahead of her, their hats pushed carefully
to the backs of their heads while they shot blowdarts at
a target tacked to a stack of hay bales. As she watched,
the taller one blew into his gun, but when the dart came
out, the breeze caught it and carried it to the very edge
of the bales where, fortunately, it did enter and stick.

"You all be careful, now," Cotannah said in a teasing
tone, slowing her steps and swishing her skirts as she
strolled over to them. "My horse is out there somewhere, and I'd surely hate for you to miss that great big
target completely and hit her instead."

They both lowered the hollow canes they were shooting through and turned to her. She didn't know either
of them, but that didn't matter. Soon she would.

She met the gaze of one and then the other with a
saucy grin. They both grinned back at her. Didn't they
always? Men always smiled at her whether she was smiling at them or not.

Except for Walks-With-Spirits.

"You don't seem to have a very high opinion of our marksmanship, Miss . . ." the taller one drawled.

His sparkling brown eyes looked her up and down. The other one did the same, but less obviously. She stopped, waited for them to come a few steps closer.

"I'm Cotannah Chisk-Ko. And, well, I don't mean to insult your aim . . . " she said, glancing flirtatiously from one to the other, ". . . either one of you, but I couldn't help noticing that all the animals are in danger for miles around, not to mention people."

They were both taken aback by this honey-voiced criticism, but only for a moment.

"I'd say some people are in more danger than others," one of them said, matching her flirtatious tone exactly.

"So, Miss Chisk-Ko," the taller one said. "Looks like you're in need of our protection."

"I was thinking much the same thing," she said, with a flashing glance from one to the other.

"Perhaps we might be so bold as to offer to escort you around the grounds today?"

"Might we take you over to the track to watch the races?" the other chimed in.

The restlessness in her heart, in her body and soul, eased just a little bit. These two would be the perfect distractions for the day. They were young and handsome and taken with her and within a few minutes she would have one or both of them swearing he was hopelessly in love with her. Yes, she would let them escort her over to look at Tay's horse and soon she'd feel much, much better about everything.

"You might," she said, "if you don't require me to choose between you. I'm afraid that would prove completely impossible."

They looked at each other, clearly startled and pleased.

"Miss Chisk-Ko," the taller one said with a grin, "you now have escorts for the races. Would you care for some exhibition shooting until the horses begin to run?"

So they vied for her approval with the blowdarts and with silly remarks and with offers of candies and lemonade, and a few minutes later she slipped one hand into the bent elbow of each young man and they all began to walk across the race grounds in step, laughing and talking like old friends. They were cousins, Daniel and Robert Bonham, prosperous mixed bloods of a prominent family, she knew that by their name. Although they both appeared to be younger than she, they would do very nicely to amuse her today.

"Let's go see my friend Tay Nashoba's running mare," she suggested, smiling sweetly at each Bonham in turn. "You gentlemen may want to place a wager on her—I hear she's fast."

"She is," Daniel said. "She won a saddle and a knife and ten dollars for me the last time she ran."

They continued laughing and talking until they reached the two sweetgum trees, but as soon as the Bonhams escorted her into the loose knot of people working around the horse, she fell silent. He was here. Walks-With-Spirits was here. She could feel his presence.

Then she saw him. The others all faded back, and she didn't note their faces or who they were—he was all she could see.

He stood at the side of the magnificent bay mare, bent over, looking at her near hock. All the group went still, then, too, to hear his verdict on whether or not she was sound to run.

After a long moment, he straightened his tall body

with the fluid grace that was his only, the grace that looked so slow and easy but that really moved faster than the eye could follow. He stood for a moment, his head tilted toward the mare as if he were listening, or thinking, then he began murmuring to her in Choctaw, patted her rump and slid his hand down over the curve of her hip and her silky leg to the hock.

A trembling ran through Cotannah, a yearning to feel his hand move on her body in that very same way, a terrible need to know that sure, slow stroking of his palm on her skin. He did it again, and her breathing stopped.

The blood in her body stopped. The sun came warm through the moving leaves above them, the birds twittered and chattered high in the branches, the smells of frying bread and roasting meat floated on the breeze, and she stood there waiting with the others—not for his judgment of the mare's condition, though—but for him to turn and look at her.

Maybe to smile at her as he had done when he held her in his ironbound arms.

But he dropped to his haunches and held the hock in both hands, feeling it gently all over with his long, brown fingers while he talked to the mare, and she replied, "Huh-huh, huh-huh," from deep in her throat.

"She's sound," he pronounced. "Let her run. That's what she loves."

Immediately, the whole bunch of them sprang into action. Someone ran a brush over the already sleek hide, someone else picked up the pad and saddle and placed them on the mare's back.

Walks-With-Spirits stood up and turned around. His fierce, bright gaze seized Cotannah's so fast that she knew he had already known she was there. He had already seen her and had given no sign.

But now he stared at her as if she were at the center

of his universe. A great clutch of fear took her heart.

He was glaring straight into the center of her soul again, and he did not like what he could see there.

"Daniel! Robert!" Tay called. "Come here and see how she's shod this time. I hired your Uncle Peck to be my farrier."

Vaguely, Cotannah was aware that the boys said something to her and she nodded. Walks-With-Spirits flicked his light-colored eyes to one of them and then the other as they left her to go to Tay, then he fixed her again with his unrelenting gaze.

Finally, he bent and scooped up his skin bag of medicines that lay on the ground, stood up and stepped directly in front of her, once more looking straight through her with his burning topaz eyes.

"You degrade yourself by going from one man to another," he said, "or I should say to two at one time."

A cold shock raced through her like no other agitation she had ever felt, a shock that struck her to the very soul.

"You're as bad as my brother, Cade," she snapped.

He didn't answer, only watched her for one more heartbeat with his eyes blazing pale in his hard, flat face. Then he stepped past her and was gone.

Chapter 6

The next thing Cotannah knew, she was alone and wandering in the trees along the Kiamichi River, holding branches back from whipping into her face, pushing blindly through the brush with no idea where she was going. Sweat was running down the sides of her neck and her breath came hard and shallow, her legs felt tired and trembly and the agonizing stitch in her side was paining her so much that she wanted to cry out.

Except that her mouth felt so dry she'd never make another sound.

She'd never take another step, either. She burst out of the trees onto the low bank of the river and let her knees buckle; she sank to the ground into a nest of dying grass.

Something was wrong with her, she thought, as she stared dully out over the slow-moving river. Walks-With-Spirits had seen it.

Hot anger flared in her again, in spite of the state she was in. He was as bad as Cade—criticizing her, judging her! But that had been a truly weak retort to fling at him, since he didn't even know who Cade was. He destroyed her ability to think, that was what Walks-With-Spirits did, because he had such unsettling powers.

Yet he thought she could do better in the way she behaved, that she was making bad choices.

The anger rose higher in her, brought a bitter bile into her throat. But now it was anger at herself instead of at him, unforgiving anger because she had let his remark cut her so deep.

He didn't even know what he was talking about. Headmaster Haynes and his abuse hadn't been a bad choice on her part—she had been a completely innocent child at the time, and she had never chosen to go to his office alone.

And she had not made a choice for the *bandidos* to kidnap her and strip off her clothes and run their rough hands over her body and press their stinking mouths to hers. None of that was her fault.

So Walks-With-Spirits could just come down here and jump in the river. He didn't have the foggiest notion of what he was talking about.

She tried to blank the memory of his terrible face and of his awful, slashing words out of her mind.

You degrade yourself by going from one man to another . . .

Oh, just remembering what he'd said and the way he'd looked at her hurt so much that even her skin felt as raw as her heart. Why hadn't she defended herself, why hadn't she told him to mind his own business? He certainly didn't want her, so why shouldn't she go from one man to another as she pleased?

Degraded, he'd said. And he had, no doubt, meant depraved and disgusting, too. Well, that was just too bad; it was nothing more than his narrow-minded opinion. Besides, he didn't know her; he'd never spent time with her or talked with her enough to have the thinnest notion of what she thought, what she was really like.

That inexplicable sense of safety in his arms and

closeness with him afterward had been an illusion, some kind of hallucination caused by the danger. He was not only a stranger to her but a strange person, a peculiar eccentric whom no one really knew. A misfit, a crazy person, perhaps. She did not have to explain her behavior to him or to anyone else. The next time she saw him she'd show him for certain that his opinion meant nothing to her. He couldn't tell her what to do, Cade couldn't tell her what to do, and neither could anyone else.

Jacob leaned back against one of the huge trees and watched Cotannah in her rose-colored dress flitting from tree to tree and person to person in the dusky pecan orchard, talking and laughing with everyone, including those obnoxious young pups, the Bonham cousins. She hadn't seen him yet, she had no idea that he had arrived or else she would be making her way toward him this minute—hadn't she come running into town to see him the very morning after they'd met for the first time?

Of course, he had fouled up that day by letting the false medicine man be the hero.

He hated that thought, but it was true. However, he had gone away on business to let time pass and let that fact fade from people's minds, including Cotannah. Now, a whole week and a half later, hardly anyone would remember. They were all talking about the horse races a couple of days ago, from what he'd already overheard this evening, and everyone he'd talked to since he arrived at Tay's annual nut-gathering social had treated him just as respectfully as ever.

He bent one leg and propped his heel against the rough bark of the pecan's trunk, and cocked his head to watch Cotannah while in his imagination he stripped her clothes off. Smiling, he shook his head in amazement.

The little minx was determined to be outrageous in

every way, wasn't she? He knew a bit about ladies' fashions from ordering for the new mercantile and who ever heard of a woman wearing a man's faded work jacket made of that blue denim cloth like the Levi Strauss work breeches? And even more incredible, wearing it with a dress that fairly shouted to his shrewd merchant's eye that it was made of the best quality silk?

What a bold little jade she was, just the kind he liked! The jacket was unbelievably alluring in its contrast to her lushly female form, plus she wore it unbuttoned halfway down and he'd caught glimpses of a positively indecent amount of smooth skin and swelling breasts where there should have been fabric of the dress.

Obviously, tonight she had chosen her costume just for him. It was a way for her to tell him that now was time. Time for him to give her a taste of what she'd been begging for ever since the minute she'd laid eyes on him.

"Jacob? I need to talk to you."

Jacob nearly jumped right out of his skin. The voice was so close and so completely unexpected that he couldn't immediately identify it.

He swung around to see Tay Nashoba standing at his shoulder. Damnation! The man had crept up on him like the unreconstructed savage that he was.

"Chief Nashoba," he drawled, fighting to keep his voice steady.

Good God! That kind of a surprise could make a man's heart stop beating!

Tay stepped out of the deepening shade behind Jacob and stood beside him, looking out at his guests, some sitting and talking, some tending the fire which would be welcome as soon as the sun went down, some gathering nuts, which was the ostensible reason for this big, annual get-together.

"People love to come to socials this time of year, don't they?" Tay said, musing thoughtfully as if he'd never said he needed to talk to Jacob. "I think it's because the coolness in the fall gives us new energy after the summer's heat."

Jacob bit back a sharp retort. He had to remember that this idiot was the chief and a great good friend of Olmun's.

And he couldn't appear too impatient, but yet he would. His screaming nerves demanded to know what Tay wanted.

"You said you wanted to talk to me?"

Tay's manner changed abruptly.

"I've been hearing some rumors," the chief said, "that you may have some friends among the Boomers."

The soft-spoken words drenched Jacob's spirits as if he'd stepped out of the house into a cold rain. His stomach tightened, and his blood pulsed faster.

"You can hear anything these days," he said, fighting to keep his words slow and level while he shook his head sorrowfully, "anything at all. Me and the *Boomers*?"

"Right. That word has drifted to my ears from more than one source."

How infuriating! How totally insulting!

"Well, your sources are wrong!"

Jacob clamped his teeth over his lower lip to stop more words from coming out until after he managed to calm down.

"Sometimes you talk progress and cooperation with the whites so vehemently that a person might interpret your views to mean you'd be in favor of giving up our holding land in severalty," Tay said coolly. "Do you realize that?"

A fearful trembling tried to take him, but he fought it

off. He hadn't been that obvious, surely! He was not that stupid, he was not!

He tried to take a deep, calming breath without being obvious about it. He had to soothe Tay's suspicions and then somehow destroy them once and for all—why, his whole life's freedom was riding on this deal with the Boomers. If he ever was to be free of Olmun's dictates, he couldn't let it come to light now.

"Chief Nashoba," he said, turning his head to look straight into the chief's piercing gray eyes. "Tay. You know I have enemies. That's been true since the day I was born—people jealous of my position and my wealth will say anything to bring me down to their level."

"I know."

Jacob listened for a moment to the echo of the chief's tone of voice in his head. Thoughtful. The chief was being very thoughtful now when only moments earlier he'd been hard and nearly decided.

He hid a smile behind his hand. Why had he worried? No more persuasive man than Jacob Charley ever walked the face of the earth. With a few more well-chosen words he could wipe this problem out of existence once and for all.

"Then it grieves me that you would give any credence whatsoever to such vicious talk," he said, trying to sound sad instead of angry. "You know me as well as anybody in the Nation."

"And you know me," Tay Nashoba said, in his usual haughty way. "I would never bring grief and shame to your father without cause, for he is truly a fine man and a Choctaw patriot. But if I find proof that you are working for the Boomers to open our land up to white settlement, Jacob Charley, even my respect for Olmun will not stop me from bringing charges of treason against you."

Now the chief's voice wasn't thoughtful at all; it was harder than flint. He meant what he said. He said it again.

"Betray the People, Jacob, and I'll see you shot."

And then the arrogant son of a bitch simply turned and walked away, as quietly as he had come.

Jacob's blood boiled high, roaring in his ears until it blocked out the happy voices and laughter of the others at the social. All right. If that was the way the Principal Chief was going to talk to him, him, Jacob Charley, of the most prominent family in the Nation, then the Principal Chief would have to be taught a lesson.

Bedding Cotannah Chisk-Ko, the Chief's houseguest, while she was under the Chief's protection, entrusted to his care by her brother, the powerful Cade Chisk-Ko, would make a fitting insult. He grinned. Not that he wouldn't have done it, anyway. But now he'd make sure the Chief would hear about it—even if he had to tell it himself.

Tay Nashoba needed to learn that he was not all-powerful.

Yes. And Cotannah's brother, Cade Chisk-Ko, was another arrogant bastard, and it'd serve him right if his spoiled little sister was violated while she was under the protection of Cade's best friend.

He smiled and turned to look for the glow of the rose-colored dress in the shadows thrown by the trees. Finding Cotannah was easy, even in the crowd and the dusk because her full skirts shone and glimmered like a blossoming flower and, of course, a gaggle of young men had gathered around her. He began strolling toward her. No doubt about it. This was going to be a pleasure in more ways than one.

*   *   *

A large, warm hand settled itself in the small of Cotannah's back, nestling there as if she had invited it. Well! Daniel certainly was becoming much more forward. She laughed and touched Robert's arm in appreciation of the joke he had just finished telling and then glanced over her shoulder, expecting to see his taller cousin looking down at her with his usual adoration.

Instead, Jacob Charley smiled at her.

"You remind me of a wild-vining rose tonight, Miss Cotannah, in your rose-colored dress," he said. "How about rambling through the pecan orchard with me?"

He let his heated gaze linger on hers for a long moment then, abruptly, he looked straight at Robert Bonham.

"You will excuse us, I'm certain, sir," he said. "Good evening."

The younger man's face flushed a deep, angry red, but he turned on his heel and strode away without a word. She was relieved to see the back of him, really, Cotannah thought—never in all her life had she met anyone with such a store of jests that were not funny in the least—but she wouldn't let Jacob know that.

She pulled away from the growing pressure of his hand and frowned at him over her shoulder.

"And what makes you think you have the right to run off my beaux?" she demanded saucily. "You may have discouraged them forever."

"That's exactly what I intended."

He captured her gaze with his and held it.

She launched a new attack, determined to get the upper hand.

"You sneaked up behind me when I wasn't looking," she complained with a pout of her lips, as she turned around to face him and took a few slow steps backwards. "I hardly think that is fair."

"I won't fight fair for you, my dear."

He spoke softly, but his dark eyes were gleaming at her so hotly that it seemed inconceivable that someone—Tay, for instance, acting as Cade's agent—didn't notice and come over to interrupt them. After all, they were right in the middle of dozens of people. A quick glance, though, proved everyone oblivious. Neither Daniel nor Robert Bonham was anywhere to be seen.

But they could probably see her and it would do them good to see they had a rival for her attentions. And, if he were anywhere around, it would do Walks-With-Spirits good to see that she would decide her own behavior, totally independent of whatever criticisms he might make.

"I wasn't aware that you would fight for me at all," she said, tilting her head and batting her eyelashes at Jacob, "fair or foul."

"With my last breath."

He spoke in a tone of deepest sincerity, then he smiled and winked at her, rogue that he was. Good. This was exactly what she needed—a man bent on no more than amusement, just like herself.

"Why, Mr. Charley!" she gasped, pretending to be shocked.

Then she mirrored exactly his rascal's smile.

"Did you do something foul to poor Daniel Bonham? One minute he was the one right there behind me, the next it was you."

"I did not. I simply touched him on the shoulder, gave him a look, and he faded quietly away into the dusk."

"You're such a powerful man! Within only a moment, you have frightened both the cousins into deserting me!"

She put her hands on her hips, pretending to be

miffed, a move to bring attention to her breasts, straining against the half-fastened confines of the jacket. The heat in his eyes burst into flames.

"Come with me, my wild rose," he said, in a husky tone. "Let's get away from these people so that we can get acquainted without all their prying eyes. I want to tell you how I feel when I look at you."

Gallantly, he offered her his arm. She took it, and they started walking toward the edge of the clearing, his eyes devouring her as they went.

It felt good to be completely, totally, the object of a man's approving attention. The Bonham boys were all right, but they were just that—boys—and they were constantly as aware of themselves and each other as they were of her.

"I never knew that you were such a natural poet, sir," she said with a flashing smile. "No gentleman has ever called me a wild rose before."

He drew her a bit closer to his side.

"Ah, my dear, but I did not call you a wild rose," he said, with a dashing smile. "I called you *my* wild rose and that is exactly what I meant."

She pulled a little bit away from him but tossed her head and flashed him a look that bade him come closer if he dared.

"I belong to no one but myself," she said.

He raised one eyebrow.

"Of course you do," he said quickly. "I'm speaking only in reference to myself versus other suitors."

He smiled down into her eyes. Then he began walking faster, leading her deeper into the rolling woods, his hand firmly over hers on his arm.

"We can't go too far from the others," she said. "Emily will be looking for me."

He stopped, suddenly, and took both her hands in his,

swinging backwards a few steps so he could look at her.

"Ah," he said, "but something tells me that you didn't wear this dress for Emily." He gave her that devil's grin. "Now, did you? Tell me the truth."

She couldn't resist grinning back. "No."

His eyes roamed over her, openly admiring every inch of her. He thought she was beautiful—it was written all over his face. Really, he was perfect for her stay here, perfect to prove to everyone that she could attract a prominent man even though she might be living under the roof of one who had rejected her. Best of all, he, like herself, was nothing but a flirt, and he would never cause her the kind of problems that Tonio had created. She held his meaningful gaze for a moment longer, then lowered her eyelashes coquettishly and looked away.

Right into the arresting face of Walks-With-Spirits.

He stood beside the trunk of one of the big pecan trees, as completely still as if he, too, had roots that ran deep into the ground. But his eyes were as alive as fire, they were burning lights in his wooden face, as bright and gleaming in the shadows of the deepening dusk as the big yellow eyes of Basak the panther sitting at his feet. Another set of eyes glowed in the darkness behind him. The coyote, Taloa, without doubt.

The flames of his eyes wouldn't leave her—they set her face and her bare throat to smoldering, the biting heat grew and grew in every pore of her skin. Beneath it, though, the inside of her body felt a sudden, deathly chill, as if she had a fever. Oh! Would he never smile at her again?

"Go away!" she cried. "You've already told me what you think of me, so you can just go away! Stop spying on me!"

She sounded like a petulant child, she knew it the

minute the words left her mouth, but she couldn't call them back. Whirling away from the touch of those terrible eyes, she caught Jacob's arm and began walking away, fast, away from Walks-With-Spirits, who was nothing but a self-righteous prude, always standing apart from the rest of the human race. *Judging, Judging.*

Well, he had no right to judge her!

"Has that charlatan insulted you?" Jacob asked. "Would you like me to demand satisfaction?"

"No," she said quickly. "No. I . . . hated that . . . altercation you all had behind the store the other day."

"Why, Miss Cotannah!" he said in a tone that proclaimed he was truly moved by her words. "You mustn't worry about me, for I can best that false prophet any day of the week with any weapon he might choose."

He didn't turn around and march right back there to try and make good on that claim, however, she noted wryly. And what a selfish pig, how full of himself he was, leaping to the conclusion that she had been afraid for his safety!

"No," she said again. "Do nothing on my account. I . . ."

She snapped her mouth closed, surprised by her own response. What was the matter with her, discouraging such delicious excitement as men fighting over her?

Jacob gave a satisfied chuckle, slipped his arm around her waist, and squeezed her to him, hard, as they began to hurry through the dusk-shrouded trees. She leaned against him as the sounds of the social faded away, erased by the sounds of sticks and leaves under their feet. "I know the perfect spot to sit and talk," he said. "I promise no one will disturb us there."

"Thank you, Jacob," she murmured.

He held her even closer, and the warmth of his body alleviated the cold inside her to a small extent.

"You just let me know if that crazy one ever bothers you again," he said, "but for now let's forget all about him. I knew the minute I saw you that you wanted to spend time alone with me tonight."

His arrogance sent a sharp shaft of irritation through her. Well, he'd soon see that she was the one in charge here.

She challenged him as they entered a small clearing in some pines where the darkness had grown complete except for the first pale rays of light from the moon.

"Tell me now, sir, aren't you assuming a great deal?"

"No. Your beautiful eyes have been begging me to be alone with you ever since the night we met."

"As I said," she repeated, with a teasing laugh, "you assume a great deal."

Without another word, he put his free hand beneath her chin and turned her mouth up to meet his. "Prove me wrong," he whispered against her lips.

Maybe she would, she thought, as he pressed her to him and began to kiss her. If she didn't like a man's kisses, she had found, she wouldn't like any other intimacy with him, either.

He kissed only tolerably well, but at least his blather and admiration had erased the sight of Walks-With-Spirits's fierce face. His kiss wasn't particularly repulsive, but it didn't make her blood heat with desire the way Tonio's kisses had done. Was it possible to learn to like a man's kisses after a while?

She desperately needed strong sensations to flood her body, to wipe out the memory of Walks-With-Spirits's arms around her . . .

The unexpected thought scared her, so she slipped her arms around his neck and made herself kiss him back.

He gave a grunt of pleasure, thrust his tongue deep into her mouth, and dug his fingers into the flesh of her shoulders, hurting her even through the thick fabric of her jacket. The next instant, one of his hands was in her hair, the other was cupping her bottom, and he was grinding his body against hers. She couldn't breathe. He was crushing her.

She realized she couldn't learn to like his kisses, after all, and then panicked even more as memories of the *bandidos* came flashing fast and hard through her mind. Panic flooded her.

She struggled to loosen his grip, to free her mouth and get some air. He wrapped her whole body closer and she felt the bulge of his manhood, growing, hardening, threatening her, even through the layers of her skirts and petticoats.

Desperate, she tried to arch her back and, to her shock, he let her—he loosened his hold on her suddenly and then just as swiftly reached out with one hand to rip open her half-buttoned jacket. He jerked it back and off her shoulders.

"Look how gorgeous you are, spilling out of that dress," he said, his eyes shining greedily. "I can't wait to get it off you completely."

As he spoke, he held one of her wrists in a death grip, ripped the jacket off her entirely, and threw it away. Then he grabbed the neckline of her dress, jamming his knuckles into the cleft between her breasts.

She fought for control, some semblance of control so she could get out of this perilous situation. What a fool she'd been to come way out here with him!

"You're hurting my arm, Jacob," she said, completely amazed by the calmness of her tone. "You need to loosen up just a little."

Immediately he let go of the arm behind her back. She pulled away.

But as she took her first deep breath for what seemed

like hours, she realized that his hand had caught her elbow in a steel-jawed trap.

"I'll loosen up, tighten up, do anything you want me to, Beautiful," he crooned. "All I want to do is give you pleasure."

His hand fumbled in her bosom, then he drew it out. It hovered like a bird of prey, then dipped down and touched the edge of her dress—he dragged one fingertip along its curve.

"Isn't that giving you pleasure?" he said.

"Jacob, let me go."

"You want more, but even you, my wild rose, are lady enough not to say so," he murmured, and with no more warning than that, he freed one of her breasts, then the other, from the bodice of her dress.

Never, ever, not even in the hands of the *bandidos*, not even in the gloomy confines of Haynes's office, had she felt so immediately vulnerable. She tried to cover herself with one hand and jerk the other hand free of his grip, but she might as well have been a dying leaf trying to defy the wind.

He tightened his grip on her arm so fast and hard it cut off her circulation and took one breast roughly into his other hand.

She screamed. She screamed her frantic fear of a man molesting her for the third horrid time in her life, and while she screamed, she slapped him, twice, three times with every ounce of strength she could muster.

"Help . . . me! Please . . . !"

Jacob clapped his hand over her mouth before she could call Walks-With-Spirits by name. But he had to come. He had saved her before, from much less danger than this. He had to be near enough to hear her. He had to. Even if she had told him to go away. He was all she could think about, he was all that could save her.

Jacob was laughing at her blows, he was dragging her down to the ground, he was talking to her all the time while he smashed his hand tight around her mouth and made her want to gag.

"Nobody'll hear you, darlin', so save your breath," he said. "Save it to pleasure me, hear?"

Panic at how utterly she'd misjudged him rushed through her veins, spiking goose bumps up through her skin. She tried so hard to twist free that her wrist burned like fire; she thought the bone would come through the flesh; but he held her easily. It was truly amazing how much stronger a man was than a woman.

And then, without warning, his weight was lifting off her and she was able to pull free. She rolled away from him over the hard ground and soft pine needles, sharp twigs and rough rocks, fighting to protect her naked breasts with one hand while the other flopped useless and numb. She tried to scramble to her feet so she could run, run. Jacob was not going to touch her again. He would have to kill her first.

Awkwardly, she fumbled at the bodice of her dress, pulled it up so that it covered all of her breasts that it would stretch over, but the effort made her stumble and she nearly fell back down again; her shoulder struck a low tree branch, and she ended up sitting slumped against the base of a huge, rough-barked tree trunk. Stunned. She must have been stunned senseless because what she thought she was seeing couldn't be real.

Somebody was fighting with Jacob, who grunted a loud, animal sound, and his head snapped back. The newly rising moon, pouring pale light down into the clearing, showed that Jacob's attacker was Walks-With-Spirits!

She lifted her good hand, stinging now from scraping and scratching on the rocks and twigs, and pushed her tousled hair out of her eyes. Could it be? The man who had turned and walked away from a gun drawn in his face was now trying to beat Jacob to a pulp?

She stared at them in wonder, as best she could. Her vision was blurry—she was shaking all over, the moonlight was patchy, her mind was whirling—but one thing was clear: he could fight like no one she had ever seen. He never stopped, never slowed down, never gave an inch, never backed up, not even when Jacob hit him hard, not even when Jacob swung a tree limb he must've picked up from the ground.

Walks-With-Spirits fought like a determined bear. He drove at Jacob, caught the limb, and levered his weight against it so fast that he took it from him. Jacob cringed and curled his arm over his head to protect it, but Walks-With-Spirits threw the weapon away, tossed it over his shoulder in a gesture of great disdain, and came at Jacob again with his fists.

Jacob got a few licks in and then there was blood coming from Walks-With-Spirits's face, dripping black in the moonlight onto the bright white of his shirt. One logical thought broke through her hazy, disbelieving brain. Was he shot? Oh, dear God, did Jacob still have his pistol? No, surely not—she had not heard the cracking report of a gun.

Suddenly, the clearing filled with more light and the glow from half a dozen torches showed people crowding into the clearing, men first, a few women behind them. Tay and Marshall Greenwood and some more men she didn't know and Uncle Jumper and Jacob's partner, Peter Phillips.

But none of them did anything! Her heart sank. They stood back at the edge of the clearing and watched, because this was a matter between two men that had to be settled by only those two.

Jacob swung his arm back enough to land a blow to Walks-With-Spirits's face, grunting loudly with the effort it took. She cringed because it landed with such a crack that it must have hurt him terribly.

Her conscience whispered that Walks-With-Spirits suffered that pain because she had screamed, because she had called to him in her mind to come and help her.

After she had ordered him to go away.

She tried to squelch the thought, for she didn't want to be beholden to him, not to a man who looked down on her and judged her a silly child whose behavior degraded herself. She could take care of herself, truly she could, this was simply a situation where she'd made a few bad judgments.

The blow rocked Walks-With-Spirits back on his heels, but only for a moment, and then he returned it to Jacob's cheekbone with a force that drove him to his knees. When Jacob touched his face and brought his hand away bloody, he let out a great, keening howl filled with fury and pain.

"You stinking, ignorant, low-down woods skunk," he screamed. "If my face is scarred, I'll kill you! I'll kill you, do you hear me?"

Walks-With-Spirits stood over him like an avenging angel.

"You are the low-down one who doesn't deserve to be called a man. A real man doesn't mistreat a woman."

Jacob struggled to his feet.

"I'll shoot you just like I shot your precious pet coyote," he shouted, his breath coming fast and hard. "You never saw me then, and you'll never see me when my bullet is meant for you."

Walks-With-Spirits froze as he stood.

"You? You are the one who shot Taloa? Why would you do such a thing?"

"To show the superstitious, old-fashioned ones the truth," Jacob shouted, panting for breath as he pulled out his shirttail and held it against his bleeding face. "I proved to the whole Nation that your animal is flesh and blood, that it's a coyote like any other and that you are a flesh-and-blood man like any other!"

Walks-With-Spirits stayed still, terribly still.

"No, you're not a man like any other," Jacob cried, his voice rising to an ugly screech. "The wild animals are your brothers because you're no smarter than they are. You don't deserve to call yourself a man."

Walks-With-Spirits ignored that.

"You would bring pain to an innocent animal, make it suffer and bleed for no better reason."

It was a flat statement of surest truth. His deep, calm voice held clear menace, it held a cold, hard promise of retribution.

"The reason was good, good for the Nation!" Jacob cried. "Clinging to the old ways will do nothing but hinder us from living in a white man's world."

"So," Walks-With-Spirits said, "you admit that you are a cruel coward."

Jacob lunged at him weakly, fists clenched, then stopped and clapped his hand to his bleeding face as if the wound prevented him. He spat on the ground as if he had to clear his mouth to be able to speak.

"You can't call me a coward!"

"I just did."

Walks-With-Spirits still spoke in that unusual, cold way that held everyone there spellbound. He held his ground without giving an inch.

Still, Jacob didn't quite dare to hit him.

"Well, I shot your coyote, and I'll shoot you next," Jacob yelled, furiously. "You don't deserve to *live*, you interfering idiot!"

"*You* don't deserve to live," Walks-With-Spirits said, in a loud and taunting voice that turned from cold to hot in a heartbeat. "The Great Spirit abhors every breath you draw since you mistreat every creature that is weaker than you!"

"I'll treat my women any way I please," Jacob shouted haughtily. "None of that is anything to you."

Walks-With-Spirits drew back his fist and hit Jacob again, hit him with a blow that made an awful thudding sound as it knocked him back to the ground. This time he didn't get up.

Walks-With-Spirits extended both arms out over Jacob and in a magnificent, ferocious gesture swept them up and held them toward the sky. He spoke in a terrible voice that cracked through the woods like lightning.

"Listen! Now you walk pathways that are black.

"You will be lonely and then you will be traveling to the Nightland.

"Jacob Charley, your spirit is dwindling. Your soul is blue.

"May the next evil thought in your mind squeeze out the breath from your body, forever."

Nobody moved. Nobody spoke.

The terrible curse was horrible to hear, magic pronounced in a spirit of vengeance was the conjury most feared.

But worse than that was the fear-stunning sight of a good medicine man doing bad medicine, that was the most evil, most forbidden magic of all. Seeing and hearing such a thing struck everyone there helpless and dumb.

Then Walks-With-Spirits bent, picked up a stick, and in the same motion scooped the end of it through the earth where Jacob's spittle had landed. He brought it up and held it high as he straightened to his full height, his amber eyes blazing.

Now he had some of Jacob's saliva. Now he could use it to strengthen the curse, he could take it to running water at dawn and cast the spell again. Then it would be even more deadly.

Cotannah felt her soul sink into the ground.

She was the one who had caused him to cast this bad medicine. She had started all this madness.

Walks-With-Spirits stepped over Jacob's prone body, bent and picked up her jacket, strode straight toward her. A hard trembling ran through her to watch him come.

It stopped when he stood over her because he scared her so much she couldn't even breathe. His eyes held her impaled on the sharp sword of his anger, his face was the fiery visage of an avenging angel. For one heart-stopping instant she thought he would strike her, too.

His eyes were like pieces of burning amber, brighter than the light from the torches that flickered on his face. Amber, awe-inspiring eyes.

His copper-colored skin stretched tight with wrath over his chiseled cheekbones, blood streaked a dark, diagonal line across his face. He looked wonderful and terrible and capable of anything.

An ache sliced through her heart like a sword's blade: She didn't know him, she didn't know him at all.

She spoke before she knew she could, astonished that she could talk because she was so scared.

"I thought you only did *good* medicine."

A new emotion came into his eyes, something she couldn't name.

"So did I."

His full lips tightened into a flat, thin line.

"Put this on," he said.

Then he dropped her jacket into her lap, turned on his heel, and left her.

Chapter 7

∽◯◯∽

Emily came running toward her, crying out, over and over again, "Cotannah, oh, 'Tannah!"

Tay called to Walks-With-Spirits, who turned to walk toward him.

Then Emily was there beside her, helping her up, pushing her arms into the sleeves of the jacket. Over Emily's shoulder, Cotannah glimpsed Peter Phillips offering a hand to Jacob, still prone on the ground.

Her fingers were trembling uncontrollably but somehow she pulled the jacket together across her bosom and buttoned it up all the way to the neck.

Then Aunt Ancie and Auntie Iola and Hattie swooped down on her.

"Don't you think it's a little late for modesty?" Iola said, her voice a scornful bark.

"Look here at the trouble you've caused, Missy," Hattie blustered loudly. "I hope you're pleased with yourself."

Ancie didn't say a word, but her face was stiff with disapproval. Her small black eyes popped furiously.

"It wasn't my fault!" Cotannah cried. "Jacob wouldn't let me go . . ."

123

"Oh, 'Tannah, you're shaking all over," Emily cried, hugging her close. "Dear Cotannah, did he hurt you? Oh, Lord, your screams are still ringing in my ears. We've got to get you to the house. Right now, right now!"

And so they did, to the house and into a hot bath and then her bed, with Emily chattering all the time and trying to keep the others from making reproving remarks, trying to keep her from listening to the sounds from downstairs and from the yard as the guests for the nut-gathering party gathered themselves together and shouted their opinions instead of picking up pecans. Finally, Emily dared to face down the older women bustling about the room. She shamed them for blaming Cotannah's dress and behavior for Jacob's boorish attempt at forcing himself on her.

"Remember what 'Tannah has been through in the past," Emily scolded. "And remember that she was trying her best to get away from him. Why else would she have screamed like she did? She was telling him 'no.' Why else would he have been trying to force her?

"Look at her wrist! He nearly pulled her hand off! The poor dear can hardly use it at all!"

So Ancie, Iola, and Hattie's recriminations subsided—for the moment, at least—to dire mutterings as they applied hot poultices to her wrist and ointment to the knot on the back of her head and made her drink an herbal tea. At last they left her, but with one last parting shot from Iola.

"You've stirred up the whole Nation tonight, causing this fight, and causing a good man to make bad medicine. Besides that tragedy, all we'll hear for days and days now is those same old arguments about whether the *alikchi* is a witch or not. Starting tomorrow, I'm taking you in hand, young lady, just as your brother asked me to do.''

Cotannah closed her eyes against that horrendous prospect, squeezed Emily's fingers in gratitude, and let the tea carry her off into sleep.

She woke suddenly, with her blood pounding in her ears signaling danger and her arms and legs tight, ready to run. She sat straight up in bed, eyes open, peering wildly into the darkness.

Tall Pine. She was at Tall Pine. Emily and Tay slept just down the hall, Aunt Ancie and Uncle Jumper were here.

No one was attacking her.

She breathed in deeply and forced the air back into her lungs as she pulled up the lavender-scented sheet she'd thrown off in her sleep. But still she didn't feel safe. Something was terribly, grievously wrong.

Then the whole evening came flooding back, and guilt bore down on her like an oncoming train. She had caused a good man great harm. She had caused him to scorn her and hate her.

Or *was* it hate and scorn in that last look he gave her?

Shuddering, she wrapped the sheet tight around her and closed her eyes but she could still see Walks-With-Spirits, his face terrible in fury, holding up his arms, putting the curse on Jacob. And him such a healer at heart! He was probably miserable with regret right now.

Or was he still in a fit of fury about what Jacob had tried to do to her?

Was his heart still full of vengeful turmoil? And oh, dear God, would he do even more harm—to himself, as well as to Jacob—by using Jacob's saliva at dawn to strengthen the death curse?

He was blaming her, the same way the aunts were, she knew it. She had caused it all.

Never in her life had she felt such guilt.

Maybe she had done some bad things, like leading Tonio to think she cared more for him than she did, but she'd never before wronged someone as purely good as Walks-With-Spirits.

Suddenly, her feelings and thoughts began shifting inside her. They were like large, flat rocks moving against and on top of and under each other, starting to shape her mind and her self into a new configuration. Her breath came faster.

This had happened to her before, at the Academy in Arkansas when the lecher, Headmaster Haynes, cut her clothes off her body with his whip and soiled her skin and her soul with his greedy, lascivious eyes. It happened to her again that day on the *rancho* in Texas when the *bandidos* ran their rough, dirty hands over her skin and forced their stinking tongues into her mouth.

But this time was different. This time all the horror and all the cataclysmic changes, inside of her and out, stemmed from something she had done.

Somehow that realization strengthened her, in spite of the guilt and regret it laid on her. But why did it have to be bad that she had caused?

The old, sick feeling ran through her. Did that mean there was something wrong with her as she'd suspected for so long?

Walks-With-Spirits knew. He had looked straight into her soul the first time they met. And at the horse races, when he'd said she was degrading herself. And then, this evening, when he'd stood towering over her.

Had it been scorn, disgust for a person with something wrong inside, that he'd been feeling?

Yes. Hadn't he sounded scornful as anything when he'd told her to put her jacket on?

Walks-With-Spirits could tell her what was wrong with her, if he would.

The thought settled one of the shifting rocks in her head and froze her whole body, as well. She needed to find out, once and for all, or the rest of her life would go on just the way it was now.

But he had been in such a fury, he had looked so scary, he had been so angry with her! Going to see him now at his cave would be like bearding a lion in his den.

Still she had to face him again, if only just to thank him. Her sense of honor demanded that.

Besides, Walks-With-Spirits had helped her twice now, maybe saved her very life twice, and she owed it to him to try to help him. His spiritual life, his life as a healer, was in danger because of her, and she ought to try to keep him from making it all worse by using Jacob's saliva at the water at dawn.

If she got there and found that he was still furious with her, that he wouldn't listen to her, the least she could do would be to thank him. And then her guilt would be lessened because she'd know that she had tried.

She had to change her ways, get herself in hand before Iola did. She had to take responsibility for her actions because she was sure enough going to have to learn to take the consequences of them. Iola and Tay, on Cade's orders, would see to that. Nobody would protect her anymore.

And she didn't want them to. She wanted to be a grown-up, capable woman, a real woman in the old Choctaw way as Cade had said. If she didn't change her ways, she'd always be no more than a spoiled child and she'd never really be in charge of her own life.

Plus, she would always feel something was wrong with her, and she wouldn't know what.

She swung her feet out of bed, reaching with her toes for the cool plank floor, throwing off the sheet and feeling for her chemise all in one swift motion, then she ran to the window to look out into the night. There was a nearly full moon, starting down toward morning. She could reach Buckthorn Ridge before dawn if she hurried.

Never, at any time had Walks-With-Spirits been so far from sleep in the dark, when most creatures were meant to rest. He had run for hours up and down the ridge, both sides of it, through the trees and along the creek, trying to wear himself out so he could drop off into oblivion. Or into dreams. Even horrible nightmares would be better than this fury that set every nerve in his body afire.

But he didn't even feel tired. He forced himself to the floor of his cave, anyway, stretched his stiff body out onto the length of his pallet, unfolded the muscles that kept knotting and jumping all over his body.

What had ever possessed him? He'd done bad medicine right in front of half the Nation. He'd been so filled with hatred that he'd nearly killed a man with his bare hands. He'd lusted after Cotannah so much that he'd longed to grab hold of her, jerk her body close to his, and kiss her senseless.

What an idiot he was!

What a bad shaman, ungrateful for the powers given him by the Great Spirit!

He was nothing to Cotannah except a handy rescuer whenever her silliness got her into trouble. She was nothing to him except a weaker creature he had saved from a stronger one. She was none of his business. He couldn't be working himself into a frenzy over her.

And he couldn't, God knew, be doing black medicine because of her.

The sick disappointment coursed through him again. How could he have done such a terrible thing? The ones calling him "witch" would cry it even louder. What if their ranks grew, now that he had behaved like one? What if his healing powers were taken from him? What if his good work was finished almost before it was begun because he had used the evil charm?

But the worst thing of all was that in one stubborn corner of his heart he wasn't even sorry! In that one corner, he still wished that he had killed Jacob with his own hands, right then and there.

Oh, God, what was this ungenerous feeling that had sunk its claws into him like an owl's into a ground squirrel? Could it be jealousy, this wild wishing to rip Jacob away from his life and his home and hurl him off the face of mother earth?

He was lost, he was lost forever from goodness, if he didn't cleanse his heart and soul and fill them with love. He must seek the help of the Great Spirit and hope the spirits of Chito Humma and Sister Hambleton also would come to his aid in trying to regain his balance and peace. Now. He must begin trying now.

He closed his eyes and threw his arm across them. Even though the interior of the cave caught very little of the moonlight, this complete darkness would make it easier to look into his own self, his own soul, easier to root out these poison weeds of hatred and agonized confusion that had sprung to life, full-grown, in his guts.

But, immediately, Cotannah's face appeared on the backs of his eyelids, her dark eyes shining huge with shock and horror. She, too, had been stunned to see him put the death curse on Jacob Charley.

She, too, had wished he could take the black words

back—he would never forget the sound of her voice saying, I thought you only did good medicine.

At this moment, in his mind, she looked very real, as real as when she sat staring up at him standing over her. It had taken all his strength, even after the horror of what he'd just done, to take his eyes off her beautiful bosom glowing pale in the dark shadows thrown by the trees. That memory made his blood grow hot for her even now. Even while regret twisted his insides into a knot.

How could he have been looking at her in the very next moment after casting a death charm?

But he couldn't stop remembering how she looked. In his thoughts she looked so real that he imagined he could hear her voice.

"Hello, the cave! Walks-With-Spirits, are you there? Will you please come out and tell Basak to let me pass? It's Cotannah."

He dropped his arm and sat straight up.

She *was* here! It was another example of how truly upset his balance had become. If he hadn't been so wrought up, he would have felt her coming through the woods.

It's Cotannah.

As if he wouldn't know that the instant she spoke!

A great white anger surged through him, washed his confusion clean. He couldn't regain his balance as long as she was around; he couldn't hear the spirits outside him or within. He had to get rid of her, she had no right to be here, no right at all.

He got to his feet, strode across the cave, and stepped out of it into the night. He saw her by the light of the moon and went toward her, walking beneath the trees.

"Cotannah. What are you doing here?"

She jumped and whirled to face him, which made him ashamed he had deliberately startled her. His words, harsh and forbidding, echoed from the rocks of the ridge.

For a moment there was silence. Such a silence that he could hear his own heart.

"You didn't have to scare me to death, sneaking around quiet as a shadow!" Then, after a moment, she said, "I came to talk to you."

The sound of her voice coming out of the night was a windsong in his ears, but it sent a storm through the rest of his senses: lightning made of desire to reach for her struck his touch, thunder made of longing to look at her forever rolled inside his sight, rain made of tears fell bitter on his tongue, smell of winter coming rushed strong into his nostrils. She would blow him away, this storm of a woman-child, Cotannah, if he didn't drive her from him right now. He couldn't risk his powers because of her.

Yet he already had.

And now she'd come here to torment him some more.

"I don't want to hear it," he said angrily. "Go away."

But he started walking toward her anyway.

She stood waiting for him, beautiful and still in a pool of moonlight. A dozen new, vehement, unnameable feelings rose in him.

"I don't blame you for not wanting me here," she said, and he had never heard her sound so purely sincere—and so sad, "but at least let me thank you for saving me again."

Did she want to talk to him that much? So much that it made her sad for him to send her away? No. He was only a convenience for her.

"I had no choice but to save you," he said. "You called my name, screamed for me to help you."

The petty, accusing tone that came out of his mouth disgusted him.

It made her angry as well.

"Well, how could I know that you would put a death curse on Jacob?" she cried out, her calm voice breaking with passion. "I didn't scream for you to do that!"

"So you didn't."

This time he sounded cold and distant. Uncaring. That was better. He must stay calm, at least on the surface, or she would draw him too close.

"Another reason I've come out here," she said, and now she sounded as cold and hard as he had, "is to beg you not to make it all worse by using Jacob's saliva."

"Then you do feel responsible in some way."

What an ass he was, what a pettish lout! Why was he engaging her like this when he'd come out of the cave to send her away?

He stopped in his tracks.

Already, though, he was too close. Close enough to look into her eyes in the moonlight. Close enough to reach out and touch her.

"I'm sorry," he said. "Let me take back those words. The curse is not your fault. It's nobody's doing but mine."

Tears welled in her eyes. Tears and trouble. Such trouble. Trouble as big as his own.

"No, it's mine," she said, in a way that threatened to tear out his heart. "In spite of what I said to you at first. Something's wrong with me that draws men like Jacob to me, men who want to mistreat me. Other men, men who are good to me, well, I mistreat them."

She was breathing hard and fast, but silently, as if scared of the sound. Perhaps she had run the last part of the way by the light of the moon. Her breasts were heaving beneath the dress she wore—a plain, cotton one buttoned to the neck this time. Beautiful breasts, high and full, calling to his hands.

"It's something wrong with *me* that made you do black medicine. It must be, for you're too good to have done it otherwise," she said rapidly. "And I'm hoping you can tell me what it is."

He stared at her, surprised, trying to assimilate what she'd just said.

"What do you mean tell you what's wrong with you?"

Her tears spilled.

"Yes. You can see into my soul. You told me I degrade myself. Why do I? What is it?"

"There's no evil in you if that's what you mean," he said. "You're only human, Cotannah."

She brushed her eyes clear and gave him a challenging stare.

"Then why did you put a death curse on Jacob?"

"Because you unsettle me," he said, which was as close to the truth as he knew how to say it. "I put the curse on Jacob because you unbalance me so much, Cotannah, that I lost my mind when he called you one of his women."

She collapsed. Her knees buckled, his words felled her like a blow from his fist.

"No!" he cried and ran to her, dropped to his knees to pull her against him. "I'm so sorry. I didn't mean that, I shouldn't blame you. I put the curse on him because I let my baser instincts take over. That's all."

He tried to force his hands to take her by the shoulders and keep her away from him instead, but his arms *ached* to embrace her—she was crying great, racking sobs, with her face in her hands. She wouldn't let him hold her, though. She pulled back and lifted her head to fix him with her incredible eyes full of pain.

"What baser instincts?"

"Hate. Jealousy."

"See? Such feelings aren't natural for you. I unsettle you because there's something wrong with me, isn't that right?" she said brokenly. "I have to know. What's wrong with me, Walks-With-Spirits? What's bad in me that causes me to hurt people and people to hurt me? Tell me. Tell me now!"

The demand rocked him back to sit on his heels.

"Don't worry about hurting my feelings. Tell me."

"Nothing's wrong with you," he said, and need to make her believe him made a knot in his throat.

She glared at him, disbelief plain, her eyes shining with determination as much as with pain.

"When I was fourteen an evil old man ripped my clothes off and would have raped me. In Texas, a few years later, *bandidos* captured me and stripped me and handled me and forced their stinking tongues down my throat. They would've raped me soon." She stopped and stared at him triumphantly.

He shook his head. "That doesn't prove something is wrong with you."

"Oh, yes, it does. Do such things happen to other women?"

"To some, I'm sure."

"Not to very many. Not at two different times in their lives—now three, counting Jacob—and in different states, everywhere they go. I can't stand it anymore. What's wrong with me?"

"You're silly and earthbound, you're in turmoil inside. You're squandering the strength of your spirit."

"And now I'm squandering the strength of yours."

The bald words, said out loud, struck his heart. True. Yes, they were true, but at that moment he didn't care.

He slid his knees apart, reaching for a closer tie to the earth beneath the damp grass, willing its strength and its wisdom to come into him through his flesh. His weak, treacherous flesh that made him realize he needed to move away from her.

Instead he bent closer to her stricken face.

"If that's true," he said, "then it's my fault. I'm letting you do it."

"Why? Why would you? What's this destructive thing about me . . . ?"

Her words trailed away as she kept looking up into his eyes.

He was watching her face in the moonlight, the sensual movements of her lips, the shape of her high cheekbones. His fingertips tingled with wanting to touch her.

Her gaze dropped to his mouth in return, and he could feel it resting there, laying a heat like the sun's across his lips.

"Cotannah," he said, "you say that you think I'm a good person."

Her eyes met his again, and she nodded.

"So if I am good and I have powers to know your heart, do you think I'd have come running to save you from Jacob if something was so evil in you that you deserved his bad treatment?"

The thought shocked her, he saw that in her eyes.

"I deemed you worth saving," he said.

A cloud scudding across the moon threw a shadow onto her face. When it was gone, she was still looking at him solemnly, searching his eyes.

"You'd save any smaller animal from a bigger predator whether it deserved it or not," she said.

"No. I'd let the laws of the Earth Mother prevail."

She didn't speak.

"Do you believe me?"

Her eyes told him that she wanted to, that she was beginning to believe him.

"Nothing is wrong with you, Cotannah," he murmured, aching to give her comfort.

But aching more deeply to kiss her lush mouth.

"I want you to know how sorry I am," she whispered. "Oh, Walks-With-Spirits, it was my fault you did the black magic because I made such a fool of myself with Jacob, and I want you to know that I am so ashamed, ashamed to the bottom of my heart. I had no right to lead him on and then yell for you to save me."

His heart swelled with pride. With possession.

"I was happy to save you."

Her dark eyes looked up into his for a long, breathless moment, and then he took her fragile shoulders into his hands because if he couldn't touch her right then, he would have died of holding back.

"I was happy you did," she whispered.

He also would die if he didn't kiss her, the blood roaring like thunder in his head told him that.

So he bent his head and took her mouth with his.

Her lips were soft, so incredibly soft that he couldn't believe it, and sweet, deliciously sweet beyond description. Tantalizingly, strongly sweet, with some tartness underneath, like sourwood honey.

He could not get enough of her, not ever. Slowly, slowly, he deepened the kiss, his whole body filling with wonder that her mouth had been created to meld perfectly with his, his mind longing to tell her so but his lips and his tongue refusing to pull away from her to speak, refusing to do any other thing, anything at all, but kiss her. He would kiss her, just this way, forever and ever.

But when the tiny little sound of welcome purred in her throat and she kissed him back, he began to kiss her in another way. He found the ripe, dark tastes of the warm mystery of her mouth, and he explored it slowly, luxuriously, as the most wonderful treasure he had ever been given.

Her arms came around him, slipped up his back and stopped, splayed soft and warm on his shoulders. She smelled of lavender and of the woods she had just run through and of her own special scent, the scent of her skin and her hair. Her breasts brushed his chest, and desire began to build in him like heat before a summer storm.

He wanted her, he wanted to lay her down, right then and there, on the dew-dampened ground. But the more of her he tasted, the more of her he would want: He knew it already, knew he would never get enough.

He could not let his feelings become so entangled with hers now, not when his whole soul was unbalanced by the awful curse he had thrown. So he summoned all the will that was in him to savor the kiss, then to pull gently away, slowly, slowly.

Oh why, why, had she come back into his life? And why had he known that she would?

He looked into her eyes and took her face in his hands, his hands that were threatening to tremble at any moment. He cupped them around her face.

"I've wanted to do that since the moment we met," he whispered. "Cotannah, I'd have died if I hadn't kissed you."

She smiled at him, her vision still hazy from the kiss. "You wanted to kiss me when I was sitting a rearing horse that was about to come down on your head?"

He laughed and ran his big hands over her hair, smoothing it back from her face with slow, deliberate motions that she wished never, ever would stop. She leaned her head into his hands, a new, deep-souled feeling of peace flooding through her. Home. As soon as he kissed her she knew she had come home.

"You truly don't remember, do you?" he said. "You fulfilled my prophecy but you don't remember it, and that makes me feel quite forgettable, myself."

She laughed, too.

"What in the world are you talking about?"

But she almost knew. Suddenly, a frisson of memory ran through her mind but she couldn't quite catch it.

"On the contrary, Cotannah Chisk-Ko," he said, slowly as if quoting the words, "someday you will seek me out."

The words rang in her head like so many cool, short strikes of the clapper in a silver bell. Then she knew, and her blood leapt in her veins, brought her hands to his shoulders again to cling to him.

"You!" she cried. "I cannot believe it's you. You stole me in the Stealing Partners Dance when I was waiting for Tay!"

His wide, topaz eyes, bright in his dark face, were probing hers in the moonlight.

"You were wearing a hat and it was dark," she said defensively. "I never saw your eyes or your face that night."

How, how could she not have known when now she knew that she had found her man? How could she have forgotten that she'd seen him before?

A great confusion of feelings began rising in her, just as they had done on that long-ago evening when her heart had been so heavy and he had taken her hand and led her to dance like a feather in the wind.

"I knew you on the Texas Road," he said.

"You should have told me then!"

"No. You have to learn to look at other people instead of only yourself."

"What do you mean by that?"

"Think about it."

But she didn't even care. What she wanted to know was how that first encounter with him had happened.

"Where did you come from that night?" she demanded. "And how did you know my name, even then?"

"I asked someone."

"Why?"

He shrugged.

"I saw you the minute I walked onto the dance ground. You looked so full of life, so full of spirit, so full of feelings of every kind, that I wanted to kiss you then."

"I was crazy in love with Tay, or at least I thought I was. You taunted me about that. You were making rude, judgmental remarks to me, even then," she said, laughing.

She made her hands into fists and pounded him gently.

"So I should have recognized you on Race Day when you told me I was degrading myself!"

He held her gaze, but a slight confusion, almost a chagrin, shadowed his eyes.

"Well!" she said, teasing him. "Maybe you have the grace to be a little bit embarrassed by your bossiness."

He grinned, such a lopsided, bad-boy grin that she wanted to kiss him again.

"I make rude, judgmental remarks only to make you think," he said.

"I am thinking now," she said. "I'm thinking all the time, and I'm going to change my ways, so you don't have to say rude things to me anymore."

He laughed.

"If you really mean that."

"I do."

They stared at each other through the thick silence that fell them.

"That's good to hear," he said. "It's a great relief to me, Cotannah. The strong life forces in you have been rushing in every direction and opposing each other—it's enough to make you explode like powder in a gun."

She looked at him for a long while without speaking.

"That's true," she said.

"So listen to your spirits inside and the ones outside you to know what you should do to send them all in the same direction."

"Is that what you do?"

"Yes."

"And are you happy?"

Surprise flickered in the back of his eyes. It made her heart turn over.

No one has ever asked him that before. No one has ever cared, Cotannah thought.

"Most of the time," he said slowly.

He's so vulnerable, really, so alone.

"When are you not happy?"

The surprise in his eyes changed to resentment.

No one ever questions him or passes judgment on him. It's always the other way around.

"You have said some very personal things to me," she said. "Turnabout is fair play."

"When I'm . . . lonely," he said, at last.

"Your friends Basak and Taloa are always with you."

"Sometimes I . . ." He looked at her straight in the eye. "All creatures at some times need their own kind," he said. "That's a new thing I'm learning lately."

She felt a clutch at her heart.

"So," she teased, to try to stop it, "you miss me when I'm not around? You get lonesome when there's no one to spy on and say rude things to?''

He smiled, but he looked uncomfortable, and his shoulders tightened. He was regretting that he'd talked about his feelings at all.

"I know exactly what you mean," she said quickly. "I learned that same thing when I first went to live at the ranch, when I met Emily and Maggie and began to see what it would be like to have friends, real friends for the first time in my life. Within days, Emily was my very first best friend, and I felt like I'd known her forever."

"So that made it even worse that you both loved Tay."

He made the flat statement knowingly, yet there was questioning in his eyes. He wanted to hear the whole story from her. And why not? He had been there, he had taken her hand, on that terrible night when Tay never chose her to dance.

And he wanted to kiss her ever since that long-ago time.

So she sat down, then stretched out to her full length in the cool grass beneath the moon, and looked back into the past.

"I had thought I would marry Tay Nashoba for years and years—since the day he came home from the War," she said. "And the minute I first thought it, right there in the middle of the street in Tuskahoma, I blurted it out to him and told him to wait until I could grow up. From that moment on, Tay was my dream of my future."

To her total surprise, Cotannah began to pour out her heart—about Tay and about Emily, about her mother's death and how she'd always missed her, and, to her own deep shock, even the details of the twin horrors of Headmaster Haynes and being kidnapped by the *bandidos*.

How could she hope to win his respect and approval if she told him all this?

But Walks-With-Spirits stretched out beside her and listened without saying a word, only making a sound now and then to let her know that she should go on. When she was done, at last, they stayed as they were for a long time. Finally, she turned and looked at him where he still lay with his hands tucked behind his head as she was. The moon was dropping low in the sky.

"Thank you for listening," she said, a little embarrassed. "I've never told all that to anyone before. So many bad things have happened to me that I always refuse to talk about them."

He smiled at her, his eyes golden in the waning moonlight.

"You're welcome."

"I never meant to destroy your peace even more with all my old turmoil," she said.

"You didn't. You brought yourself peace, instead."

She nodded slowly, surprised, as his words sank in, that they held so much truth.

"You're right," she said, "I did."

His next remark deepened her surprise to consternation.

"Next time we talk I'll tell you my childhood and how I came to the New Nation."

Next time! He wanted to talk with her again. Her breath caught. He might want to kiss her again, too.

A look passed between them then, a new kind of look that held no judgment, no reserve from him and no flirting from her. A look of knowing, as if they knew each other now, although he had told her very little.

A look that shook her to the bone.

"I . . . I need to get on back to Tall Pine," she said.

"It'll be morning soon, and neither of us needs to give any more grist to the gossip mill."

He got up, then, and so did she.

She felt such a warmth in the air between them, but it wasn't the tension that precedes a kiss. It was more the feeling between friends.

He felt it, too—she knew because of the way he smiled and said, "Go safely, Friend."

She smiled back at him and began walking away, but the word caught and held her as if he had taken her heart in his hand.

Because it was right, they were friends, he was her first new friend, real friend, since . . . Emily. But how could a real friend of hers possibly be a man? A man who kissed her like no man she'd ever known.

Halfway to Tall Pine, a realization hit her.

Walks-With-Spirits had been her friend from that first day's supper. He wouldn't have censured her or criticized her behavior if he didn't care something about her; he wouldn't have told her she was degrading herself if it hadn't bothered him to see it. Another thought followed that one like thunder after a bolt of lightning.

He had been her friend from the very beginning two years ago because during the dance he had asked her needle-sharp questions about Tay. To try to make her think about Tay's actions and feelings toward her. If she had listened to him and used her head, she might have saved herself a lot of grief.

During the dance.

She tucked her hair behind her ear and began to race away from him.

The dance Walks-With-Spirits had danced with her, the dance he had also predicted they would share again someday, was the Wedding Dance.

Chapter 8

❧⟶∘⟵❧

I t was an hour after daybreak when she slipped into the house through the back door because she had wandered slowly across the fields in the dawn light, thinking about everything and feeling how the sliding stones of her consciousness had settled. Listening to her inside spirits, as Walks-With-Spirits had put it. The talk with him had helped her immensely, but she was proud of the fact that she'd known when she went to see him that she would take charge of her life. Now she would do it. There would be no more men like Jacob anywhere near her, ever again.

The sound of voices coming from down the hall startled her, and she closed the door silently behind her and stopped still until she could know who was up and about. She didn't want to see anyone right now, not even Emily. She wanted to go to her room and remember Walks-With-Spirits's kiss one more time and then sleep.

"We're here to petition you, Chief Nashoba," a rough male voice said. "You must tell the witch called Walks-With-Spirits to leave the Nation. He must be gone before Grandfather Sun comes and goes three times more."

Cotannah's stomach lurched. The voice was truly vicious.

144

It was coming from Tay's study, the large room across from the parlor where he conducted a great deal of tribal business. She glanced through the window lights on each side of the front door at the opposite end of the hallway from where she stood and glimpsed several saddled horses tied in the front yard.

Tay's rich tones sounded then, answering the rude command with a calm as great as that man's agitation, saying, "There're as many of the People who believe Walks-With-Spirits is an *alikchi* as there are who think he's a witch."

"Last night he proved what he is!" the man shouted. "We saw that he possesses strong medicine and that it's black medicine. Jacob Charley is young and strong, yet the witch whipped him soundly, quickly. Too quickly for a human to do."

Someone else spoke up.

"The witch said that Jacob Charley, one of our most prominent citizens, does not deserve to live, and he put a death curse on him. Next thing we know, the witch will kill the innocent Jacob, by his hand or by his incantations, if we don't run him out of the Nation."

"Seems to me that it was Jacob who threatened to shoot Walks-With-Spirits like he did the coyote," Tay said mildly. "Maybe it's Walks-With-Spirits who's in danger."

"Ha! Didn't you see? Didn't you hear? Jacob is in danger from the curse!"

Then several voices spoke out all at once, all angry. Immediately, then, came the sounds of chairs scraping on the floor and footsteps. Cotannah dashed down the hallway and into the empty parlor.

She didn't want that bunch of fanatics to see her—why, they'd probably say she should be sentenced to a

whipping for calling the dangerous Walks-With-Spirits
down on poor, innocent Jacob's head!

Standing against the wall, she held her breath until the
group of five men, followed by the ever-courteous Tay,
had filed past the parlor and out the front door onto the
veranda. There Tay talked to them for a moment more—
she could see him through the window—and then they
mounted their horses and rode out of the yard.

Tay, frowning thoughtfully, came back into the house,
and she stepped out into the hallway to meet him. He
raised his eyebrows in surprise and smiled at her.

"Tay, I am so sorry about all that happened last evening," she said. "It's my fault that these people are
coming here putting you in such an impossible position."

"Cotannah," he said, "a Principal Chief is in an impossible position the minute he's elected."

"Maybe so, but those men sounded so adamant about
forcing you to run Walks-With-Spirits out of the Nation!
By acting like a stupid flirting fool, I've caused all this
controversy about him to be stirred up again."

He took her hand in both of his and patted it consol-
ingly.

"No, none of this is your fault," he said. "Walks-
With-Spirits is always the subject of controversy because
people don't understand him. Come with me to the
kitchen for coffee, and I'll tell you about the first time
I ever saw him."

"You're as gallant as ever, Tay," she said, as they
walked down the hall side by side. "But right now that
can't distract me. I'm too worried that that bunch will
try to force Walks-With-Spirits out of the Nation themselves, when they find out that you won't do it—they
sounded so mean and vicious when they said the word,
'witch.'"

Then a worse thought hit her.

"Oh, Tay, do you think Jacob would try to make good on that threat to shoot him the way he did his pet . . ."

She paused, practically hearing Walks-With-Spirits's voice saying that the animals were his friends, not his pets, ". . . the way he shot Taloa?"

"No," he said, and he sounded so calm and sure that he allayed her fears instantly. "Now that Jacob's said that in front of witnesses, he'd be scared to carry it out because Olmun, his father, believes Walks-With-Spirits is a true shaman, and Olmun's money has always supported Jacob."

He stepped back for her to go ahead of him into the kitchen, but she stopped in the hallway.

"Thanks for the offer of coffee, but I think I'll just go to my room now," she said. "I want to ask you one more thing, though. What was Walks-With-Spirits saying to you after the fight last night?"

"He was telling me in no uncertain terms to keep a closer eye on you, Miss 'Tannah," he said, smiling down at her affectionately. "He's afraid you'll get into even bigger trouble next time."

She didn't even feel the resentment she usually felt at being treated like a child; instead she felt a thrilling warmth that Walks-With-Spirits was so protective of her. But that was because she had this new strong, calm confidence. Because she was different now.

"There won't be any next time," she said, smiling back at him. "I did a lot more thinking than sleeping last night, and I've changed my whole outlook. I won't be getting into trouble anymore, I promise you."

Surprise, and then gladness, flashed across his face.

"I'll count on that when it comes to men like Jacob," he said. "But it's hard for me to imagine you, the famous Cotannah Chisk-Ko, not attracting any trouble at all.''

They both laughed, and she gave him a quick hug before she turned and ran up the stairs. Life was full of irony. Two years ago, she would never have dreamed that Tay and Emily, who had betrayed her, would already be her best friends again.

Except for Walks-With-Spirits, who she had thought felt only scorn for her. Would he turn out to be her best friend of all?

For most of Saturday and Sunday, she spent her time alone, getting accustomed to the rearrangement of thoughts and attitudes in her head. Her promise to Tay further confirmed her new resolve to take herself in hand—she could already tell that it wouldn't be hard to do.

And that was because of what Walks-With-Spirits had done for her. In some mysterious way, he had made her believe in herself and her instincts again the way she did when she was ten years old and eleven and twelve and thirteen, before she'd ever gone to the Academy in Arkansas, before she'd ever seen Headmaster Haynes.

Monday morning she was up before dawn, leaning out her window to breathe in the crisp air of the frosty fall morning that called to her like a song. It was cold, she thought, shivering in her nightgown as she ran to the armoire and pulled out her beloved old cord breeches that always seemed too heavy for the Texas weather and the loose jacket that matched; an outfit of Cade's when he was a boy.

When she was growing up, wearing them had made her feel closer to her often-absent brother, and on this glorious morning the thought of him actually made her smile. He'd be surprised when he found out she didn't need him to boss her around anymore.

This would be fun, riding out and seeing the frost on the leaves, watching the fall coming to the trees and mountains. This was one thing she loved about the Nation over the ranch in Texas: the definite change of the seasons and the always-shifting weather.

She grabbed a faded cap knitted from red wool that someone—maybe some ancestor of Tay's—had left on the top shelf and stuffed her hair up under it so she didn't have to mess with it and miss the sunrise, ran from the room and down the stairs on tiptoe, hoping no one would wake. She didn't want any company on this early-morning ride but if she ran across Walks-With-Spirits somewhere out there in the woods, now that would be fine.

Riding Pretty Feather across the open fields in the cold, fall morning, galloping toward the bright pink eastern horizon, got her blood pumping even higher and, as the sun rose and lit the sparkling land, she rode all the way to the boundary of Tay and Emily's property, the narrow, swift-running Tulli Creek that had to be forded on the way to Tuskahoma. Pretty Feather must've caught Cotannah's exuberant mood—she raced straight on into the water and began dipping and tossing her head the way she always did when she wanted to play, throwing cold water back onto Cotannah every time.

"You silly girl, will you stop it?" Cotannah said, laughing, and began pulling her around.

The mare went back up the sloping bank as fast as she'd gone down it. Cotannah bent to avoid the low branch of a mulberry tree, but it caught her anyway, pulled off her cap, and tore at her hair, sent it tumbling in all directions over her shoulders and face.

"Whoa!"

Pretty Feather knew that tone of voice, and she began to slow immediately, turning easily in a circle as Cotannah's knees squeezed her, but by the time she'd gotten her hair out of her eyes and gone back, the cap had dropped from the tree into the water, which was fast carrying it away. Cold air swirled around her head.

"Well, I hope you're happy, Miss Priss. Now my ears are going to freeze!"

In answer, Pretty Feather dipped and tossed her head once more and pawed at the frosty ground. Cotannah sighed and turned the mare's head toward the house.

"I hope nobody at Tall Pine is sentimental about that cap."

But nothing could destroy her fine mood on such a morning, and she and the mare began wandering through the woods, Pretty Feather delighting in making the squirrels run for the trees, Cotannah loving the sight of the sunlight hitting the leaves, which seemed to be turning deeper colors right before her eyes.

She wished Walks-With-Spirits was here to see them, too. Talking to him had made her feel as free as she felt this morning, and she marveled again at the fact that she had told him everything in her life. Never, ever, had she done that, not even with Emily, but even more astonishing was the fact that she'd told it all to a man. Never, ever, was she straightforward with any man. But without a moment's hesitation, she had been completely forthcoming with Walks-With-Spirits.

The desire to be with him again suddenly stabbed through her, so fast and deep that it made her hands tighten on the reins. She took in a long breath of the cold, crisp air, turned Pretty Feather around, and started back toward the house, where she could find someone to talk to, someone to distract her from thinking about him and wondering when she'd see him. She could still taste his kiss.

She slowed Pretty Feather to a walk and gazed into the long line of oak and elm trees growing along the fence line between this pasture and the grounds of the house, stared at their low, leafy branches as if they could whisper secrets to her when the breeze moved through them just right. The frost was brightening them fast and furiously, turning some of them yellow and others all shades of orange and red. They were so beautiful that she filled her eyes with the colors, tried to memorize the way they looked, trembling in the breeze, flashing their frosty sides in the early-morning sun.

A flash of a deeper, golden yellow moved in between two tree trunks, in a different way from the rippling leaves. She blinked and looked again, slowed Pretty Feather even more so she could see through a break in the timber. There it was, farther away toward the house, only a glimpse of a vanishing patch of gold. Low to the ground. Vanishing behind the log smokehouse.

Her heart gave a quick, hard, pounding beat. Could the gold have been Basak? Walks-With-Spirits might be going to Tall Pine to see her!

That thought made her stop the mare and put her hands to her hair, running her fingers through it to comb it as best she could. Oh! She looked awful in these boy's clothes, with her hair wild and loose.

But she didn't care. He liked to talk with her more than to look at her, as all the other men did.

What if she went into the house and there he was at the breakfast table? Maybe he would stay around and they could go walking in the woods and talk all day long!

She smiled as Pretty Feather carried her toward the house. After he told her the story of his childhood, perhaps she could get him to explain how he knew everything. Two years ago, he had predicted that she would seek him out one day and she had done so. That boggled her mind—it seemed impossible in one way and in another, totally natural. Ever since that moment when he had looked into her soul out on the Texas Road, it had seemed natural that he would know everything. But how could that be?

Pretty Feather ambled to a complete stop. Absently, Cotannah pulled the mare's head up and stuck her heels to her sides to get her to move on, while her mind clung to Walks-With-Spirits. Where had he come from? What had his childhood been like? She couldn't wait to hear his story.

And he might be at Tall Pine right now! She smooched to Pretty Feather and lifted her into a trot, rode through the trees, opened the gate, went through and closed it behind her and looked ahead to try to see him. There was no sign, but that meant nothing—Basak and Taloa would lie hidden in wait for him, and he'd had time to go inside already, since he had no horse to tend. Smoke was rising from the kitchen chimney, and Daisy was shaking the tablecloth off the back porch.

A palomino gelding that she knew belonged to Peter Phillips stood tied at the stable hitching post, a light steam rising from his back in the cold air of the morning, a saddle upended on the ground on his off side. Phillips squatted beside it, brushing the horse's leg.

"Good morning, Mr. Phillips, you're out early today," she said, as she rode up beside his horse.

He turned and glanced up at her, smiling.

"Good morning, Miss Cotannah!" he said, sounding especially jovial.

"I see you're out riding early because you don't need any more beauty sleep."

Out of habit, she began smoothing her hair and tucking it behind her ears.

"I lost my hat," she said, "and I didn't even have a ribbon with me, so I'm a bit wild-looking, I'm afraid."

"Not at all, not at all! You're always beautiful, no matter what."

She smiled at him.

"And just what are you doing out so early?" she asked flirtatiously.

"Oh, I'm getting so excited about the new mercantile that I can't sleep, so I decided I'd just as well go on into town and get to work."

He ducked beneath his horse's neck and came around to the side of the palomino next to her, brushing it quickly where the saddle would go. Then he hurried to help her dismount.

"Yes, ma'am," he said. "If you'll pardon a personal remark from a tired, sleepless old man, I must say that you're so lovely that every time I see you I wish I was twenty years younger."

She laughed as she stood in the stirrup and swung down, accepting the hand he offered for balance as her foot touched the ground.

"I *always* accept personal remarks like that one," she said, with the coy glance that was her habit. "You're looking fine today, yourself, kind sir."

He did look quite handsome for an older man, although this morning his hair was a bit tousled and wet with sweat around the edges.

"Well, that's good," he said. "A merchant who looks handsome will surely have many ladies coming into his store to buy his wares."

"That's exactly right," she said, with a smile. "And as soon as you open your mercantile I'll be the first one at the ribbon counter."

They talked and laughed as she insisted on unsaddling her own horse so as not to delay him, and he put the saddle on his own mount.

"Well, Miss Cotannah, I'm off to town now," he said. "You come and visit my store anytime, even before the ribbon counter is filled."

He mounted and smiled down at her. Then he sobered as he spoke.

"Don't you let so much as one fleeting worry about Jacob Charley keep you away from the mercantile," he said earnestly. "I can promise you that he'll never bother you again."

A chill ran through her at the memory of Jacob's hot, rough hands tearing at her dress and pressing into her flesh.

"Thank you, Mr. Phillips," she said. "It's a great comfort to me to know that."

"Very well, then, it's agreed," he said, in his usual happy tones. "I'll treat you to a tour of the mercantile on opening day!"

He turned his horse and rode down the driveway toward the road.

Cotannah watched him for a moment, finished putting her tack away, and brushed Pretty Feather quickly, so she could hurry and get to the house. Mr. Phillips was a nice man, she thought, and he didn't deserve to be trapped in a partnership with a lout like Jacob Charley.

Thoughts of Peter Phillips didn't occupy her mind for long, however. She thought about Walks-With-Spirits as she finished up with her horse and ran to the house.

"'Tannah," Emily called, "we're in the kitchen."

Emily was sitting at the table in the middle of the room, teaching Sophia to feed herself—an especially poignant scene considering the baby's splinted arm. Rosie stood at the stove, cooking, Daisy was putting jellies and jams, pots of honey and sorghum, and bowls of butter onto a tray to carry to the dining room. Cotannah's heart fell. Walks-With-Spirits was nowhere to be seen.

"'Tannah!" Sophia cried, in a perfect imitation of her mother, and promptly slapped a spoonful of oatmeal into her hair.

Emily rolled her eyes at Cotannah, then looked at her daughter.

"For a little girl who woke up hours early, screaming for her breakfast, you aren't getting much of it into your mouth."

In answer, Sophia dropped the spoon, put her hand into the bowl and scooped a handful of the cereal up and into her mouth. Emily sighed.

"Most of the time I would swear that this child is Maggie's, not mine."

Blithely, Sophia waved the spoon at Daisy who was heading toward the dining room with the tray.

"Maggie's! Child is Maggie's," she cried.

All three of them laughed.

"Tay left way before daylight, then Sophia woke up so early I feel as if I haven't slept all night," Emily said, her shoulders sagging wearily.

"Where'd Tay go?"

Cotannah asked the question automatically; she didn't care what the answer was. She only cared that Walks-With-Spirits wasn't there.

"To Tuskahoma."

"Why in the world did he start so early?"

Emily hesitated.

"There was to be some kind of a sunrise ceremony on the banks of the Kiamichi south of town, an incantation to drive Walks-With-Spirits away. Tay was determined to try to talk some sense into the ones who assembled for that.''

Cotannah's stomach constricted as she remembered the hate-filled voices of the men who had come to Tall Pine to talk to Tay.

"I feel so bad about the trouble I've caused you and Tay . . .''

"It isn't your fault!" Emily said fiercely, and started to say something else when the sound of hoofbeats, rapidly approaching, stopped her.

"Rosie, will you watch Sophia?"

Rosie nodded, and Emily and Cotannah both went toward the front of the house to see who was coming onto the place at a speed that usually meant trouble. They were on the front veranda when three horsemen galloped hard into the yard and rode right up to the foot of the steps.

"Oh, 'Tannah, it's the Lighthorse!" Emily gasped when she saw their armbands, appliquéd with the bright yellow-and-blue seal of the Nation.

"Has something happened to my husband?" she cried, running to the porch post nearest the steps and grabbing it for support. "Is the Principal Chief . . .''

"Chief Nashoba's all right, ma'am," a tall, broad-faced, glum-looking Lighthorseman said.

All three of them sat their lathered horses for a minute, letting them blow.

"We're looking for the man called Walks-With-Spirits," another one said, and flashed a charming smile at Emily. "Seeing as how he's known to visit at Tall Pine from time to time, we thought he might be here right now."

"No," Emily said. "He isn't. Why are you looking for him?"

The third Lighthorseman, slightly older than the other

two, hard-eyed and quick-moving, spoke impatiently.

"Jacob Charley was found dead in the street at Tuskahoma around daylight, without a mark on him," he said. "There was no signs of a fight, no wound, no reason for him to be dead, and his gun was still in his pocket. He looks to be dead by magic."

Emily gasped.

"Well, you can't think Walks-With-Spirits killed him!"

The Lighthorseman made his horse move abruptly.

"Half the Nation heard the medicine man throw a curse on him and saw him take Jacob's saliva to use when he did it again."

Cotannah stood stunned in her tracks.

After a moment, Emily said, "Jacob is dead?"

"Yes," the impatient one said, "and we have to bring in the man who said a death incantation over him Friday night. If he's not here, we'll try his cave hideout."

He began pulling his horse around to ride away.

Emily's voice stopped him. "Listen to you," she cried, "talking about his cave hideout! And death incantations! You sound as if Walks-With-Spirits is guilty! Your job is to make arrests and carry out the sentences of the court—the Lighthorse haven't had the power to try a person or pronounce his punishment for years now, remember?"

Cotannah felt she ought to help her. She ought to help Emily, who was trying to defend Walks-With-Spirits. But she just stood there frozen, body and mind, unable to form a sentence.

"We met Jacob Charley's partner, Mr. Phillips, in the road right back there," the glum man said, "and he tells us he doesn't know of any other enemies Mr. Jacob Charley had."

"Well, he does! I've heard he has plenty of enemies!" Emily shouted at him.

Gentle Emily was shouting at a person in authority.

"Go and arrest some of those other enemies and leave Walks-With-Spirits alone! He would never kill anyone, he didn't mean that incantation!"

Cotannah didn't know that she would—or could—move, but the next thing she knew she was standing at the top of the steps beside Emily. She didn't recognize her voice when she spoke, but she knew it was hers.

"You'd better leave Walks-With-Spirits alone," she said to the Lighthorsemen. "He's an *alikchi*, you know, and you don't know what he can do . . . to you."

All three of the Lighthorsemen turned to look at her, fast.

"*Alikchi* or witch, we know he's dangerous, sure enough," the charming one said quickly. "That's why we're moving in on him before he can get word that we're coming."

The man's smile had vanished completely, and his companions shifted nervously in their saddles, began pulling their horses around.

"Don't let anyone go from here to warn him," the older, impatient one ordered, looking straight at Emily. "We would get there first, anyhow . . ." then he added grudgingly, ". . . ma'am."

"He didn't do it," she said stubbornly. "Leave him alone. And don't try to tell me where and when people can go from this farm."

"We're only doing our job, Mrs. Nashoba," the charming one said. "We must investigate him because of the magic and all. Believe me, we'd rather not, with him having such powers as he has."

"You don't know he's guilty," Cotannah said. "So don't treat him as if he is."

"We know what everybody in the Nation knows, Miss," the older one said sharply, "on Friday, Walks-With-Spirits was yelling at Jacob Charley that he didn't deserve to live and putting a curse on him, and today, Monday, Mr. Charley is dead. From no visible cause."

They circled their horses around and tipped their hats. Then they were gone, long-trotting fast in the direction of Walks-With-Spirits's cave.

"If he should come to Tall Pine before we find him, tell him he's under order of the Lighthorse to wait for us here," one of them yelled back over his shoulder.

"They're part of the faction that believes Walks-With-Spirits is a witch, aren't they?" Cotannah asked. "I think they are."

She was still talking in that stranger's voice and it was because she already knew the answer to her own question. The horror of it made her hands begin to shake.

"Quick, Mimi, we've got to warn him," she cried.

She turned and grabbed Emily by the arm, pulling her toward the door to the hallway that led to the back of the house and the horses.

Emily dug in her heels.

"No, it's too late, they've got a start," she said frantically, "and even if he ran, they're determined to hunt him down."

Desperate, she glanced from the Lighthorsemen to Cotannah and back again.

"Tay!" she cried. "We've got to get to Tay. He may not know they've already found him guilty. He can talk to the judges and tell them the Lighthorse are biased."

Then she took a deep, shuddering breath.

Cotannah wished she could do the same, but she couldn't breathe at all. She couldn't think, and she couldn't breathe.

But somehow she had to get hold of herself because

she had to help Walks-With-Spirits. She might not be able to see into his heart the way he could see into hers, but she did know one thing about him and she would stake her very life on it: he would never kill anyone. He had said the black magic charm out of fury and anger; he hadn't meant it.

And she'd been with him until almost dawn. He hadn't used Jacob's saliva in another incantation. She would stake her life on that, too.

"What if a lot more of the people are thinking he's a witch now, because Jacob is dead?" she managed to say.

"We have to change their minds," Emily said tersely.

They rushed into the house, asked Ancie, who had just gotten up and come in search of the baby, to watch Sophia all day, told her and Rosie the news, then ran for their horses.

She and Emily rode to Tuskahoma, where they found Tay—who already knew the leanings of the Lighthorse— and they listened to the talk and the shouting and arguing as more and more of the People gathered in town upon hearing that Jacob Charley had been found dead in the middle of the street when the sun came up.

She and Emily and Tay all argued, too, talking until they were hoarse, reminding everyone that Walks-With-Spirits was an *alikchi,* that he could never kill anyone, that he was a healer, not a destroyer. Tay left them to go to Olmun Charley, when his nephew drove the old man into town to claim the body of his son.

Cotannah watched Tay help Olmun down from the carriage and put his arms around the old man. She knew where she was, she knew what she was saying when she spoke, but nothing really came clear or stuck in her mind until a shout rang out along the main street that the Lighthorse were coming in with Walks-With-Spirits. He was under arrest.

Everyone in town, everyone in the Nation it now seemed, stood three deep along both sides of the dusty street to see the arrival for themselves. Cotannah's vision blurred, but she couldn't stop staring, couldn't stop looking at this sight that couldn't be.

Walks-With-Spirits was mounted, the first time she'd ever seen him on a horse, and he rode as if the horse was an extension of his body. She had expected as much, since he was so in tune with all other creatures. He was surrounded by the lawmen, he was bareback on a white horse that she recognized as having been in the pen with Pretty Feather that morning. They'd obviously borrowed it from Tall Pine on their way back to town so none of them would have to ride double with the prisoner.

Thank God he didn't have to ride with any of them!

Her gaze devoured him although her heart stood still with fear that when her eyes reached his face he would look as desperate as she felt.

But he didn't. His handsome face looked chiseled and solemn, but his shoulders were straight and broad as the length of an ax handle. He held his head high and looked directly at people as he passed.

They hadn't bound his hands, and that was a comfort to her. But that didn't mean anything—every Choctaw accused of a crime was assumed to have the honor not to try to escape, the honor to come in to Tuskahoma whenever he was told to be present for his trial, and the honor to return again to accept the court's punishment whenever it was decreed to take place.

People began falling in behind the little procession as it passed and inevitably, as if they'd been carried there by a river's current, Cotannah and Emily found themselves in the middle of a crowd outside the white frame building that held the courtroom and the other tribal offices. The Lighthorsemen and Walks-With-Spirits stopped their horses at the foot of the steps.

"The witch will be shot," somebody yelled. "He'll be judged guilty at the trial."

Cotannah's blood ran faster. That couldn't be true. It could not.

But another man shouted agreement.

"Now he's proved he's a witch, and we know his magic is evil."

"Olmun Charley will see to it that justice is done," a different voice called.

"Yes. Now Olmun Charley can see that the man he's been calling *alikchi* is a witch!"

That was a woman's shrill voice. Dear God, how many of the People believed it?

Cotannah's stomach turned as she looked around her, reading the dozens of faces intently turned toward the courthouse. They looked hard and mean, scared and determined. None of them was looking at Walks-With-Spirits with sympathy. They looked as if they could watch him be declared guilty and shot to death without turning a hair.

Chapter 9

❦

"**T**his investigation won't take long, my brothers!" some other voice called. "They've found a witness."

Quiet fell over the crowd, immediate and complete.

A man Cotannah didn't know, a man who moved with authority, came out of the building and stood on the steps. A moment later, a younger man, one who looked familiar, followed and stood beside him.

"Who's that?" she whispered to Emily.

"Moses Prettywater, the head of the Lighthorse," she whispered, "and you know that workman from Jacob's mercantile—he's the one who said the bricks couldn't have fallen on you and Sophie unless someone moved them."

"Yes. I couldn't think who he was."

"William Sowers saw Jacob Charley fall dead," Moses Prettywater said, in a loud, carrying voice. "I asked him to step out here and tell you all about it because I know that many among you are decrying the fact that my men have arrested a medicine man."

He paused for a moment, looking over the crowd.

"We don't want any trouble here today while we're

163

performing our duties with this arrest," he said. "After William speaks, we'll let the shaman speak, too."

"He's certainly taking elaborate precautions not to look prejudiced," Cotannah said bitterly.

Emily squeezed her hand to comfort her.

William Sowers moved forward into the morning sunlight. His narrow dark eyes stared out at the street as if he could still see what he was about to relate.

"I came to work right after good daylight this morning," he said. "I was in front of Brown's when I saw Mr. Charley come out of his mercantile. He paused and called back to somebody over his shoulder, then he walked on out into the middle of the street like he was crossing to come talk to me. Next thing I knew, he stopped right quick and then he just crumpled up and fell on the ground."

"Who was he talking to?" a man's voice yelled.

"I don't know. After I ran to try to help him and saw he was gone, I went in and searched the store, but the place was empty."

An older man, his face horrible in anguish, appeared in the wide doorway of the building. Tay moved up beside him, one hand supporting his elbow.

"William," Tay said, "what was it that Jacob called out to whoever was behind him?"

William gave a start of surprise and turned around.

"I don't know, Chief Nashoba. All I caught was the tail end of it and it sounded like he said, 'out of the Nation' or something close to that."

"Poor Olmun," Emily whispered. "Poor, grieving old man. There must be no worse pain in this life than to see your child lying dead."

Suddenly, for the first time, the reality of the truth Cotannah had been holding in her mind struck her heart. *Jacob was dead.* Jacob was dead and this pitiful old man, eyes glittering bright with sorrow and anger, didn't have a son anymore.

"Did you look carefully all through that store?" he shouted suddenly.

William Sowers looked at him.

"Yes, sir, Mr. Charley. Nobody was there."

"Maybe. Or maybe it was somebody who had the power to change himself into a *shilup*, a ghost."

Olmun Charley glared down at Walks-With-Spirits, still seated on the horse at the foot of the steps.

"Aren't you the evil one in disguise?" he said. "I thought you were an *alikchi*, and I told everyone I met that that was true. Now you prove me wrong in the cruelest way."

He and the crowd waited in silence for Walks-With-Spirits's answer. None came.

"You put a curse on my son," he said. "Three days later, he is dead."

Cotannah couldn't bear to do it but she couldn't stop herself—she stood on tiptoe to see Walks-With-Spirits's reaction. His face told her nothing. But his handsome, chiseled features, hardened in place to accept Olmun's blows, struck at her heart.

"The only good thing I can find about this awful day is that it falls during the six months of the year that the Court is in session," Olmun shouted. "Justice for my son will be done and done quickly." His hard, black eyes ranged over the faces below him.

"I want to tell every one of you who ever heard me say that Walks-With-Spirits is an *alikchi*, a good man, a medicine man, a man of magic that now I know better. He is a witch! He is evil!"

A murmur of agreement ran through the crowd.

"His medicine is evil, and he killed my son!"

"Mr. Charley," Tay said, speaking loud enough for

all to hear. "The Lighthorse must look into this. Jacob may have died of natural causes. There is no wound on his body. We don't know what killed him."

"I know he was murdered by magic and I know who is guilty!" Olmun said it in a quavering scream, his glaring eyes again fixed on Walks-With-Spirits.

"Listen to him! He doesn't deny it! Has he one time said that he did not kill my son?"

A loud murmuring ran through the crowd.

"No," they said. "He surely hasn't denied it."

Somebody else laughed, and it was an ugly sound.

"He thinks it's all right to kill but not to lie."

The murmuring grew louder.

Tay let go of Olmun and stepped forward, eyes blazing, both hands in the air signaling for silence.

"I can't believe what I'm hearing here today," he shouted. "You should be ashamed to judge this man guilty before he's even seen the inside of a courtroom. Why do we have a Constitution? Why do we have laws?"

He paused and glared at each portion of the crowd before he shouted some more.

"Are we really the red savages that the white Boomers who covet our land say that we are? Do you want to prove them right when they write that in their vile rag of a newspaper?"

The cold anger in his voice made everyone fall silent.

"What has happened to our minds?" he demanded. "When have we decided that the courts cannot make such a judgment?"

He waited a long moment for that to soak in, then he spoke again, not as loudly but with just as much determination.

"Let the Lighthorsemen finish investigating this crime," he said, looking directly into his people's eyes.

"And don't let me hear any more talk about who is guilty until the Judges have spoken."

He reached out and touched Olmun's arm again.

"I have no more respect for any other elder of this Nation than I do for you, Grandfather," he said, using the old-fashioned term of respect. "Please hear me. Do not say more. Do not say words you will wish someday that you could call back out of other men's ears."

Olmun seemed to wilt, suddenly, and he turned and went back inside the courthouse.

"Walks-With-Spirits is a witch!" someone shouted, as the Lighthorse started dismounting and motioned for him to get down, too.

"Our people root out witches when we find them in our midst!"

"Of course he's a witch," someone else yelled. "He sucked out Jacob's breath by magic."

Cotannah's nerves snapped. She stood up on tiptoe and looked fiercely all around her at all the dreadful faces.

"Walks-With-Spirits is not a witch!" she yelled. "Can't you all see that he could never kill anyone?"

Her voice broke with the weight of her fear for him. She pushed her way through the crowd to where Walks-With-Spirits could see her, then climbed up onto the bottom step.

"Tell them!" she cried, pleading to him with her voice and her eyes. "Tell them you didn't kill Jacob."

He looked straight at her with his face solemn and calm.

"The earth is the mother of us all," he said, "and the Great Spirit is the father. We are only a part of the Creation, we stand in a world that is only a part of Life."

Stunned, sickened by disappointment that he didn't say he was innocent, she waited for more. Everyone there, everybody in the Nation, waited for more. But he didn't say another word.

The murmurings rose up again, all over the crowd, most them against him, most of them saying that if he was innocent, he would say so. Dear Lord in Heaven, what if the Judges thought the same and found him guilty?

Panic beat in her throat like a trapped bird's wings. He was in this danger because of her stupidity in teasing Jacob. God help her, the consequences of her actions just went on and on.

Tay said a few more things in a loud voice, then the next thing she knew, he and Emily were on each side of her. The Lighthorse took Walks-With-Spirits into the courthouse, and the crowd began scattering, forming smaller knots of talking people in front of every store, all up and down the street.

Tay started them walking down the middle of the street, toward the rail where she and Emily had left their horses tied.

"Why didn't he say he's not a witch?" Cotannah cried. "Why? Now even more people think he is because he won't deny it. All on the basis of one bad curse! Why did he just talk in riddles?"

"Walks-With-Spirits always makes cryptic remarks," Emily said, tugging on her arm so she could catch Cotannah's eye and try to calm her.

"I don't care! The least he could do is to say he didn't kill Jacob, if he didn't," Cotannah said furiously. "And I know good and well he didn't and you all do, too."

They walked a little farther in silence.

"Don't you?"

"Yes," they said, speaking in chorus.

"Walks-With-Spirits would never kill anyone, and he

didn't really mean that death curse," Tay said. "I'd stake my own life on that."

"For one thing, he believes too strongly in the Great Spirit and the Earth Mother and the natural rhythm of things, as he just said in what you called his riddles," Emily said. "He wouldn't presume to decide the time when Jacob should die."

"Then why won't he say that he's been wrongly arrested?" Cotannah cried, breaking free of their hands so she could walk ahead and see both their faces at once. "Why wouldn't he at least say that I was right when I was proclaiming his innocence in front of hundreds of people?"

"All I could gather from his riddles was that he believes his arrest is also in the natural order of things," Tay said. "So I guess he thinks he'll somehow 'naturally' be found innocent; therefore, he doesn't need to protest and say that he is."

"I'm afraid that most people will believe he did it anyway, no matter what," Emily said thoughtfully. "All they can think of is the curse he put on Jacob."

"But it had no force. He didn't mean it! And he must say so or it'll hurt him, and badly!" Cotannah said.

Tay put on a forced smile to try to comfort her.

"Maybe he'll say it yet," he said. "The Lighthorse are questioning him now and perhaps he'll tell them he didn't kill Jacob, that the curse wasn't one he invested with any of his spirit."

Cotannah gave a disgusted snort.

"I doubt it. And fat lot of good it'll do to tell just them," she said. "Those Lighthorse are so scared he's a witch and will use black medicine against them for arresting him that they'll probably tell the Judges he confessed, no matter what he says, just trying to get rid of him once and for all. What can we do? We have to do *something* to clear him!''

Emily put her arm around Cotannah's waist.

She growled in frustration and beat her fists against her thighs. ''He makes me crazy,'' she cried. ''I can't bear to think of him being called a witch, or, God forbid, being found guilty of murder!''

''Right now there's nothing else we can do,'' Tay said, ''until the Lighthorse finish their investigation. Maybe they'll find out how Jacob really died and who the real killer is and let Walks-With-Spirits go.''

''And maybe we'll all sprout wings and fly from here to Tall Pine,'' Cotannah said sarcastically. ''Maybe we should just turn these horses loose right now and rise into the air.''

They walked up to hers and Emily's mounts.

''I'm assuming you're sending us home now,'' Emily said to Tay, ''since you've brought us to our horses.''

''Yes,'' Tay said. ''Go on and take care of Sophia and oversee the place. Send Cornelius back here to run messages for me and have him bring me some fresh clothes, just in case I sleep in my office for a day or two. I'll be home as soon as I can.''

''Don't leave Walks-With-Spirits,'' Emily said. ''And try to talk him into defending himself.''

''I'll do all I can for him,'' Tay said, and looked straight at Cotannah as if to comfort her.

She stepped into the stirrup, swung up into her saddle.

Nothing on earth could comfort her except an official ruling that Walks-With-Spirits was innocent. She tried to think how to make that happen all the way back to Tall Pine.

A line of terrible thunderstorms with wicked lightning and whipping, slashing rains moved across the Nation

that evening, hitting Tall Pine just after dark. The day
had grown warmer and warmer until at sundown the air
felt sultry as spring.

"Sounds like the Great Spirit and the Earth Mother
are as upset as we are," Cotannah said tightly, as she
and Emily ran upstairs to close the windows while Rosie
and Daisy got the ones downstairs.

"I'd think so," Emily said. "It's a travesty of nature
for a man as good as Walks-With-Spirits to be accused
of murder."

She longed to see him, to listen to his low, beautiful
voice. Now, more than ever, she wanted to know him,
to understand him. Maybe she would after he had told
her about his childhood.

The lightning and thunder and the rain lashed the farm
unmercifully, coming in waves, for what seemed most
of the night. Then, around morning, the cooler air moved
in behind a storm as it usually did in the Nation. This
time, though, the rain lingered on and on, falling in solid
sheets from the gray sky. The creeks and rivers rose and
filled up and ran raging, overflowed their banks and
spread through the bottomlands belly deep to a tall
horse.

"Nobody can go anywhere for days and days, except
in a boat," Cotannah said, pacing from one window to
the next on the morning of the third day of rain.

"I know," Emily said, rolling a ball of yarn to Sophia, who was sitting waiting for it on the floor. "It's
surely a good thing I sent Cornelius to Tay just as soon
as we got home."

Cotannah whirled to stare at her.

"Do you think they've decided to have a trial for
Walks-With-Spirits?"

"Olmun will have been pushing for it," Emily said,
so quickly that Cotannah knew she, too, was obsessed

with whatever was happening in Tuskahoma. "And Court is in session. They were hearing other cases when the Lighthorse brought Walks-With-Spirits in."

She glanced up at Cotannah, worry showing in her brown eyes.

"If they didn't let him go, he could already be on trial."

Cotannah's breath left her.

"Even with most people not able to get there?"

Her voice sounded pitifully thin.

"It'd probably be for the best," Emily said. "Can't you imagine all the carryings-on of the witch-hunt with half of the Nation going in to watch the trial?"

Cotannah turned back to the window and glared out at the water.

"It's best I'm not there," she said, "I couldn't sit still for it."

"He may have already been cleared," Emily said hopefully. "There may have been no trial. As soon as he can get here, Tay will bring him home—if he'll agree to come."

From then on, until the rain stopped the next day at noon, they hardly talked of anything else. The following morning Cotannah got out of bed after what seemed her hundredth night of tossing and turning and having bad dreams, got dressed to ride before she even thought what she was doing, and went to Emily's room. Instinctively, she knew, before she even knocked, that Tay had not come in during the night.

Emily opened the door. She, too, wore a riding habit.

They laughed when they looked at each other.

"I'm worn out from thinking about it," Cotannah said. "Let's go. If we have to swim, we'll swim."

They were outside within minutes, and mounted, not even bothering with breakfast. The day was bright and cool, with wind blustering at them from all directions.

"This is going to whip my frazzled nerves into a frenzy," Cotannah said, as they loped off the property and started down the road toward town. "I don't know how I've managed to wait this long to find out."

"Um. We're going to be covered with mud from head to toe," Emily said, as her horse's hooves threw another glob onto her skirts.

"Slow down," Cotannah agreed, much as she wanted to hurry. "This road's so wet the horses're liable to slip and break a leg."

So they did slow down and they tried to talk, but in the past days of being trapped in the house they had said every single word there was to say. Finally they relapsed into silence and slogged on, gasping and crying out at the cold water splashing on them when the horses swam the roiling Tulli Creek. By holding their feet up in the air, though, they escaped being soaked.

An hour later, Cotannah spotted horses through the trees, on a curve of the road directly across from her and Emily.

"Mimi! There! Horses! I didn't get a good look at them, but I'd swear they're both white or maybe gray. I know that's them, I know it!"

They rode leaning over, peering, but it wasn't until both parties came into the bend of the curve that they could see each other.

"It is," Cotannah cried, "there they are."

She had the weirdest feeling then, at the moment she saw Walks-With-Spirits, a feeling like she didn't even know who she was or what she was doing, a sensation of riding to meet a man she knew better than she knew herself when she didn't really know him at all. Why did she have this sudden sensation at the sight of him that she had come home at last?

But Emily gave a glad cry and urged her horse to hurry, and Tay trotted fast to meet her, so Cotannah rode up to Walks-With-Spirits. She stopped beside him, his horse facing one way, hers the other.

He looked at her with his topaz eyes bright in his open, handsome face.

"They turned you loose," she said, and with the words came a rising sense of relief and tears that threatened to overcome her exhausted nerves. "Thank God."

He kept looking at her, then he blinked as if he'd only just then heard what she said.

"For one moon only," he said.

She stared at him in turn, for the longest time, trying to force those words to make sense. Then they fell into her heart, one by one, like sharp hailstones of ice.

"They found you *guilty?* No! No! It can't be."

He looked at her some more but nothing changed.

"Tell me it isn't true!" she cried, twisting in her saddle to look for Tay.

"Tay! Is it true . . ."

But it was. Tay had given Emily the same news because she was weeping, leaning on him from her horse to his.

This had to be changed, Cotannah thought. This was wrong. Somebody had to do something! She turned back to Walks-With-Spirits.

But he slid down off his horse as calmly as if nothing in the whole world worried him and walked through the mud to the edge of the woods, where he stood looking into the trees. Giving a long, musical whistle that sounded like a mockingbird, he cocked his head to listen as if he expected an answer.

Cotannah watched him while recognition of the whole horror spread through her like a burning, itching rash on the inside of her skin. This was her fault. He was sen-

tenced to be shot because of her. She had drawn him
into a fight and got him hurt and caused him to betray
his beliefs and do black magic and now she would be
the death of him.

This was *all* her fault. This was the disaster Cade had
predicted, the consequences of her behavior that he'd
warned her about.

Yes. One moon from today, she, Cotannah Chisk-Ko,
would be just as much a murderer as whoever had killed
Jacob, except that she would be worse because she
would have killed a good man, a man who had never
brought harm to anyone. The cold truth made her sick
to her stomach.

At the same time it made her shake with rage at the
injustice of life. Why was it the innocents who always
had to suffer? Look at all the bad things that had happened to her when she was just an innocent girl! And
now the ignorant, superstitious witch mongers had made
her into a guilty woman, guilty of killing an *alikchi*!

She slapped her heels to Pretty Feather and rode over
to him, bending down to shake him by the shoulder.

"You can't be standing around waiting for the day
they're going to shoot you!" she cried. "Walks-With-
Spirits, you have to leave here. Come with me—I can
take you to Texas!"

He frowned and brushed her off as if she were an
annoying fly, then squatted on his haunches as Taloa and
Basak burst out of the brush and into his arms. She
thought she would choke on her panic while he hugged
them and let them lick his face.

"You should have sicced those two onto the Lighthorse instead of letting them arrest you," she shouted.

He was rubbing his hands into their fur, crooning in
Choctaw, telling them how good they had been to stay
hidden in the woods until he called them, taking his

sweet time, carrying on as if he hadn't a worry in the world. It was enough to send her into a fit.

"Walks-With-Spirits!"

He acted as if he didn't even hear her.

Desperate, she whirled her horse toward Tay and Emily.

"You have to help, please. Oh, Mimi, Tay, this is all my fault!"

Tears broke through the knot in her throat and poured into her voice, drowned the rest of the words on her tongue.

A sudden calm flowed over her. If it was her fault, then she would have to be the one to do something about it. She would have to find out what really did happen to Jacob if the Nation's Judges and Lighthorsemen were going to believe that he died of Walks-With-Spirits's curse.

The next moment, Walks-With-Spirits was beside her, standing at her stirrup. He reached up and laid his hand on hers, and the touch made the calm in her go even deeper. So did his words.

"Don't blame yourself. Jacob Charley's actions were his own, my actions were mine. I'm the one who put the death curse on him."

She seized that moment of his full attention.

"You didn't mean it," she said, staring intently down into his topaz eyes. "You told me yourself that pronouncing that incantation was just your baser instincts taking over for an instant. Such an empty curse couldn't kill him."

He listened to her, for all the good it did.

"It might. I said the words, and in my anger I did wish him dead."

"But the moment you calmed down you didn't."

"No. But maybe by then it was too late."

"You didn't use the saliva at dawn, did you?"

"No."

"So," she said, "he died of something else. Maybe he had an illness he'd never noticed before."

She turned to throw a questioning look at Tay and Emily, both of whom were listening carefully.

Tay shook his head.

"Jacob was never sick."

"He was young and strong," Walks-With-Spirits said. "It may have been the curse that killed him. I certainly can't say that I'm innocent."

Cotannah turned her hand and closed her fingers around his.

"Incantations take their power from the spirit, don't they?"

"Yes."

"Your spirit is good, good to the bone. I knew that even more surely after you set Sophie's arm. A good spirit can't kill someone."

He didn't answer.

"Then maybe it's my time to leave this world. This world is only part of Life."

"I don't want to hear that again," she said. "I intend to find out all I can because I know you didn't kill Jacob and I know there's more to all this than meets the eye."

He shook his head slowly, giving her the slightest smile.

"My spirit will never be killed. And I must feed it with harmony, with the bright trees and the smoky breezes of the fall that is coming."

His piercing bright gaze never wavered.

"Well, I must try to find out what really happened to Jacob."

Stating that out loud, meeting his eyes as she said it and then Tay's and Emily's, deepened her feeling of calm. She had a purpose now. For the first time in her life she had a real purpose.

"Come on, everyone," Emily said, her voice shaking. "Let's go home and have a hot breakfast, then we'll talk about this. Rosie's coffee will make us all think better."

So Walks-With-Spirits threw his leg over his horse and rode beside Cotannah, with Basak and Taloa at the white horse's heels. Tay and Emily, talking quietly, rode a little way ahead.

But she couldn't think of anyone but Walks-With-Spirits. He rode beside her like some rustic god of the woods, his fringes swaying like the leaves in the wind, all the colors about him blending in with the trees behind him.

His hand had felt indomitable on hers, massive and warm and now hers felt cold without it.

Tay's voice came floating back to them, he was talking loud enough for Emily to hear him over the sounds of creaking saddles and squishing hooves.

". . . Jacob was connected to the Boomers," he said, as Cotannah listened.

Instantly she quickened her mare's gait to catch up to him.

"What? How?" she called. "How was Jacob connected to the Boomers?"

Tay shot her an annoyed look over his shoulder.

"I don't know how or even whether it's true," he said. "All I know is that I've heard the rumor from three different directions."

"Who? Who told you that?"

"Cotannah, I've already tried every way I could," he said, "but I've never been able to trace the whispers back to a source."

"Well, let's figure it out," she said. "If Mimi and I

help, too, surely we're bound to find someone who knows more about this."

"Jacob would've tried to keep it a stone secret, obviously," Tay said dryly. "I doubt we're bound to find out."

"What connection could he have had with the Boomers?" Emily said.

Cotannah tried to think. "What could he do for them and what could they do for him?" she said.

"All they could want from him was treason to the Nation," Emily said thoughtfully. "They want our land; they want all the Indian Nations dissolved."

Tay nodded.

"Maybe they were paying him to try to talk up the whole idea of individual allotments," he said, "but I never heard him go quite that far."

"No, but he preached cooperation with the whites and assimilation with them every chance he got," Emily said.

"Yes!" Cotannah cried. "He did that at supper the first day I was here, remember?"

"All right, now, let's think," Tay said. "Jacob was talking assimilation and cooperation with the whites, and he was criticizing his father for encouraging the old ways and believing that Walks-With-Spirits is an *alikchi*. Maybe he was planning to progress, a few months from now, to preaching the benefits of individual allotments. Maybe he would've warned us all that we could never survive if we continued holding our land in common as a Nation."

"But then the Boomers wouldn't kill him," Emily said. "If he was killed. If he wasn't murdered by magic, which none of us believes, how did he die? Maybe his heart stopped of natural causes even if he did look young and healthy."

"Maybe he was demanding more money, more than he was worth," Cotannah said. "And they threatened him and he died of fright. Jacob was a coward."

"Or maybe some patriot threatened him," Tay said. "Some loyal Choctaw who believes in the old ways and who accidentally found out about Jacob's deal with the Boomers. Maybe that was who was in the mercantile that he called back to."

"We need to question some of the Boomers about Jacob and see if they act suspicious," Cotannah said. "That might lead us somewhere."

"The Boomers hate Tay with a passion," Emily said. "They'd never talk to him, and they'd probably recognize me, too."

"They don't know me," Cotannah said.

"They won't talk to any loyal Choctaw," Tay said.

"But I have enough white blood that I don't look Choctaw for sure, do I?" Cotannah said, as Walks-With-Spirits rode up beside her. "Couldn't I pass for a . . . well, part-Spanish, perhaps? From Texas. I'll be a cattlewoman from Texas."

"Yes," Emily said, absently. "Oh, if we find that Jacob was being bribed by the Boomers to encourage cooperation with the whites, that will crush Olmun all over again. It'll kill him."

"Yes," Tay said, frowning in sympathy. "There's no greater Choctaw patriot than Olmun. How he could have had Jacob for a son, I'll never know."

"Who is a Boomer?" Cotannah demanded impatiently. "Where can I find one?"

All of them laughed at her eagerness.

"Hold your horses," Tay said, "I think it's too dangerous for you to be going around those people asking questions alone. Let's see, I'll find a man to escort you . . ."

"To where?"

"I think the place to start would be McAlester, the newspaper offices of the *Oklahoma Star*. That filthy rag was created for no other purpose than to agitate for the dissolution of the Indian Nations."

"Its editor, Millard Sheets, makes virulent, vicious attacks on Tay," Emily said, her tone clearly aggrieved. "Not just on his political positions but on him as a person."

"They print the news of every murder that occurs in any of the Nations in all big print like a headline," Tay said. "Trying to prove to the white world that Indians can't govern themselves."

"What will you tell him, 'Tannah?" Emily said. "How can you ask him about Jacob?"

"I'll think of something on the way to McAlester— it'll take nearly a day to get there."

"We'll talk about it over breakfast," Tay said, as the big house at Tall Pine loomed into view. "We'll help you make up your story, and we'll send for a man to go with you, too."

"I'm going with her," Walks-With-Spirits said.

All three of them turned to stare at him.

"She's going on my account," he said, in explanation, looking at Emily and Tay, each in turn, with his calm, wise eyes. "Therefore, I'm going along to protect her."

For a single moment happiness burst through Cotannah's veins like a strong wine in her blood.

Chapter 10

Early the next morning, Cotannah, Emily, and Tay waited at the back steps of Tall Pine with the two horses. Cotannah's overnight satchel was tied to her saddle and a long leather bag containing biscuits filled with ham, apples, cornbread and fried chicken was tied to Walks-With-Spirits's horse. Emily checked the fastenings one last time.

"Don't worry, Mimi," Cotannah said, pacing up and down the yard, ostensibly to keep warm but mostly to fight her restlessness to be off—and, she had to admit, her eagerness to see Walks-With-Spirits. "If we lose one bag, we can live for a week on what you've packed in the other."

"You think that now, but riding in the cold makes a person hungry and Walks-With-Spirits . . ."

"May not be coming," Cotannah interrupted, worrying out loud. "Maybe he's changed his mind."

"He'll be here," Tay said. "The sun's barely up yet."

The back door opened and all three of them turned. Peter Phillips was emerging from the house, nattily dressed, as usual, for his day in town at the new mercantile.

"Well, well," he said, closing the door gently behind him before he walked across the porch, his plump stomach bouncing a little with each stride. "Saddled horses at this hour of the day! Who's going where on this beautiful fall morning?"

His cheerfulness irritated Cotannah unmercifully in spite of the fact that usually it amused her.

"Why are you so happy?"

He gave her a sharp glance as he bounded down the steps.

"Point well taken, my dear," he said, and let his round face fall into solemn lines, "but I can't let the loss of my partner cast a pall over my professional life, wouldn't you agree? No customer is attracted to a store filled with an atmosphere of gloom."

"That's true," Emily said. "Jacob's death is very sad, but both you and Olmun must go on."

"Yes, and it's Olmun I'm most concerned about," he said. "I don't know if he'll ever have the heart to return to business or not."

"Give him time," Tay said, looking up from tightening the cinch on the white horse's saddle. "Will you be opening the mercantile soon?"

"Probably in about two weeks. The building is completed except for the brickwork and while that's being finished I'm arranging the stock inside."

The two men and Emily talked a moment more, their breaths rising in frosty puffs in the cold air while Cotannah continued to pace. After a moment Phillips, preparing to leave, pulled on his gloves, and put on the felt hat that he carried.

"I need your warm red cap this morning, Miss Cotannah," he said, with a dramatic little shiver that made his stomach jiggle again. "It's a whole lot nippier out today than I had expected."

He tipped his hat to her.

"Be sure you bundle up for your ride," he said. "I only hope you aren't going on a secret shopping trip to Fort Smith or McAlester before I can even get my mercantile open."

Cotannah smiled back, suddenly glad for the distraction.

"I wouldn't," she said. "I have my heart set on being your very first customer."

He beamed at her.

"That's wonderful! Well, you ride safe. I'll see you at supper."

He waited for a split second as if expecting an answer, then he tipped his hat to Emily and strode away toward the stables, whistling a ragged tune.

"He's a naturally jolly person," Emily said, "but he really is sorry about Jacob."

"I didn't mean to criticize him—I wasn't even thinking about Jacob when I asked him why he was happy," Cotannah said. "He just took it that way."

"Here's Walks-With-Spirits," Tay said.

Cotannah swung around to look across the pasture. Walks-With-Spirits was surprisingly close, running toward them with that sure, unhurried, silently graceful flow of muscular power that marked his every movement. With his light step he looked as if he were caressing the face of the Earth Mother. Where the mist rose in the low spots, he appeared to be floating a little bit above the ground. He truly was like a shadow.

Her breath caught in her chest and made a hard knot there, tears stinging her eyes. He would soon be a shadow gone from this world no matter how bright the sun might shine.

Unless she saved him.

Walks-With-Spirits reached them then, looking more

handsome than ever in clothes she'd never seen before: faded denim breeches and a gray wool coat with the stand-up collar of a white shirt showing at the neck. He smiled as the three of them looked him over in amazement.

"I dressed to blend into the town," he said, "so no one will take notice of me . . . " He grinned and flashed her a devilish glance. ". . . and if I have to rush in and rescue Cotannah, maybe it won't bring the white men's attention back here to the Nation."

"Well, you won't have to rescue me, I can take care of myself, thank you very much," Cotannah said, giving him a saucy look in return.

She couldn't help staring at him. How did he think no one could notice him? He had an air about him that drew attention more than fringed buckskins—or even war paint on his face and feathers in his hair—ever would. Women, especially, would watch him every minute.

"Where are Taloa and Basak?" she asked.

"They'll stay at the cave," he said, "so no one will be tempted to shoot them."

Her heart drummed hard against her ribs when his soft, rich voice caressed her ears. He was wearing his hair pulled back and tied with a rawhide thong at the nape of his neck instead of in braids, too, in another attempt not to draw attention to himself or his Indian origins. Cotannah felt another rush of excitement go through her. He was, by far, the handsomest man she'd ever seen.

"I've got a hat, too," he said, patting the soft leather bag he carried swinging from his shoulder, "to complete my disguise. I intend to stay near you in that town, Cotannah. I won't let you out of my sight."

Those words warmed her so that she almost forgot what they were doing there.

Finally, at the same moment, they turned and began walking to their horses. Tay and Emily followed.

"You can go to Mary Sudbury's tonight, remember," Emily said, as she stood between their horses with a hand on each animal's neck as if to hold them there.

Emily could hardly bear for them to go without her, Cotannah thought, because she took it upon herself to protect everyone she loved.

"Mary's only three miles from McAlester, and if you all stay there, no one can gossip about the two of you spending the night away from home."

"Well, I sure don't want that, with my reputation completely unsullied as it is," Walks-With-Spirits said wryly, as he swung up onto the white horse.

"Nor I," Cotannah said, "since so far the worst they say about me is that I'm a shameless jade whose teasing ways cause fights and killings."

They all laughed a little and the sound of Walks-With-Spirits's deep chuckle calmed Cotannah even more. Maybe he knew his life would be spared, the same way he'd known for two years that she'd seek him out, she thought, suddenly. If he did, he'd better tell her!

She twisted in the saddle to try to read that in his face. Their eyes met, and a quick feeling of warmth sparked between them.

"Don't worry, you'll both be vindicated," Emily said.

"Watch your backs," Tay said.

Walks-With-Spirits answered with a quick gesture of his hand, Cotannah bent and hugged Emily's neck, and they rode off with Emily calling after them, "God-speed!"

They went out of the yard and down the driveway at a long trot, side by side, through the chill of the autumn morning with the sweet smell of woodsmoke from Tall Pine's kitchen floating on the air with the homey sounds of cows lowing to be milked and roosters crowing, riding into the unknown. She smiled at him.

"Thank you for coming with me."

He threw her a slanting glance.

"I thank you for what you're trying to do for me."

Then he held her gaze.

"How can you be so sure that I didn't kill him, sure enough to risk your life?"

She shrugged. "I just know you didn't."

Because you're the most gorgeous man I've ever seen. Because you have wise and magical eyes.

"And don't tell me again that your curse may have killed him. Whose side are you on, anyway?"

He grinned.

"I'm just amazed that you think you know me so well."

"I know I do," she said confidently. "I can sense your true nature."

"Yet . . ." he said, frowning now, "you don't sense the true nature of other men, men like Jacob, men whom you tease without knowing the danger."

Heat rose in the skin of her throat and suffused her face, she turned away. "You're different."

He laughed. "But not different enough for you to recognize me when you saw me again."

She whirled in the saddle to meet his eyes.

"I never saw your face that night we met, *remember*? And I did know there was something familiar about you that day on the Texas Road."

He laughed even more, and she finally grinned back at him.

"You're different, too," he said, cocking his head to one side and looking her up and down as if to note every detail that would make him say such a thing.

The pleased tone of his voice, the bright heat deep in his eyes, the intensity of his stare all melted her thoughts.

"How do you know?" she asked, at last. "How many women do you know, anyway, Walks-With-Spirits?"

He smiled.

"Not too many."

"Well, then."

"But I see lots of things. Most women aren't bold and brave like you, most aren't straightforward in their talk because they try to hide bad feelings and not upset anyone, most are . . . nowhere near as beautiful as you."

She sat transfixed, staring at him.

He was praising her for exactly the qualities that Cade and Aunt Ancie and everyone else usually criticized. And, she thought, as her heart gave a quick, hard stroke of delight, he considered her beautiful.

She couldn't think of another thing to say.

"Cotannah," he said, "you're different in another way that pleases me greatly. You don't fear me as a witch, you don't stand in awe of me as an *alikchi*."

Tears stung her eyes. Oh! How lonely he must be! And now most people wanted to kill him!

"You please me, too," she said, "because usually I'm taken to task for being bold." She swallowed hard and forced a smile to try to drive away the urge to cry. "But not for being straightforward. I'm not honest with any man but you."

He watched her face as the horses jogged along, side by side.

"I don't say personal things to any woman but you," he said. "Usually I do my healing with animals and the land."

They held a long, steady look and Cotannah felt, suddenly, that they had exchanged some kind of vow. A frisson of fear ran through her. She cared too much for him. With him, she was home.

"You'd be good for people if you did say personal things to them," she said. "You made me really angry at you at first, but if you hadn't said I was degrading myself, I might never have tried to take responsibility for my own actions."

"But you're overdoing that responsibility now," he said softly, his light brown eyes still fixed on hers. "You can't prove me innocent when half the Nation heard me saying that death curse."

"Yes, I can," she cried, welcoming the frustration that sprang up in her, trying to make it grow hot enough to blot out all her other feelings. She urged Pretty Feather to more speed and rode out ahead of him down the middle of the road, but almost immediately he caught up.

"You saved me twice, Walks-With-Spirits, and I am jolly well going to save you this time!"

"What if you're killed, too?"

She whipped her head around to look at him.

"I thought you said you weren't going to let me out of your sight."

"I'm not. This trip. But later the Boomers could send someone into the Nation to find you. If Jacob really was involved with them, you might make them think you know too much."

"I'm not afraid of Millard Sheets," she said scornfully. "He'll never know who I am or what kind of information I'm really looking for."

"And how will you get it, then?"

"Flirt it out of him."

"Why did I ask?"

But he wasn't censuring her, she could tell by his tone, he was teasing her.

She smiled at him, but his face had fallen into its accustomed solemn, chiseled lines.

"Sheets is an Indian hater. What if he feels superior to the Spanish, too, assuming he does believe that's what race you are? What if he considers himself too good to flirt with you?"

She threw him a quick glance.

"You mean the way you always do?"

He grinned, actually grinned, at her. It changed his face to that of a mischievous little boy, a roguish young man, a . . . dangerously handsome, dimpled devil who could play havoc with her heart. Then the light in his eyes turned to heat, heat that set fire to the core of her, body and soul. Something leapt in the air between them, some magnetism strong enough to touch crackled in the air.

And a startling truth fell into her head.

Why, his spirit was kindred to hers! He had that calm, that wisdom, yes, that incredible, mysterious peace, but within it, or beneath it, he was filled with passion, too.

If he held out his hand just now he could take hers. He could hold her hand in that sure, warm grasp that had saved her and Sophia from the falling bricks. If he stood in one stirrup and leaned toward her while their horses were keeping pace like this, he could take her lips in a kiss. Another of his wonderful, hot, sweet kisses. The thought of it streaked through her blood like a falling star.

But he didn't move, he only looked at her.

She had to break that look, she had to, or she'd be the one reaching for him.

"You . . ." Her voice sounded low and husky and strange. She cleared her throat and tried again. "You need to pull your hat down and stay as inconspicuous as you can in McAlester," she said. "In case someone sees us together on the road and notices us again in town."

"Perhaps I should go in with you," he said. "The color of my eyes shows my white blood from some ancestors in the past."

She chuckled.

"But the color of your skin and the bones of your face scream of many Choctaw ancestors born into the woods and hills of the old homeland."

"All right. I'll pretend not to know you, and I'll wait on the street near the newspaper office like any Choctaw come to town for trading waits for his wife."

Like any Choctaw waits for his wife.

She tried to shut out the insane echo in her head, but she couldn't help turning to look at him again.

"Don't worry. I'll be watching you and Millard Sheets through the window," he said. "If he so much as touches you, I'm coming in."

His jaw jutted out and he flashed her a fiercely protective glance that shot straight to her heart.

For the rest of the ride Cotannah tried either to keep them moving too fast for much talking or, when they slowed to rest the horses and stopped to eat a quick noon meal, to keep the conversation completely impersonal. Most of the time she didn't have to worry—they were riding fast because covering thirty miles on horseback through the mountains would take all day long and the trails through the woods were narrow enough in most places that they had to take them single file.

They arrived on the outskirts of town as the day was sliding into late afternoon and immediately separated to ride in from different directions on the busy main street.

Cotannah tried not even to glance around her for Walks-With-Spirits, but he was in front of the office of the *Oklahoma Star* when she found it. He had found a vantage point leaning against a post not far from some loiterers on the street corner, and he blended into his surroundings very well.

She dared to look at him again as she rode Pretty Feather up to the hitching post. He was an *alikchi,* that was for sure, else how could he look like such a part of a town when always before he'd looked so like a natural part of the wild?

He was wearing the hat now, a brown, wide-brimmed sueded leather pulled low over his eyes, and his hair was tucked in beneath his coat collar at the back of his neck. It would seem to any passerby that he was completely absorbed in whittling at the stick he held propped against his thigh—he stood on one foot and placed the other behind him flat against the post, every line of his big body completely loose and at ease. The knife in his hand moved slowly, with a certain sureness that struck a longing deep at her core.

Looking at him standing there made her go weak all over.

Knowing, although he gave no sign, that he knew she was there made her ache to touch him.

Finally, she tore her gaze away and got down, tied Pretty Feather to the hitching rail, and crossed the board sidewalk to the door, glass across the top half, etched with the words in script, *Oklahoma Star.* When she opened the door, a tiny bell rang. Two men occupied the room, one seated across the room at a printing press with his back to her and the other at a desk facing her.

The one at the desk was a tall, thin man who immediately stood up and walked around to the counter that ran across the front of the office.

"Yes, miss," he said. "How can I help you?"

"It's Mrs.," she said, tilting her head to smile up at him. "I'm Mrs. Maggie Harrington, owner of the Double H Ranch in South Texas."

He offered the slightest suggestion of a bow but did not return her smile.

"They call me Millard Sheets," he said abruptly.

"I've come to you for some advice," she said, pasting the smile onto her face.

"About what?"

She walked up to the counter and put both hands on it, leaned toward him until he bent his head to listen.

"About who among the Choctaw might be willing to overlook that silly law they have against leasing grazing land to outsiders."

He drew back and looked down at her sharply.

She gave him her best smile one more time.

"We've had a dry year at home," she confided, softly enough that once again he had to tilt his head again to hear her, "and I've come all this way to find grass for my cattle that would be on the way to market—only to find out that they have this stupid law!"

She stepped back and glanced at the man working at the printing press, then used her prettiest, most indignant pout on Millard Sheets.

"You don't have to worry about Ernest there overhearing us," he said, in a flat, bored tone. "Everybody in this establishment is here to tell the world that the redskin savages have no business trying to run a country on their own. Any fool can see that they could make a lot of income leasing out all that good grazing land."

"Good!" she cried enthusiastically. "So can you tell me the names of some of the more progressive Choctaw landowners who are also good businessmen?"

The man was a stick. A lump of unfeeling clay. He

still hadn't smiled at her and now it seemed that he might not answer her question. He wasn't going to. She could feel it.

She smiled at him again anyway.

"As you can imagine, I *don't* want to get into trouble by approaching the wrong person," she said, "and I've been assured by several citizens of McAlester that you have your finger on the pulse of every kind of business transaction that transpires for miles and miles around here."

He favored her with the barest of nods.

So, flattery must be the best tactic to use on him, but at this rate she would be too old to ride horseback before he gave her the name of someone to see. It would be a true miracle if that name was Jacob Charley.

She took a deep breath to steady her breathing.

"Surely you know someone among the Choctaw who resents all those stupid laws they have?"

He almost smiled. But he didn't speak.

"Now, I do have one name already," she said, wasting another smile on him before she opened the bag hanging from her wrist and took out a small piece of paper, "the person who gave it to me said that this man is a very shrewd Choctaw businessman and that he has lots of grass." She looked up with wide, innocent eyes. "Can you advise me whether I should mention leasing grazing lands to him . . ." she paused and touched her chest delicately, "leasing them to me, a white woman . . . or not? If I tell you the name, could you tell me if that proposal would offend him?"

Nothing. The stone of a man made no response whatsoever.

Cotannah glanced down at the paper, unfolded it and pretended to read.

"Jacob Charley," she said, and looked up again,

hopefully, into Millard Sheets's narrow eyes. "Have you, by any chance, heard anything about him?"

A slight flicker of . . . interest? Disgust? She couldn't name it, she couldn't even say whether it was positive or negative, but the first emotion she had seen in him flashed across his narrow face at the mention of Jacob's name.

"I've heard he's dead," he said, in that same flat tone.

A true shock ran through her that he should know that fact, even though logic told her that, in spite of the storms and the floods, everyone in the boundaries of the Choctaw Nation and all the other Indian Nations had heard it by now, no doubt. But she pretended that she was surprised at the news.

"Don't tell me that!" she cried, putting her hand over her heart.

He leaned toward her, this time.

"Fell dead in the street without a mark on him!" he thundered. "They tell me the whole Nation believes it was a curse of death that killed him—one of them Choctaw medicine men slapped the bad word on old Jacob Charley."

"Oh?" she managed to say. "Is that so?"

"Now can you imagine the sane, white, God-fearing citizens of the United States letting such superstitious red savage riffraff control all that good grassland and coal and timber and water?"

She searched his reddening face.

"No-o-o."

"Damn right you can't," he roared. "Read the *Star*. I've written the best editorial calling for the destruction of the Indian so-called Nations that ever saw print."

Then, with no warning at all that he was about to change the subject of the conversation, he reached under the counter and pulled out a dog-eared ledger book, threw it down in front of her with a resounding thump.

"Little lady, let's find you a Choctaw with a shred of sense," he said, throwing it open and starting to thumb through. "If there is such an animal. We need to get some more intruder cattle onto that Choctaw grass."

He gave a loud snort of derision as he thumbed through the pages, then glanced up to glare at her again.

"Can you feature that they call them intruder cattle if they belong to a white person?" he demanded. "When, from the dawn of recorded time, it's been the goddamned red Indians who're intruding on a white man's world?"

Stunned, Cotannah stared at him.

"Pardon my French, ma'am. But I can see you agree with me, and I'm gonna do all I can to help you."

He wet his finger and went through some more pages.

"Here," he said finally, "we've got one Choctaw who thinks he can read English, I reckon—he's a bona fide subscriber to the *Star*. If he's willing to pay real money for a Boomer newspaper, I'm thinking he's smart enough to know the Nation's days are numbered, and he's trying to learn how to act like a white man."

He turned the ledger around so she could read it and marked the name with his long, pale finger.

"Folsom Greentree."

Cotannah looked at the name and the mailing address, Greentree Crossing, both listed in a clerk's fine script.

The name was familiar, but she couldn't quite place it at the moment.

"I'm thinking this redskin might lease you some land, or he'd know somebody who will," Sheets said.

She took a deep breath to try to calm the sudden sickness in her stomach and accepted the pencil he offered. She noted the information on the piece of paper that supposedly carried Jacob's name on the other side.

Dear God in Heaven, how had any Indian survived this long with people like Sheets stirring up the land-hungry white people?

"Thank you," she finally managed to say, and stuffed the paper back into her bag.

"You're welcome and good luck to you. The more white holdings and white settlers we can get in here, the quicker these Indians'll have to become Americans and abide by the laws like the rest of us do."

She turned around and walked out, sick now for another reason, too.

Finding any information about Jacob was going to be a lot harder than she'd thought.

Walks-With-Spirits saw Cotannah's face clearly as she came out of the newspaper office. She looked stricken. And she let the door bang shut behind her as if she didn't have the strength to reach back and close it.

His stomach tightened to a cold knot. Was this the meaning of that strange portent he'd felt the first time he ever saw a copy of this newspaper? Had she been harmed in there? But how?

The white man hadn't touched her, he had watched him carefully. And if he had insulted her with words, surely her face would have had that fiery look of flashing fury or the quiet one of seething anger, the one where her fine-boned jaw went tight and set and she spoke in a slow, disdainful drawl.

He turned his head slightly so he could see her walk all the way to her horse and mount up. She moved with the same supple grace as usual, but it was as if she had drawn her body in onto itself, and she shivered once after she was in the saddle. The day had turned out to be one of those capricious ones that he'd found typical of the New Nation in the fall—a frosty morning followed by a summerlike afternoon—so she couldn't be physically cold.

The shudder made him wish he could go and put his arms around her to comfort her, but he folded the knife and put it in his pocket, stood away from the post, and walked toward his horse instead, resisting even a glance back. More and more, he wanted to touch her, and he had to gather all his strength to fight the desire. Comfort as it would be to him, it would only make her anguish worse one moon from now.

He set his jaw and looked in upon himself. The thing to do was to remember why he had come with her in the first place, the two reasons. One, the portent. He had come to protect her in case it had been a foreboding of danger to her. Two, because his honor demanded that he accompany a woman who was risking her own safety to try—impossible as it was—to save him from execution. Wanting to touch her, wanting to be with her were temptations he'd known in advance.

So. Now he must think about his purpose here. What could have hurt her so much in the newspaper office? Was it something she'd read in that book the man had put out on the counter? Or was it that she found nothing at all to help her in her quest? His heart went out to her, but maybe such a disappointment would make her give up the search before it brought her even more pain.

He reached his horse, threw himself onto it without putting his foot into the stirrup, and, as soon as he gained the extra height, turned his head to see her through the crowd moving in the street. Why couldn't she know that she couldn't change his fate when so many of the Nation had heard him put the curse on Jacob? Trying to explain that to her was the same as letting a leaf drift from his fingers to blow away on the wind. Now he must make her believe it, or she would wear her body down and make herself sick.

Her horse was so brightly colored with bay and white spots that he picked it out immediately from among the other animals near the west end of the street. A mule-drawn wagon pulled to the side to let a horse and buggy pass it by and then he could see Cotannah on the paint horse. He gave a little sigh of relief. Already, she had recovered a little—she held her shoulders square and her head at that splendid angle that gave her such a proud air.

That air was what made men like Jacob so determined to conquer her, but her real pride wasn't strong enough to keep her from needing their attentions. If only she would be able to keep her resolve to behave differently, to take responsibility for protecting herself!

For a moment he sat still and watched her moving away from him, wending her quick way in and out among the animals and vehicles and people, all of whom looked drab compared to Cotannah. Drab and hurried. How could they live in this crowded place, with its constant noises of squeaking wheels and human voices? Why people ever made towns, he did not understand.

He turned his horse and started moving in the other direction toward their meeting place, the grove of red oak trees outside of town. Staying apart seemed an unnecessary precaution now, considering that no one in this whole noisy town was paying him the slightest notice at all and no one seemed interested in Cotannah. If she wanted to go back to the newspaper office, though, for more information, it was good he hadn't given her any Choctaw connection.

But she mustn't go back, not to a place that had affected her so badly. On this trip, while they had so many hours together, he must make her see the truth, so she wouldn't return to any part of this pursuit anymore.

Chapter 11

While she waited for Walks-With-Spirits, Cotannah slumped in her saddle and, on its horn,
smoothed out the piece of paper she still held crumpled
in her hand. Folsom Greentree.

The name sounded familiar, but she couldn't place
him. Was it possible that he was reading the *Star* to learn
the white man's ways, as Millard Sheets said? Or was
Sheets working with the Boomers in some way?

Or had Folsom Greentree subscribed to the *Star* in
order to read, as Tay did, the plans of the white settlers
greedy for the land belonging to the Choctaw Nation and
to the Cherokee Nation to the north and the Chickasaw
to the west? Was Greentree plotting to counter those
plans? Was he a strong Choctaw patriot or a man who
would break Choctaw law?

Would he be courteous to her when she rode onto his
place or would he run her off?

Millard Sheets was a horrible man. How could he hate
Indians so much?

"You're staring a hole into that paper," Walks-With-
Spirits said. "Does it have a secret written on the other
side?"

Her heart leapt and started thudding against her ribs, she whipped around in the saddle to look at him. He sat his horse just a stone's throw from her inside the little grove of whispering trees.

"Why in the world did you sneak up on me like that?" she cried. "Even Pretty Feather didn't hear you coming."

"To put the color back into your cheeks. When you came out of that newspaper office your face was the color of eggshells."

"Eggshells?"

"Not birds' eggs—chickens'," he said.

"Some chickens lay brown eggs. Brown is a color."

"I'm talking about white chicken eggs. Thin-shelled ones ready to crack into pieces at the slightest touch of a fox's teeth."

Her heart was slowing and tears were threatening, but she smiled at him, he was trying so hard to distract her.

"That Millard Sheets is so vile I can't tell you—he's a fox in the Nations' henhouse, all right. Oh, Walks-With-Spirits, I felt ready to crack into pieces when I came out of there, cold all over and about to throw up."

His face hardened.

"But now you're all right? How is he vile, in what way? What did he say to you?"

"That Indians are savages, intruders on the land intended for white people, all the old insults."

His shoulders relaxed, as if in relief.

"Nothing you haven't heard before?"

That made her laugh a little.

"No," she said, "nothing new to my ears."

Her anger began to return.

"Just infuriating, humiliating . . ."

"Now, now!" he interrupted. "Let's not give him

that power over us. He can't take it if we won't give it."

The thought stopped her.

Walks-With-Spirits rode closer, his eyes warm and bright, almost smiling now.

"Who is he that we should take to heart his opinion?" he said. "He is no one to us, he is nothing but a scavenger with a withered spirit, who has no harmony with the earth."

She felt warm inside for the first time since arriving at the office of the *Star* and the tension began to leave her. She smiled at him.

"Let's ride through the woods and up along the ridges," he said, "where we can see the mountains stretching blue and far and smell fall coming on the wind."

"Oh, I wish we could," she said, "but no." She looked at him, straight and without a smile. "Don't try to distract me," she said. "Just because I didn't find out very much from Sheets doesn't mean I'm giving up, and you volunteered to come with me, so you can't go riding the ridges, either."

"I came because I'd never forgive myself if you got into danger on my account."

"Well! You're already in danger on my account, and I'll never forgive myself if I don't get you out."

He nudged his horse and rode closer still. Peeved as she was that he was trying to stop her search for the truth, she still wanted to reach out and touch him, to lay her hand on his smooth, heavily muscled forearm beneath his rolled-up shirtsleeve.

"Cotannah. Don't do this to yourself. It's bad for you."

She gathered her reins and pulled Pretty Feather's

head around, turned her back on him and started trotting out of the trees.

"I'm going. You can come with me or not."

From the corner of her eye she saw him begin to follow.

"This isn't good for you," he said.

"Don't repeat yourself," she said. "We're going to see a man named Folsom Greentree, but it's too far to get there before midnight. Tonight we'll go as far as my old homeplace."

He rode up beside her, his jaw tight and his eyes hard. He was angry. Really angry.

"All right, then. We'll lie upon the ground when we get there and let the Earth Mother speak to you since you won't listen to me."

The hopeless fury she'd felt at the *Star* swirled up inside her again.

"Stop it! Just stop it! Nothing's going to make me quit, can't you see that? This is one time I'm not going to let them win, not if it kills me, too!"

"Let who win?"

"The wicked ones, the ones with the power! Fate, or destiny, or whatever it is that's always making innocent people suffer. I'm sick to death of it!"

He stared at her and then gave an abrupt nod, agreement or understanding or acquiescence, she couldn't tell. And she didn't care.

"My cousin Robert lives in our old cabin now, but he's gone to Muskogee to the Indian International Fair," she said quickly. "Let's get going so we can reach it before dark."

She set her jaw and put her heels to Pretty Feather. Walks-With-Spirits followed.

Then, after only a mile or so, he was riding at her side, not looking at her, not saying a word. His huge shoulders were relaxed beneath the white cotton shirt, his body barely moved and only in keeping with the rhythm of the horse.

His presence began to soothe her.

"I'm sorry I yelled at you," she said finally.

He glanced at her and nodded.

"I think I'm so upset because Sheets reminded me so much of Headmaster Haynes," she said. "He despises our people—he thinks we're savages who have no right being in the white man's way to claiming every square inch of the earth and fencing it in. Like Haynes, he could, without a twinge of his conscience, take out a whip and use it to strip an Indian girl naked."

He made a sound between a grunt and a growl, and she turned to see his eyes blazing and his face hard again.

"I want to protect you," he said suddenly, fiercely. "Now. Forever. I want to protect you from ever again breathing the same air as men like Haynes and Millard Sheets."

She gaped at him.

"I've had such angry, fighting thoughts of Haynes every time he crossed my mind since you told me about him," he admitted, and then when he looked at her again, his eyes held as much surprise as she felt.

"What happened to the advice you just handed to me," she said, gently teasing him. "Why do you give him that much power over you?"

He laughed, and her blood raced with delight. He cared about her. He really cared! That was why she felt she had come home when she was with him.

"I cannot tell you," he said slowly, searching her face with his fierce topaz eyes. "All I know is that you have unbalanced my harmony, Cotannah Chisk-Ko, as no one else has ever done. Before I saw you, I never had such thoughts of fighting other men.''

She smiled, but she didn't know whether she wanted to or not. She felt elation and sadness for destroying his peace and guilt and happiness all rushing around in her heart.

''Nor did you have thoughts of putting death curses on them,'' she said wryly. ''It is all my fault, after all. Now you admit it.''

She grinned at him and asked, ''Why do you give me that much power over you?''

He looked at her for a long, long moment, his eyes warm as amber sunshine.

''I never intended to give it,'' he said. ''You took it the first time I saw you, Cotannah.''

That melted her heart.

''I want to keep that power,'' she said softly, through lips gone stiff with unshed tears. ''And I want to keep you in this world. Don't you understand? I could not bear it if the Court carried out your sentence.''

She held his gaze while she drew a deep, ragged breath.

''Cotannah,'' he said, ''you are breaking my heart.''

''Don't worry about me. But tell me: what if I can't prove that your curse didn't kill Jacob before this next moon is past?''

''Then I'll know that my passage to the next world is part of the harmony of earth and sky.''

He gave her a smile that stopped her breath.

''The Great Spirit and the Earth Mother, they have the power, Cotannah. The powerful people only think they do.''

She ignored that.

''How can it be part of the natural harmony for you

to die because the Judges mistakenly think you killed Jacob? That makes no sense!''

"Our spirits are not wise enough to know that."

"Mine is! I know that!"

He laughed again, soft and low.

"Now that's why I wanted so much to dance with you that night we met," he said. "I could not keep my hands from reaching out to touch you, for the life force in you was stronger than in Long Man river."

A sharp, sweet shock shot through her even though he'd told her that before. She hadn't known that he had longed to touch her. Was he longing to touch her now?

"How did you know that my life force was strong?"

"Your eyes flashed like lightning looking for someone, searching, always searching. Your feet stomped against the face of the Earth Mother, trying to make her give you your wish."

"You could see it that plain that I was out of my mind in love with Tay," she said slowly, remembering. "When all the time he only loved me as a sister. How I could have been so unseeing, so stupid, I'll never know."

"That, too, was part of the natural harmony," he said.

"No!"

Her cheeks flamed with hot embarrassment, even after all this time, recalling her devastated pride.

She looked down at the ground, watched Pretty Feather's small hooves cutting into the grass, one swift, trotting step after another. When she glanced up at him again he was looking at her, his topaz eyes gone soft and dark.

"Yet it must be," he said.

"How can you say that? How?"

"Because all that has happened to you has made you this Cotannah today."

"What does that mean?"

"You are Cotannah: a beautiful body inflamed with a fervent spirit. You have bubbling passions brave with hope, right-loving thoughts bright with honor. Never have I known another woman like you."

She would remember all of that forever, she would think about it time after time. She would remember the sound of his voice; it stroked her skin as if he had reached out his hand.

He said it again while his horse moved beside hers through the golden afternoon.

"Never has there been another woman like you."

His affirmation sent her heart soaring to the sun.

They rode up to the cabin at dusk. It lay in the shadows, folded into the quiet valley like a bird in the nest. A horse ran along the crooked, split-rail fence, nickering, and Pretty Feather answered as they passed.

"Robert had better be gone for sure," Cotannah said.

"Why?"

"I want us to be alone."

The minute the words spilled off her tongue, she bit it, incredulous that again she had blurted out to him exactly what she was thinking.

"I can't believe I said that." She ducked her head, unable to meet his eyes.

"I can believe it," he said, with a low chuckle. "Even on the night we met you were speaking bold and straight to me—but then you called me an old black crow and told me to get away from you."

He threw her a glance, his eyes flashing bright in the dusk.

"Now you want to be alone with me. I like *this* straightforward talk of yours much better."

She felt heat rising into her face.

"I only meant that it's going to be a good evening to make a fire and sit and talk," she said quickly, as he sidepassed his mount up to the gate and bent to open it.

"Of course," he drawled, leading the way into the horse pen, "and if Robert were here, we couldn't build a fire or speak a word."

He laughed, and so did she.

"You know what I mean! You promised to tell me about your childhood, and you know you wouldn't if Robert were here."

"I might. For all I know, Robert is a rapt listener."

"He isn't," she said, dismounting in front of the open-sided pole barn. "Cousin Robert is a bigmouth who has to do all the talking himself."

Walks-With-Spirits stepped off his horse.

"Oh, now I understand. You want to do all the talking yourself with no interference from Robert."

"What a thing to say," she cried. "Just listen to you—you talk lots more than I do, and you know it!"

Laughing, they walked to the horses' heads and stopped, facing each other, standing close, very close. He smelled the way he looked—like a woodsman— pines and mountains, and juniper, she thought. Like sweet, pungent cedar branches mixed with that special scent that was his alone.

"But I like to listen to you," she said slowly, as she drank in the sight of the dusky light falling across his high cheekbones and straight, broad nose, across his full, sensual mouth and hard jaw and chin, "even if you do talk in riddles sometimes."

"I like to talk to you," he said, in a voice so low and smooth it sent heat moving through her flesh, "even if you are only interested in my childhood."

"That's not true!"

"What else?" he said, smiling, teasing her with his

eyes and his voice. "What else are you interested in, Cotannah?"

Without a thought, she lifted her hand and traced the line of his cheekbone, just with the tips of her fingers. A lightning strike of excitement ran up her arm, straight to her heart. He felt it, too—in the dusky, purple light his eyes shone like stars.

They stared at each other, stunned. For an endless moment she couldn't take a breath, couldn't move, could only press the tip of her finger against his warm, smooth flesh and feel his hot blood running like a river of enchantment through his skin to hers.

Then he reached for her, took her by the arms, rubbed them up and down to warm her, but that was only to prolong the delicious anticipation, and she knew it.

"You're shivering," he said, and that was true, too, but she hadn't realized it until then.

He drew her closer.

Her gaze clung to his.

"It . . . it turns cold fast when the sun goes down."

"Let me warm you, Cotannah."

His eyes, heavy-lidded and hot, set a fire at the very core of her, before his mouth, his incredible mouth, met hers and melted her bones. He kissed her, and she clung to him and kissed him back and lost all connection with everything else on earth.

He smelled of horse and dust and the wool of his coat and of his own special scent that never failed to go to her head. He tasted of his own self, too, purely sweet and darkly mysterious.

He took all her breath and all her strength and at the same time he made her very heart sing and fly. He found her tongue with his, twined them together, and her whole body melded with his.

This. This was all she wanted, ever, ever, and she was never going to let him go.

But at last he savored her lips one last time and then drew back and held her away.

"I can't kiss you now without doing more," he said. "Go. Go on in and start the fire. I'll see to the horses."

Every instinct in her screamed for her to stay. Her bruised lips opened to argue, her hands moved to reach for him again.

But he was right. It was too dangerous, for her very soul wanted to be with him, and he might soon be gone.

She turned and ran toward the house, wanting to stay but afraid of what would happen if she did. The tips of her fingers and her breasts and her thighs and her belly tingled. She could still feel him against her; her lips held the taste of his and so did her tongue. She was trembling all over, and she barely could breathe.

The cold night closed around her before she reached the porch, and she pounded up the steps and across it by pure instinct, opening the door and moving across the room to light the lamp. Robert was gone and they would be alone and what would they do?

Nothing. They mustn't. Walks-With-Spirits had been right to send her away from him.

Her hands were shaking but she found the matches and lifted the glass chimney to light the lamp. The old, familiar room sprang to life all around her.

Then she moved toward the hearth, where the banked fire glowed. No. Walks-With-Spirits hadn't been right to send her away because it felt too right to be with him, too destined for them to lie together, skin against skin.

But she'd better be careful with that destiny. She had never before made love with a man whom she loved. So how would she survive when he was gone?

Shoving the thought away, she knelt and grabbed the

poker, began to stir up the fire. Adding more kindling, watching the flames come to life as tiny tongues of yellow and red, she tried not to think of him at all.

Because then she'd have to think of him being shot one moon from now. She put two new sticks of wood on the fire and stared into it harder. Old Grandmother Stonecipher who lived over by Piney Branch could read the past and the future in the fire, it was said.

"Will I be able to save him?" she whispered to the blaze she was creating. "Will I get to keep him with me for the rest of my life?"

Try as she would, though, she could see no answer in the shimmering sparks or the flames. Cool night air rushed in and fanned them higher, but still she saw no shapes, nothing.

"Cotannah."

He stood in the doorway, his arms full of wood, the saddlebags swinging from his shoulder.

She went to him, slid the strap from his shoulder to hers.

"Come in. Welcome to my old home."

He smiled and took in the whole room with his eyes, drew in a deep breath of the smell of the house. The wind rose in the eaves and made small creaking sounds in the walls.

"I can feel you here," he said.

She laughed.

"That's because I am here."

"No, I mean I feel you in the past. The little girl and then the big girl Cotannah, helping Aunt Ancie with the cooking and Uncle Jumper with the garden."

"And pestering Cade to take me riding with him," she said, her voice giving way a little when she thought about those days. "Whenever he was home."

A profound sorrow swept through her as she turned

and started toward the kitchen with the bag of food, dropping the other one into a straight chair sitting by the window as she passed by. Walks-With-Spirits carried the firewood to the hearth.

"Was he gone a great deal?"

She stopped in the kitchen doorway and looked at him.

"Yes. Aunt Ancie always said that his Wandering Year lasted for ten years."

"Did you have friends close by?"

"No," she said, and went on into the kitchen to see what food Robert had left.

She found blackberry jam and tomato preserves, both of which must have been made by Aunt Sally, Robert's mother, and some baked sweet potatoes and parched corn. Standing there, looking at the food, she tried not to remember the bountiful table Aunt Ancie had set and tried to forget how lonely she had been during all those years that she'd lived here.

Now, even if they didn't make love, she would be lonely beyond belief if she was separated from Walks-With-Spirits.

"Cotannah."

She turned to see that he had come into the kitchen without her hearing him.

"I know how you must feel," he said. "I would be sad right now if I went back to my old home."

Tears filled her eyes.

"Did you have friends close by?"

"No. There were plenty of children in the town, and I played with them sometimes, but I was always separate, too. No one else was being raised by a medicine man and a missionary woman; no one else was being taught how to heal and how to say incantations. No one else was an orphan from nowhere."

She clutched the soft leather food bag with both hands.

"But now you and I are friends," she said, "and that means the world to me. Not even Emily can see my true feelings the way you do."

Her swollen lips felt awkward from the effort she was making to hold back the tears, but she managed to smile. He looked so sympathetic, so worried about her. He looked so dear.

"We are truly friends, aren't we, Walks-With-Spirits? But I don't know how. I never thought a man and a woman could be friends, did you?"

He returned her smile with one of his solemn looks.

"I never thought about it," he said.

"Did you ever tell another woman she was your friend?"

The corners of his mouth turned up in amusement.

"No."

"Have you ever told another woman that she was different from all the others?"

He shook his head.

"No."

She gave him a mischievous grin that made her throat relax and her tears recede.

"Have you ever told another woman that she was degrading herself?"

His trace of a smile vanished, and he shook his head again.

"I wouldn't have said that to you if it hadn't been such a blow to look up and see you, not on the arm of one man, but of two," he said, his voice hardening as he spoke. "And neither of them Jacob Charley, with whom you had already made a foolish scene in front of my very eyes."

He pivoted on his heel and went back into the main room.

She stood frozen for a moment, listening to the echo of his voice in her head. Why, he was jealous! And he was admitting as much! Could that be true? Walks-With-Spirits, who lived in harmony with all the earth, *jealous?*

The thought boggled her mind but as she looked at it over and over, she knew that she was right. Still staring at the place where he had been standing, she picked up a jar of jam, turned it over in her hands, and set it down again on the tablecloth with a soft thump.

"Walks-With-Spirits," she called, as she ran to find him. "Was it really a blow to you to look up and see me with the Bonham cousins?"

"Yes!"

He was kneeling in front of the fire, his eyes blazing as he turned to look at her. He gave the logs a vicious punch that made sparks fly everywhere, up the chimney, inside the big firebox and out onto the plank floor.

"I felt a white-hot rage," he said, slapping one of them out with his bare hand.

She went to kneel beside him.

"You were jealous."

"Yes."

And then, with no warning at all, he reached out, touched her cheek lightly with the rough tips of his fingers. "Come here, Cotannah," he said, his voice gone hoarse as a stranger's.

"I am here. I'll always be here, as long as you need me."

He took her face in both his big hands and tilted it up for another kiss.

Chapter 12

❦

The wild scent of his skin—dark, primitive, deep woods and wind—entered her blood on the pungent incense of the burning logs. The flames of the fire, blinding bright and dancing, leapt in his eyes as he bent toward her, and then her sight was gone. Her sight and her breath, both gone.

But she didn't need them. This, this was what she needed, Walks-With-Spirits's mouth on hers once more. His mouth knew hers now and his lips and his tongue gave her such pleasure that her heart beat slow and hard to hold time still and savor it. This was more than pleasure, though—he was marking her as his with the fierce grip of his hand cradling the back of her head, with the authority of his tongue as it found hers and claimed it as his own. She drank that possessive kiss like a parched hummingbird would drink nectar.

Pleasure and wanting, startlement and knowledge all surged through her in one mighty wave after another. No one, no one had ever affected her like this before, this honest stealing of her very soul from her body. No other man had this power.

And then her mind, too, was gone, into his keeping.

She couldn't think anymore but she didn't want to, this was all she wanted, this kissing with him that pulled her to him, that melted her to him, body, soul, and spirit. Slowly, slowly, he drew back just a little and traced her lips with the tip of his tongue. Desire burst inside her like a flower coming open, and she let him dip in and taste her, drew him nearer again with quick, tantalizing touches of her tongue. His mouth was made to meld with hers, this was why they'd both been born.

He made a rough, ragged sound, deep in his throat, and turned his whole body to hers, cradled her head in both his callused hands, now, to keep her mouth beneath his. Her arms felt heavy, so heavy she couldn't hope to lift them yet she couldn't hope not to, for she had to touch him, had to hold him somehow captive as he was holding her.

She managed to wrap them around his neck at last, but it made him deepen the kiss so, made him moan in his throat and caress her so tenderly with his tongue and his hands in her hair that she could only cling to him and let him melt her very bones. She had no choice, she could only let him kiss her on and on, let him keep her in this heavy haze of pleasure that had no ending. This kissing with him was all she wanted, forever.

Forever.

Her eyes opened wide. She pulled back from him. Slowly, reluctantly, he let her, opening his eyes then to search her face. She could only look at him, she could not speak.

Never, ever had she felt this . . . this pull before. This kiss ran far deeper than any other from any other man, all the way deep into her spirit.

Fear blew through her like snow in a blizzard.

Why did it have to be, this truth that she'd known ever since that very first kiss at his cave? Why did her life have to turn out so that he was the one man she truly ever loved?

Oh, dear God, he was sentenced to die a few days from now!

She closed her eyes against the beautiful sight of him and reached weakly for the rock ledge of the hearth to help her get up and away from him. Wouldn't that just be the way things always were for her? Wouldn't that just be another of the bitter ironies that had speckled her life if Walks-With-Spirits, her one true love, was held guilty of Jacob's murder to the very end and she had to give him up to the Lighthorse with their rifles?

Cotannah walked away from him after the earth-shattering kiss they shared. Walks-With-Spirits heard her in the kitchen rattling dishes so hard that he knew her hands were shaking, but he didn't have to hear that to know she was as shaken by the kiss as he. And he felt as if his bones lay in pieces inside his limbs, pieces so small that they could never come together again.

Except to reach out and pull her to him.

His lips hurt for another kiss, his tongue cried out for another taste of her, his arms ached to hold her. His very blood burned with the sudden, coursing need to know how it would be to lie down with her—here in front of the fire, to press her whole body against his, to strip off their clothes and feel the yielding of flesh against flesh and the shimmering heat of the fire on one side, the cool nipping of the night breeze from the window on the other. Or to carry her outside into the night beneath the waxing moon and make sweet, sweet love with her until the moon went down and the sun came up.

The thought set fire to the inside of his skin, gave his body complete control over his spirit.

He couldn't let himself think this way, he could not.

If he kissed her again and again, he would hold her and do more and that would only make it harder, much harder for him to meet his fate with a serene mind and spirit. A stab of panic cut through him. Could he regain his harmony? It had been disturbed ever since the first time he had laid eyes on Cotannah, yet whenever they kissed, he had never felt so attuned to his soul, body, and spirit, to the Earth Mother and the Great Spirit.

Yet now, at this moment, he had never felt such a tumult.

Nor had she, judging by the noise she was making.

His kiss had moved her deeply. If he ever hoped to help her prepare to go on with her life without him, he must not so much as touch her again.

She appeared in the doorway with a bucket in her hand.

"I'm going for fresh water," she said, her eyes wild in the glow from the lamp.

"Let me."

"No! I have to do something," she cried.

She ran across to the door and out into the night.

He got up and paced back and forth in front of the fire, his whole body aching for her. But if he ever hoped to dissuade her from this hopeless quest to save him, he must not touch her anymore. He bent his head to his hand in despair. Now he didn't want the quest to be hopeless, he wanted to stay in this world, to stay with her, and, if that was so, how could he ever pass to the other world with a scrap of true peace left to him?

This was so shallow, so wrong, to be so enamored of the sensations of his mortal body that he let desire steal his peace. He tried to cling to that thought but as he stared into the flames his spirit saw that his feelings for Cotannah were more, far more, than those of his mortal body. Truly, she fit into his soul although he could not know why or how.

She came back into the cabin like the whirlwind she'd become, filled the coffeepot and hung it over the fire, went back into the kitchen without a word. He followed, and the minute he stepped silently into the room, she knew he was there. She turned to him, conflict raging in her beautiful face.

"Tell them the truth when we get back to Tuskahoma," she said. "Please, Walks-With-Spirits. Half the Nation or more will believe the words of an *alikchi*. Tell them you didn't mean the curse, so it didn't kill Jacob. Tell them because that may be our only chance."

"Don't," he said, gripping the doorframe to keep from going to her and taking her into his arms. "Please, Cotannah, don't worry like this."

"I can't help it. Will you tell them?"

Pure despair sharpened the edges of her voice.

"How can I? What if it's true? I did say the incantation, after all. You heard me."

She gripped the edges of the table with both hands. Her soft skin—oh, his fingertips and his lips knew how soft it was!—stretched tighter across her bones, hardened the beauty of her features.

"Did you hear me when I said that you are too good in your spirit to ever kill anyone? I saw you with Sophie and I sensed how much you wanted to stop her pain. I felt your righteous wrath when you saved me from Jacob. You were angry—that's all the curse was, just angry words coming out of your mouth. That incantation didn't have your spirit in it, so it had no power."

She was trembling, and her voice shook, her eyes were wilder still. At this rate she would never stay whole through the hard days to come.

It would be easier for her not to carry so much hope

that might be misplaced. He walked to the table and leaned toward her, held her eyes with his. "I wish I knew that as surely as you do," he said. "But you didn't see inside my heart as I said those words over Jacob. At that moment, Cotannah, I wanted him dead."

He stared deep into her eyes, willing her to listen, to know this.

"I felt so protective of you and so jealous of him— never, ever have I felt so strongly about anything," he said. "Those feelings I had were strong enough to kill him, no matter what we both would like to believe."

"Jacob had enemies," she said stubbornly. "He was not a good person, Shadow, dear. His own actions killed him, not your few words."

A sharp, new sensation ran through him. A thrill.

"What did you call me?"

"Shadow," she said, smiling. "You appear and disappear silently, like a shadow."

He smiled back.

"A nickname."

Her smiled broadened.

"Yes. A nickname for you, Mr. *Alikchi*, sir."

He couldn't stop smiling at her, couldn't stop hearing the affection in her voice. But he mustn't forget what he was about, here, mustn't let her fall in love with him. And he mustn't fall in love with her.

"Listen, Cotannah, my darling, and listen well," he said. "No matter what I might say to the judges it would make no difference. That death curse convinced too many people that I am a witch."

She looked at him with the storm still raging in her eyes, then, gradually, it died down. "I go by my instincts that you once called earthbound," she said, speaking slowly, as if working out her conclusions in her head as she spoke. "Those instincts tell me that there's more to

Jacob's death than meets the eye. They tell me it wasn't a natural death, because he was young and healthy and very strong. So I'm going to keep on looking to see what I can find out.''

''Usually I'm all in favor of hope,'' he said, around the lump that was forming in his throat. ''But in this case it's going to make you hurt so much more, Cotannah. Look at the state you're already in.''

''I'm sorry about that,'' she said. ''Out of old habits, I've let my feelings get out of hand here, but I'm in control again. Really, my darling, I'm calm inside. I really am. Finding out how Jacob died, trying to prove that you didn't kill him—that gives me a purpose like I've never had in my life before.''

He heard it all, but it was the endearment, the sweet quoting of the words that he had said to her that rang in his ears like a bell. Her voice was filled with so many feelings that he knew she not only meant them but that she understood everything he was trying to tell her as well.

She nodded, as if she had read his mind.

''Jacob had enemies,'' she said again, but very calmly. ''Everyone knows that.''

''So tomorrow you'll go on to see this Folsom Greentree?''

''Yes. Will you go with me?''

''Yes. I'm going to protect you until the day I die.''

Quick tears sprang to her eyes.

''Please prepare yourself, just in case,'' he said softly. ''One thing to remember is that I can't ever be at peace or find my balance again if I sully my honor by swearing that my curse didn't kill Jacob when I don't know for sure if that's true.''

She went pale around her eyes, at the sides of her nostrils.

"That helps me some," she said, just as softly, "but not as much as clearing your name will do. Even if I, God forbid, should fail to find out what the secret is about Jacob's death, I have to leave no stone unturned. Cade told me that my thoughtless selfishness would cause a killing someday, and now it has. I have no choice but to do everything in my power to stop it from causing the Lighthorse to kill you."

He stared at her in the kitchen's lamplight, willing her to understand. Praying that she would hear him.

"And I have no choice but to uphold my honor. One reason I now see—and it is because of you—is that if I refuse to run away, if I practice the old Choctaw way and return to accept my sentence after being set free for my last days, I will help to strengthen the old traditions against the culture of the white man."

He paused to let that soak in, telling her with his eyes not to speak.

"When I say this thought came to me because of you, I speak true," he said, too quickly, because it scared him to think how much she already had come to mean to him. "Most of the time the healing I do and the connections I make affect animals in the woods and the Earth Mother, but not a human person."

Her lips parted and her eyes grew huge and shiny. For an instant he feared that he had made her cry, but she didn't. She was listening intently, taking in his words, thinking about them.

"When you met me on the road that morning beside the Tulli Creek and said that you believed your flirting with Jacob had caused my death sentence, I understood, suddenly, how one person's decisions could be said to cause another to act in a certain way, that people's lives do tie together when they live in a community."

He waited, but she only looked at him, her eyes narrowed thoughtfully. He felt a stab of surprise at her quietness. And hope. He was getting through to her.

"Now, because of you and your honor, which demands that you try to get me out of this death sentence because you think you got me into it," he said, "I want my actions to affect other people's lives. I see that I strengthen their honor when I satisfy my own."

"So," she said softly, "you will die so that your life will affect other people."

He nodded.

"Because of you," he said.

"But don't you see?" she said, triumphantly. "That proves that you agree with me: it is my actions that have brought you to this terrible pass."

His heart clutched as an awful sincerity suffused her face.

"That means that now you also must agree that I cannot stop trying to save you."

She searched his eyes.

"You understand that now, don't you, Walks-With-Spirits?"

"Yes."

She smiled, a glittering, unexpected pleasure to see, a new smile like sun coming out on snow. His heart gave a quick, hard stroke and began to beat faster and faster.

"So you'll start to help me now. You'll use your powers and help me at Greentree's place?"

He couldn't trust himself to speak, so he answered with a nod. He would go with her to protect her and help her all he could to make her happy, even if he did still think that there might be no information to find because he might've killed Jacob.

The main reason he would go was to protect her. That came first. And he would help because this search was something she had to do. He wasn't going because he couldn't bear to be separated from her now.

No. It was not that at all.

The next morning, riding through the countryside
with Walks-With-Spirits seemed like a dream to Cotannah. They left the cabin behind and turned the horses
toward the dazzling, new sun, and when they did, he
took her completely into that present world and left all
the past behind. And the future, too. She didn't even
think about what they might find at Greentree's
Crossing.

From the moment she'd called him to breakfast from
his bedroll which he had spread in the yard, he had
showed her this familiar country she'd grown up in as
if it were a brand-new place. He'd suggested that they
sit on the cabin's porch to eat so they could watch the
squirrels gathering pecans in the yard and his talk about
them, or maybe just the rich sound of his voice, had
smoothed all the thoughts of the death sentence from her
mind.

Or maybe it was the sight of him that had filled all
her senses until she couldn't worry anymore. Now, one
glance at his strong brown hands on the reins made her
think of how he caressed her face, one glimpse of his
sensual mouth made his taste spring strong to her lips,
and she was lost in the delicious awareness of being
alone with him in a beautiful country where the breeze
blew brisk and cool and morning had come.

The woods grew close to the path and then, in the
open places, they could see out over the layers of purple
mountains that rose and fell, higher and higher, until the
color paled and faded away into the sky. They took a
faint trail through the wooded hills that she remembered
from her childhood, a shortcut to the road that led to
Greentree's Crossing.

"When I was growing up, the muscadines were thick over there in that little gully," she said. "I never tasted anything so delicious in all my life as they were when we came out to pick them on a frosty morning."

He nodded.

"Frosty muscadines are a gift from the Earth Mother. Like falling stars from the Great Father Spirit."

She laughed.

"I've never thought of wild grapes and falling stars in the same breath," she said.

"Frosty muscadines," he said, "dusted with ice stars, they are the color of the sky at night."

She sensed him shift in the saddle, felt his eyes on her.

"Aren't they?"

His voice held an edge of humor, the teasing tone that never failed to draw her to him. She couldn't have kept from looking at him then, not for all the grapes and stars in the world, not even if she'd been trying to ignore him, which she certainly wasn't.

Yes. His lips were curved up at the corners in a trace of a smile and his topaz eyes twinkled with mischief like that of a small boy. She smiled back at him and clutched the horn of her saddle so she wouldn't reach out to him with her hand. They had to keep going, truly they did.

Without warning, the path led abruptly up the side of a steep, densely wooded hill and he went ahead of her, holding back tree branches and finding the faint trail. When they were almost at the top, he reined in and raised one hand to her in a signal to halt.

It took a second for her to realize he'd stopped, that he was silent, and then the fear she'd been carrying in the pit of her stomach since his arrest leapt, full-blown, up into her throat.

"What?"

Instinctively, she kept her voice low and then said no more, but her hands were trembling and her thoughts were flying wild. Had someone followed them? Maybe the real killer had seen them leave Tall Pine together and surmised that they were looking for him!

Or maybe Millard Sheets knew that she wasn't Spanish at all. Maybe he had sent some Indian haters to follow her to Folsom Greentree's and find out what she was really about!

But Walks-With-Spirits didn't seem afraid. He cocked his head and listened for a long moment more and then she heard it, too—low, panting groaning and clacking sounds of sticks struck together, almost like claves at a dance. Then some moaning and grunting and one furious bellowing made her know whatever it was that had stopped them wasn't human at all.

Walks-With-Spirits signaled with his raised hand and they rode a little farther up the trail. From there they could see what it was: two buck deer, their antlers locked in combat, pushing and pulling to try to get themselves free. Only a moment of watching showed that they were hopelessly caught, their racks so snarled and twisted into each other that it was impossible to see where one stopped and the other began.

Their hides were darkened by sweat, their small hooves had dug great holes scrabbling desperately in the dirt.

"Stay mounted," Walks-With-Spirits whispered.

He slid silently from his horse and walked toward the two, speaking to them softly. Not in English, not in Choctaw, but in grunts and snorts and growls. She held her breath. The deer seemed half-crazed, rolling their big brown eyes sideways at him, throwing dirt into the air and making awful noises. They moved back from him a little bit, still struggling, but he walked steadily toward them.

She reached for the light rifle in the scabbard of her saddle. For the first time since arriving in the Nation she thought of it and was glad she was carrying it as she did on solitary rides at the ranch.

But she didn't need it. The deer began to calm as Walks-With-Spirits raised his voice and made them hear him. He walked closer, never hesitating, still talking to them. By the time he was close enough to run a hand over each of their withers, they stood quiet beneath the big oak tree.

Walks-With-Spirits stroked each of them twice, talked to them some more and then reached for the tangled racks, pushing and pulling until the muscles of his shoulders bulged and color flooded into his face. He wrenched at them mightily and his arm muscles seemed on the very verge of bursting his shirtsleeves, stopped, took a deep breath, and wrenched at them again.

At last they came undone. Suddenly, the deer realized they were free.

They stood in place, breathing hard. Then they threw their heads up high and stood looking at him. Fiercely. For one endless moment they stood and stared at him, exhausted muscles quivering, sweaty hides shining in the streaks of sunlight while Cotannah wished she'd pulled the rifle, after all.

But then some snuffling sounds passed among the three of them, Walks-With-Spirits grunted some last message to them. The deer wheeled in their tracks and vanished into the woods, each in a different direction. Cotannah sat her horse, staring in wonder.

"They're grateful," Walks-With-Spirits said, as he walked toward her across the crackling leaves that had already fallen.

She gaped at him.

"How did you do that? How did you know their language?"

"Cotannah," he said, smiling, "you need to learn to listen as well as to see. You could speak their language, too, if you wanted."

He leapt onto his horse without pulling himself up with his hands, with only one light balancing touch on its neck.

"You should be a likely one to speak the deer's language," he said, teasing her, "since you were a girl baby wrapped in a deerskin at birth."

She laughed.

"But even if you were a boy baby wrapped in a cougar skin, when you were separating those two deer you almost became a deer yourself. I thought you were a shape-changer there for a moment."

"Or a shadow of a deer?" he asked, with a grin.

"Yes, Shadow," she said, grinning back at him. "You became a shadow of a deer."

They sat still, smiling into each other's eyes, feeling close and safe. Her breath went short again, almost vanished. Looking into his eyes was like looking into a deep forest pool that stood still and quiet all the way to the bottom. Looking into his eyes made her see peace.

"One time in the Old Nation I came upon a deer who was dragging the rotting skeleton of his dead enemy around by his antlers," he said. "I didn't want that to happen again here."

Cotannah couldn't look away from him. She still could hardly breathe. Suddenly, every inch of her flesh, every pore of her skin, every part of her brain was desperate to know all about him. Longing to know. Trying to imagine where all he had been, what all he had done.

"What did you do with the one who was fastened to his dead enemy?"

"I shot him with an arrow and sent him to the next world," he said, and a great shock ran through her to hear that he, the healer, had done such a thing.

He shook his head at the astonishment in her face.

"It was the only merciful thing to do," he said. "The burden had driven him mad."

He started them moving again at a brisk trot through the bright-colored trees.

"Think of that when you think of dragging your past around behind you, Cotannah," he said. "It's the source of many obstacles for you. Love yourself and look to the future instead."

But I want you to love me!

She bit back the impulsive words as a great surge of anger washed over her. The way he'd sounded, he didn't intend to be around when she was loving herself and looking to the future.

"Listen to yourself and take your own advice," she said bitterly. "I'm not the one volunteering to strip to the waist and have a white cross painted over my heart!"

When they rode up the hill at Greentree's Crossing and saw that the big house and the grounds were crowded with vehicles and horses and people, Cotannah looked at Walks-With-Spirits and pulled up her horse.

"You can wait for me out here if you want," she said. "You don't need to hear any more accusations that you're a witch."

He smiled at her and shook his head.

"I can't bear to leave you right now," he said simply. "You don't need to bear this burden all by yourself, and I promised you I would help."

Without another word, they began to ride closer.

"It's a funeral cry," he said, at the moment she saw the reason for such a gathering.

A brush arbor stood near the cemetery at the edge of the woods behind the house and long tables laden with food sat out in the open, where the relatives and friends, who were not presently wailing and crying over the grave, were sitting around visiting with each other and feasting. They rode toward them side by side.

A buzz of excitement swept across the grounds as soon as people began recognizing Walks-With-Spirits. A man got up to greet them, a man who walked slowly across the grass to meet them with the authority of the landowner and host. She remembered him clearly now that she saw him.

"I am called Folsom Greentree," he said. "Have you come to mourn my wife's mother?"

"I am called Walks-With-Spirits and this young lady is Cotannah Chisk-Ko, sister of Cade Chisk-Ko, niece of Jumper and Ancie."

Cotannah tried to be unobtrusive as she looked the man over, searching for . . . what? He wasn't going to wear a sign saying, "Boomers' Friend," was he? He looked much the same as when she was a little girl, except that he was a little more jowly and his paunch had grown larger.

"No, Mr. Greentree," she said, "we weren't invited to the cry. We've come because we need to ask you something."

He turned without acknowledging the introduction and stared at her, waiting. She swallowed, hard, and tried not to notice the hard look in his eyes and the ungiving cast to his face.

"We would like to ask if you know of any connection between the newspaper called the *Oklahoma Star* and the man called Jacob Charley."

Folsom Greentree only stared at her in silence.

She looked at Walks-With-Spirits, but he appeared not to have noticed the man's rudeness nor her beseeching glance—he was looking over the crowd that was beginning to gather around them. Then Greentree spoke.

"Why has he brought you with him—to do his talking?"

Cotannah's temper flared.

"I brought him with me is more like it," she said, fighting to keep the irritation from her voice in hopes that he still would ask them to get down, that he would sit and visit with them.

Preferably, in some private place. More people were drifting from the tables toward them, standing around close, openly staring at her and Walks-With-Spirits.

She wanted to scream at them to go away instead of watching and eavesdropping and making quiet comments behind their hands. If she couldn't get any information from Folsom Greentree, what in the world would she do? This was her only clue to follow.

Mournful wails floated toward them from near the mother-in-law's grave, the muttering in the crowd grew louder. Cotannah caught the word "witch" and the word "*alikchi*" more than once. Evidently, Folsom Greentree did, too.

"And why have you brought him to my place?"

Her hopes for a chat in which she might learn something died. Greentree avoided looking at Walks-With-Spirits—he must be one of the contingent who thought he was a witch.

"Walks-With-Spirits did not kill Jacob Charley," she said, raising her voice so that everyone there could hear her. "And we are thinking that perhaps the Boomers might know who did. You subscribe to the *Oklahoma*

Star, so perhaps you have read something in it that could help us.''

He glared at her for the longest time, incredulously, as if he could not believe her audacity.

''Are you deaf?'' he said. ''Didn't you hear this witch put a death curse on Jacob Charley right in front of your face?''

She stiffened her backbone against the scorn in his voice. And the fear. He was afraid of Walks-With-Spirits.

''You think I am a friend to the Boomers,'' he said roughly. ''Well, Missy, did you ever think I might be their strongest enemy? I read that paper to see what trick they will use next to try to take our land.''

His triumphant tone as he finished talking and crossed his arms across his chest brought murmurs of agreement from the people surrounding them. Once more, his glance touched Walks-With-Spirits and slid quickly away.

''The witch killed him.''

That hostile whisper rose in the air, coming from several voices.

''No, you fools. He is an *alikchi,*'' someone else said clearly.

Arguments began in the growing crowd. Cotannah glanced worriedly at Walks-With-Spirits, but he was still looking calmly at one person and then another.

A small child, a little, toddling boy, bobbled into view, obviously trying to run and play with some other children who had darted out from behind the adults. All the children moved toward them but the smallest one was left behind, limping along at a hobbled gait, reaching out with his little arms to try to hold back the child nearest him. Walks-With-Spirits began watching him closely.

"Go on, now," Folsom Greentree boomed, making her turn back to him. "Go back to your family, Cotannah Chisk-Ko, and don't run around the country with a witch. The Court has decided who killed Jacob Charley."

"But they're wrong!" she cried. "I know . . ."

His expression and his voice turned thunderous.

"Turn your horses around and ride out! I want no witches throwing death curses on my place."

Her throat aching with painful disappointment, Cotannah pulled Pretty Feather around, starting to do as she was told. But she couldn't give up.

"Walks-With-Spirits is an *alikchi*!" she shouted. "And he did not kill anyone. Tay Nashoba, your Principal Chief, believes he is innocent!"

All eyes turned to her.

"Do any of you know of an enemy of Jacob Charley's who might have caused his death?"

"Not by witchcraft," some hard voice yelled. "You're riding with the only witch I know!"

From the corner of her eye she saw Walks-With-Spirits move and she thought he was going to turn his horse, too, but instead he leapt down and walked straight toward the hobbling child, who had thrown himself into a lurch of a gait in a determined effort to run. A sudden silence fell, then individual voices rang out.

"Don't let him touch that child!"

"Sunflower! Keep him away from your baby—he's a witch."

"Let her alone! Maybe the *alikchi* can heal him."

Walks-With-Spirits reached the child and held out his arms. The baby stopped trying to run and stood looking up at him.

"He'll say a death curse!" a woman's voice screamed.

A young woman who Cotannah took to be Sunflower, the mother, quickly pushed her way through the crowd and Walks-With-Spirits began talking to her. She nodded and he reached down to pick the child up, he stroked the toddler's cheek and spoke to him, too, then held him out for his mother to hold him while he felt of his legs. He extended them—one, clearly, was two or more inches shorter than the other. He began speaking to the mother, again, but he was too far away for Cotannah to hear what he was saying.

All the cries of advice and the mutterings and murmurings stopped when Walks-With-Spirits turned around and stared into the crowd.

"I will not harm this child," he said, and his rich voice carried all over the grounds.

Then he turned back to the mother, gave her a nod of the head as a signal, and, as she held her child, Walks-With-Spirits took the boy's shorter leg in both hands and, his lips moving in a chant, pulled on it, worked with it, massaged it at the hip. The child gave a sharp, high cry of pain.

A burly man pushed forward toward them, but when Walks-With-Spirits turned around and met his gaze, the man stopped in his tracks, glowering. Walks-With-Spirits's very stance, his height, and the way he held himself was intimidating enough, Cotannah thought, but the straight, hot look from his topaz eyes would catch a wet field on fire.

He gazed all around him, then, and even the last of the whispers and noises died away. Soon the woman bent over and set the child onto his feet again. He tottered and swayed.

"Now see what you've done, Sunflower . . ."

Whoever was calling to the mother hushed then, be-

want to grow up and take responsibility for the consequences of my own actions. All I'm doing is assuaging my guilt.''

She touched her heels to Pretty Feather and flew past him down the sunny road to Tall Pine stretching endlessly ahead.

Chapter 13

∽◦◦◦∽

They rode hard, all the rest of the day and into the night, arriving at Tall Pine a little before midnight. The dogs roused and started barking when they were coming up the drive, and by the time they reached the house Tay and Emily were on the porch, coming down the steps to greet them. Walks-With-Spirits dismounted and spoke with them briefly while Cotannah was removing her numb body from Pretty Feather's back, and then, without a word to her, he was gone.

She stood leaning against her horse, watching as he led his mount through the spotty moonlight toward the barn lot, handed the reins to the sleepy stableboy who met him halfway, and walked on until he vanished into the dark. Like a shadow. He was gone from her.

Her whole body felt hollow, light enough to blow away on the slightest breeze, yet it was too heavy for her to move even one foot or one hand. The whole night was empty, now, even if the sky held the moon and stars and high, scudding clouds, even if the air smelled of cedar and dew and mint from the garden. The whole world was empty, now.

" 'Tannah?"

She jerked upright and looked around at the sound of her name.

"I'm sorry," Emily said, as she took her by the arm. "Poor Cotannah, were you about to go to sleep standing up?"

"I guess," Cotannah muttered.

"We must get you to bed," Emily said, leading her toward the steps as if she were too feeble to decide what to do on her own. "Unless you want something to eat first. I'm sorry Walks-With-Spirits wouldn't stay."

"He said he needed some solitude," Tay said, handing Pretty Feather's reins to the stableboy who came for her. "But he has a long walk, and it's awfully late. I had hoped we could talk over the trip."

"We didn't find out one helpful thing," Cotannah said. "And he healed a little boy, so there'll either be more people saying he's a witch or a few more saying he's an *alikchi*. Either way, it probably won't make any difference."

"Where did he do that?" Emily asked.

"At Greentree's Crossing. We went there because Folsom Greentree subscribes to the *Oklahoma Star*."

Tay came to her other side as the three of them entered the house.

Cotannah gave a great sigh.

"Come into the kitchen and give me a snack and I'll tell you all about it."

She wasn't hungry but hoped food would fill up a little of the emptiness and she couldn't go up to her room and be alone right now, she just couldn't, even if she was so exhausted she could hardly stand.

So Emily heated milk and made hot chocolate while Cotannah washed up on the back porch and Tay took it upon himself to set out the cold roast beef and home-made yeast bread, imitating Daisy while he did so, which made them all laugh. But that was not enough to comfort Cotannah. She poured out the whole story of the past two days—except for the kisses and intimate talks—and tried to make herself think of nothing but the task of proving Walks-With-Spirits's curse had nothing to do with Jacob's death.

"I couldn't get a feel about Jacob having a connection to Millard Sheets," she said in conclusion, slumping wearily against the back of her chair while she sipped the hot, sweet drink. "Sheets could have known Jacob well or he could never even have heard of him before he was killed. He's an impossible man to read—that is, until you get on the subject of Indians in general, and then he's a walking barrel of hate. All I know is that he'd do anything to destroy the Nations."

Tay shook his head.

"Well, then, I'll have to dig deeper to get to the source of the rumors that Jacob had friends among the Boomers," he said.

Cotannah drained her mug and set it down, then flattened her palms on the table to push herself up from the chair onto legs so tired they threatened to give way at any moment.

"If you'll try to find out more about that tomorrow, I'll start working on Jacob's enemies in business."

She turned to Emily.

"Mimi, you said he's known to have several. Do you know who they are?"

"I know Sally Redhawk's son was in a cattle deal with Jacob that went bad," Emily said thoughtfully. "Who else quit dealing with him, Tay?"

"Nate Bowlegs. He refused to lay the bricks for the new mercantile because Jacob wouldn't pay him the contracted price for some work he did for him before."

Cotannah's exhausted brain almost refused to take in

the information she'd asked for, but she forced it to work. She had to keep thinking to hold her feelings at bay.

"Can you all look into those two? And I'll have a visit with Peter Phillips to try to get some more names. He's bound to have looked into Jacob's business dealings before he went in partners with him."

"But if he does know something, he won't want to tell it," Emily said, getting up to start clearing the table. "Remember that he told the Lighthorse he didn't know of a single enemy Jacob had except for Walks-With-Spirits."

"Oh, that's right!"

Cotannah considered that.

"But that was when they first told him that Jacob was dead—he was too shocked to think. And he's always really gallant and charming to me, so I can get him talking, I'm sure. I get the feeling he likes me."

Emily looked up.

"Be careful. Don't let him like you too much or lead him to think that you're trying to . . ."

"Don't worry, Mimi, dear. I won't go walking alone in the woods with him."

"Well, then, you have my permission," Emily said, and flashed her a smile that was more sympathy than encouragement.

"Sleep well," Tay said, and he, too, seemed to pity her.

She fought back tears as she went on upstairs ahead of them and, though she was growing more and more exhausted by the minute, she managed to keep her mind on puzzling out what would be the best way to approach Peter Phillips. The instant her head hit the pillow, though, her rational mind turned itself off, and her aching heart took possession of her body and her thoughts.

She had promised herself to be upright and honest and responsible from now on but she had lied to Walks-With-Spirits when she said that she was compelled to save his life only to assuage her guilt. Even if she'd had nothing to do with the dangerous predicament he was in, she would still be just as determined to save him from death.

The false words ran through her mind, again and again, as she lay there agonizing because she could not call them back. That was the only lie she'd ever told him, and that fact proved how special he was to her.

She lied to most men all the time.

At dinner that evening, she started working on Peter Phillips.

"You must be ready for a good, hot supper and an evening of sitting on the porch watching the lightning bugs dance," she said, smiling at him as she offered him the bowl of mashed potatoes with butter melting on top.

He smiled into her eyes as he took it.

"Do I look that weary?" he said. "It's just that you're so young and fresh, my dear. That makes us elders frail and pitiful in your eyes."

"Oh, listen to you go on, now," she said, flashing him an openly admiring look. "You aren't old at all, and you certainly aren't frail! I was just referring to the fact that now you must have twice as much work to do since . . . you have no partner now."

His pleasant face fell into mournful lines.

"That's so true. I still haven't fully realized that Jacob isn't coming back and that I must see to every detail myself."

"None of us can realize Jacob isn't coming back," Emily said, from her place at the foot of the table. "His death is the most shocking we have had here in the Nation for a long while.''

Phillips's only response to that was a heavy sigh. He turned his attention to his food, and although Tay made one more unobtrusive try at getting him to talk about Jacob, he said nothing. The table conversation became general and went straight to the question of Walks-With-Spirits's guilt or innocence.

Most of the boarders and visitors expressed a strong belief in his innocence, to agree with Tay and Emily if for no other reason, but Peter Phillips didn't add his voice to the chorus. When the meal ended, pleading a need for fresh air, Cotannah wandered out onto the side veranda.

To her delight, Phillips joined her almost immediately.

"You mentioned fresh air, my dear. May I escort you on a walk through Miss Emily's flower gardens?"

She accepted his proffered arm.

"That's most thoughtful of you, Mr. Phillips."

And it was. She would be within screaming distance of the house, yet they'd have enough privacy that he might say something he wouldn't say in public.

But he asked her a question before she could think of one for him.

"Did you and your shaman friend have a successful trip to McAlester?" he said, watching her narrowly as they descended the steps.

He saw the surprise on her face and chuckled.

"My spies are everywhere, my dear," he said, teasing with his voice and his twinkling blue eyes.

She forced a laugh that she hoped sounded natural.

"My, my," she said, returning his narrow look, "I had no idea you were that determined to prevent me from shopping anywhere else but your mercantile."

He laughed, too.

"No, I'm not quite that greedy. And I'm not a fortune-teller, either."

He gave her a broad smile, but his eyes were assessing her as if to see whether she actually believed him or not.

"To tell you the truth, Bogue Henry came into town and mentioned that he'd seen you and Walks-With-Spirits riding west onto the McAlester Road, but I had no idea whether that was where you went."

She smiled at him, thinking quickly what to say next. Knowing the ubiquitous grapevine that ran through the Nation, he had most likely already heard that she'd been seen in McAlester and soon he'd hear the whole story of the visit to Greentree's Crossing.

Suddenly she stopped in her tracks and gripped his arm a bit more tightly, gasping as if a new idea had just occurred to her.

"You know, I wonder if you could help me?"

Confiding in him might lead him to confide in her in turn.

"I would be honored."

"Yes, of course you could help," she said, with her most dazzling smile. "Why didn't I think of this before? You would know whether Jacob had any enemies, wouldn't you, and who they are?"

He patted her hand and smiled down at her in his avuncular way.

"I don't wish to upset you, my dear, but in answer to such a serious question I must speak honestly. It seems to me, as it does to many other people, including the Judges of your Choctaw Court and the people who heard the death curse put on Jacob, that your medicine man would fall into that category."

"I know it seems that way," she said, sighing softly and letting her gaze drift off to fix on the middle distance for a moment, "but—not to speak ill of the dead, you understand—I'm sure I've heard rumors that Jacob had other enemies of long standing."

She glanced up at him quickly, hoping to see his real feelings in his eyes.

"As an astute man of business, you would have looked into Jacob's reputation before throwing in with him for a partnership, I dare say."

He favored her with a blazing smile and stuck out his chest proudly.

"You are rather astute yourself, my dear."

Then, just as quickly as he had smiled, he frowned.

"Did you learn anything helpful yesterday?"

For an instant, his blunt question stopped her heart. He knew. Somehow, she had the feeling he already knew where it was she had gone. Could it be that he and Jacob both had had some connection with the Boomers?

He quickly explained, as his blue eyes filled with sympathy.

"I overheard Tay and Emily talking about your mission," he said. "My dear Miss Cotannah, I hate to see you getting so involved in this ugliness, no matter how much regard you may have for the medicine man."

His voice dropped lower and he spoke very gently.

"You do know that it's possible his curse killed Jacob."

"Why, Mr. Phillips!" she said, forcing a smile. "I would never have guessed that you were so superstitious."

"I heard the curse with my own ears," he said solemnly. "It sounded very efficacious to me."

A decision leapt, full-blown, into her mind, almost before she knew she was considering it. She would give the Boomer connection one more chance—if Jacob had been allied with them, it would give two possible sources of danger for him, the Boomers themselves and unbending Choctaw patriots like Folsom Greentree. A subscription to the newspaper really meant nothing, but it was all she had.

"I really do trust your judgment, Mr. Phillips," she said sweetly, "and your experience. Did you ever hear or see any evidence that Jacob could have been working with the Boomers somehow?"

His eyes widened.

"The Boomers? What a preposterous idea! My dear, Jacob was raised by his father, Olmun, who is one of staunchest . . ."

"But Jacob didn't always agree with Olmun, remember?" she interrupted. "Right here at Tall Pine, at the table of the Principal Chief, Jacob would talk about how we need to adopt even more of the white man's ways if we want to survive. You know Olmun didn't approve of such talk."

When he made no answer, she pushed on.

"If Jacob said all that, it could have been preliminary to openly advocating individual allotments, couldn't it? The Boomers would have paid well for him to do that."

"Yes," Phillips said, frowning thoughtfully and drawing her hand more firmly through his arm as they went down the broad, stone steps that led from the flower garden into the grassy side yard, "but I believe Jacob did love his father, and he wouldn't ever have dishonored him by saying such a thing openly even if he did believe it."

"Jacob dressed in fine fashion, though," she said, slowly, as if just now thinking the problem through, "and he may have had other expensive tastes as well."

Phillips smiled, shaking his head, and gave a low, mirthful chuckle.

"Jacob was entirely dependent financially on Olmun, you know, and he wasn't the kind of man to jeopardize that."

"Oh, I see."

"I'll share something with you if you'll promise not to tell," Phillips said abruptly. "May I entrust a confidence to you, Miss Cotannah?"

Her heart gave a quick, hard beat. Would he, could he, finally tell her something that would help save Walks-With-Spirits?

"Yes," she said breathlessly. "Oh, yes. I won't tell."

"Well, then."

He bent his head so he could speak low in her ear, as if dozens of eavesdroppers surrounded them.

"I know for a fact that Olmun supplied the money for Jacob's third of our three-way business partnership," he said. "Jacob didn't want it known because he liked to appear independent, but it's true."

For an instant she looked at him in dismay. Everyone knew that, it was no secret at all! But she bit her lip before she said so—maybe he knew other things about Jacob that he would eventually tell her.

"I promise you I won't breathe it to a soul."

His face took on a mournful expression.

"Our new mercantile was extremely important to Jacob. He wouldn't have risked losing his place in it by betraying his father to connect himself somehow with the Boomers."

"You're probably right, Mr. Phillips," she said encouragingly.

"Peter," he said, "please do call me Peter, my dear."

So she did, and she kept him smiling and strolling through the grounds with her until the early dusk had begun to fall and the voices of the others who were sitting on the porch, as they often did after supper, drifted out to them.

"We must go in," he said, "as it's unseemly of me to keep you out alone after dark, but before we do, I have one private word of advice, dear Cotannah."

She stopped still to listen.

"I'm fond of you, Cotannah, and I'd hate to see you hurt. Don't invest your fine heart in trying to save the shaman, my dear, because there's probably nothing anyone can do."

He laid his hand over hers.

"He must have killed Jacob with his curse, my darling girl—the Judges of your people have found that he did." He paused significantly. "After all, there wasn't a wound or a mark on Jacob's body and he was young and healthy and strong, so how else could he have died?"

"I don't know," she said, biting her tongue to keep from saying anything else.

She mustn't alienate Phillips, not yet. He was the only person who had been close to Jacob that she had a prayer of questioning, and he might eventually say something that would help her and Walks-With-Spirits.

"A young woman like you should be filling her pretty head with thoughts of frocks and flowers and beaux."

She bit her lip to hold in a sharp reply. He might help her yet, she told herself. He might help her yet.

"But, you see, I feel a certain responsibility in this case," she said softly, giving him a pleading look, "even though it was Jacob's behavior that caused the famous fight that ended with the curse. I'm sure you understand."

"I do," he said, holding her gaze with his blue eyes that gleamed hard like marbles in the dim light, "and I admire you for it."

She looked at him trustingly and waited.

He took her hands in both of his and she prayed he wouldn't feel the impulse running through her body to pull back from him.

"Promise me that you will think carefully about what I've said. How could a normal, regular human being kill a healthy young man without a weapon? It's got to be the curse that did it, Cotannah. There's no other explanation."

He frowned at her in the dimming, dusky light.

"Don't be running around this countryside alone," he said. "Promise me that, too. Lots of people hate the witch, you know, and everyone knows you're his friend."

"All right. Thank you, Peter. Thank you very much."

Her heart was hammering in her chest as they began walking back toward the house and the gathering on the porch. She had not accomplished anything with this little charade—not one bit more than with the long ride to the *Star* and to Greentree's Crossing.

Walks-With-Spirits held on to the low branch of the tree that sheltered him in its shadow, pressed his hand around it until the rough bark's pattern imprinted itself in the skin of his palm. It did no good, though. The bitter feeling of jealousy ripped him loose and he clicked his tongue to Basak and Taloa, the three of them started walking through the gloomy dusk toward Cotannah.

Phillips was taking her to the house, to Tay and Emily and their guests. Therefore, the older man wouldn't be alone with her anymore. However, knowing that didn't slow him one bit. It didn't lessen the strange, intense disquiet in his spirit and in his body that had gripped him, sharp as eagle's talons, the minute he had come into sight of the two of them strolling and talking alone in the dusk. How dare the old lecher hold both her hands in his!

He walked up behind them, heard Phillips say, ". . . so I never knew of any real enemy Jacob might have made . . ."

At that moment Cotannah sensed his presence and whirled to look behind her. She laughed, a light, tinkling sound of delight.

"Shadow!" she cried. "I should've known it was you."

Phillips turned, too.

"What the *hell* are you doing, Boy," he shouted, "trying to scare us to death? Lord! You're sneaky enough to be a killer, that's for damn sure . . ."

A thrill of mean satisfaction ran through Walks-With-Spirits.

"Didn't you hear me coming? Are you having trouble with your hearing, Old Man?"

"No! Who could hear you? And you'd better take those animals out of here before they hurt somebody!"

And Phillips raved on, talking only to himself now.

For Cotannah was looking at Walks-With-Spirits with her huge dark eyes luminous in the purple twilight, and he was looking at her. His heart began to beat against the cage of his ribs like a rabbit in a snare.

He had been aching to run to them and wrench them apart since he saw Cotannah looking up at the man and his head bent close to hers. Now it was as if Phillips had vanished into thin air. At the moment he was longing to bend over and kiss her full lips, still parted in surprise. Or just to touch them, even, with his fingertips instead of with his mouth would be enough to ease his yearnings. Perhaps.

A deep, ragged breath sighed through him like a whispering breeze.

"Sneak up behind a man with those yellow-eyed monsters at heel, will you?" Phillips shouted. "I ought to smash that solemn face of yours to smithereens!"

Walks-With-Spirits spared him a glance.

"You're welcome to try," he said.

He could hardly believe the belligerent words as they came out of his mouth. What was happening to him? His spirit and his body both were swirling in turmoil, and the prospect of a fight fired his blood, felt like a coming relief.

But Phillips was all talk.

"Well, uh . . . uh," he stammered, and took a step backward, his hard, pale eyes flicking from Basak to Taloa and then back again, "I wouldn't want to distress Cotannah. I won't fight with a lady present."

"That's very unselfish of you," Walks-With-Spirits said, taunting him.

And observing him. Closely.

The man was afraid of more than Basak and Taloa. He was hiding something—that was clear in his anxious, erratic movement as he turned his face away.

Walks-With-Spirits's blood rushed through his veins, flamed hot as the sun. Did the slimy white-eyes have designs on Cotannah? Had his appearing here so suddenly thwarted some nefarious plans?

He forced himself to take a long, ragged breath.

This must be a full-blown attack of jealousy, he knew of no other name to put to it. This tormenting selfishness must be jealousy, and he was helpless against it.

"Come, my dear," Phillips said, offering his arm to Cotannah. "Let me get you back to the others now."

Cotannah didn't even glance at him. Her eyes were on Walks-With-Spirits. "I need to talk with Walks-With-Spirits," she said.

"Very well."

Phillips snapped out the words as he was already leaving them, disappearing into the growing gloom.

"I'll tell Tay where you are," he said, in a tone like a warning.

"He must think I'm in danger from you," she said, her gaze unwaveringly fastened to Walks-With-Spirits's.

You are. Let me tell you now, you are.

"I don't know," he said, looking deep into her eyes with a feeling like silent laughter moving him inside. "He seemed very concerned about me and my troubles. Perhaps he thinks *I'm* in danger from *you.*"

And I am. It is the Great Spirit's own truth that I am.

The laughter inside him was a pitiful bravado in the face of that fear.

She took a step toward him.

He reached out and touched her mouth with the tips of his trembling fingers.

It wasn't enough. He had been wrong about that. It was not enough.

Desire flooded him, stiffened his loins, weakened his legs. His lips flamed with the need to kiss her again.

But that way lay madness, he was living proof of that now. And the quick intake of her breath told him she knew the same thing.

She was helpless, too, however. Her lips closed against his fingertips in a kiss light as the brush of a butterfly's wings. She kissed them again.

He thrust his fingers into the silky mass of her hair and cradled her cheek in his palm. He ran his thumb over her fragile, high cheekbone, traced the pert shape of her nose. The smooth, unspeakable softness of her skin moved against his hand as she snuggled her face into it and sent a warm melody singing through his blood.

He tilted her head back on her slender, beautiful neck and took her mouth with his.

And she took his heart away. With one, tiny welcoming whimper, deep in her throat, she reached right out and took his heart from his chest to keep forever.

She kissed him with a sweet, honest urgency like a promise and his eyes burned with tears.

How had he ever walked off into the woods without her? How would he ever do so again?

But someday soon he would have to.

Slowly, his arm burning all the way to his shoulder, he dropped it to hang useless at his side. He looked her up and down, devoured her face with his eyes and then forced them to fix on the ground, on her pale skirts swaying like a candle's flame against the grass, its color changing from green to black in the quick-falling darkness.

"What did you want to tell me?" he asked, his voice too husky to recognize. "Or did you just say that to get rid of Phillips?"

"No. I want to say that I lied to you, and I'm sorry," she said. "You are the only man I never lie to, and I won't do it again."

"Why not?"

"I . . . want us always to trust each other."

Always.

The word hit him like the sharp blow of an oak branch across the back of his neck.

Bless her innocent heart. Always would be one moon's worth of days and nights and that was all. That was why he must not touch her again—for her sake, not for his.

He'd known that all along. Why was he so weak when he was with her?

"What lie did you tell me?"

"I said that I'm going to keep on trying to save your life only to assuage my guilt."

He could barely hear her for the roaring of realization in his ears.

One evening, one, wrapped in the warmth of her smile and basking in the light of her eyes inside the cozy walls of the cabin, and one kiss—the very first one at the horse shed that had fired his blood and shattered his bones—had ruined him. When the afternoon shadows began to grow long today, he had come to her like a goose returning to its mate.

"And what did you have to say to Peter Phillips?"

Her face fell.

"He just kept telling me that the curse killed Jacob," she said. "He wouldn't tell me a thing about Jacob's enemies."

She came a step closer, her skirts swishing against the grass with a whispering like the voice of a spirit.

"I've got to go see William Sowers," she said fiercely, "and ask if he overheard anyone arguing with Jacob. He worked for weeks building the mercantile and, aside from Phillips, he probably spent more time around Jacob than anyone else in these past few weeks."

"Don't go alone," he said simply.

He knew when he said it he would go with her if she asked him. William Sowers was trustworthy, but it was a long way to his place and no telling what witch-hater would watch for Cotannah to ride by. He would not let her be in danger from someone else like Jacob Charley.

She looked at him, her eyes like shining dark pools in her pale face.

"If you went with me, I wouldn't be alone."

"And ride back from there in a thundering silence as we rode for hours from Greentree's Crossing?" he said softly.

Her face changed, one quick emotion after another racing across it like birds flying across the sky. He saw it, he felt it, when the one realization he was willing upon her swept down and settled on her heart.

"No," she said slowly, "we won't act like that anymore. Ever. No matter what happens, let's promise each other that. It's a waste of precious time."

He couldn't help himself then, as hard as he tried to make himself be strong. He reached out and pulled her to him, wrapped her in his arms, and cradled her head against his heart.

Over and over again he stroked his hand through her hair, feeling the silk of it on his skin like the blessing of sunlight on a bitter cold day.

Chapter 14

I t was in that moment that she knew how much she loved him and that she would never love anyone else. He wanted her, yes, just as Tonio and the other men who had held her had wanted her—she could feel his desire in the thrumming tension of his muscles and the hardening of his body against her. But unlike the others, he wasn't concerned with pleasure, he hadn't taken her into his arms for that reason. What Walks-With-Spirits cared about was her, her spirit, her real self.

She tightened her arms around his slender waist and nestled her cheek deeper into the solid solace of his chest, let every thought roll right out of her head. He was what she had needed all her life long.

He stroked her hair with his big hand over and over again, and the ease it gave her flowed from her scalp down her neck, down the length of her spine, collapsing her against him until they were melted together so surely they would never come apart. For an endless while he held her there, in the purpling twilight, and she clung to him, warm and safe, while the evening air grew briskly chill.

She clung to him until she had soaked up his closeness

to fill her, until his presence had eased her heart and filled it lipping full with the sweet knowledge that this, this was love, come to her at last. This magic connection between them was love, this comfort and wanting and needing to give to him was what she had feared for so long.

But she shouldn't have. Loving Walks-With-Spirits didn't make her afraid. She lifted her head and leaned it back into his cradling hand, looked up into his half-open eyes.

"I love you."

A smile, a quick, blinding smile that made her go weak in the knees came over his face and lit his eyes.

"I love you, Cotannah. That is the truth—in my body, in my spirit, in my harmony."

She laughed.

"What? I don't disturb your peace anymore?"

"You disturb every inch of me," he growled, and pulled her even harder against him to prove it.

She wrapped her arms around his neck and went up onto tiptoe to meet his blazing kiss, his mouth lusciously moist and so hot it branded her, his body a rooted oak, strong enough to cling to in a rolling wind. He was as famished for comfort, for love as she, he crushed her to his chest and devoured her mouth with lips and tongue and teeth.

Then suddenly he stopped, as if sorry to have been greedy, and changed the kiss without ever breaking it, changed it to a slow, lovely savoring. But not a gentle one—a tasting of lips and a twining of tongues that made shivers of pleasure run all through her blood.

She ran her hands over the bulging muscles of his shoulders and his back, stroked the satiny club of his bound hair, then jerked the rawhide thong from around it to drive her fingers through it before she began to caress the back of his big neck, glorying in the sheer strength she found in this vulnerable part of him, his skin sleek beneath her palm, his hair soft and shifting across the back of her hand. He scraped his teeth lightly over her lower lip and made a rough purring sound deep in his throat when he felt her trembling.

Then he trailed the tip of his tongue around the shape of her lips and dipped inside again, shoving both hands into her hair to catch her head in his hands as he had done that very first time in the cabin and he held her there, helpless and willing, while he plundered her mouth and drew her soul right out of her body. Deep, deep at the woman's core of her she opened to him, wept for him to come in.

He cradled her head in one hand, then, and with the other reached to cup her breast. She turned a little to give him the aching tip, and he ran his rough thumb across it. The glory of the touch blazed through her like a fire.

Then a blow hit her at the backs of her knees.

" 'Tannah! What you doing? 'Tannah!"

Even with the voice rising into a hopeful wail, and the small body with its rough splint supporting one arm pummeling her legs through her skirts, it took a while for her to realize that Sophia had joined them. Walks-With-Spirits tore his mouth from hers and clasped her to him, holding her head in the hollow of his shoulder, shaking all over now, as she was, while he circled his hand on her back.

"Sophia!" Emily's voice called from out of the dusk. "Where are you, you little rascal girl?"

"Mama!" Sophia screamed. "I found 'Tannah."

Then Emily's voice, and Tay's, sounded from someplace very near, and Walks-With-Spirits spoke to them over her head.

"Tay," he said. "Do you know where William Sowers lives?"

"Over near Standing Rock Mountain," Tay said.

Then Emily cried out.

"Oh! Oh, my goodness, we are so sorry! We didn't mean to intrude. We just never dreamed . . . Sophia! Come here."

But Sophia's one healthy small arm was firmly clasped around Cotannah's legs and Walks-With-Spirits was loosening his hold on her. With a last squeeze of a hug, Cotannah let him go and turned to bend down and pick up the baby.

Emily reached out.

" 'Tannah, let me take her away . . ."

Cotannah laughed. She couldn't keep from laughing, the joy rising in her was growing so great.

"No, it's all right," she said. "Sophia's come all the way out here in the dark to find me."

"Dark!" Sophia agreed.

Tay was talking to Walks-With-Spirits, their bass voices rumbling quietly in the dark. The moon and stars were coming out overhead, and the sharp night air carried the scent of pines and junipers. Cotannah took in a long, shaky breath of it and held Sophia's face to hers.

Life is wonderful, right now at this moment. For this one instant, everything is all right, for the first time since I was born.

"What is it about William Sowers?" Emily asked.

Cotannah told her.

"Walks-With-Spirits and I are going to see him early in the morning," she said, when she had explained. "I found out nothing from Phillips, but William has been around Jacob nearly as much as Peter those last weeks before his death, and he may know of some enemy we haven't heard about."

"He might know something," Emily murmured. "But William's a responsible person. I think he would've come forward by now if he did."

Cotannah felt disappointment flood her face at that news.

"I'll go talk to Olmun tomorrow and find out if he knows of any more enemies Jacob may have had," Tay said quickly. "But it wouldn't hurt to talk to William, too."

A little silence fell.

Emily shivered and wrapped her shawl more tightly around her.

"Well, we'll surely all keep on looking under every stone," she said. "You must really question Olmun, Tay, and make him answer you."

She sighed.

"Now it's hard to get Olmun to admit that Jacob ever had a falling-out with anyone when everybody knows he had to intercede for him many a time in one dispute or another. He's rescued Jacob from scrape after scrape, but now he refuses to remember any of that—he seems to be trying to proclaim Jacob a martyred saint."

"Daisy told me that in town she heard Olmun saying that Jacob would never have tried anything with me if I hadn't led him on," Cotannah said.

Emily patted her arm.

"Don't you take that to heart," she said. "Like I said, Olmun's refusing to see reality."

Cotannah sighed.

"About Jacob he is, but he's telling the real truth about me," she said.

Then she marveled that she could speak of it so calmly, that the guilt didn't overwhelm her. It was still there, but its cold fingers couldn't even dent the warm feeling that filled her. Walks-With-Spirits was in this terrible predicament because of her, yes, but now the power of her love for him would make her strong enough to save him.

"I don't care if you were making eyes at Jacob like crazy, if you were wearing that shameless dress or even if you told him you wanted him to ravish you right then and there on the ground," Emily cried. "When you started telling him no, then he should've taken his hands off you!"

Cotannah smiled and hugged her friend. "I love you, Mimi," she said. "You are the most loyal friend I ever had."

Then she marveled that she'd said that, too, and that she'd meant it. It seemed incredible that there'd ever been a time that Emily had betrayed her. It seemed even more incredible that there'd ever been a time when she'd thought she loved Tay.

"Tay?" Walks-With-Spirits said. "May I impose on your hospitality and sleep in the shed with my friends here tonight?"

"You bet. We'd like to have you."

A new, raw happiness filled Cotannah, a feeling so powerful it made her believe she could rise and fly. He was going to stay at Tall Pine tonight and go with her to see William Sowers tomorrow.

That's all she ever wanted for the rest of her life: Walks-With-Spirits with her tonight and tomorrow.

They turned and started walking toward the big house in a tightly knit group, Emily, as usual, making small talk.

"We'll all have hot chocolate and popcorn," she said. "It's way too early to go to bed yet."

"Choc'late!" Sophia crowed, and Cotannah danced a few steps with her in her arms.

Walks-With-Spirits didn't ask to stay the night at Tall

Pine so he could come to her bed tonight or she to his—
she knew him well enough to know that. But he had
asked to stay because he was feeling the very same way
she was feeling about him: he could not bear to go away
and leave her, to be in another place where she was not
there.

They loved each other. Neither of them would ever
be able to go away and leave the other, not ever again.

By the time the sun had climbed halfway up the sky
the next morning, Cotannah and Walks-With-Spirits
were within three miles of their destination. The closer
they came to the big hill called Standing Rock Mountain,
the more excited she became. Not once, had he agreed
with her that William Sowers just had to know something that would help them, but she knew it was true.

"I know you think it, too," she said, finally, "so you
might as well admit it."

He threw her a slanting glance that she couldn't quite
read.

"And how do you know what I think?"

"The first thing you said to Tay when they found us
kissing last night was to ask him where William Sowers
lives," she said triumphantly.

"That's true," he said, and he smiled at her in a sad
way that scared her, "but I said it not because I believe
Sowers knows something that will help us but because
for that first moment, when I had just torn my lips from
yours, I had to hope that he did. Because I can't help
but hope for many, many years of kissing you or die."

Shock brought stinging tears to her eyes.

"Well, what about this moment, this one right now?"
she cried. "Don't you still feel that way?"

His topaz eyes blazed at her.

"Yes! I could kill right now and deserve my death sentence for one taste of your mouth."

She melted in her saddle.

"But I don't know whether William Sowers will help us. I don't know what we'll find out, if anything, and I'm worried sick that you have your heart so set on finding a secret enemy for Jacob."

"I know we will!"

"Cotannah," he said, "I cannot bear for you to be disappointed. Please try to wait and see."

They said no more, and she rode beside him with a little smile on her lips, for she knew she was right.

"There's the Standing Rock Mountain," he said, after a little while.

She followed his glance to the low mountain curving blue-purple against the sky. He rode out ahead of her and turned off the road onto a grassy track that led into the woods.

"Here's the trail to the Sowers place," he said. "Tay said it's less than a mile from here."

They rode single file through the woods without talking any more and soon came out into a rail-fenced clearing, a pitifully poor little solitary farm. There were a few head of cattle grazing in a long, narrow pasture, two milch cows, some chickens and guineas and two mules and five goats scattered about the property. The log cabin home sat in front of a small grove of oaks on a rise to the west of the ramshackle barn and pens. Behind it lay a scraggly attempt at a fall garden.

Walks-With-Spirits started his horse down the slight incline. Cotannah followed on Pretty Feather. As they approached the cabin, a man hobbled slowly around one corner of it into the front yard, gazing straight ahead, holding a forked stick in his hands. Not William. An old man with his hair in two long, white braids.

The old man saw them then and stopped in his tracks. A woman stepped out onto the porch as they halted the horses. She looked almost, but not quite, as old as the man who had begun walking toward them. His face had wrinkles upon wrinkles, but his eyes looked alert and sharp.

When he stood in front of them, Walks-With-Spirits spoke to him.

"Hello, Grandfather," he said respectfully. "We are looking for a man called William Sowers. Does he live here?"

The old woman came closer to the steps and peered out at them.

"Why?" she said, her voice quavering a bit. "Why are you looking for William?"

"Only to talk to him, Auntie," Cotannah said, also using a term of respect for her age. "We think he might be able to help us."

"About what?"

"About who might have had a disagreement with Jacob Charley a little while ago in Tuskahoma."

The old woman's gaze froze to Cotannah's.

"Jacob Charley is dead," she said flatly.

"We know that, Auntie."

The old woman stared at Walks-With-Spirits then, as if she hadn't noticed him earlier, gasped, and clapped her hand over her mouth, started muttering behind it.

Walks-With-Spirits spoke to the man again.

"Would you call William out here so that we can speak to him? Tell him I am called Walks-With-Spirits."

At that news, the old man also drew in a deep, sharp breath.

"My grandson, William, has gone away," the old man said, in a voice full of sudden fury. "Out of the Nation."

Cotannah's heart dropped into her feet.

"Where?" she cried, leaning off her saddle toward the old man. "Where did he go?"

"To find work that pays in money," the old woman announced clearly. "To save our farm."

The old man turned on her as quickly as his creaking bones would permit.

"You needn't tell everything you know, Mama."

"I needn't but I will," she said, mimicking his sharp tone. "William made a gambling debt against our home, so he is the one who must pay it. He went to Arkansas to find work in the timber."

She glared at them, as the old man was doing.

"William has gone and left us because of you." And she pointed a crooked, bony finger straight at Walks-With-Spirits. "You killed Jacob Charley, and now William has no work for the cold months."

"No! He didn't kill Jacob!" Cotannah cried.

The old man gave her a long, straight look.

"He put a curse on him, a death curse, was the way I heard it."

Cotannah stared at the old man and then at the woman on the porch. Her stomach was churning.

"He didn't mean it. The curse isn't what killed Jacob."

It was the old woman who answered.

"Yes, it is. He said the incantation and it killed Jacob Charley and William was out of work and that's why he had to go leave us."

Cotannah stared into the old woman's button eyes.

"William was already out of work and Jacob Charley's death had nothing to do with it. The carpenter work on the mercantile building has been done for a while now."

The old woman's bright eyes gleamed with triumph.

"That's what you think, Missy!" she said. "Jacob Charley had promised William barns to build—work enough to last him all winter and next spring, too. Now that Jacob's dead, Olmun said he don't want no more barns. And since William left us the well has gone dry," the woman's relentlessly accusing voice went on. "I think he put a curse on William and the well, too."

"No, he didn't!"

Cotannah looked to Walks-With-Spirits, but he was looking sorrowfully at the old woman's face.

"Papa ain't able to haul water from the creek all winter," she said. "We must have a new well."

"Are you preparing to dowse for water?"

Walks-With-Spirits asked the question in a voice filled with . . . guilt? Was he feeling truly guilty for the plight of these people who were accusing him?

He was. Even though he was innocent.

Cotannah's heart twisted with pity and anger. Now he'd be thinking again that the curse might've killed Jacob, all because of this old woman's ramblings.

The forked stick trembled in the old man's hands. He shakily nodded his head.

"Yes, I am dowsing. I am too crippled up to haul it from the creek."

"Let me," Walks-With-Spirits said, and Cotannah's heart stopped.

Had she actually heard tears in his voice? Yes. One glance at him as he dropped the reins and stepped off his horse confirmed it. Dumbfounded, she stared at him.

"No," the old woman said. "You can find the water because you're a witch, but it'll be bitter if you do. Go away."

Walks-With-Spirits ignored her and walked toward the man with his hand outstretched.

"Usually, the stick will move for me," he said. "Is this green limb from a peach tree?"

"Yes. But somebody told me any green limb will work."

"I don't think so," Walks-With-Spirits said. "It needs to be peach."

"It is, but it will not move for me. I can do no good."

"Give it here," Walks-With-Spirits said, and took it into his lean, brown hands. "It will move for me."

The old man held on to it for a moment, obviously torn between hope for water, fear and resentment against Walks-With-Spirits, and dread of the old woman's tongue. His bright eyes flicked to her face.

"It'll be bitter," she said again.

But she spoke in a weaker tone this time. She, too, had been about to give up hope for finding water.

Hardly able to believe her eyes, Cotannah whirled Pretty Feather around in a swirl of dust and watched the torture in Walks-With-Spirits's face as he moved along with the forked stick held out in front of him. Her heart pounded fiercely, the blood roared in her head. Dear God in Heaven, how could he feel so sad and guilty about something he didn't do?

Even so, he was walking the earth with the same air of being one with it as he had with his mount when he rode horseback. The long muscles of his thighs bulged beneath the buckskin of his breeches with each light step he took, each of his feet reached out with an unfaltering motion to caress the next spot of ground through the thin soles of his moccasins, lingering for a moment each time as if he could feel a message the Earth Mother was sending to him through the bent, short grass, as if his feet could feel the water flowing below it.

His hands held the two branches of the forked peach tree limb, the single end sticking out straight and level in front of him. He looked ahead, into the middle distance, with a tortured look on his face. Back and forth he walked, slowly. Very slowly. Concentrating as if he knew, really knew that the Earth Mother would give him water.

The old woman began a keening hum under her breath, the old man watched in silence, his shoulders slumped with weariness, shaking his head. He must've already tried that same route for water to no avail.

Walks-With-Spirits was opposite the south corner of the porch, a short stone's throw from the cabin, when the stick moved. The tip wiggled, up and down, once, twice, and then the whole thing twisted so hard that it nearly tore free from Walks-With-Spirits's hands. The end of it dived straight at the ground until it disappeared into the grass and stuck, quivering, into the earth.

The old woman cried out.

"Oh, it'll be bitter water!"

She threw her apron over her head and began to wail.

The man hobbled to the shed out back of the cabin and came back in a moment with a spade and a mattock in one hand and a shovel in the other. Walks-With-Spirits took the spade from him and began to dig.

"The water is here," he said.

He threw up his head and looked at the old woman.

"It won't be bitter, Grandmother," he called. "Don't worry."

It was then that Cotannah saw the tears pouring down his face.

"I'm sorry if I caused you to be left alone," he said, looking from one of the old people to the other. "I didn't mean the curse I said over Jacob, but then again, I did."

Cotannah waited for what seemed an endless time with panic rising into her throat, watching him. A mad, wild despair came crushing down on her, a black despair as absolute as his grief. He believed it. He believed that he was guilty, and he had to dig this well to try to make things right again.

His tears hadn't slowed one bit, they were wetting the ground beneath his spade. They shone on his cheeks when he raised up to throw a spadeful of dirt out of the hole.

She stood in her stirrup, threw her reins to the ground, and stepped down. Walking straight to the old man, she took the shovel from his hands and went to the deepening hole for the well, bent her back and began to shovel the dirt away from the edge so Walks-With-Spirits could keep digging.

He turned to her, surprise in his liquid amber eyes, gratefulness in his face. It wasn't until then that she realized that she, too, was weeping.

In the dark of the night, they rode back to Tall Pine with only the most desultory talk between them. Cotannah was almost too exhausted to speak, yet she couldn't be quiet. She had to reach out to him with her voice because there was no other way. He hadn't touched her or really looked into her eyes since the digging began.

"It's a good thing the water wasn't too far down," she said, trying to make her tone light. "Otherwise, we'd have had to move in with the Sowerses, and I don't think the old woman would have welcomed us as houseguests."

For a long moment he didn't respond.

Then, with his rich voice so full of feeling that it resonated right into her bones, he said, "Thank you for helping me, Cotannah. You certainly didn't have to—it's my job to do."

"What do you mean is? We found the water!"

"But the lower shaft of the well must be walled with rock all around, and they'll have to move the windlass from the old well to the new one. I'll build a wooden curbing, too, to keep things from falling in."

"Shadow! It's not your fault that William Sowers risked his grandparents' farm in a gambling debt! And it isn't your fault that he's gone, either!"

"It very well may be."

That was all he would say.

And for the next two weeks, he went back to the Sowers place almost every day. He came and lived with Basak and Taloa at Tall Pine, although he never slept in the house, and during the days he did all he could to make up to the feeble old couple for the loss of their grandson. She spent her days working with Tay and Emily, riding for miles and questioning people, turning over every rock in the Choctaw Nation in a search for clues to the truth about Jacob's death that proved over and over again to be totally fruitless.

In the evenings, though—ah, in the evenings—he was with her. They roamed the pastures and forests and creeks until the early dark fell and then sat in the yard or in the parlor for hours, sometimes talking and talking, sometimes in silence. The rest of the family thoughtfully stayed at a little distance to give them time alone, and finally Walks-With-Spirits had told her as many details of his three years in the New Nation and about growing up in the Old Nation under the tutelage of the medicine man and the missionary woman as she had told him of her own past. She began to understand how he could accept Jacob's death as his responsibility, and she began to see how deeply he was disturbed from his impulsive use of black medicine. There was a terrible tension in him now that hadn't been there before.

It made her wild to comfort him, but nothing she said seemed to help him much.

She was also wild with desire, as was he, she could tell, but through some unspoken, instinctive fear that they both felt, physically they stayed apart. Once in a while, they touched hands, once in a while, they dared to hug when they parted, but that was all. More than that would pull them in too deep, and both of them knew it. More than that would shatter the strength they needed to do what they had to do.

The fleeting days and nights continued to pass. Suddenly, and far too soon, there were only ten of them left. During that day, Cotannah and Emily and Tay all sat around together in near silence as if someone already had died. There was nothing else to try, nowhere else to turn.

"We mustn't give up," Emily said, reaching out to squeeze Cotannah's hand. "We still have several days left."

"But we don't know what to do with them!" Cotannah said, her lips so stiff with the need to weep that she could barely form the words.

"Something will happen," Emily said, trying her best to smile. "Something is bound to happen soon."

"Yes," Cotannah said bitterly. "They're going to kill him if I can't talk him into running away."

At supper that evening, she thought for a moment that he had come to grips with his desire to live, that she wouldn't have to try to talk him into it, after all. She had sensed, from the time he'd come into the house telling of seeing and hearing the first flock of geese going south, that he, too, recognized this day as some kind of watershed.

Sure enough, when the meal was done and the boarders had gone from the dining room, leaving only the

immediate family, he said that he wanted to tell them
good-bye.

"At dawn tomorrow I'll be leaving," he said quietly,
his calm eyes resting on Tay, then Emily. "But I want
you to know I'll hold both of you in my heart forever,
and I'll never forget what you've done on my behalf."

Cotannah's heart gave a quick, hard leap, and then
began beating twice as fast. Thank God! He was going.
He wouldn't die, after all.

A great relief began to grow in her, a relief changing
to pure happiness with every excited beat of her heart.
And he hadn't looked at her, yet, so he wasn't including
her in this good-bye.

She could go with him, or if he insisted, meet him
somewhere. That would be best, perhaps, in case the
Lighthorse went looking for him when he didn't appear
on the appointed day—alone, he could vanish into the
mountains and leave no trace.

Yes. He could move deep into the wild mountains,
cross them, cross Red River, and drift through Texas
until he met her at the ranch!

"I'm relieved, very relieved," Tay said. "I don't
think I could bear to see you executed for something
you didn't do."

"No, you don't understand," Walk-With-Spirits said.
"I *will* honor my word, but I won't see you again before
that dawn of the rifles. I'll go straight to Tuskahoma the
evening before."

Tay's gray eyes darkened to the color of slate, and he
frowned, considering what to say. Cotannah watched
him, her gaze clung to him, as if to see salvation in his
eyes—it took that long until she could make her heart
believe what her ears had heard. Then she whirled on
Walks-With-Spirits.

"Why didn't you say that to begin with? Why did

you get my hopes up?'' she cried, her voice a scream of pain. ''How could you?''

Her fingers scrabbled for purchase in the heavy table-cloth, knocking over glasses and cups as she leapt to her feet, pushed her chair over backwards, and fled the table, the dining room. And the house.

Blindly, she flung open the front door, left it swinging, threw herself across the porch and down the steps into the early dark. She ran as fast as she could without the slightest thought of what might lie ahead of her in the night, ran as if her hair was on fire, as Aunt Ancie would say, but it wasn't her hair—it was her heart.

The moment Cotannah cried out, Walks-With-Spirits realized what he had done. He leapt up and ran after her, his blood roaring in his head. How thoughtless could he be? How could he have been so cruel?

He had meant to give her time to assimilate the idea before he took her aside for a private farewell, but he had made it all worse instead, and he would never forgive himself. He followed her into the early-autumn dark, lightened by the new-rising moon.

Was this to be the way they'd part? After all they'd been through? After the long talks and the love between them, the unforgettable kisses . . .

The taste of her sprang to his lips at the thought, and his jaw hardened. They loved each other too much to part like this, no matter how upset she was. He was going to tell her good-bye and she him—he would not let it end with her running away.

He caught her just as she reached the tall pine tree where he had nursed Taloa that day Jacob shot him. That day when Cotannah had stood over him and thanked him for calming her horse, talking and smiling and trying to make him flirt with her. That day that now seemed a hundred years past.

Sobbing, running blindly, she stumbled over the tree's protruding roots. Before she could fall he caught her by both shoulders and spun her around into his arms.

But she was having none of it, even though her whole body trembled and her breath came in long, shuddering gasps, she pummeled at his chest with her fists and he felt every blow as a strike at his heart. Her hair came loose from its fastenings and fell in a dark curtain across her face.

He grabbed her wrists and held them down at her sides, murmuring to her, saying her name again and again, tasting its honey on his tongue while the sound of it broke away pieces of his heart. Finally, finally, she lifted her chin and shook back her hair to glare a savage warning at him.

"You had better just turn me loose! Unless you've chased me all this way to tell me that you're willing to run away and live out your life somewhere that those ignorant witch-haters can't find you, you had better let me go, Walks-With-Spirits."

Her eyes blazed dark fire; they threatened him with merciless annihilation.

He pulled her wrists together into one of his hands and held them behind her while he brushed back her hair with the other so he could see her face. She threw her head and arched her back, jerked her arms to try to shake him loose. The tips of her breasts brushed his chest, a touch which immediately filled his whole body with agony.

"You had better just calm right down," he growled at her. "Unless you do, I'll hold you right here just like this until the sun comes up in the morning."

Chapter 15

But he couldn't. He couldn't hold her long without taking her mouth with his, without laying her down right here on the ground.

And that was exactly what he would do if he kissed her one more time.

She bucked and arched into him again.

It took all the will he had, and all the strength, but he pulled her down with him to kneel in the thick bed of pine needles, where he could hold her a little apart from him, hold her until he could tell her what he had to say, until he could make her hear him.

"Well?" she demanded. "Will you run away?"

She was as full of life, as passionate about what she wanted as she had been the first time he'd ever seen her, she was vibrating with desires. But now he was the cause, not Tay. All the strengths, all the feelings in her, even her fury, was gathered to love him.

The thought rocked him back on his haunches, loosened his hand around her wrists. She tore her arms free and reached for him, gripped his shoulders until her fingernails cut into his flesh.

"Will you? Go away? Oh, dear God, will you, please?"

Her tear-streaked face blazed at him.

"I've done everything I knew to do to try to prove your innocence, but it's no use," she cried. "Running away is the only thing left."

He took in a long breath and blew it out again, forced his hands flat on the mothering earth to keep them off her. She let go of him then, with her hands but not with her fierce eyes.

"No. To save my life that way would ruin it."

"How can you say that? You don't know for sure. Not until you try it."

"I know that my peace would be gone if I had to be looking over my shoulder for the Lighthorse and always on the run. I'd rather have one more week on this earth in peace and harmony than many, many years of running and knowing that I broke my word and acted without honor."

She went completely still and, for a long, long moment, knelt there like a carving made of wood. Tears welled in her eyes, and she held out her hand to him without turning her head, as a sightless person might. He took it and held it quietly in both of his.

"For the first time I truly do believe that all hope is gone," she said, her voice breaking.

Then the passion flared again.

"Where? Where will you go for your last week?"

"Deep into the south of the Nation, to the wild and beautiful country along Blue River."

He longed to touch her cheek, but that might make her jerk away again, or make her jump up and run away, and he couldn't risk that. He must make her see why he had to do this or, honor or no honor, he'd never have peace again.

But when he spoke, it was to blurt out what was on the tip of his tongue.

"Cotannah, I want you with a craving that makes my body burn. I love you with a passion that tortures my heart."

She answered with a quick intake of breath and a desperate clutching of the hand he held.

"But I must leave you for this last week because I am in such turmoil inside, my *holitopa*," he said. "When the tears took me that day at the Sowers place, for the first time I knew how much tumult boiled deep inside me."

"Hasn't the work you've done for them helped you find peace?"

"Yes. But it hasn't restored it, and I must find my balance again before I die."

He spoke again, as gently as he could.

"Cotannah, you'll understand if you'll let yourself. I must keep my word and return on the appointed day."

"Because of your honor and your peace."

She said it tonelessly, in a strange, flat voice that tore out his insides more completely than any scream or shout of anger could have done.

"Yes. And because of the influence I can have on our people who need the strength of the traditional ways."

She looked at him for a long, long moment, her eyes unfathomable, her face magnificently solemn.

"I'm going with you," she said.

The calm, sure words sliced his heart open and let the love inside it spill out onto the ground.

His spirit began to soar. She wanted to go with him even if he wasn't running away!

"You like to have a human companion, remember?"

Her hot, dark gaze was searching his, her face was pale with the force of her feelings, too pale.

"Yes, but not at such a time as this."

If she went with him, it would make it hard, so hard

to act for the sake of honor and not of love. Why, right now, his pulse was beating so fast he could barely breathe. What choice would he make at Blue River if she begged him again to run away with her?

"At first I was devastated that you didn't ask me to go with you," she said. "And then I realized that it was like digging the well—you thought that this was your burden to shoulder alone. So I'm volunteering to help you."

In that moment, in a flash of mingled happiness and despair that struck him like lightning, he knew she was right. For his sake. But he wasn't so sure that going with him would be good for her.

It would help him immensely. He was wise enough to know he was still a flesh-and-blood man, and before he could make his peace he must get straight with the root of his unsettlement. And that was Cotannah.

He loved her so! And she loved him. It was a magic that none of Chito Humma's teachings had taught him to make.

But going with him would only make it much harder for her when they had to part. He shook his head and spoke fast, before he even knew whether he had formed a coherent thought.

"I need to live, really live, these last few days in this world," he said, "to take the autumn air into my lungs and feel the sun's fingers warm on my skin."

But I need to feel your fingers more. Being with you is now my warmth.

She looked at him, waiting.

"I need to taste the wild muscadines tart on my tongue, I need to stand on a ridge and look away far into the blue sky, so blue it pulls a person's breath from his body."

You are the one who takes my breath away. And the

taste of you is all I need to feed me forever.

He couldn't say it though, much as he ached to do so, for it would only make her more determined to go with him.

And then, suddenly, he couldn't say anything more, for all the words felt like lies on his lips.

She was watching him, searching his eyes by the scant moonlight that was filtering in beneath the limbs of the tree.

"I can't let you go, Walks-With-Spirits, not until they snatch you away from me, don't you understand? I love you."

And I love you. I love you.

"That is even more reason that you should stay here," he said softly, resisting, with a bravery he didn't know he had, the need to say the bigger truth.

"Cotannah, you understand that, don't you?"

"Yes, but it's my decision," she said, speaking with a new, calm quietness. "Because I'm the one who will suffer the most when it's over."

That can't be. No one could hurt more than I'm hurting right now.

Her huge brown eyes were looking into his heart, calling to him.

His arms shook with the need to reach and hold her, his legs ached to wrap themselves around her.

Finally, he leaned forward until his knees were touching hers. He couldn't live a minute longer without some kind of linking of their bodies—this would be the only one, he promised himself, he wouldn't let himself touch her in any other way.

"Absolutely not. Stay here."

She shook her head.

"During this next week, if you could make just one remark that woke me to the truth and made me take responsibility for myself and guard myself, if being with you could teach me to sense other people's inner spirits the way it has taught me to sense my own and yours, then you have much more to teach me.''

The simple words stopped his heart.

''I've been so miserable for so long, Walks-With-Spirits,'' she said quietly. ''Won't you please go on teaching me how to truly live?''

His heart turned over in his chest and his blood sang with happiness.

''That's the most seductive thing you could ever say to me,'' he said slowly, trying to honestly search his heart but already knowing that he would do as she asked because it was best for both of them. ''I could help you and also leave some of Chito Humma's and Sister Hambleton's teachings to live after me.''

''Yes.''

''That'd be the only reason to take you with me that might satisfy my conscience.''

''Good,'' she said, and smiled as if she had won a great victory. ''I want to gain some more freedom from the restlessness that I'm starting to conquer because if I don't, it will kill me once you're gone.''

His heart broke, then. ''Oh, Cotannah,'' he said, his chest so tight he couldn't breathe.

''I'm only just learning from you how to feel what's inside of other people—who is real and who isn't,'' she said. ''And how to listen to the spirits inside and outside me. Help me find peace and get a balance at the core of me so that if I can't be happy without you, I can at least be content.''

''And you think we can accomplish all that in these few days we will have?''

''Yes.''

"Then come and be my companion," he said, "and I will teach you all I can."

And I will love you all I dare.

They arrived at the spot Walks-With-Spirits loved on Blue River in the middle of an autumn afternoon so radiant that it seemed they could float on the air.

"It was on a day like this one that I found this place," he said, as they rode down into the grassy cove formed by a bend in the river, "and I stayed here through the Cold Time that year. Until then I hadn't camped anywhere for more than two nights since I'd been in the New Nation."

The mention of the past pierced the protective bubble of pretense that Cotannah had formed around herself during their long ride. She had deliberately thrown her whole self into taking in every sight and smell and sound of each mile to make it last longer and to make her mind fix on the present, only the present, pretending that it would last forever.

Now the ride was over and the week, their one precious week, was beginning. Once it began, it had to end. The thought consumed her for a moment, made her hands shake and her heart turn cold.

"What's your favorite thing about being here?"

Her voice shook, too, but she steadied it and tried to push the fear away. She had to pay attention, had to memorize every word he said, every gesture, every motion of his gorgeous body so she'd be able to close her eyes and hear and see him again. Her mouth was indelibly imprinted with his kisses, she had relived them a thousand times already, and maybe her skin could even hold on to the feel of his hands, assuming, that is, that he touched her again. So far, he'd been extremely careful not to.

"The animals, I guess."

She glanced down at Basak and Taloa, who had flanked him every step of the way.

"Is this where you found them?"

He glanced at them, too.

"Oh. No, they both came to me at the cave. I meant the ones who live here. This valley has lots of different inhabitants."

"Maybe that's why you stayed so long—the ones who live here relieved your loneliness."

He shrugged, then laughed a little.

"Maybe. Cotannah, you worry more about my being lonely than I have ever thought of it."

"Because I've been lonely, too, even with my family around. I feel for you because I imagine it'd be even worse to have been physically alone."

He had led the way across the grassy space to the edge of some trees scattered across the side of a sun-kissed hill that faced the river. Now he reined in and sat quietly, looking around them in every direction, searching out every detail with his straight gaze.

Then he turned it on her.

"I didn't know the difference then," he said, "but I do now. Loneliness would kill me today if you were not here."

They looked at each other for one long, still moment while those words wound themselves like twining arms around Cotannah's aching heart. Then he held out his hand across the space between their horses.

"Welcome to Blue River."

She put her hand in his big, warm one and leaned into his strength while she stepped down out of the saddle. When he let her go so he could dismount, too, she felt nearly as bereft as if he'd walked away.

"Are we going to camp in these trees here?" she asked.

"Yes. Here at the bottom of the hillside where the grass is thin and the ground is rocky."

"Look out there in the valley how green the grass is underneath," she said, going to stand beside him, "but its tops are a mist of brown forecasting what's to come."

She bit her lip. What's to come she would not think about.

"You're right," he said, "the mist of brown is so thin it looks like the hovering sweep of a spirit hand."

He was looking around as he had when they were still mounted, drinking in the beautiful valley with his eyes, and she must do the same. She must fix her mind on the present.

"And the yellow maples and red sweet gums are the fires the spirit hand has lit," she said.

That made him smile at her.

"You're learning already," he said. "Did you ever think that on a day like this it seems that everything in the world is light both ways?"

"What do you mean?"

"The air's so bracing that it seems able to carry a rock easy as a feather or a leaf. Our bodies feel light, as if we could walk on it. And every tree and bush is so full of light for our eyes that it looks as if the sun has bent down and breathed part of itself into the leaves."

"I've thought they looked like lamps," she said, "or candlesticks with every leaf a separate candle flame."

"I used to question Chito Humma," he said. "When I was little, I used to believe that the trees came alive and walked around when they looked like that."

She laughed. "I think you were right. Look at that big elm up there—I'm pretty sure it's moving."

He laughed and bent over and kissed her, once,

lightly, on the tip of her nose. A tingling shock ran through her.

"Now you're making fun of me," he said, and looked at her so intently that the heat began to rise in her blood.

He felt it, too.

"I can't seem to keep from touching you," he said, "but I'm going to stop. I promise."

"Don't."

"I must," he said. He tore his gaze free of hers and looked over the top of her head into the distance. "If we become . . . lovers, it'll be even harder to part."

If we become lovers maybe we won't have to part!

The thought leapt to her tongue from the depths of the stubborn determination for which she was notorious. She bit it back and turned to stare out across the bright valley while she recognized the secret hidden from herself.

Why, she hadn't given up, after all! She had told him she believed that all hope was gone and when she said it she'd thought she was telling the truth, but she wasn't. Her expectation of saving him was so strong it couldn't be killed, no matter what he said or did.

So she shook back her hair and turned to smile up at him.

"But if we came here to really live these few days, how can we not become lovers?"

Twin flames, brighter even, than the sweet gum trees, leapt to life behind his eyes.

"We can't."

He took her by the shoulders with a desperate grip.

"I am not willing to risk your heart that way," he said, his voice dropping to a menacing growl. "Don't mention this to me again."

His eyes were fiercely sharp and they pierced her through.

"You! You can't risk my heart because it doesn't belong to you!" she lied.

"Good," he said briskly, letting her go as he turned away. "You keep it safe, then, and that'll be one less thing I have to worry about. We came here so you could learn from me," he said softly, in a voice so quiet that at first she thought she had only imagined that he had spoken. "So look."

For a moment she couldn't even see him for the blur of frustration in her eyes, and she simply stood there trying to quiet her pounding heart. Finally she could follow his steady gaze: he was looking across the length of the narrow valley to the woods that closed in on its southern end.

It was quite a long time that she saw only the trees, slender birches with their leaves changing back and forth from yellow to silver in the breeze, with their peeling trunks mottled white and cream and every shade of brown. She glanced at Walks-With-Spirits once, but he was the stern teacher now and only flicked her a quick look and stared at the same spot again.

She did the same, and, although still nothing had moved but the wind and the leaves, this time she saw it. Them. Two deer, their tan coats blending in with the sun-drenched trees, their heads high and alert, their big eyes shining bright, their nostrils flaring wide for the new scents in their valley.

"Yearlings," he said, using that tone that was less than a whisper again. "Twins. That's your first lesson—find out if they want to be our friends."

"But you haven't taught me how yet!"

"You'll be ready for teaching when you've tried on your own."

They watched the deer, and the deer watched them.

"We're downwind," he said. "Anyway, they may

never have smelled a human being before.''

The deer were pulling at her, even through the turmoil raging in her heart. That first, sudden glimpse of them, frozen against the trees, would never leave her—the wildness in the stillness and the shape of them had vibrated through her whole body.

''Just watch me,'' she said, trying to speak in that same soft way he'd used.

Her blood running fast with the excitement of this welcome to the wilderness, she began walking toward them, moving slowly, carefully, hardly moving at all. They stayed in place, their big brown eyes fixed on her.

The trek seemed interminable, but she was covering ground, she could tell by quick glances at the river's crooked bank from the corner of her eye. The sound of the water had lessened a little, she felt less of the wind because of the curve of the hill.

Her heart lifted, then began to race. She was learning already. The deer hadn't moved. Before she met Walks-With-Spirits, she would never have thought even to try this.

The yearlings twitched their nostrils, but otherwise they didn't move. Slowly, slowly, she lifted her hand toward them, to let them catch her scent before her whole body might threaten them with its closeness.

Her feet brushed through the grass but even she could barely hear the sound they made. She glanced toward the river again. Halfway. She was almost halfway across the open space between Walks-With-Spirits on one end of the valley and the deer on the other. She could do this. He was going to be so surprised!

If only she had some grain in her outstretched hand. Or some acorns or pecans. Something for them to eat, something to tempt them to come closer, something to distract them a little bit from her.

Her arm trembled. Her legs shook, too, from moving so slowly after having ridden for so long. They had been almost numb when she got down off Pretty Feather's back. But none of that was any excuse. She would make friends with these deer, and Walks-With-Spirits would be so glad.

He needed to teach her just as much as she needed to learn. She'd discovered that when he'd agreed that she could come with him, she had felt the need spring to life in him like a fever when she'd told him she wanted to learn what he knew. He needed her in lots of ways.

Tears stung her eyes, she blinked them back. Never, ever, would she forget his voice as he told her that loneliness would kill him now if she hadn't come here with him.

One of the deer gave a snort of alarm and then they bolted. They were gone. Vanished, before she could even blink

"O-oooh!"

She stared at the trees for a short, useless span of time, then she whirled to look at him, beating both fists against her thighs, shouting in frustration.

"That makes me so mad! I can't believe they would run off when we were doing so well!"

He was walking toward her, laughing.

"Don't you dare laugh at me! I almost had them!"

That made him laugh harder.

"I did! You saw it for yourself. If I'd had some food, they'd have stayed right where they were and by now they'd have been eating out of my hand!"

He walked up to her.

"Admit it, Walks-With-Spirits!"

She was fighting tears again, and she didn't want him to see. What was the matter with her? She never cried easily like this.

"It's just that I wanted so much to succeed, to show you that I have a little bit of the gift . . ."

He finally quit laughing when he saw her distress and he put his arm around her shoulders.

"You did great at the beginning. All you did wrong was stop sending messages to their spirits, you stopped sending them your thoughts and listening for theirs."

"Is that all?"

"Well, you crowded them a bit, too," he said, and started them walking back toward the horses and their camp site.

"I couldn't have moved any more slowly."

"No, but you could've stopped. When you got to about here, you could've stopped and let them come to you."

She looked up at him and quit walking as the words rang in her heart with more truth than just that about the deer.

"You have to respect their feelings and let them make some of the judgments. You have to listen to what they're thinking and give them some chance to move toward you if you want to be friends with them."

Every bit of that advice was true of Walks-With-Spirits, too, and she knew in that moment that she had to give up the thought of deliberately trying to make them be lovers even if it was for the purpose of trying once more to convince him to run for his life. It would be wrong to set out to seduce him as she'd done to other men.

Yes, it was true that if they forced themselves to stay apart and spent this whole week looking at each other and agonizing to touch, then they wouldn't really have lived life to its fullest as they'd set out to do. But, no matter if she was willing to risk the even deeper hurt to her heart at the time of parting, this decision was not for her to make.

If he came to her bed while they were at Blue River, it would have to be because deep in his own heart he felt it was right.

Unloading the horses and setting up camp, making the fire and warming the food Emily had sent, then eating it and cleaning up the dishes kept them occupied until well after dark. Then they spread out their bedrolls and sat on them beside the campfire, drinking coffee and talking quietly about the deer again.

"Remember this about any of the animals we come across," he told her. "Listen to their spirits and stand still and let them come to you. You're the one who is new here in the place where they live. Be still and send them thoughts that you're a friend and let them come to you in their own good time."

She drew up her knees and wrapped her arms around them.

"Next time, I will."

"It may not happen to you the very first time you try it, but eventually you'll be able to know what their spirits are saying."

She nodded.

"I've learned to do it with you," she said.

She felt his quick look, but she didn't turn to him.

"Ever since you caught me at the tall pine," she said, "I've been listening to your spirit. It tells me that I'm the center of your concern, the same as you've been telling me with words, yet you also must satisfy your honor and find your peace."

Then she looked at him. The fire was throwing streaks of light onto his face, but his eyes were in shadow. She could feel their power, though, just the same as she had on that first night they met.

Suddenly she ached so to touch him that she thought she would die if she didn't.

"This afternoon when you said you weren't going to touch me again, I decided to tempt you until you changed your mind."

He tilted his head, and, in the firelight, she saw his quick, amused glance.

"Am I to take this as a warning?"

"No. *I* changed my mind. I respect your decision, and I don't want to cause you to do something you'd regret."

His slight smile changed to a grin.

"You're very sure of your powers."

She grinned back at him.

"Yes, I am."

She leaned back on one arm, angling away from him to show the silhouette of her body against the light of the fire.

"I know that you are flesh and blood, no matter how strong your spirit is," she said.

"Ah, but I've had years and years of practice in putting my spirit in charge," he said.

However, his eyes caressed the shape of her long legs with the knees languidly bent, anyway—she could tell by the tilt of his head, even if his face was no longer in the light. And she could tell by the heat as it roamed slowly over the curve of her breasts that his glance was lingering there.

It made her hold her breath.

It made her breasts tingle, and her hands itch to touch him.

Slowly, deliberately, she straightened up, crossed her

legs in front of her, and leaned the other way, toward him.

"Ah, but your spirit wants me, too," she said softly. "Will you admit that's true?"

He chuckled.

"No?" She leaned closer still, close enough for him to smell the fragrance of the flowery perfume she'd used from the bottle in her saddlebags. "I would hate to have to torture an admission from you," she whispered. "It's not nice to lie."

His laugh was throaty and low.

"You are torturing me right now. Is that admission enough for you?"

"Well, I'd say it's a start," she drawled.

His eyes were hot and bright in the dusk of his face. They caressed her mouth. However, his big, hard-muscled body stayed still.

For a long, long moment, their eyes held in a look that stopped her heart.

"This is how it is with me, Cotannah," he said, at last. "I gave in to my flesh and my spirit lost control and that's when I put the curse on Jacob. If I give in to my flesh again, and make love to you, it'll be like putting a curse on you that makes it harder for you to bear our parting."

Consternation started her blood flowing again.

"But you're not a spirit!" she cried. "You're a flesh-and-blood man and you can't always tamp that down. You shouldn't."

"I should," he said, and his face filled with torment. "I'm supposed to be a healer, not a destroyer. And I used *bad medicine*. Me, a shaman with gifts given to me so I can do good, only good."

"I didn't behave right, either," she said. "I was trying to get you jealous by the way I acted with Jacob, and that kept me from sensing his badness. But you sensed it, you knew he was a terrible person. See, your spirit was working, after all.''

"But not enough to keep me from killing him.''

"You didn't,'' she said, letting all the belief she had in him show in her eyes. "You didn't kill Jacob because you didn't mean for him to die.''

He watched her eyes and searched her face, she saw the desire to believe it leap to life in him.

"Do you really think so?''

"I know so. You don't have a bad bone in your body—I sensed that with a powerful force when you set Sophie's arm that day. I know it. My spirit tells me.''

He grinned.

"Is your spirit strong enough yet to change your behavior?''

She laughed. "Soon it will be, with you teaching me. I'm just glad I'm getting straightened out at your hands instead of Auntie Iola's.''

He laughed, too, a low, silver sound that fired her blood.

"So you think my hands can change you, do you?''

She dropped her gaze to look at them, huge and hard and brown, with beautiful, long fingers and callused palms. Then she looked into his eyes again. Desire went tumbling through her body like a runaway wheel that wasn't quite round. "I know they can.''

She parted her lips the slightest bit and wet them with the tip of her tongue. He watched, but he did not move at all. He was thinking it over, she could see that, and he was beginning to know that making love with her was right.

"And I know that they should,'' she said. "I need to teach you that giving in to the instincts of the flesh doesn't always bring on something bad.''

left to gleam in the firelight,'' she said. ''Every tree limb I passed would reach out and catch it.''

He smiled dreamily.

''Cotannah. Beautiful Cotannah. Every thing and every person wants to reach out and catch you as you pass. Especially every man.''

His eyes gleamed with a fierce heat. He dropped his arms around her suddenly, and turned her face away from his, pulled her back against his hard body. He fit her head into his shoulder, brushed her hair behind her ear before he pressed his cheek to hers.

His whole body was taut with desire now, she could feel it vibrating through him, through her, between them, like the plucked string of a bow. But he didn't touch her in any other way.

''I know you're right about our bodies coming together,'' he whispered, ''but Cotannah, I would never forgive myself if I broke your heart.''

Chapter 16

Her blood stopped pumping. He couldn't deny her now, he just couldn't. Not after the change of heart she'd seen in his face.

Yet, he stayed very still, the chiseled bones of his face pressing into hers.

"You won't. I'll die of a broken heart if you don't love me, Shadow."

"I do love you. With all my heart, my soul, and my spirit. But if I love you with my body, it'll make it worse, much worse, for you when I'm gone. Then I won't have to suffer, but your flesh and your skin will long for me, too, as well as your mind and your spirit."

"They will anyway," she whispered, her lips almost too stiff with despair to speak. "All of me is longing for you now so much that it's devouring me."

She pulled away from him then, although the loss of his hard warmth made her feel so bereft she could cry, and shifted her body to face him, took his dear face in her hands.

"I know how you feel," she cried, and she willed her voice not to break. "You think that our coming together will make it harder for me, but it's harder for us both without tasting him, he grazed her lips with his. Once, twice, and then again.

"And this?" he whispered. "Is this tempting you?"

"Yes! Yes! I'll even beg if you want me to."

"Not necessary," he murmured. "I'll give you anything you want with open arms."

Except your life.

But instantly the wretched thought was gone and he was hers forever, a part of her, because he knew without thinking what she needed before she herself knew. He held her like a treasure too precious for price, he cherished her like a woman too passionate for playing at love.

And that told her, suddenly and well, in a way that felt so different in her blood from the way she already knew it in her mind, that this time, indeed, she was not playing at all. This was going to sear her very soul, this was going to bind her to him for all the rest of the days and nights that she drew breath.

He kissed her mouth to satiation, then he held her breast in his hand and suckled it until she cried out his name and thrust her fingers into his hair to hold him there and never let him go. Until she begged him to stop and then implored him to do it some more.

"More," she murmured, with her greedy, bruised lips already craving another kiss, "more."

She wanted more of his kisses and his touch, more of everything he was doing and was going to do with her. She wanted to be part of him, she wanted to be inside his skin and have him inside her.

The voluptuousness of his power, the dark delight of his body struck into her heart like a shivering lance. This was more, more than she'd bargained for, more than she'd ever imagined. Maybe more than she could bear.

More than she could ever hope to control, she knew that already.

But there was no stopping now.

Her palms hungered to know every ripple of sinew, every bulging of muscle, every stretching of tendon, every shape of bone beneath his flesh. Never before had she felt this need, this pulsing of desperate desire that she could not command. She could only give herself to it, go with it wherever it carried her.

Her fingers thrust into his hair, brought his mouth back to hers, but before she kissed him, she had to whisper against his lips.

"Love you," she said. "Walks-With-Spirits, I love you."

Never before had she made love with a man that she loved.

Never before had she loved a man.

And with those two thoughts her mind left her. Walks-With-Spirits was kissing her again with a leisurely, lazy, possessive pleasure that made her blood run fast and hot and her breath slow to stopping.

But even breathless, even existing without air, without sight, hearing or speech, she never had felt so gloriously alive inside and outside her skin. Alive and dangerous. Alive and able to do anything.

He knew before she did that she had to have him at her breast again and this time he took the other rigid, begging tip into his mouth to send those arcing sparks of fiery happiness flying through her body until the pleasure grew so great she could not bear it. No, it was the other wantings he was creating with his teeth and tongue that she could not bear, for she needed his mouth at the wet center of her woman's body and his hands on her, on every bit of her skin that was not already pressed against his.

Walks-With-Spirits knew that, too, for he knew her too well, far too well. He slipped his free hand along the curve of her waist and then, as she arched up and into his mouth more fully, he cupped the swell of her hip and pressed her against his hardened manhood. Then he moved his mouth back to hers in a kiss so slow and gentle and hot and succoring that it melted her very bones into the ground.

Her mouth melded with his and then they parted, only far enough for delicious torment, only long enough to prove that they could come back together again and again. Always. They always came back together again.

Until, at last, with his hands caressing her shoulders and his legs wrapped around hers, as if to enclose her in a living circle of his body, he began to trail kisses along the line of her jaw and then over the vulnerable curve of her throat that she offered to him. Tiny, laving tastings of his tongue to her skin. He wanted to love every inch of her, those kisses told her. He wanted to know and to love all of her.

He made his way down into the valley between her breasts, which were aching for his attentions again, but his mouth moved past them, on down and down, not varying from its straight path. Until he reached her waist.

Then he stopped and got up onto his knees beside her, raised his head to look at her. She laid her hand against his heart and felt it bucking against the cage of his chest-bone.

Very gently, with a touch so intriguing, so tantalizing that she trembled and let her hand fall away from him, he stroked her thighs, the delicate, responsive insides of her thighs, which were yearning for him. Which she opened to him. He knelt between them and looked down at her.

"Cotannah," he said.

That was all. Just "Cotannah."

But his eyes gleamed with the amber of the fire, and his chiseled cheekbones silvered in the starlight when he cocked his head and looked at her as if she were the most wonderful sight he ever had seen. A smile touched the corners of his full, sensual lips.

Then he bent to bestow a perfect, tender kiss on the sensitive spot halfway between her belly button and the core of her woman's body, hot and wet and weeping for him. A kiss as a gift holding all of his love.

And then he slipped inside her and gathered her up, all of her, swiftly into his arms, held her hard and fast as they began to move together in the ancient, timeless rhythm that now was new as the slender moon rising. She wrapped her arms and legs around him and clung to him, drew in great breaths of the scents of his skin and his hair and his breath before she kissed his neck and licked his shoulder and filled her mouth with the taste of his sweat and then of his lips and tongue until his essence rushed in her veins with her blood and swirled in the marrow of her bones.

He plunged deeper and she welcomed him, clung to the immutable, solid strength of his dear body and loved it with hers, stroke for stroke, and flash for flash until they went soaring, fused together, spinning up and out through the dark sky into a sparkling spangle of stars.

He woke with Cotannah's breasts warm against his side, her face buried in his shoulder, and her back and rounded bottom chilled by the autumn night air. With his free hand, he managed to reach the other quilted bedroll and pull it over them.

Then he lay, looking up into the blue-black, silvery haze of the night, gradually coming back into his mind now that his blood was no longer roaring in his head, glorying in holding Cotannah in his arms. What they had done had been magnificent, and he wasn't going to worry now that it would make her pain worse later on. No matter that it was too late now, anyway, but such worry would only ruin the time they had left. She had made him realize that.

She had wanted this, too, she had told him in words and she had told him, oh, dear Lord, how she had told him with her body! And she had given it careful thought.

Triumphant heat bloomed in his veins. He had done well. He had known by instinct what to do, and they had fused, body and spirit, in a fire of passion. Now he knew why people set such store by this showing of love with their bodies. It was a mystery, he thought, as he slowly stroked her sweet skin while she lay sleeping with her arm splayed out across his chest—a wonderful, mysterious magic, in which somehow the mating of bodies made spirits mate as well.

Or maybe their spirits, already drawn together by love, were what created the wondrous sensations of their bodies.

Either way, it was joy, pure joy, and he was so glad that he had partaken of it. And that he had given it to Cotannah. Truly, though, it was Cotannah with her wise words who had given it to him, to both of them.

He let the wandering thoughts drift around and around in his head while he luxuriated in the feel of the soft quilt on one side and Cotannah's even softer skin on the other. Their bed was already growing warm. Snuggling deeper into their nest, he shifted her position a little, pulling the quilt closer around her, leaning her head back against his arm so that he could see her face.

"Walks-With-Spirits?"

His name was a murmured question, but then she

flung her arm around his neck with a satisfied sigh that proved she knew full well who he was.

"Is it morning?"

He chuckled and picked up her hand to kiss each of her fingertips in turn.

"No, you haven't slept long. Look up and see the stars."

She opened her eyes, he cradled her head in the curve of his shoulder.

"Crescent moon," she said drowsily, "white feather moon."

"Mmhm," he said, and bent his head to drop a kiss onto her hair.

She froze, then, quit breathing in his arms, and for a heart-stopping moment he thought she was rejecting the caress.

"Look!" she cried. "Look at that star!"

He glanced up to see a star so bright that it stood out from the others like a beacon.

"Why didn't I see that before?" he muttered, half to himself.

"Because it's for both of us, because we're meant to see it together!"

He stared at it.

It stared back at him, shining white-bright, not twinkling, not moving at all up there in the far, far away night blue sky.

Cotannah sat straight up, shivering in the sudden chill, and lifted her hand as if to try to touch it.

"That is our star, Walks-With-Spirits; it's here for us."

She whirled around to challenge him, her hair sweetly tousled, the quilt hanging half-off one beautifully curved, milky shoulder. She clutched it desperately against her chest like a talisman.

"Did you ever see it before? That mighty, blazing star?"

"No."

"Then it's a sign. For us. Because we love each other! Because we made love."

He sat up, too, and pulled her, trembling, into his arms to warm her. To try to stop the words he knew would come.

"What does it mean?"

"It means love . . . and life! It means you aren't going to . . . die," she said, choking on the dreaded word. "It means we'll both live . . . and love each other for years and years and years."

He rested his chin on top of her head so he wouldn't have to look into her great, shining brown eyes while his heart broke into tiny pieces inside his chest.

"Don't . . . get your hopes up again, my sweet *holitopa*. Please, Cotannah, don't."

The star stayed with them all night. Cotannah fell asleep as soon as the excitement of finding it had become the great hope that had settled, warm and sustaining, in her heart. She nestled spoonlike into the curve of Walks-With-Spirits's body, wrapped both her arms around one of his hard-muscled ones, and slept, deeply, until just before dawn.

When she woke the night was at its blackest, clinging desperately to the sky for its last hour, the moon and many stars beginning to fade. But their star shone on, splendidly bright and immovable.

For a long time, she didn't realize that Walks-With-Spirits was awake.

"It's an irony, isn't it?" he said, and his low, rich voice rumbled softly in her ear as his chest rose and fell against her back. "I'm the one who's supposed to be teaching you."

She waited, but he didn't say any more.

"Does that mean you believe me now, about the star?"

"I want to," he said, "but that's not the most important thing. I had no right to tell you not to hope. Your spirit is brave, and it flies high; I shouldn't stand on the ground and try to shoot it down."

She turned within his embrace to face him and snuggled deeper into their cozy bed until her head rested in the crook of his arm. She grinned at him in the light from the fire.

"Fly with me," she said. "We might see your friend Hawk that you claim sits on your shoulders. I hope he comes to visit while we're here in his valley."

He gave her a look that made her blood run hot again.

"You're the only friend I need."

When he bent his head to kiss her she met him halfway.

They got up and dressed, shivering in the frosty morning, after the sun splashed its first light into their faces, made a quick breakfast of scrambled eggs and bread toasted on sticks, ate it ravenously, and set out on foot across the valley meadow.

"The wild horses may not be anywhere near here anymore," Walks-With-Spirits said, swallowing up the ground with his long, effortless stride, "but this valley and the one over the next ridge will have good grass during the Cold Time, and they wintered here last year."

Cotannah stretched her long legs and tried to keep up.

"I guess so. The turkey grass is knee-high here."

Suddenly, she whirled around and walked backward,

staring at Pretty Feather grazing near the bank of the river.

"What if they're behind us instead of over this ridge? Would your wild stallion try to steal my mare while we're gone?"

He shrugged and walked faster.

"Who knows? She's hobbled, so I doubt he could take her far."

"But what would happen if he did? Could we get her back from him?"

"No," he said, in a teasing tone, "we'd have to stay here forever."

Cotannah looked around, at the sunshine glinting off the silver frost that covered every leaf, every blade of grass, every rock. At the intriguing white mist she loved to watch rising along the length of the river. The deep wine red of the sumacs and the brighter oranges and yellows of the oak and sweet gum leaves shimmered beneath the frost like sweet promises, the evergreen junipers looked blue in places, so thick was their burden of berries.

The sky picked up the blue again, one shade deeper, and the mountains showed every blue in existence, rolling on and on until they darkened with distance into purple and indigo. And back there, at their camp, their fire glowed, safely banked within its circle of stones.

"That's fine with me," she said, drawing in a long, deep breath of the forest-scented air. "There's nowhere I'd rather stay forever."

They walked on in silence, then, afraid to say any more lest they ruin this first precious day.

The herd of wild horses was grazing and playing exactly where Walks-With-Spirits thought it would be, in the circular valley on the other side of the nearest wooded, rocky ridge paralleling the river. Halfway down the other side, he signaled her to be quieter yet, and when they slipped through the trees at the bottom of the hill and peered out through a screen of close-growing cedars, the horses appeared to be completely unaware of them.

Cotannah had to clap her hand over her mouth to stop her gasp of delight. The adult horses had their heads down, lazily grazing, scattered across the frosted grass like different-colored jewels spilled out on cotton—burgundy bays, yellow buckskins with black points and dorsal stripes, blue and red roans, blazing red sorrels, blacks and whites, solids and paints. The sun streaked their pasture and set their hides to gleaming, picked at the edges of the frost crystals that had formed on their backs in the night, made them twinkle.

"But look over there," Cotannah said, trying to speak in that way of Walks-With-Spirits's in which the sound was less than a whisper. "That's the best of all."

He nodded. Of course. He had spotted them before she had.

They were three young ones, yearlings, like the deer, and every bit as quick and graceful, dancing and prancing between the trees and the herd, running in spurts and then sliding to a stop, slowing down only to pretend to kick and bite at each other, bursting with pent-up energy that threatened to explode from beneath their little hides. They were so silly, so full of vigor—they had to have been playing hard for quite a little while, they'd gotten themselves hot enough to have steam rising from their backs.

The sight of that steam stirred some picture in the back of Cotannah's mind, something she couldn't quite catch long enough to know it. She shook her head and looked again, especially at the yellow dun colt, but the connection or the memory or whatever it was wouldn't come to her. She tried again, almost got it. Then it was gone completely.

Then she forgot about it because the spotted baby and the yellow one reared at the same time, stood on their tiny back hooves and pawed at each other with their forefeet, sending out high, baby squeals of masculine challenge. Cotannah looked at Walks-With-Spirits, and they both stifled laughter.

The stallion thought that was ridiculous, he threw up his head and called to the rowdy colts in a tone that sounded like a reprimand and that made it even harder not to laugh out loud. He was a dictator, that stallion, she could tell by his attitude. A tall, muscular buckskin, he had stationed himself behind the mares and young ones, grazing off to one side, watching them constantly. From time to time he lifted his nostrils to the wind and his eyes to the hills, searching for danger anywhere in the mountainous country that surrounded his herd.

Now, after he watched the yearlings for a minute and saw to it that his get were causing no harm, the horse turned to face her and Walks-With-Spirits. He whinnied softly, his gaze directed exactly at their hiding place.

"He's asking us in," Walks-With-Spirits said.

"I'm not crazy about visiting him," she said.

He laughed, and said, "You're with me."

And so they left their hiding place and walked slowly out to the herd, first stopping at the stallion for him and Walks-With-Spirits to renew their acquaintance. After that, they wandered at will among the wild horses, talking to them, even petting them, and none spooked, none ran away, none even tensed a muscle in fear—except for the babies, who frolicked away into the trees again when Cotannah slowly started toward them.

"This amazes me in one way and then, in another, it

doesn't surprise me at all,'' she told Walks-With-Spirits. "Why should it? Any man who has a mountain lion and a coyote for traveling companions ought to be able to talk to wild horses.''

Everything they did that day amazed her, as did the next and the next. They explored the hills in the four directions from their camp, they saw deer and rabbits, squirrels and possums, every kind of wildlife that lived in the Nation, and they lay on their backs at night looking up at the sky while Walks-With-Spirits told her legends about stars that danced and boys who were sent from earth to visit the sun and moon.

Walks-With-Spirits came to dread the coming of darkness, though, and he began to pray for clouds or fog because no matter how many stories he told her or how many lessons she learned, they were never enough to distract Cotannah from her obsession. The special, brilliant star that she called "our star" remained fixed in the place where they'd first seen it, high in the sky to the southeast of their camp. One night after another, every night, they looked up and it was there.

"It's going to give us a revelation," she would tell him, turning to him with her face alight from within. "I tell you, Walks-With-Spirits, it's going to show us how to save you."

But no revelation came.

So he would take her in his arms and they would share the miracle of making the growing love between them a physical thing, a passionate thrill and a splendid comfort. And a triumphant victory.

Surely she was right, he would think, afterward, when he lay sated and exhausted, with her in his arms, with her sweet, sweaty cheek resting on his. This celebration of life had to be a victory over death.

Then he would realize that he was only repeating her

thoughts and her worries in his mind, that he was for-
getting that the bullets of the Lighthorse would not be
killing him, but sending his spirit from this world into
the next. It seemed like death, though, thinking that he'd
be leaving Cotannah behind.

She was enchanting him, mesmerizing him, fascinating him, and it was all he could do to keep his mind on
what he should teach her.

So, one afternoon in the middle of the week, while
they were making their daily exploration of the river
with its quiet pools and rocky waterfalls, he determined
to fix both their minds on her lessons, on preparing her
to live the rest of her life in this world without him. She
was becoming far too accustomed to being with him,
just as he was to being with her.

"Why do you think that we come to the water to say
incantations?" he asked her.

He was stepping from rock to rock out in the middle
of the river, where he could see through the clear water
to watch the fish swimming by.

"For the same reason we come to the water to get a
drink," she said, very sure of herself, looking up at him
from where she was wading at the edge of the river with
her thin, soft breeches rolled up above her knees. "Because water is life."

The afternoon sun fell across her face in streaks of
light and shade, the red and yellow leaves behind her
shone like ripe fruit on the trees. Her eyes gleamed huge
and dark in her perfect face, her loose mass of black hair
framed it like a picture. She had tucked an old shirt into
the waistband of the breeches, explaining that both had
belonged to her brother Cade when he was growing up,
and she looked infinitely more appealing than ever. The
sunshine outlined her lush breasts straining against the

pale blue cotton, their fullness contrasting with her tiny waist.

His hands hurt, ached, to trace that sensuous curve.

A twisting torment of desire burned through him, fast and hot as a lightning strike. She saw it.

"I dare you," she drawled, smiling at him across the chattering, rushing water of the river.

He smiled back at her. How could he not let her distract him from the lesson? A man would have to be carved of wood to resist her for a minute.

"To do what?"

She lifted her hands to the waistband of her breeches and slowly, slowly, began to unbutton them.

"Go swimming," she said huskily. "Isn't this a hot day?"

He began moving toward her, not even glancing down to see his stepping-stones, just feeling for them while his eyes feasted on her. She finished with the buttons and peeled the cloth down and down . . . she wore nothing beneath.

"You have no mercy," he said, and he hardly recognized his own voice it was so gruff from wanting her.

But the wanting would wait. It would grow, no matter what either of them did or said. And the day was hot and tart and lighthearted and there wouldn't be many more like it.

He held out his hand and she took it.

"You have no mercy," he said, again. "And neither do I!"

He pulled her to him and jumped from the rock into the rushing middle of the river, laughing as she screamed and clasped him around the neck hard enough to strangle him, gathering her safe into his arms as they went under, her hair swirling upward in the water. When his toes hit bottom he pushed against it and sent them back up to break the surface.

"It's too cold!" she cried, as soon as she could speak, beating her small fists on his shoulders, his back, any part of him that she could reach. "The water's too cold!"

He was numb. Absolutely numb and desperate to get out of the wet clothing weighing him down. He was freezing, and he'd nearly frozen her. Whatever had possessed him?

"You wanted to go swimming," he said, trying uselessly to keep his teeth from chattering as he lunged toward the bank and water shallow enough to keep his head above. "Didn't . . . you?"

That made her attack him with even more energy and try to kick him with her legs locked around his waist. She had glued herself to him, it was a wonder he could even move.

But he forced his unfeeling feet over the rough bed of the river, began dragging them up and onto the next pile of rocks and gravel, heading toward the bank that now seemed miles away. Cotannah gasped some more air into her lungs and began pummeling him again.

"You knew how cold it was out there in the middle," she yelled, but now she was laughing, too. "You knew it, and now you can know that I'm going to get you for this!"

Cold as he was, he was already beginning to feel heat from just holding her.

"O-oh, I never knew you were so mean," she said, renewing her grip around his neck. "I never would have come out here with you if I'd known you were so mean."

His feet stepped on more rocks, then on blessed

ground. He held her tighter and began to run up the bank.

"Yes, you would," he said. "You would have come with me no matter what, wouldn't you now?"

They had reached the trees and the piles of leaves and needles beneath the limbs, leaves and needles heated all afternoon by the sun. He fell forward into a patch of full sunlight, rolling with her safe in his arms.

"Quick," she said, the moment she'd landed on the dry earth, "off. Off with these clothes!"

He tore at the buttons of her shirt while she pulled at the tails of his, trying to get it away from his skin long enough to take it off over his head.

"Good thing you aren't wearing skins," she said, still gasping for each breath. "I'd never get them off you."

"Yes," he said, breathing hard, "yes."

He tried, but he couldn't say any more. She jerked his shirt off, and the sun hit his back.

"Hurry," he said, giving up on trying to fumble the small buttons through the wet cloth of the buttonholes.

She wore nothing beneath the shirt, either, and her breasts brushing against his fingers made them shake so he couldn't make progress. Damn the thing! He grew hard wanting to cup them in his hands and suckle their hard tips even through the cloth, but she was shivering harder now as the wind hit her clothes.

He reached for the top of her breeches, still halfway down onto her hips where she'd rolled them when he pulled her into the river, and used both hands to peel them off her, down and down her long legs while he caressed her trembling body with his eyes.

"Now you," she said, and flung her shirt off her arms and away. In the same motion she reached for his own soaking breeches.

"Yes," he said again.

At last, his came off, too, with both of them working at them, and the sun bathed them in heat and she pressed her naked, trembling body to his once again and there was no more need for words anymore. The sun was nothing compared to the burning she created in him, even with her flesh still chilled from the river.

She wrapped her legs around his and her arms around his neck, burrowed into him as if she wanted to share his very skin. He stroked her back, her limbs, rubbed them with his hands until her skin felt warm again. Then he held her tighter, closer, and kissed her wet hair until she finally lifted her head and gave him her mouth.

Chapter 17

He fell on it as a starving man would fall on a
meal, greedily and with no conscious thought,
tasting her desperately, pulling the essence of her being
into his own self like a life-giving drink. Then she was
kissing him back, frantic herself, giving him her tongue
and then demanding his, twining them together while her
hands began stroking his skin.

Her hands were smooth, as he knew them to be, but
this time they tore at his heart and ripped it apart, left it
lying in two separate halves like an opened shell. But
he couldn't stop to consider. Not now.

Now, he had to have her, now all he could do was
love her. He cupped her bottom in his hands, lifted her
away from him and laid her down, hovered over her for
just long enough to look into her eyes, into the beautiful
brown depths of her eyes and see the love that was vibrating through him reflected there. He came into her
with a keening cry meant to be the sound of her name.
She took him in, closed around him hot and wet, clasped
him in her arms and pulled him gloriously close.

Into a raging storm. Her spirit was hot and wild, her
body was all curves and delicate bones beneath silk skin,

his hands too slow, too few, to take it all in. Such hunger! How could he have such hunger and the feast of her mouth at the very same time, how could he have such wanting when she was giving him so much?

She was so slim, so supple, so lovely and she was his, only his.

His to learn, his to meld with and explore. His to move with to a drumbeat that only the two of them could hear, his to sing with to a heartsong that only the two of them would ever know.

Then she arched beneath him and trembled like a bowstring he had plucked. It aroused him beyond measure and he plunged into her harder, deeper. The storm came back on him, full force, a storm of crashing thunder and searing lightning, a lightning that lanced through his flesh and bones to reach his heart and leave a jagged trail across its charred and molten parts. Yet the last of the unbalance she had brought to his peace burned to ashes. His spirit melded with hers as his seed flowed into her body. He called out her name, a gladsome cry that echoed from the mountains.

For the longest time they lay in each other's arms, sated, dazzled by love, dazed by its magic and the heat of the sun. The wind stirred near the earth and then lifted into the trees, swirled backward to caress their sweat-sheened skins and whisper legends of love in their ears.

"This is what the old men said when I was a boy," Walks-With-Spirits said, repeating its message to Cotannah, "the Ancient One does not fail to make it known when a man should say to a woman, 'You must think of me from your very soul as I think of you: truly you and I are set apart.' "

The moment the words left his lips he wished he could call them back.

Not because they weren't true—never had he spoken

a deeper truth—but because he couldn't bear to see the fires of new hope that they would set to burning in her unguarded eyes. Which they did.

But she spoke with uncharacteristic quietness.

"We are," she said, lifting her hand to touch his cheek, "set apart and bound together. Will you go away with me?"

"We are," he mimicked gently, touching her face in return, "put on this earth to accomplish certain tasks. The Ancient One has brought us together so we can help each other know what our tasks are and do them."

She only looked at him for a long, long time, with her fingertip tracing the shape of his face, looked at him with those great, dark eyes that were seeing all the way through him, now. But the passion to save his life was seething in her blood again, now that their time was growing so short. He could feel it running high and hard beneath her skin.

She must have been up long before him the next morning for when he woke, she had set coffee to brewing over the fire and she was creating a second invitingly delectable smell that was floating through the little valley. It drew him out of his sleeping bag although he wanted to lie there forever and watch her while she thought he still slept.

"Good morning, Cotannah," he said, when he had pulled on his breeches. "What are you making?"

Her face lit like a lantern when she turned to him, smiling. His heart nearly stopped, then started up again with hard, pounding beats. He, himself, only himself— the sound and the sight of him—had put that light in her eyes!

"Good morning to you, Sleepy Shadow," she said, teasing him with the huskiness in her voice. "I'm making chocolate fritters for your breakfast, so hurry and get washed up.''

He grabbed his shirt and headed straight for the river because he didn't trust himself to go any closer, much less to touch her. If he did, they would never get to breakfast before noon and she seemed very serious about her creation. Chocolate fritters! Whoever heard of such a thing?

And that was exactly why, although it was only one of a thousand reasons why, he could not bear to think about leaving her. She was an elemental force, like the land and the always-shifting, sometimes violent weather here in the New Nation: he never knew what she would do, and so he was fascinated with her all the time.

He did allow himself one quick kiss when he returned to the fire and she returned it enthusiastically but she was most involved with her cooking for him.

''Now, sit right here and let me serve you your surprise,'' she said. ''I made this recipe up all by myself.''

''I didn't know you could cook . . . at least, not original concoctions.''

He kept a solemn face and put sufficient wonder in his voice but he didn't get a rise from her—she knew he was teasing her, she knew him too well by now.

''No need to insult my past efforts,'' she said, with a grin. ''In fact, you'd better not because this is so delicious you'll be begging for more, and if my feelings are hurt too much I can't make them.''

Obediently, he sat down opposite her, crossed his legs, and accepted the plate she gave him. It held long pieces of thin, rolled up dough, crisp around the edges, sprinkled with chocolate and sugar.

''Hold it still,'' she said, and held a tin dipper over the plate to drizzle a thick chocolate sauce, which gave off more of that heavenly smell, onto his fritters.

"It's butter and chocolate and sugar filling the dough and chocolate and butter and my own secret spices in the sauce," she said. "You gave me the spirit gift of talking with the horses, so this is an earthiness gift from me to you. I want to show you how to please the body in other ways beyond making love."

He pretended great surprise, then hung his head in an extremely exaggerated mock disappointment.

"We've moved beyond making love! Surely not, why I . . . I don't know if even chocolate can compensate me for that . . ."

Then he seemed to recover, gave her a big smile.

"Yet, on second thought, I think it can," he said. "That smells absolutely delicious."

"Don't ever say that," she warned, "or I'll take your plate back and you'll never know how wonderful it tastes!"

They laughed together, then, and she fixed a plate for herself, and they ate, groaning and exclaiming with pleasure, until the fritters were all gone and the only sauce left was what was left in the dipper. She scraped some out with her finger and held it out to him.

He kissed her fingertip and then closed his lips around it, holding her eyes with his while he sucked the last of the delicious, thick chocolate onto his tongue. She held still for one moment longer than necessary, then brought it to her own mouth.

"The taste of you is like the chocolate," she said, "a burning, bitter sweetness that permeates my soul."

"Ah, Cotannah . . ."

And so he had to make love to her again, there in the glittering wind of the autumn morning, because he could not contain his joy.

*   *   *

The bright star shone steady in its place again that night. Cotannah touched his arm and motioned for him to look as soon as the dark came deep enough to see it.

"This is what the old women said when I was a girl," she said, " 'Truth is a bright star.' "

"I believe that," he told her, assuringly. "It is our star. And it is truth. But maybe it is telling us that we're together just for here, just for this time. I will love you with all my heart, forever. But every day, everything around us changes, even stars, my *holitopa*."

She looked down and picked at the bedroll they sat on, cross-legged.

"I know," she said, and the soft sadness in her came to lodge in a hard lump beneath his breastbone, "and this time together with you, here, has changed me. It'll sustain me. It's more than most people have in a whole lifetime, and if I have no choice, I'll make it be enough."

Cotannah couldn't believe she'd said that and meant it at the time. A heartbeat later, she was wild to wrap him into her arms and hold on to him forever, screaming that she could never let him go. But yet she could, that peace really was there, like a rock to cling to deep inside, the peace that being alone here with him had brought her. The focus on what was really important, what would last a person for a whole, long life. That was the real spirit gift he had given her.

She didn't want to have to hold on to that peace right now, though. Tonight he was here in the flesh and their star was shining and she wanted to live, really live. She got up and walked purposefully across the camp to her saddlebags, took out a vial, returned to the fire and poured some oil into a tin cup, then held it over the flames. Soon a heady, spicy fragrance filled the air.

"That smells delicious," he said, "but if it's a bedtime snack, I think I'd prefer more chocolate.''

She laughed.

"This isn't something to eat, Greedy Shadow."

He laughed, too.

"This morning I'm Sleepy Shadow, tonight I'm Greedy Shadow. Don't you have any good descriptions of me?''

"How's Passionate Shadow?"

"Great! But I'm too lazy to live up to it right now."

He stretched his arms and turned around, lay down on his side on the bedroll and propped up on one elbow to watch her.

"Or, then again, maybe not," he said.

She laughed.

"I have something else in mind."

"Oh? Surprising Cotannah. How's that for an apt description?''

She swirled the oil in the cup, tested it with her finger and found it pleasantly warm, stood up and walked over to him. She stood over him, looking down into his uplifted face.

"Take off your clothes," she said.

"I thought you had something else in mind."

"I do. Trust me."

"That is the scariest thing you've ever said to me."

That made them both laugh.

"Take off your clothes and lie flat on your back," she persisted.

"Is this another of your gifts of earthy pleasures?"

"Yes. It may turn out to be your very favorite."

"I don't think so."

His tone was such a low, rough caress that she could hardly think what she was about.

"As long as we don't get completely beyond making love, I know what my favorite is," he said.

"You're becoming obsessed," she said, teasing him.

Then she bit her tongue, afraid she'd raise his old demons of doubt again.

"See, this'll be good for you," she said. "Maybe it'll get your mind onto something else."

"I doubt that," he drawled. "You've taught me about the pleasures of the flesh too well."

She set the cup down, got down on her knees to unbutton his shirt.

"Not with your seductive fingers moving on my skin, taking my clothes off my body, it won't."

Finally, laughing, pretending to struggle over what they should be doing, the two of them together managed to divest him of his clothes.

"Your turn is coming," he promised. "I get to do whatever this is to you in return. Right after I make love to you."

"If you're able," she said. "I intend to have you so relaxed you won't be able to lift a finger."

And so comfortable on this earth and so addicted to my touch that you won't be able to leave me.

She banished the torturous thought immediately. That wasn't worthy of the new person she was becoming.

But it was typical of the old, determined Cotannah, who was known for never giving up.

As was the next thing that popped out of her mouth.

"Look at our star," she said, as she dipped the fingers of both her hands into the warm perfumed oil. "Let's wish on it. That's another thing the old women said when I was a girl: 'Wish on a bright star.' "

She paused, sat back on her heels, and looked up at the star as he was doing.

"What shall we wish?" he said, a quiet edge of warning in his voice.

She ignored it and boldly said what was uppermost in her heart.

"Let's wish we had the rest of our lives together. Where would we be, Shadow? What would we be doing?"

He went very still.

"Don't do this, Cotannah."

She smiled. "Pretend. Pretend you aren't going. I want to pretend you'll still be on this earth with me."

"Don't," he whispered. "Don't, Cotannah. You're hurting us."

"I'm hurting anyhow. On top of the peace you've helped me find, I'm hurting anyhow."

So much pain sounded suddenly in her voice that it must have filled him with pity.

"All right," he said slowly. "If I stayed on this earth until I was old . . ."

She turned to him and began to rub his muscles with the perfumed oil, wanting now to distract him from the fact that he was talking about things he didn't want to talk about, participating in a fantasy he thought would only hurt them both.

"You would be where?" she said, to encourage him.

"In the New Nation. Living near Tuskahoma, probably, although I used to think I'd come back here to Blue River and stay someday. That's how you've changed me, Cotannah. My dream always was to use the gift of my hands to heal, but now because of you, I'm connected to people and I would use it for them as much as for the animals and the land."

He paused for a moment.

"I'd heal as many as I could and give spiritual gifts to as many as would take them, but I'd stay close to the animals and the Earth Mother, too."

Then he looked into her eyes.

"What would you be doing?" he said.

"Loving you," she said, without hesitation. "And your children. And I might have a school for girls, older girls," she said suddenly, although the words shocked her totally because she'd never known she'd had that thought before. "Emily's the teacher, so she would teach them their lessons and I would teach them about men and how to protect themselves and how to become persons of their own."

His tense muscles began to relax beneath her hands as he laughed.

"Sounds like Emily would be doing most of the work."

"Not so! My part would be harder by far."

"I doubt that Emily will think so."

"We'll have a new kind of finishing school," she said, as visions flashed through her mind of the good such a school could do. "Instead of teaching girls to please everyone, we'll teach them to please themselves!"

"Is that the same as teaching them to be selfish?"

"No. It's teaching them to survive. They can still be good, strong, unselfish women in the old Choctaw way."

The phrase reminded her of that day on the veranda at Las Manzanitas with Cade, a day that now seemed to belong to another life entirely.

"We'll dedicate the whole school to Cade," she said, laughing a little. "After all, he's the one who sent me back to the Nation to learn. He just didn't know it would be you who was here to teach me."

And so they teased and laughed and dreamed of a future that might not, probably would not, come to pass, and the star shone on. Cotannah learned every inch of his wonderful body, soaked the shape of it into her palms and her fingertips and stored it in her own flesh.

Then, when it was hours later and he had caressed her
all over, too, with the wonderful, fragrant oil and then
filled her up with his love again, she lay in his arms
while he slept and gazed at the bright Blue River star.
She never took her eyes from it and she prayed to the
Great Spirit to give her the strength to give him up if
she had to, but she prayed harder for the wisdom to
know what to do to keep Walks-With-Spirits out of
range of the Lighthorsemen's rifles.

The star was gone when she woke alone the next
morning, the sunlight was sparkling everywhere on the
dew and on spiderwebs made during the night. She sat
up and blinked at the bright strands connecting leaf to
leaf, woven lace thrown over the bushes like veils.

She felt as if she were still in her dreamworld—stray
images glittered everywhere in her mind, scraps of vivid
dreams flashed through her memory. The yearling horses
running, steam rising from their backs. A grown horse,
a golden palomino, calling to them in a high, urgent
whinny, steam rising from its back, too, although it was
walking slowly behind the young ones. The red knit cap
of Emily's or Tay's or whoever's that she'd helped herself to and then lost, floating in the fast water of the
creek.

It had all been about to fit together just before she
woke.

And Peter Phillips. She had dreamed of Peter Phillips,
too.

Suddenly she saw Peter Phillips with the steaming
horses, leading the three babies toward her, calling to
her, smiling broadly.

Then the dream faded and real memories began coming back to her.

Phillips squatted beside his palomino, brushing its legs, saddle upended on the ground, steam rising from the horse's back.

She thought about that picture for a moment.

Steam. Because it had been a cool, fall morning, and the horse was hot.

He must have brushed away some sweat before she rode up.

The horse was hot. Phillips was not saddling up to ride out; he must have just ridden in.

On the morning Jacob died!

She froze in place, closed her eyes, and went over every detail of that meeting. She had told him she lost her hat. Exactly that. Her hat.

And when she and Walks-With-Spirits were leaving Tall Pine for McAlester, he had said, "I need your warm, red cap." She knew that's what he had said. "Your warm, red cap."

She had never worn the warm, red cap before. The only way he could've known what her lost hat looked like was that he had seen it floating in the creek. The creek that lay between Tall Pine and Tuskahoma. The creek would've carried it away soon, so he'd been right behind her when she'd turned and started back to the house. He must've ridden fast while she dawdled in the beautiful morning woods, hoping, perhaps, to have his horse brushed and turned out and himself in the house at the breakfast table before she came back.

Peter Phillips had ridden to Tall Pine from Tuskahoma while William Sowers had stood over Jacob's body in the street. Maybe Peter had been the person inside the mercantile whom Jacob had called back to over his shoulder.

Her blood stopped. Really, she'd never thought of it before, but no one had ever really questioned Peter Phil-

lips about Jacob's death! The Lighthorse had asked him
if he knew anything about Jacob's enemies and he had
said he didn't. She herself had asked him that, too. But
no one had questioned him with the idea that he might
have been the killer.

He could've killed Jacob for his share of the mercantile.

But surely Olmun would be the partner to inherit his
son's share in the event of his death.

Perhaps they'd quarreled over how to conduct the
business.

But how could he have killed him?

Her heart sank into pure despair. There wasn't a mark
on Jacob. Jacob, strong, healthy, young Jacob. That's
why everyone, including the Judges, thought Walks-
With-Spirits had killed him: because if there wasn't a
wound on him, he must have died by magic.

However, she would bet anything she owned—she
would bet Pretty Feather, even—that Peter Phillips was
in Tuskahoma, with Jacob at the mercantile on that fate-
ful early morning, that Peter was the one to whom Jacob
spoke his last words.

She sat straight up in the bedroll.

Another thing that made her believe that—Peter Phillips knew that Jacob hadn't died by the black medicine.
He must know it. Because, even though he hadn't hesitated to say right out loud to her that Walks-With-
Spirits surely was guilty of killing Jacob by magic, he
wasn't scared that Walks-With-Spirits would do the
same to him. He had felt perfectly free to insult Walks-
With-Spirits to his face in the garden at Tall Pine!

She threw back the covers, leapt to her feet, and ran
toward the river. "Walks-With-Spirits!" she called.
"Walks-With-Spirits, where are you?"

She had run halfway to the riverbank before she realized she was buck naked. Skidding to a stop in the wet grass, she turned and ran back toward the camp, hoping to find her shirt, at least, before he responded to her call.

Which was pretty silly, she told herself, considering he had just left her bed.

His dark red hunting shirt was the first garment she found, so she snatched it up and jerked it on over her head. It fell to her knees.

She pulled on her breeches under it, anyway. She might as well find her moccasins, too, because they'd be packing and leaving and the sooner the better. Frantically, while she braided her hair and tied it with a scrap of rawhide thong, she tried to think how many days were left before his one last, precious week was up. They had no time to waste getting this information to the Judges.

She had lost track of time since they'd been alone here in their own private world, she had tried to forget about time except to wish it would stop, but to the best of her hurried calculations, if they started traveling now, they'd arrive at Tall Pine with a day and a half, at least, and two nights remaining before the dawn designated for the execution.

Her whole body shook as she pulled the moccasins on and laced them up to her knees. They needed to be on the trail now. First, they ought to search the mercantile and see if there was any evidence that pointed to Peter Phillips—which the Lighthorse had not done on the day of Jacob's death. They needed to search Peter's room at Tall Pine, too.

She glanced up at the trees along the river, saw a place where the sunlight struck the leaves to purest gold, and then Walks-With-Spirits appeared in front of the birches and elms even though she'd seen no movement at all. Her gaze clung to him. She could never get accustomed

to the way he could magically materialize of out nowhere.

Their horses grazed a stone's throw from him, but
they'd never even pricked their ears in his direction to
let her know he was there. Animals never betrayed him.

"Shadow! Come here!"

Once again she ran, this time straight to him. He
laughed and held out his arms.

"Did I hear you calling me to breakfast?" he said,
teasing her as he scooped her up and swung her around.

"No time for breakfast today! We need to be on our
way back to Tall Pine. My *holitopa*, I think Peter Phillips knows how Jacob really died. I feel in my heart that
he's guilty of the murder!"

She threw her arms around his neck and hugged him
as hard as she could.

He stiffened.

"Cotannah," he said, "no. Please, please my darling.
Don't do this to yourself."

He set her on the ground and took her by the shoulders.

She dragged a long, ragged breath into her lungs to
steady herself.

"Listen to me," she said, laying her finger across his
lips to stop his protests. "You don't know what I've
remembered."

Quickly, she told him all of it.

She watched his eyes and made herself admit what
she saw there. Exactly what she'd feared: pity.

"Don't look at me like that! Aren't you listening?
Walks-With-Spirits, we need to go back now!"

"Darling. My darling Cotannah. Listen to me. If Phillips was coming instead of going from Tall Pine that
morning, if he insulted me with no fear, those things do
not prove him a killer."

A look of exasperation replaced the pity in his eyes.

"Think, Cotannah!" he said. "How can you prove that Phillips did this—if he did—in the short time we have left? The Lighthorse have never even suspected him, so it would take a lot to convince them. Don't waste our last days together, 'Tannah. Think about that. How could you prove it?"

That stopped her, but only for a moment.

"I'll . . . I'll make him confess!"

"How?"

"Well . . . he likes me, I'll get him talking . . ."

"You've already talked to him, and he certainly hasn't blurted out a confession. Why would he tell you anything different now?"

"I'll flirt with him now. I've never done so before, and he's always trying to flirt with me."

His face took on a fierce look she'd never seen before and his fingers tightened until they dug into her flesh.

"No! Don't be flirting with him. You might get into another situation like the one with Jacob."

"I can manage Peter Phillips," she said, knowing that she could.

More and more emotions crowded into his face like storm clouds in a darkening sky. She ignored them— she could talk him out of his doubts on the way.

"Come on, Shadow, let's go! You're right when you say we don't have much time but I think a couple of days will be plenty once I turn my wiles on crafty Peter Phillips."

"I'm not going with you. I'm having no part of this false hope that is only going to hurt you more in the end."

For an instant, fear, fear cold as the frost of a November morning touched her.

She started to answer him, had it on the tip of her

tongue to beg him to come with her, to help her, then she stopped and took a deep, shaky breath. Somehow the peace was growing inside her. If she had to do this alone, she would. She could. She was strong enough now.

And she would get the truth out of Phillips, if she had to seduce him for it. Men said lots of things in bed that they wouldn't say anywhere else.

He saw the thought the minute it entered her head.

"You belong to me," he cried. "I don't want any other man touching you! Don't do this Cotannah!"

Sheer consternation stopped her heart.

"But it wouldn't mean anything," she cried in return. "And I'll be careful . . . I'll be in control . . ."

He wrapped his arms hard around her and pulled her against him as if he were drowning and she was a rock, caressing her with his big, hard hands, begging her with every touch not to go.

"I have to do this, Shadow, my love. I am not going to let you die without a fight."

"I can't let you go," he muttered, while he was kissing her hair.

"Then come with me."

"I can't do that either."

She hugged him as hard as she could.

"Don't worry, don't fret. In my heart I know he's the killer, and that same instinct tells me I can prove he is . . ."

He pulled back, gave her a little shake, and she stared up into his blazing eyes.

"You belong to me," he said again. "Promise me you'll never forget it."

Then his hands tightened on her arms.

"I don't mean that after I'm gone you shouldn't love someone else, sometime . . . I mean . . ."

"I never will," she said, and she knew in that moment that it was true. "You're the only man I'll ever love, my Shadow."

His eyes filled with agony.

"But it's so selfish of me . . . I shouldn't have said that to you. Yet, I can't help it, I mean it . . ."

She laid her finger across his lips.

"You have to believe in me," she said simply. "You won't be gone. You didn't kill Jacob, and you aren't going to die for it."

"I may have killed him."

"No. I've jumped to a lot of conclusions, I admit," she said, looking straight into his eyes, willing him to feel the confidence she was feeling. "And I've led us on a lot of wild-goose chases since Jacob died. But you have taught me much, my Shadow, and I know who did this murder now. I know it with my earthy instincts and with the spiritual strength you've helped me find."

He didn't say a word, only looked deep into her soul, that same way he had looked at her that day on the Texas Road.

Finally he spoke, in that rich, low voice that sounded like a song.

"All right. This search has helped you to grow, just as I realized that night at the cabin, and this decision is the result."

"The search made me grow only because you came with me," she said. "But now that you've taught me, I can finish it alone."

All she could do was look at him. At his wonderful, gorgeous, hard-chiseled face.

"I'll see you soon," she said. "Shadow, I love you."

He gave her a smile so wonderful, so full of love that it would be burned into her memory forever.

"I love you," he said. "Cotannah, I'm standing here handing you my heart."

Those words struck her soul like a thrown lance and lodged there. They hollowed her out and then broke the shell of her into pieces, so that she couldn't leave him.

But she had to go so that she could save his life, so she could keep him with her for all her life.

He saw it in her eyes. He pulled her closer, bent his head, and kissed her once, hard and fast, but deep, as if branding her as his, and then he let her go.

"Ride safe," he said.

She turned and ran for her horse.

Chapter 18

J ust before dusk, Cotannah rode into the yard at Tall Pine numb with exhaustion from traveling so fast, yet with the peace in her heart never wavering. Tay and Emily both came out of the house to meet her and, when she refused to rest or eat until she had talked to them, they stayed in the privacy of the yard listening to her reasoning that Peter Phillips was the murderer.

"You know that the strength of the incantations is always in the thought," she said. "Walks-With-Spirits doesn't have a bad bone in his body, so his curse did not kill Jacob. I know in my heart now that Peter Phillips did, and I'm going to search his room and the mercantile to find out how he did it."

"I agree that Walks-With-Spirits never meant Jacob to die," Emily said, "and I really don't believe that the curse killed him."

Then she added gently, "But 'Tannah, what happened to him? There wasn't any wound."

"I've thought about it all the way back here," Cotannah said. "Maybe Peter stabbed him in the heart or the temple or another really vulnerable spot with a tiny awl—there were tools at the store—or a hatpin or something that left an unnoticeable hole."

335

"'Tannah, darling, please don't make yourself sick, now,'' Emily said, searching her face with huge brown eyes full of worry. "You look so tired."

"Don't try to distract me!" Cotannah said. "Don't you think it could've happened like I just told you?"

"It could've happened," Tay and Emily said, speaking at the same time.

"It could," Cotannah said eagerly, ignoring their worried looks. "Or maybe Peter told him something that made him so angry he had a heart attack. I just know that Peter was the person in the store whom Jacob was calling to over his shoulder."

"I think you may be right," Emily said.

But Tay threw her a glance that said, don't encourage her, as he stood up and held out his hand to Cotannah.

"Better come in and rest now," he said, teasing her gently as she let him pull her up from her chair, " 'Tannah, remember how sick you were when we got you back from the *bandidos*. We can't bear to go through that again."

The thought of that horrible time when she felt so low in her spirits that she didn't want to live gave her a moment of sharp insight into how far she truly had come, how much she had changed. And all because of Walks-With-Spirits. She would not let him die.

"Don't worry about how I feel," she said, "and don't worry that I'll be hurt more if I try this and fail. I won't fail. I know it."

"All right," Emily said. "We believe you. Let's all go into the kitchen, and while you eat something and Rosie pours a hot bath for you upstairs, we'll talk about the best way to go about looking for evidence against Peter."

"Maybe we can search his room now," Cotannah whispered, as they climbed the steps to the porch.

"No, he's in it," Emily whispered back. "He went up early tonight."

"Then I must see him at breakfast," Cotannah said. "Wake me up early, and I'll ask him if I can go into town with him. I intend to make him believe that I've given up on Walks-With-Spirits and that I'm turning to him as my new romantic interest."

"Be careful," they said in unison.

Cotannah laughed.

"You two and Walks-With-Spirits should form a little choir," she said. "But none of you should worry. I can deal with Peter Phillips just fine."

The truth of that gave a lift to her heart as they went into the house. She might be so tired that her legs were trembling and her head was swimming, but she'd never felt so strong in all her life.

The next morning while getting dressed, Cotannah imagined a dialogue in which she, Emily, and Tay asked such clever questions at breakfast that Phillips slipped up, then broke down and confessed. She recalled every suspicious statement the man had ever made. At last, on her way down the stairs, she closed her eyes and tried to clear her mind and heart as she had learned from Walks-With-Spirits. The most important thing was that her spirit be open to listening to Phillips's.

She had chosen a new, dusty gold–colored day dress that Emily said made her eyes and hair black as midnight. It had a high neckline, because it was made for fall and for daytime, but it fit so snugly at the waist and over her breasts that it would definitely draw a man's eye. Phillips would notice her and be doubly glad that she wanted to flirt with him.

And he was.

"What a delight to see you!" he said, as she entered the dining room.

Hastily, he scraped his chair back and stood up to hold hers for her.

"What are you up to, this fine morning, Miss Cotannah, my dear? Did your friend return to Tall Pine with you?"

In other words, *Are you still defending the medicine man and searching for a killer?*

"No," she said, flashing a smiling glance up at him as she slid into her chair, "now I'm all alone."

"Ah! That won't last," he said, jovially, as he sat back down and picked up a platter of bacon and eggs. "A woman as beautiful as you will never be without an escort for long."

"I hope not," she said, tilting her head in her best coquettish manner. "As a matter of fact, Mr. Phillips, I was hoping that you might be my escort today."

He beamed at her and then, with a sketch of a bow, took the liberty of serving her plate.

"It would be my distinct honor to serve as your escort, my dear girl," he said. "Do you have a destination in mind?"

She batted her lashes at him, then cocked her head and gave him a long look right in the eye that brought even more color into his ruddy cheeks.

"I never did get my own personal, private tour of the new mercantile," she said slowly. "Do you think today would be a good time for that?"

He barely glanced at the table when he set the platter down.

"Today would be perfect, my dear Cotannah. Absolutely perfect."

She was so excited that she could barely eat, and her hand shook each time she tried to drink her coffee, but

Peter Phillips took that to mean that she was enormously eager to be alone with him and winked at her several times while he ate to let her know that he understood. Finally, the meal was over, and he handed her into the buggy that he had ordered brought around.

"I didn't want us to go horseback today, since you rode so many miles just yesterday," he explained, as he climbed in and took up the lines. "And, wouldn't you agree that it's much more pleasant for us to sit together?" He scooted over on the seat close enough for his thigh to rest against hers. "What do you say to that, Miss Cotannah?"

She smiled up at him brightly, then reached out and touched his arm. "I thank you for your consideration, kind sir."

They bantered and talked and flirted all the way into town, arriving at the mercantile an hour or so before the time that he usually opened the door to customers. A clerk, working in the front of the store, was already there, which she hadn't counted on, but Phillips immediately sent him away on an errand that would take a good, long while.

"I don't intend to share your company," he told her when the man was gone, "not when I've finally got you all to myself."

He touched her hand as he said that and he held her elbow as he showed her around, from one section of the store to another, and he let his arm brush the side of her breast as he encouraged her to choose a ribbon from the ribbon case to go with her dress. She began to get desperate. Nothing had looked the slightest bit suspicious yet, and she'd tried to glance into every corner of every room of the mercantile. But the storage room that ran across the length of the back of the building was huge and filled with thousands of different items, and the store itself held thousands more.

While Phillips tied the ribbon in her hair, she took several deep breaths and tried to think. Anything incriminating would be hidden from the eyes of the clerk. Anything incriminating would probably be in Phillips's private office, which opened off the main store by a door he had pointed out in the back near the double doors to the storage area.

"You haven't shown me your office yet," she purred, turning around to take the mirror he was offering for her to look at the effect of the ribbon's satiny color against the darkness of her hair. "You only showed me where it is. Do I get a tour of it, too?"

He leaned so close to her.

"You get anything you want, you beautiful creature. You only have to give me a hint."

She fought down a little shudder of revulsion.

"I'd love to explore your own private place," she said. "I know it'll tell me so much about you."

He straightened his back and offered her his arm in a dramatic, exaggerated gesture of gallantry.

"Come with me, Miss Cotannah."

She clung to his arm and let him lead her to the doorway of his office and then into it, across the polished threshold. Just as they entered the spacious room, she cried out, stumbled and made an exaggerated show of holding on to him.

"Ooh, it's my ankle!" she said, gasping, pretending to be in great pain. "I've hurt myself. Oh, Peter, I turned my ankle."

She sucked in her breath as if the hurt was almost unbearable and reached feebly with her other hand toward the big swivel chair in front of the desk, whimpering pitiably all the time.

"I don't know how I did that," she said, as she sank into the chair. "But it's hurting so much I feel I may have broken it."

He was all solicitous attention and concern, wanting to see the injury for himself and do something about it, but she screamed each time he reached for her ankle.

"Peter, please run to Mrs. Smoke's boardinghouse and see if she has any ice," she begged. "Or at least some cold water from her springhouse. We must keep the swelling down so this won't ruin our whole day."

"Of course, of course, but my dear girl, I do hate to leave you alone."

"I'll be fine. I'll sit right here, and I won't even try to move around. Please, Peter, just try to get me some ice."

Finally he was gone and she dropped both feet to the floor and swung around to begin going through his desk but first she ran a thorough glance over every shelf, every table, every item sitting out in plain view. Of course she saw nothing that looked like an instrument of murder. If he still had it, wouldn't he have hidden it in a drawer somewhere?

Her heart sank at the next thought.

Or wouldn't he have put it back on the shelf in the store among other tools of its kind? If that were true, she'd never find it.

She shook off the panic pulling at her and opened the lap drawer of the tall, rolltop desk. Pens, paper, business forms and correspondence.

She began opening the other drawers, the ones down the right side, looking in the cubbyholes as she did so, and then glancing into the drawers, moving their innocent contents around a bit and then moving on. In the bottom one, a glint of sunlight off glass caught her eye immediately and she moved the envelopes that lay half across on top of it.

A white skull and crossbones shone up at her, a small skull and crossbones in the middle of a small, dark brown glass bottle with a cork stopper in the top. Her blood stopped running.

Poison!

In a large, bold script the narrow label beneath the skull and crossbones proclaimed, **Monkshood**.

For a long heartbeat she sat there staring at it, then she snatched it up in her hand and opened her drawstring bag with the other, thrust the bottle deep into it, and pulled the strings tight again. Poison. Phillips could have poisoned Jacob if the two of them had been eating or drinking together early that morning. She looked in the drawer again. There was a half-empty bottle of whiskey there, too.

Quickly, she rifled through, but nothing else in the drawer interested her. Her head was whirling and she could barely breathe, much less think, she was so excited but she kept the presence of mind to close the drawer and slip her bag back onto her wrist before she swiveled the chair around to face the door where Peter would reappear. Her heart beat so hard and fast she thought it would break her ribs.

Why, why in the name of heaven hadn't anybody thought of this before? Poison, of course.

She herself should have thought of it the instant she first heard someone say that it had to be the death curse that killed him because Jacob was young and strong and healthy. Young and strong and healthy and dead, just like Ruffy Sloan.

After all, she had been at Las Manzanitas when Ruffy, one of the white vaqueros, had poisoned himself with too much medicine. With her own eyes she had seen

him laid out in the parlor for the funeral, looking exactly
as if he had fallen asleep, and with her own ears she had
heard, over and over again, how impossible the death
must be because Ruffy had been young and strong and
healthy and too mean to die. The very same could be
said of Jacob.

She froze in the chair, her mind racing. She'd tease
Peter Phillips, all right, but in a different way from what
she had planned. She would taunt him with her knowledge, and she'd drop enough hints to let him know that
his bottle of poison was missing and she'd torment him
into confessing that he was the guilty one. She would
start at dinner, and he would have to respond in front of
everybody. Maybe she could even lure him into her
room to try to get the poison back and she and Emily
and Tay could catch him doing it.

It was all she could do to restrain herself, but she
remained seated in the chair until he returned with a
handful of ice chips in a handkerchief.

"I got some," he called happily from the front door
of the store. "Mrs. Smoke said for me to carry you to
her house if you'd like to lie down."

"No, no, I just want to go home," she said, making
her voice tremble a bit. "I want Emily and Aunt Ancie.
I know you must open your store now, Peter, but if you
could have someone drive me home . . ."

She let the sentence trail off and took the ice from
him, bent to take off her slipper and apply the ice to her
ankle. Suddenly, she held the ice with only one hand
and reached for the handle of drawer that had held the
poison with the other.

"If you have another handkerchief here anywhere, I
could tie this pack around my foot . . ."

"No!" he cried, and his hand shot out like a snake's
striking head to stop hers. "No, not in there. Here, I

have another handkerchief in my pocket.''

She kept her eyes lowered behind her lashes but she felt him look at her sharply. Good. Now he would surely look into the drawer and see that the bottle was gone before he came back to Tall Pine for dinner, and his nerves would be on edge.

After much pretended pain and after sitting with her foot propped up on a stool for several minutes until she could declare the hurting was much less, he finally went out into the street and found Mud Martin and his wife, Beuly, who were heading out toward their own farm, which lay just on the other side of Tall Pine.

''This way, you'll have the buggy to come home in,'' Cotannah told Peter Phillips as he carried her out to the Martins' wagon. ''Don't be late for dinner, now, because I'll feel bad that I've been the cause of delaying the start of your workday like this.''

''No, no,'' he assured her. ''Not at all.''

But he settled her into the seat next to Mrs. Martin and went back inside the mercantile without any more flirting or a lengthy good-bye, with only a cheery, ''You take care of yourself, now, Miss Cotannah!'' thrown over his shoulder as he left her.

She felt her lips curl in a triumphant smile.

Was he rushing back to his office to see if the poison was still in the drawer?

Cotannah decided on the way to Tall Pine to keep her own counsel for a while. If Emily knew for sure that Cotannah had the poison, that knowledge would show on her honest, open face and for the moment, Cotannah wanted to keep Peter Phillips guessing a bit. Of course, if he did go right in and look in the drawer, he'd almost know that Cotannah was the culprit, but yet he wouldn't know for sure. It could've been stolen during the night.

The more she thought it through the more she knew that she'd do more good with her baiting of Phillips if everyone else at the dinner table remained in the dark. After dinner, if Phillips hadn't incriminated himself, she'd tell Tay and Emily about the poison. But if things went well, Phillips would trap himself right there in front of everyone.

So she went back to Tall Pine and searched Peter's room, to no avail, and then tried to take a quick nap to sharpen her wits. She locked the doors and windows to her room to protect the poison bottle when she went downstairs to supper. The family and the boarders were gathering, but Phillips was nowhere in sight.

A terrible, sharp-clawed fear took hold of her heart—what if her stealing the poison bottle had scared him so much that he left town? What if he was halfway to Texas by now?

But he wouldn't just run off and leave the mercantile that he had invested in so heavily. Surely not. Besides, she couldn't prove a thing about his guilt, and he knew that.

Her heart soared, anyway. Soon she wouldn't need to prove anything because she'd frustrate Phillips into blurting out the whole story before he knew what he was about.

The man beside her, a traveling preacher called Brother Jones, held her chair and she sat down. She smiled up at him in thanks and then couldn't stop smiling. She wanted to lick her lips like the cat who stole the cream, she wanted to jump up and shout. Walks-With-Spirits should be on his way to Tuskahoma by now, but he was not going to die. She was going to save him.

Finally, after what seemed an eon, when she felt she could not bear the waiting another minute, Phillips drove the buggy into the yard, washed up, and came in for dinner. He looked a bit drawn and strained, Cotannah thought.

"We were getting worried about you, Mr. Phillips," Emily said. "Did you have trouble on the road?"

"No, no, simply too much business," Phillips said, in an approximation of his usual, hearty tone. "But then that's the best trouble a store owner can have, don't you think so, Miss Emily?"

He smiled and nodded at Cotannah, too, as the only other woman at the table since Aunt Ancie and Uncle Jumper had eaten earlier and gone outside to play with Sophie, and the schoolteacher, Jane Strahorn, was away visiting with a student's family. Cotannah met his pale blue gaze and smiled at him.

"Yes," she said. "There's a lot *worse* trouble you could have."

He held the look for a moment too long, searching her face with steel in his eyes. A flush gradually grew redder in his cheeks.

Cotannah softened her smile and gave him an innocent, wide-eyed look. "Mr. Phillips gave me a wonderful tour of the new mercantile," she announced to the room in general, "and a souvenir gift to remember it by."

His eyes slashed at her face like twin swords the instant those words left her mouth.

"What is it?" Emily asked.

"The ribbon in her hair," Peter Phillips said to Emily, but his eyes never left Cotannah's face.

She smiled at him again.

He turned away from her at last and began filling his plate from the bowls and platters the others began to pass to him, but the tension between them was beginning to make itself felt and everyone fell quiet while they tried to figure out what was going on. Emily, especially, was glancing questioningly from Cotannah to Peter Phillips and back again.

Maybe she should have told her, Cotannah thought. She didn't know quite what to say next. What if Phillips fell silent and wouldn't talk anymore? What would she do then?

"The town was filling up with spectators for the execution when I rode through there this afternoon," Brother Jones said. "It's a shame that more people will turn out to see a criminal shot and sent to hell than for a camp meeting where they can learn how to send themselves to heaven."

Tay answered him.

"Many of us think that Walks-With-Spirits is not a criminal, that he is innocent of murder."

"I don't know how you can still say that," Peter Phillips snapped, with uncharacteristic irritability. "He put a death curse on Jacob, and the boy died without a wound on him. What else could have killed him? The people that found him said he looked like he'd just fallen asleep."

"It really was the weirdest thing, Jacob falling dead in the street like that when he was so young and strong," Cotannah said. "But, you know, this morning I remembered a young, strong vaquero who died on Las Manzanitas last year—he also looked as if he'd just fallen asleep. There was no shaman within miles of the rancho and no death curse for him."

Emily sighed. "That is so sad. Did they ever know what killed him?"

"Poison," Cotannah said, and looked straight at Peter Phillips.

He glanced up from his plate with daggers in his eyes.

Fear trembled in Cotannah's stomach for a moment, but she held the look.

"Who did it?" Emily asked, and it took Cotannah a second to realize she was referring to Ruffy and not Jacob.

"Ruffy killed himself," she said, slowly, still looking at Peter. "He rode in from town after the girl he'd been courting rejected his proposal of marriage and ate some monkshood."

Peter Phillips's face turned red as the sunset Cotannah could see through the window behind him. He swallowed hard and then coughed, almost choked on the bite that had been in his mouth when she'd named the poison.

"Is monkshood a wild plant that grows on the *rancho*?" Emily asked.

"I believe so," Cotannah said, although she had no idea what it was because Ruffy had died of too much laudanum.

Peter Phillips made a strange little noise, deep in his throat.

Emily turned to him.

He continued to stare at her, and his face grew redder still.

"Why, Mr. Phillips," the innocent Emily cried. "Are you all right? Do you have a fever?"

He coughed some more and took a sip of water. He seemed to lessen his color through the sheer force of his will as they all watched.

"I'm fine," he said, calmly, and looked at Emily, then at Cotannah, with a cool, steady gaze. "Just fine, thank you."

His pale blue eyes spoke to Cotannah as clearly as his tongue could have done.

I know you have it, but I also know that you can prove nothing. Nothing at all.

Everyone saw the look, and no one but Cotannah knew what it meant. The tension came back with a vengeance, it lowered silence over the table like a shadow. Finally, Emily, always the perfect hostess, started a conversation going again and kept it firmly away from the coming dawn and death and poison until the plates were cleared away and dessert had been served and eaten.

Cotannah's heart sank. What could she do now? Obviously, Peter Phillips didn't intend to break down and confess. When Emily rose from her seat, everyone followed suit, and Phillips left the room with the other boarders, chatting along as if he hadn't a worry in the world.

A sudden picture flashed across Cotannah's mind: that of Walks-With-Spirits in a cold, dawn wind, stripped to the waist, his heart marked by a cross of white paint. Bravely facing the rifles of the Lighthorsemen. Her heart gave a hard, painful clutch.

Not while she still had breath in her body, she thought. She had Phillips worried and long before dawn she would wring an admission from him somehow.

Perhaps she shouldn't have let him know that she had the poison, she thought, as she waited for the others to leave so she could draw Tay and Emily aside. Maybe she should've stuck to her original plan to seduce him.

But then she decided that it wasn't too late for that. She could always resort to her old, flirtatious ways, and if he questioned her about the poison, insist that she had no idea what he was talking about. If she were clever enough about it, that might make him angry and lustful at the same time and the more emotional he was, the more likely he was to make a mistake. He was upset already, that much was certain, and even though he'd sent her that calm challenge of a look and had started visiting with the others as if nothing was wrong, she just knew that she could push him a bit more and he would shout out something in anger that would form a trap for himself.

"I'm onto something and I'm not giving up," she said quietly when Rosie had gone into the kitchen with an armload of dishes and she, Emily, and Tay were alone. "You two watch and listen for surprises this evening, because I may end up in Phillips's room."

They questioned her curiously but she wouldn't say any more right then—she couldn't because she wasn't sure what tack to tell them she would take. No, she admitted to herself, she couldn't tell them because she needed to do this all herself. She had been the cause of all this horrible trouble and making it all come out all right was the only way she could redeem herself.

Just the mention of going to Peter's room brought back so many terrible recollections that they paralyzed her for a moment. Her whole body turned cold at the thought.

She shivered and rubbed at the goose bumps that were springing to life on her upper arms as the unwanted memories took over her senses: Headmaster Haynes, advancing on her slowly while he brandished his whip, the big *bandido* with the hairy hands, taking hold of her chin and jerking her mouth up to his dirty, stinking kiss. Herself in the bed at Las Manzanitas after Tay and Emily had rescued her, surrounded by the whole worried family who knew that she wasn't really herself, that she was only a shell, a wraith lost in the long, empty, sinking feeling of not caring what happened next, of wanting nothing but to drop through the face of Mother Earth.

She stiffened her spine and pushed the past away. This was not then, this was now, and she would live, truly live this moment, as Walks-With-Spirits had taught her. She wouldn't let the past make it any worse than it had to be.

And she would not be ruled by fear. She was stronger than that.

She was stronger than she'd ever known she could be or she'd never have been able to leave Walks-With-Spirits before someone tore her out of his arms. She'd left him to try to save him, and that was exactly what she intended to do.

Her new peace was still there, deep down, and it would give her the strength to do what she had to do.

She gave Emily a quick hug, whirled, and ran to the stairs to go up to her room. Phillips had gone out onto the veranda with the rest of the company, just as he usually did—to keep up the appearance of normality, the crafty devil—and she'd use this opportunity to search his room again. Perhaps she had overlooked something significant the first time.

But still she found nothing in his room that would help her. The bottle of monkshood was all she had. When she got back to her own room she sank down onto the bed and tried to slow her pounding heart. She would have to approach him when he came upstairs and she told herself, over and over again, that she would go through with seducing him, all the way, if she had to. She could do it.

Even though it wouldn't be much different from being forcibly bedded, which was her greatest fear. She could face it, though. To save Walks-With-Spirits, she would face it gladly.

Emily sighed and shifted from one foot to the other without taking her eye from the narrow crack between her door and the jamb.

"Darling, don't wear yourself out," Tay said. "Phillips is still on the veranda, and we'll hear him when he comes up."

She turned and threw him a quick glance across their dim bedroom.

"Sh-h-h!" she whispered.

Then she put her eye to the door again. A second later, she saw movement at the edge of her vision and then Cotannah's slender form gliding silently past. Her heart stood still. She waited long enough for her friend to reach the top of the stairs, then closed the door a little more and turned to whisper to Tay again.

"There she went—why won't she tell us what she's up to? She's going downstairs, do you think she's going to confront him out on the veranda? What's she doing?"

He crossed the room silently and slipped his arm around her.

"She said for us to wait for a surprise. We'll find out soon enough."

Emily leaned back against the blessed comfort of his hard, lean body, but for once she couldn't relax in her husband's arms.

"How can you be so calm about this when there are so few hours left for Walks-With-Spirits?" she asked.

"Cotannah is the stubbornest person I've ever known," he murmured. "And she's determined to save him, so she will. She just wants to do it all by herself after finding out whatever she found out today."

"Well, obviously," she drawled. "Goodness, Tay, what an insight!"

He held her closer, with both arms around her, and dropped a kiss onto the top of her head. "All right, you just be as sarcastic as you want," he said. "But settle down. We're right here in the house with Cotannah and we won't let her come to any harm."

"I wish we could say the same about Walks-With-Spirits," she said sadly. "Oh, Tay, I just have to go out there and help her!"

"Help her do what?"

"I don't know. Whatever it is she's doing."

"So if you don't know what it is, you can't know whether she needs your help or not."

"I am in no mood for any logical thinking," she said.

She was only in the mood to do something, *anything*, to help her friend but she knew Tay was right. She had to wait until Cotannah asked for her help.

It seemed days, weeks, even, but just when she was losing control and about to go downstairs to see where Cotannah had gone, a faint sound, like glass clinking, floated to Emily's ears. They saw Cotannah move silently across their field of vision, making one more small clinking noise, and the shine of light from the hallway lamp glinted off a bottle and some glasses in her hands.

"Whiskey!" Emily whispered. "She's going to lie in wait for Phillips to come up. Now that's the last tactic she ought to take, considering what she's been through in the past. Oh Lord, Tay, what if she gets him drunk and he rapes her?"

Chapter 19

It seemed to Cotannah that the night would stretch on forever and that Phillips would spend every second of it on the veranda. From her window she could hear his voice joining in the desultory conversation which kept returning, again and again, to the coming dawn's execution. To her own amazement, none of it upset her terribly. Phillips was sitting down there thinking about her and that bottle of poison, no matter what words he was saying, and at dinner she had definitely seen that he was shaken. She would get the truth out of him long before dawn.

She smiled to herself. He probably was staying downstairs so long to give her time to go to sleep so he could sneak in and steal the bottle back from her.

While she waited, she thought about Walks-With-Spirits and spoke to him with her spirit.

I'm with you, my holitopa. Think of me and know that is true. We are truly set apart to be together, you and me, and in only a few more hours we'll be side by side for years and years to come.

Every little while she sent him that message and in between she tried to ready her mind and her body to deal with Peter Phillips. It wouldn't be long now.

Finally she heard his heavy footsteps on the stairs. She ran to the mirror and smoothed her hair, adjusted the neckline of her dress. A few minutes after he entered his room she would go to see him.

To her shock, though, his footsteps stopped in front of her own door. She turned to stare at it and stood frozen, suddenly she realized that she was holding her breath, waiting for his knock.

It didn't come. The knob squeaked, then turned, the door opened and he stepped in, closed it quickly, and reached behind him to turn the key in the lock. His face looked extremely pale in the lamplight.

He was smiling, though.

"I stopped by to ask about your ankle," he said. "When you left the dining room after supper I thought you'd made a remarkable recovery."

She gave him a blinding smile of gratitude and, pretending to limp slightly, took a step toward him in spite of every muscle in her body screaming for her to turn and run.

"I've recovered very well, thank you so much for asking," she said, gesturing for him to sit at one of the chairs at the little table by the window. "It's all to your credit that my ankle hardly swelled any at all, that ice you brought so quickly saved the day."

He began to stroll toward her, not the chair.

"And you repaid me by taking something of mine."

The hard-edged coldness in his voice chilled her through. Perhaps it wouldn't be so easy to seduce him after all.

But now she had no choice.

She tilted her head and put on her most flirtatious air. "Why, sir, I don't know what you mean."

"I mean you didn't hurt your ankle at all. You only

wanted me out of the way so you could go through my things.''

She forced her lips to smile and her voice to drop to a husky intimacy. ''I wanted to see your private space so I could learn more about you,'' she said, ''not to go through your things, Peter.''

''Where is it?''

''Where's what?''

''The bottle you took from my desk.''

She clapped her hand over her heart as if shocked. ''Whatever are you talking about?''

''At the dinner table you mentioned monkshood.''

She widened her eyes. ''The poison?''

''Yes, the poison, you little vixen.''

''Just talking about poison makes me need some fresh air,'' she said, turning away with a swirl of her skirts to go to the window. ''As I'm sure poor Ruffy Sloan did, too.''

She threw the window open wider.

''Do you think Jacob was poisoned, too?'' she asked, and turned to look at him.

But he had come up right behind her, fast, and his protruding belly pressed against her back as he reached up with both arms and pulled the window all the way down. He locked it.

''You're going to give me that bottle, and you're going to do it now, Missy.''

He sounded so cruel that her heart leapt into her throat, but she leaned into him seductively. ''If I did take something of yours, did you ever think that it was only so that you would come to see me?'' she purred. ''Maybe I only wanted to have a private talk with you.''

''So you could hold me up for money?'' he growled, stepping back from her, trying to see into her eyes. ''Is that your game? You think I'm a rich man because I've got a new brick building and a store full of expensive merchandise?''

She drew back, threw her hands in the air and pretended great shock. ''Whatever are you talking about?''

His eyes narrowed to slits. ''So that's it. Well, let me tell you, little girl, I'll tear this room apart and your beautiful body, too, before I'll pay you one penny for that bottle. You're barking up the wrong tree.''

''Well, the best I can tell without understanding the subject of this conversation, you're insulting me,'' she said, making her voice rise, trying to sound angry instead of afraid. ''You may leave my room, now, Mr. Phillips.''

He came toward her again.

''Not without what I came for, I'm not leaving. And I may just help myself to you while I'm here.''

He grabbed her upper arms with his fat, soft hands and jerked her to him with a strength that stunned her. She tried to turn her head away but he clasped her close to his rounded front with one hand and used the other to hold her chin in a vise grip and kissed her wetly, right on the mouth, so grindingly hard she couldn't even get her breath.

Pure panic raced along her nerves.

Walks-With-Spirits stood in the open field that stretched from the back of the courthouse in Tuskahoma to the edge of the woods. He shouldn't have come in so soon, he thought. Even though he'd promised to come in the evening before the dawn of his execution, and the Lighthorse had been waiting for him, he should have waited until right before first light.

Because now he couldn't think, and he couldn't regain his balance.

He turned his back to the lanterns hanging in scattered

trees near the building and tried with every scrap of strength left in him to remove this place and these Light-horsemen from his thoughts so he could be at harmony in his spirit. He faced the south, the direction called white, the color of happiness and peace.

He said the incantation for removing enmity from his heart, said it silently four times.

Now. Listen! I am Walks-With-Spirits.

All the White Pathways are mine!

I am wrapped in White Pathways!

Black Red Mockingbird! You have just come to make my soul beautiful!

After he finished, he stood still with his eyes closed, hoping for harmony in his heart.

Yet turmoil still filled him, unmerciful in its constant onslaught.

Cotannah.

He had thought he'd found his peace about her and even about her stubborn determination to find evidence against Peter Phillips, but this tumult came from Cotannah.

And it was rooted in more, much more, than her sadness about his death. Also, it was more than his own reluctance to be going from this world and leaving her behind.

He slipped out of his moccasins and pressed the soles of his bare feet to the face of the Earth Mother, praying for wisdom to come to him through the ground, feeling for balance. Oh, Great Spirit, he was losing the true balance that he'd achieved at Blue River.

He waited for the peace to come and slow the rapid beating of his heart.

When it didn't come, he knew. The turmoil he felt was danger.

Cotannah was in danger, and a vision was coming to him.

The vision came clear, but only for an instant. Walks-With-Spirits stood with his head bowed and his eyes closed to look at it.

Sure enough, Cotannah was with Peter Phillips. She was trapped in the man's arms. Peter Phillips was holding her against her will, he was kissing her . . .

A lancing of jealousy cut through Walks-With-Spirits's heart but it soon faded. The real blow was the striking lightning of fear that burned through him. Evil was stalking Cotannah, the man meant to harm her.

"Turn around here and look at me, *Medicine Man*."

The growling voice came from directly behind him, and it froze the vision on the backs of his eyelids. It refused to change. He waited another minute, but it would not tell him more. Then it was gone.

Slowly, resting his weight on the balls of his feet, he turned around.

Two Lighthorsemen stood there, directly in his face, straddle-legged and tense, as if they expected him to fight.

"Take off your shirt," said the tall one.

"Aren't you a little early with that order?" Walks-With-Spirits said.

To his deep aggravation, the sound of the rough voice not only had stopped the movement of his vision, it had intensified the tumult inside him. His muscles had gone taut and were strumming like bowstrings.

Cotannah needed help.

He had to go to her, he had to help her, he had to run!

"That's not for you to say," the shorter one said. "I can cut the rag off you if I need to."

That one's voice held just the smallest tremor. He was afraid, Walks-With-Spirits realized.

And so, come to think of it, was the other. They were starting to worry about being the ones who must shoot him—just in case he might be able to use his powers here after he'd gone on over to the next world.

"Maybe I'll make my shirt disappear by magic," he said.

Each of them stared at him, their own shirts billowing about them in the stiff breeze coming out of the south. It was cold, that before-dawn wind, and that was why they wanted his shirt off him now—just to punish him a little for being a shaman, or a witch. Whatever they thought him to be, they knew he was stronger than they, and so they craved power over him.

The shirt he wore was the soft skin of one of his brothers, the deer. Its fringes lifted and fell in the fingers of the wind. He crossed his arms, grasped it by the tail, and pulled it off over his head.

"Which of you wants to wear it and see what luck it brings to you?"

They both took a step back.

He smiled a little.

Then he let the shirt fall and walked forward, right between them, right into that cold wind from the south.

"Over there on that blanket," the rough-voiced one shouted, "so we can sight the distance."

Several men and horses were standing in the middle of the field, a pale square spread on the ground at their feet. Walks-With-Spirits walked toward them.

The moon was bigger now, and it gave enough light to make white streaks between the gray shadows and the yellow stripes of the lanterns. The blanket, he could see as he reached it and walked onto it, was woven of threads the color of raw cotton.

Good. It was close to white. That was a good omen.

"Kneel," commanded one of the Lighthorse waiting at the chosen spot.

Slowly, Walks-With-Spirits went to his knees.

A man he'd never seen before stepped away from one of horses and came toward him, holding something in one hand.

Finally, he could see that it was the pot of paint. The man stopped in front of him, dipped two fingers in, and drew a white cross on the naked skin over Walks-With-Spirits's heart.

Once his heart was marked they moved back and left him alone, so Walks-With-Spirits knelt there with his eyes closed and tried to calm himself enough for the vision to come to him again. When it did, it was the same.

No, the image was the same but the sense of danger to Cotannah was stronger now. Peter Phillips truly was evil.

Walks-With-Spirits's muscles reacted, his instincts guiding them, long before the men standing around talking to each other near him knew what he would do. He was on his feet and running, he was throwing himself into an empty saddle on a ground-tied horse before one even noticed that he had even moved.

Phillips had killed Jacob. It was as clear to him now as the moon and stars overhead. He would have sensed that truth long ago whenever he was near the man if he hadn't been consumed with jealousy at seeing him with Cotannah. Cotannah had unsettled his peace ever since the moment they met.

But now his only peace was with Cotannah.

And Phillips would kill her, too, if he didn't get to her in time.

"Hey! Hey, there! What th' hell . . ."

More shouts rang in his ears and then men were running toward him from every direction, yelling, as he picked up the reins and wheeled the horse around.

"Hold it! Hold it or I'll shoot!"

Walks-With-Spirits spoke softly to the horse, who immediately did as he was asked and reared high into the air.

From his back, Walks-With-Spirits began to shout an incantation in the Choctaw tongue.

> *"Ha! Listen! I am sent by the Ancient One*
> *to bring justice to this Nation!*
> *"I am the Red Horse Running, you cannot*
> *catch me.*
> *"The eyes of the Seven Eagles will be in my*
> *body,*
> *"Ah-hulu! Run from my path and save your-*
> *selves!"*

Then the horse was flattened out along the ground, galloping toward Tall Pine and Cotannah.

They were beginning to leap onto their mounts and chase after him, the Lighthorsemen and the others, but this horse was fastest of all. The Great Spirit had led him to the best running horse, the Great Spirit was giving wings to this horse.

And the Great Spirit was laying the portentous words on his tongue.

> *"Now! Listen! I am the Avenger!*
> *"I have come to remake the Medicine for the*
> *People!*
> *"I am not to be interfered with!*

"Diamondback Rattlesnake, with me you rest!"

His pursuers dropped back a little bit, he could tell by the sounds of their horses' hoofbeats. He smiled. Good. Let them be even more afraid. Giving such respect was good for them.

After what seemed a lifetime, Cotannah was able to pull her mouth free and step out of the trap of Peter Phillips's arms. It surprised her that he let her go so easily.

"Why, you do take a girl's breath away," she cried, trying to smile.

He reached out and let his hand fall, deliberate and heavy, on her shoulder.

"You strike me as the kind of little tart who likes it rough," he said. "But just in case I'm wrong about that, you might want to give me back what you took from me."

Her mind raced as fast as the blood pumping wild through her veins. What tack to take? Should she go on the verbal attack? Could she get him into a shouting match loud enough for the rest of the household to hear?

Maybe she could provoke him into yelling that he was the one who killed Jacob.

"I'm not giving you anything."

He advanced on her, pure menace in his slitted eyes.

"You damn sure are."

"I can't," she said quickly, "if I don't even know what it is you're after."

"You damn sure know, all right."

"Peter, you have to stop talking in riddles. Please."

He turned abruptly, and her heart lifted because she

was thinking that he was going to give up and leave, but she should have known better. He went to her armoire, jerked open the door and starting pulling clothing out, throwing clothes in every direction.

"I'll find it," he said, "and then I'll make you pay for not telling me where it is, for making me look for it."

"What if I already gave it to Tay?"

"You didn't. I watched his face at supper. He's in the dark."

"Several hours have passed since supper."

"I don't care if you gave it to the Judges themselves. Nobody can prove a thing against me."

He continued to toss her things everywhere.

"So this . . . whatever it is that you think I stole from you could be evidence in a crime? Perhaps a murder? Jacob's murder?"

He ignored her completely and continued searching until he'd gone through every corner of the armoire, then he moved on to the chifforobe.

"You think you're so clever, Cotannah," he said. "But you've outsmarted yourself this time, gal. You should've confided in somebody instead of trying to get more out of me than I intend to tell."

"What in the world are you talking about? You're the one who came to my room, if you recall."

"But you were all ready for me," he said, turning away from his task to look around the room as if counting the hiding places left.

"I was not. I had no idea that you were coming here."

"Do you normally keep a bottle of whiskey and two glasses sitting on your table?"

As he spoke, he strode across the room, grabbed her by the arm, and pulled her down into one of the chairs.

"Let's have a little drink, darlin'," he said roughly.

"It'd be a shame to waste the hospitality you've prepared."

Her blood began roaring in her head. She was completely losing control over this situation that she'd felt so confident about. No, to face the truth, she had lost control of it several minutes ago.

He poured each glass half-full.

"Drink up," he said, and he suddenly sounded as jovial as ever. "And think about whether you want to give me back what's mine or have me beat it out of you."

A devil of rebellion took over her tongue.

"I don't know what makes you think I won't scream the house down," she said. "Besides, you'd better not mess with me. I learned to fight from the Mexican vaqueros, and once I escaped from a whole bunch of *bandidos*."

"But not from me, honey," he said, lifting his glass and tossing down his drink. "You won't escape from me."

He scowled at her and his eyes turned to ice.

The thought crossed her mind that perhaps this was the time to scream for help.

"Drink that," he said.

She took a sip.

"All of it," he demanded.

She drank a little more.

"Tell me how you think you're going to get out of this," she said, "before I yell for Tay and all the other men in this house."

"You won't yell for anybody as long as you think there's the remotest chance you can get me to talking while we're alone," he said. "Because I proved to you at supper that you can't trick me into talking in public.

You're a stubborn girl, Cotannah, my love, and that will be your downfall.''

She smiled at him and lifted her glass, pretended to sip at the drink.

"Your downfall was keeping that bottle," she said. "Why did you? Did you plan to use it again?"

He smiled a smile cold enough to freeze a summer day.

"Why, what are you talkin' about, Miss Cotannah?" he said, in a eerie imitation of her voice. "Use what again?"

Then his face went solemn and hard.

He poured himself another drink, then left the glass on the table and reached across it to take her wrist in a painful, twisting grip.

"Drink that one, and I'll pour you some more," he said. "Don't give me any guff about it."

"What'll you do if I don't? Put a little monkshood in it?"

"Very funny. Drink that."

She tried to pull free, but he was so much stronger than she that she couldn't believe it. He looked fat and flabby, but his muscles weren't.

It wasn't panic that she suddenly felt. It was a simple certainty that she was making no progress, that she could not make him confess or trick him into confessing and that it was time that she got some help.

"Drink it yourself."

She threw her drink in his face and jerked her arm free, leapt up to run for the door.

But he was also quicker than she'd ever thought possible, and he caught her before she could get the key in her hand, clapped his hand over her mouth.

"You've done yourself in, now, sweetheart," he growled, and she knew it was true.

So she twisted in his arms and kicked at his shins, elbowed him in the ribs and bowed her back until she freed her mouth enough to scream. At first, for one horrible, frozen second, she thought she was too scared to make the slightest of sounds, but then she got out one loud cry before he tried to close her mouth again.

She bit his finger and he pulled his hand back and she screamed.

The next instant he was smothering her with both hands but it was all right because somebody was running in the hall, somebody was rattling the doorknob.

"It's locked!" Emily screamed. "Cotannah, oh, 'Tannah!"

"Damn it, Phillips, open up!"

It was Tay's voice, roaring.

Then the roaring was inside her head and everything went black.

To Walks-With-Spirits's great shock, not one of his pursuers had fired a single shot, and now he was thundering into the house yard at Tall Pine. None of them was even in hearing distance yet, even though he felt sure they were galloping their horses on his trail as fast as they could. Or maybe not.

He grinned to himself. Maybe they had deliberately stayed behind far enough so that he couldn't cast a spell on them.

Probably. He had shouted at them when they'd first left Tuskahoma, at the top of his lungs, that he was sent on this mission by a medicine vision, and then, when no one answered, he had begun chanting again, in the Choctaw tongue, every charm of protection that he knew. So far, it had intimidated them into staying far back and not shooting at him.

"Only an *alikchi* could make such an impossible escape!'' one of them had yelled, and then they had all been silent.

As he rode into sight of Tay and Emily's house, he gave a great, shuddering sigh of relief that the Light-horse were afraid of his powers. They had followed him somewhere back there, but they wouldn't keep him from saving Cotannah, thanks to the powers of the Great Spirit.

And to the powers given this gallant, spirited horse who had carried him so swiftly. He was surefooted in the darkness, and he'd raced even faster when the trees thinned and the moon and stars gave them light. The time had dragged at first, then it had passed in a flashing moment, it seemed, and Walks-With-Spirits's heart was in shreds when the two of them jumped the horse over the fence and galloped up to the house at Tall Pine.

He was off the horse and running before they reached the steps to the veranda; he pounded across it and burst into the house. Blocking everything else from his mind, he tried to open his spirit, tried to feel where, exactly, Cotannah was.

Upstairs.

But something was wrong, he couldn't get to her this way. He stopped in his tracks at the bottom of the stairs.

"Phillips! Open the door!"

Tay's voice.

"Break it down," Emily screamed. "Brother Jones! Come help Tay break down this door. It's solid oak."

Loud pounding knocks and more yelling echoed through the house.

He whirled on his heel and ran through the empty parlor, stepped out through the window onto the veranda, darted across it, and immediately shinnied up one of the posts to the veranda above it, threw himself bodily over the baluster rail. Cotannah was in the room im-

mediately to his right, he could feel her spirit calling to
his.

Below him, the Lighthorsemen and the others were
just turning into the long driveway from the road, with
their horses' feet all drumming against the earth. He
breathed a little prayer of thanks. They hadn't stopped
him, and now he would save Cotannah.

The window was closed, and one slight tug proved it
was locked. He could see Cotannah's feet and her full
skirt hanging off the bed, with Phillips looming like an
evil monster above her upper body.

Choking her!

"Phillips!" he yelled. "Turn her loose or the Black
Lightning will strike you!" Then he hid his face behind
his shoulder and drove his elbow into the glass, his spirit
reaching ahead to feel hers.

*It's all right. I'm here. Cotannah, my darling, my pre-
cious one, I'm here.*

She swam back into consciousness in a haze of happiness wondering where the rock that had fallen on her
throat had gone. Her whole neck was hurting horribly,
yet the pain of it passed her by, wiped out by joy. She
opened her eyes to the lamplight when the tinkling bells
began to ring and tried to think what was happening.

The next breath caught in her hurting throat, she
gasped for more air and turned her head.

Walks-With-Spirits burst right through the window,
half-naked, flying straight through, shattering glass
everywhere, hurtling magically through the air with his
bare feet tucked up against his tight bottom and his arms
reaching for the prize like a stickball player straining to
catch the ball. Except that this time his prize was also
his prey, and he was stretching his big muscles to get
hold of Phillips with hands like a hungry eagle's claws
instead of a playing stick.

He was here! Oh, thank God, Walks-With-Spirits was here! By what miracle? How had he ever gotten away? Or had he not gone to Tuskahoma yet?

She wasn't sure how much time had passed. All she knew was that he had come to save her and he was right here in her room, wearing only his breeches, fringes flying, his face fierce as Basak's on the attack.

Phillips turned to meet him, but he never had a chance. Walks-With-Spirits collided with him like a tornado hitting a house.

There was another horrible thud, right then, this one at the door, which came crashing in to fall flat on the floor with an awful screaming noise of tearing wood that sounded almost human.

Helpless to speak or move, Cotannah glimpsed Tay and Emily and Brother Jones all watching Phillips and Walks-With-Spirits fight. Emily's face was frighteningly pale.

She saw Walks-With-Spirits, with Tay helping him now, throw Phillips face down and start to tie his hands behind him with Tay's belt. Emily ran to her, tears pouring down her cheeks.

Tay jerked the belt tight around Phillips's wrists and stood up, setting one booted foot deliberately in the small of his back to hold him down.

Then Walks-With-Spirits got up and came toward her. He broke her heart. The cross of white paint stood out against his gleaming copper-colored skin, marking the target, and it made her tremble to think how close he had come to losing his life, how close she had come to losing him.

He filled her eyes. Every step he took moved something inside her, some deep core of her that had stayed locked away for a long, long time, perhaps since she was born.

Or since she was old enough to know that she had no mother.

And no father.

For the first time since Phillips grabbed her, she was able to take in great gulps of healing air, able to breathe deeply in a calming rhythm that soothed her soul. No, no. It was the sight of Walks-With-Spirits, alive and unhurt that comforted her beyond belief.

He was scooping her up then, into his arms, he was holding her close, so close, that they were one body once more. She nestled her cheek onto his naked chest, gloried in the feel of her skin against his skin, and laid her ear against the steady, pounding beat of his heart. Safe, it said. Safe. We are both safe now.

Slowly, the shivering inside her began to subside. He held her even tighter, rocking gently back and forth on the balls of his feet while he held her in his arms.

Emily hovered near her.

"Her throat is nearly crushed!" she cried. "You can see the marks of every one of his fingers on her neck!"

The room quieted completely.

"Get up, Phillips," Tay growled, dragging the man to his feet as he spoke. "Get up and tell us why you were choking her."

Phillips's face was so red with rage that it was almost purple.

"Because she's a sneaky, lying little thief!" he cried, in a tone so aggrieved that a person would think he was the one who'd just been strangled and choked half to death. "If I could've found that bottle of poison, I'd have poured the rest of it down her throat."

Tay slammed him against the wall.

"What poison?"

"The damned monkshood, that's what poison! The poison that killed Jacob! None of you simpleminded idiots ever even thought that he might've been poisoned, now did you?''

"Why'd you want to kill your own partner?"

"He was trying to back out of our deal with the Boomers. I couldn't do without that money after it started coming in—I didn't have a rich father to give me anything I wanted the way Jacob did."

He said the last as if it absolved him completely.

Tay glared at him.

"What deal with the Boomers?"

"The deal for Jacob and me to talk up white settlers and individual allotments."

"They were paying you both for that?"

"Yes! A lot of money! And that fool Jacob was going to quit on them just because you had heard rumors about it."

"So you were the person in the mercantile he spoke to right before he died?"

"Yes."

"Had you gone there to meet with your Boomers?"

"Yeah, and I kept him quiet while they were there, but when they left us, we were having a drink and Jacob repeated what he'd told me after the pecan-picking social—that he was going to quit them very soon. If he'd gone through with it, the Boomers would've killed us both! Really, listen to me, everybody . . .''

He was calming down, now, and he looked around the room for a sympathetic face.

". . . if I hadn't killed Jacob, the Boomers would have. He wouldn't have lived much longer no matter what. They would've killed us both."

Cotannah motioned for Walks-With-Spirits to set her down, and she stood on her own feet in front of him. Her legs were trembling, but she slid her feet apart for

balance and dug in her heels to stand straight. He placed
his hands on her shoulders for support.

"Well, Walks-With-Spirits wasn't about to be killed
by the Boomers!" she cried in a voice so hoarse she
couldn't recognize it. "You're the one who was about
to kill him!" Her throat hurt terribly, but she couldn't
be quiet. "You'll go to Fort Smith and stand before
Hanging Judge Parker!" she announced, as if she were
pronouncing sentence on him herself. "*He'll* hang you
high, and that's what you deserve, Peter Phillips!"

Then fists pounded on the front door and Rosie let
the Lighthorse in. They rushed up the stairs and into the
room, stopping in their tracks when they saw the situation. While Tay talked to them and turned over his prisoner to them, Emily hugged both Cotannah and
Walks-With-Spirits, together, and then the two of them
just stood still, wrapped tight in each other's arms.

"Come downstairs, everyone, and have something
warm to drink," Emily cried, as she stepped between
them and the rest of the people in the room. "We truly
have cause to celebrate the morning."

Cotannah glanced out the window with its jagged
edges of pane sticking out from the wooden frame, past
the bits of glass on the floor starting to sparkle now with
the faint pink-and-yellow light of the dawn. The others
were beginning to follow Emily out of the room but it
didn't matter to her who was there and who wasn't. The
only person she could see was Walks-With-Spirits.

She looked up at him and cupped her hands around
his dear face.

"Was our star out? Did you see it on the way here?"

"All I saw on the way here was you."

She started to pull him toward the window, then realized that his feet were bare and the broken glass was
everywhere. Tears sprang to her eyes when she thought

of what he'd risked to save her, and she reached to touch every one of the small, bleeding cuts scattered over his shoulders and arms. Some even on his face.

Soon she would attend to them, but right now their star was about to fade before the sun.

"Let's go out to the veranda from the hallway," she said.

They walked hand in hand, out onto the second-floor veranda and across it to look up at the sky. She slid into his arms again the moment they stood at the rail. He laid his palms flat on her abdomen and pressed her hips into the hardness of his body while they looked for their star.

"I don't know if we can see it from here . . ." she said.

"There," he said.

And, indeed, there it was, shining gloriously in the southern sky, their own Blue River star.

"Thank you, for my life," he said.

"And thank you, for my soul."

She gazed at their star for a moment, and then she tilted her head back against his shoulder to look up at him. He brushed back the strands of her hair that the wind was blowing across her face and bent his head to kiss her.

Epilogue

South Star Hill
Choctaw Nation
Late Spring 1877

Cotannah snuggled deeper into Walks-With-Spirits's arms, with her back against him spoon-fashion, and took several deep breaths of the cool, fresh air drifting in through the windows of their new bedroom. Outside, the birds chittered wildly because it was almost morning and entirely spring.

They were echoes of her happy heart.

She drew up her knees and hugged her rounded tummy, marveling that she could have had so little such a short time ago and now be rich beyond counting.

But she counted anyway, on her fingers, silently, so she wouldn't wake her husband. Her husband! Just thinking the words made her smile.

He was first on her list of riches, tied with the baby coming this summer. The three of them, plus Aunt Ancie and Uncle Jumper, now asleep in the smaller log cabin that William Sowers had built for them a stone's throw away from this huge one, would be a good beginning on the big family she'd longed for since her girlhood days, when she'd begged Cade to come home and stay, the days when she'd prayed for the Great Spirit never to let him go out wandering again.

Cade!

She froze in place, her blood racing. Then she twisted around, threw off the sheet, and sat up, shaking Walks-With-Spirits by the arm.

"Shadow, wake up! Oh, darling, I just remembered what day it is. Maggie and Cade will be here today."

Her words must have been a bolt of lightning because they brought on a roll of thunder. The rattling thunder of wheels. The muffled thunder of horses' hooves.

"They're here! How can that be? Why, it's barely even daylight!"

"It's all right," he murmured, in his most soothing tone. "It's all right, darling. It'll take them a while to drive down the lane."

He sat up sleepily and looked at her for a moment before he reached for his breeches.

She jumped out of bed, grabbed a wrapper, threw it around her shoulders, and ran on bare feet to the window to see if they were in sight.

"Oh, the rocks on this ridge make the sound carry so far!" she cried. "I can't tell where they are."

He cocked his head and listened while he put on his clothes.

"Sounds like they're halfway in from the road," he said.

"I'll stir up the fire and put the coffee on," she said. "I want to impress Cade with how domestic I am."

Walks-With-Spirits laughed as he followed her to the kitchen.

"He's going to be so glad to see you, 'Tannah, he won't care if there's breakfast or not."

"Well, I will," she said. "I tell you, Shadow, you don't know all the criticisms my bossy big brother made of me the last time I saw him. I intend to make him eat his words."

But when the coaches rolled in and her beloved Cade's deep, familiar voice called, "Hello, this house! It's the Chisk-Kos from Texas out here," every silly intention she'd ever had flew right out of her head.

When she and Walks-With-Spirits were standing in their own front yard welcoming Cade and dear Maggie and the rambunctious five-year-old twins, Cole and Miranda, plus two-year-old Doak who was toddling after his brother and sister as hard as he could, she knew once again that nothing said or done in the past was important anymore. All that meant anything was that all of them were together, right here, right now.

Cade kept his arm around her shoulders as they turned to go into the house, even while he was talking to his new brother-in-law.

"Sorry we couldn't get here for the wedding," he told him. "But now I'm glad we waited so we can see this beautiful place of yours."

"We've only been moved in for a couple of weeks," Cotannah said. "Emily and Tay were so good to put us up at Tall Pine until we chose which section of the tribal land we wanted to improve and got our house and barn built. And Ancie and Jumper's cabin and the hired man's, too, of course."

"Are you raising crops or cattle or both?" Cade asked.

"Cotannah's started a horse herd for breeding saddle horses to sell, Uncle Jumper's overseeing the hired man in a big vegetable patch and we're raising hay," Walks-With-Spirits answered. "But mostly we raise wild animals, rocks, and trees."

"And babies," Cotannah said proudly, as Maggie reached out to squeeze her hand.

Cade looked down at her and grinned.

"Babies? Do you think it's twins?"

"Oh, my goodness, I don't think I'm strong enough for that," she said, laughing, looking at Cole and Miranda running through the house ahead of the adults, squealing and calling to each other as they explored the new place. "I'm hoping to have mine one at a time, but I want a whole houseful of them."

They walked through the archway from the parlor into the huge kitchen with its two enormous rock fireplaces centered in opposite log walls, the shiny new cookstove in the far corner, and a beautiful, round oak table ensconced in the very middle of the room. The new sunlight was coming in the south windows to make the lamplight unnecessary, the smell of coffee and frying bacon filled the whole house.

"I'm going to make flapjacks," Cotannah said, with an arch little glance at Cade. "And once Cade has washed the dishes we'll all go up to the school and you can meet the students that are mine and Emily's and Miss Jane's."

Maggie burst out laughing.

"Cade insisted on getting up very early this morning and coming in here at dawn so he could tease you about sleeping late and not cooking breakfast," she said, "but I do believe you're ready for him."

She stood on tiptoe to give him a quick kiss.

"Your little sister's got it all under control, and the joke's on you, Cade."

He laughed and hugged his wife in one arm, his sister in the other.

"Maggie, do you recognize our 'Tannah?"

He stopped in his tracks, then, and held Cotannah out

in front of him with both hands on her shoulders.

"I feel I hardly know you," he said, "for years and years you did nothing but have a good time and indulge yourself and now, all of a sudden, you're a wife, soon a mother, a teacher, a breeder in the horse business, a cook and . . . what are you doing, trying to make up for lost time?"

"No," she said, and reached for Walks-With-Spirits's hand, held it against her cheek. "I'm only trying to live, truly live, the time I have now. It's something I learned from my husband, the healer."

Dear Reader,

If you loved the Avon book you've just finished, then you should know that Avon's commitment to publishing the very best in romantic fiction is ongoing. Each and every month brand-new Avon romance novels become available at your local bookstore.

Sensuous, powerful, and packed with emotional intensity, Karen Ranney's love stories are a must-read for lovers of historical romance. MY WICKED FANTASY, her latest, has a rakish hero, a strong-minded heroine and not-to-be missed love scenes. Don't miss this compelling romance and discover for yourself why *Affaire de Coeur* has called Karen an "uncommon talent."

Westerns are always a favorite setting, and Nicole Jordan's latest THE HEART BREAKER comes complete with a rugged cattle baron who needs a wife and mother to keep the ranch in order. But when he enters into what he thinks is "just" a marriage of convenience he soon discovers he's gotten more than he'd bargained for.

Rosalyn West's new miniseries THE MEN OF PRIDE COUNTY is sure to captivate readers who like strong heroes who find redemption through love. A bitter Civil War veteran returns home to Pride County to find that the woman who owns his heart, and the entire town, have branded him a traitor. He must regain his honor—and her love—in this unforgettable love story.

And for lovers of *contemporary* romance . . .

Award-winning author Sue Civil-Brown, who you might also recognize as Rachel Lee, has written a sexy, light-hearted romance, LETTING LOOSE, filled with rollicking good fun. Jillie MacAllister has a new life, a new job . . . and is newly single after dumping her philandering, no-good ex-husband. But when a matchmaking maven decides to fix Jillie up with the sexy Chief of Police Blaise Corrigan, her life gets even more confusing . . . but in some very wonderful ways.

Happy reading!
Lucia Macro
Avon Books

AEL 0198